Praise for Sarah Maine

'An echo of Daphne du Maurier'
Independent

'Sarah Maine is a master of Scottish historical fiction'
Sunday Post

'A sweeping and atmospheric story of family ties, interwoven mysteries, love and redemption'
Quick Book Reviews

'Maine writes beautifully about the wilderness'
The Times

'Skilfully balances a Daphne du Maurier atmosphere with a Barbara Vine-like psychological mystery'
Kirkus

'A beautifully woven tale that crosses the continents. Atmospheric and vivid, the characters will stay with me for a long time . . .'
Sue Lawrence

'Reworks the conventions of historical romance in a novel that regularly undercuts expectations of what is to come'
Sunday Times

'An utterly gripping dual time story about secrets, mistakes, redemption and possible forgiveness . . . It all blends into a fabulous tapestry that will keep you spellbound until the very last page'
Christina Courtenay

Also by Sarah Maine

The House Between Tides
Beyond the Wild River
Women of the Dunes
Alchemy and Rose
The Awakenings

The Forgotten Shore

Sarah Maine

HODDER &
STOUGHTON

First published in Great Britain in 2023 by Hodder & Stoughton Limited
An Hachette UK company

This paperback edition published in 2024

1

A CIP catalogue record for this title is available from the British Library

Paperback ISBN 978 1 399 71765 6
ebook ISBN 978 1 399 71763 2

Typeset in Plantin light by Manipal Technologies Limited

Printed and bound in Great Britain by Clays Ltd, Elcograf S.p.A.

Hodder & Stoughton Limited
Carmelite House
50 Victoria Embankment
London EC4Y 0DZ

www.hodder.co.uk

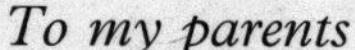

To my parents

PROLOGUE

Rosslie, 1940

Archie

It was the nights he dreaded. In the darkness there were no shadows in which to hide, no sun to blind the inner eye, only the moon's bleak light chinking through the curtains bringing no comfort.

The frights were inescapable. They'd followed him to Rosslie, hidden in the train's luggage car, and even here, in his boyhood bedroom, they'd found him. As soon as his eyes shut they'd emerge from the darkness and begin a flickering reel of hideous images that played relentlessly, mercilessly, in his head. A boy, face down in the sand; a mother's son pleading; a lover staring up, dead-eyed, at indifferent clouds.

He tried to turn in his bed, forgetting for a moment that he couldn't.

Was this the price of survival? Endless nocturnal visitations that denied him peace, and always the question: why had he survived and others not?

Better to stay awake. Terror came cloaked in darkness; there was no escaping it. He tried leaving the light on but sleep couldn't be denied for ever and as soon as his eyelids drooped they were onto him, tearing at his guts to reach his very soul. He seemed doomed to an eternal re-living, a never-ending reprise of anguish and pain . . . Night after night he woke panting, bathed in sweat, every nerve straining. Perhaps he'd stop taking the damned pills. They gave some respite from pain but he suspected they made the nightmares worse and weirder, and, as their effect wore off, his leg throbbed anyway. Better just to endure it . . . Whisky helped, though perhaps that fuelled the frights. Damned if he'd give up drinking, though. Half a bottle of his father's single malt had done the trick tonight, numbing the heart-sickness and the pain just long enough for him to get some sleep.

But he knew the frights would be there, waiting in the shadows, biding their time.

CHAPTER I

Rosslie, Argyll, 1980

Eva

'Ladies and gentlemen, your attention, please.'

The hall fell silent. Heads swivelled, faces turned forwards and Eva watched as the auctioneer scanned the gathering, gauging the anticipation, letting it build. 'We begin with lot number one, a charming landscape attributed to Sir James Guthrie. Note the distant view of Rosslie House out towards the headland. Dated to just before the Great War and presumably painted when he is known to have visited. While unsigned, it has all the hallmarks of Guthrie: his broad, confident brushstrokes, the tonal quality and . . .'

Eva surveyed the hall while the man continued his practised patter; there was excitement in the air. The sale had brought punters from all over Scotland. Some had come up from London, David had told her, scenting desperation and bargains to be had. The rows of seating set out in the oak-panelled hall were packed and all eyes were fixed on the central staircase, its wide bottom step serving today as a makeshift podium. Austere portraits lined the walls, eyeing the proceedings with cold disapproval.

'So, who will start the bidding?'

David leaned sideways, reeking of cigarettes and grubby pubs. 'Flogging the family silver,' he murmured. 'Duncan Maxwell's that dark-haired, stony-faced chap at the foot of the stairs; between a rock and a hard place, he is.'

Eva had wondered if it might be him, the heir apparent, and decided that he was a good-looking man – though with a rather aloof demeanour – somewhere either side of forty. He looked tense, though, as well he might, and his resemblance to the portraits was unmistakable: same high forehead, same long nose. He was, in essence, a younger version of his father, the late Sir Andrew, whose portrait was prominently placed on the staircase and whose demise had precipitated this sale of paintings. His death, in his ninety-sixth year, was hardly unexpected but had left the family in a fix.

There was enthusiastic early bidding but interest soon faded and the bidding stalled. 'Thank you, sir, with you at a thousand. Who will give me eleven hundred? Come now, ladies and gentlemen, that's hardly a *large* sum for such a delightful painting, whose value's increasing even as we sit here.'

David leaned close again, too close. 'Entering stage left, the grieving widow. Still a cracker, eh?' Lady Jillian Maxwell had that sculptured sort of face that aged well; her silver hair had been stylishly cut, her make-up carefully applied, and she took a seat with a cool nod to her neighbour. A renowned patron; an avid collector, David had said, and Eva admired her elegant red outfit, chosen perhaps to express defiance in the face of the family's very public financial difficulties. Eva studied her, making mental notes for the article that would come from this afternoon's outing, and watched as a fair-haired young man pulled up a chair beside her and whispered in her ear. Her ladyship's face lit with a smile and she tapped his arm in affection, or admonition; it was impossible to say.

David had seen him too. 'Keith Maxwell,' he informed her in a whisper. 'Younger son. Pain in the arse, according to Duncan.'

'Going once . . . and twice.' The auctioneer left a tiny final pause before letting the gavel fall. 'Sold to the gentleman in the tweed jacket. Thank you, sir. And now we come to lot number two.'

David whistled as another painting was placed on the easel. 'My God, that's a Peploe! If I'd the cash, I'd bite his hand off. How can she part with it?' Eva shushed him, conscious of dark looks and disapproval from their neighbours. 'Needs must, I suppose, until they find the missing link.' A long career in journalism had given David Mallory a rock-hard shell and he regularly mortified her. The auctioneer glanced their way, sensing a bid but David shook his head and dropped his voice to a whisper. 'Whatever they raise today'll only pay off immediate debts, I'm told, and it's capital they need. Can't see how they'll keep things going unless the man's found.' David might claim Duncan Maxwell to be his friend but there was ghoulishness in his tone.

Bidding was brisk for the Peploe and Eva saw Duncan Maxwell exchange a nod with his mother as it fetched a rather better price. One or two further paintings came and went, most selling at knock-down prices, and there was then a brief interlude during which caterers filled glasses and the auctioneer's easel was adjusted to take a larger painting. David sipped at his drink, his fourth or fifth, she'd lost count, his eyes continuing to skim the crowd. 'They're all talking about it,' he remarked, returning to the earlier topic. 'You can hear it, eh, taste it and smell it, and they're just loving it! Their very own Lord Lucan.'

'Except this man's not suspected of murder.'

David shrugged. 'Must have done something disgraceful or why vanish? What's the story, eh? Massive row, I expect, but over what? Duncan just clams up, claims not to know and Lady J ain't for telling either – eats journalists alive if they ask. Proper shitstorm until he's found.'

The final lot was now in position and the auctioneer cleared his throat, adjusting his smile. 'Ladies and gentlemen, an exciting late addition!' The easel had been draped with a cloth and the man allowed a murmur of curiosity to swell before he whipped it away. 'A very rare opportunity to acquire a little-known but certified work by the renowned William McTaggart. We're calling it lot number—'

A commotion erupted at the front of the hall. The auctioneer broke off and Eva craned her neck to see that an elderly gentleman with a walrus moustache had got to his feet and was jabbing towards the painting with his cane. 'You can't sell the *McTaggart*!' he declared and swung round, scanning the punters, and then addressed the hall. 'Known it these fifty years or more. Used to hang in the dining room.' The auctioneer's assistant went over to him and spoke in a low voice that Eva couldn't hear.

David leaned forward, his eyes alight. ''Ello, 'ello.'

At the front of the hall the dissenter was shaking his head and continuing to protest. 'Jilly said they were selling *her* paintings, from her own collection, not the ones from the house. Where is she?' His eyes swept the company again, not seeing where she sat ramrod straight but expressionless. Duncan Maxwell stepped forward to speak to him but the old man was not to be won over. 'And can you *prove* it's yours, Duncan?' he demanded, audible to all. 'If you can't, then it belongs to Archie – it's part of the estate! Known it half my life, I tell you. Hung over the sideboard in the dining room. Always admired it.'

'Oh, lordie, lordie.' David looked around gleefully as the argument continued and the muttering spread. The purchasers of the unsigned Guthrie and the Peploe came forward and joined the huddle, as did one or two other buyers, and Eva saw Duncan Maxwell run a harassed hand through his hair. The auctioneer stepped back, distancing himself from the whole unsavoury business, leaving his assistant to fence with the moustached gentleman who would not let the matter rest. 'I *know* he's missing, young man, everyone does, but Archie's a ruddy war hero, for goodness sake. Can't flog the damned thing behind his back.' David had pulled out a notebook and was scribbling rapidly. Duncan Maxwell's response was inaudible but the old man's voice carried well. 'Yes, I *know*. So where is he, eh? If you ask me, Duncan, after almost forty years it's time he was found.'

The auction descended into chaos and Eva could only feel sorry for the Maxwell family. Such a very public humiliation. She began to feel like a grubby voyeur rather than a decent journalist. Not so

David, he was in his element. If she could have left without him, she'd have done so, but they'd come in his car and so she was compelled to watch as he fought his way to the front of the hall where the argument was intensifying. She saw him accost the auctioneer, shrug off the disdainful rebuttal to turn, undaunted, and work the punters, swiping a drink off a passing tray as people milled around in a buzz of excitement. Some began drifting towards the door. 'See how they run,' David muttered, as he passed her, squeezing her arm. 'This is gold-dust copy, girl; this'll sell the paper all on its own.' She backed away and waited in a corner, shamed by his antics.

Things came abruptly to an end. The auction was halted, a postponement, the auctioneer announced, adding with a haughty detachment that the *family* apologised for the confusion. Once matters had been resolved, a future sale would no doubt be announced but his tone made it clear that his auction house would not be involved.

The maybe-Guthrie and the Peploe were left, shamed and unclaimed, propped against the easel and the cloth was discreetly replaced over the McTaggart.

When David finally came to find her, he was high as a kite. 'I'll drive us back,' she said.

'Nah, nah. I'm fine.'

His car was the last to leave Rosslie House. He made a flamboyant turn, skidding on loose gravel before speeding off down the drive then cut in front of a tractor as they rejoined the main road. 'Woohoo! What a show, eh? They pulled out, you know, both those buyers, the Peploe and the Guthrie, and one or two others. Walked away! Nothing scares off the punters faster than a dodgy title. And poor old Duncan was left standing there with his trousers down, worse off than before cos he'll have the auction house to pay. And *they* were *not* amused, I can tell you . . .'

So much for the alleged friendship, she thought, glancing at David as he punished the clutch. His pen would be merciless, and it was unlikely now that she'd get the promised shared byline; David would fly this one solo.

He'd briefed her on the background as they'd driven over that morning. 'Andrew, Fourth Baronet of Rosslie, died a month ago. Old soldier. Fought in the Great War and so forth. Eldest surviving son, Archibald, VC, hero of El Alamein, inherits, except for the juicy fact that he went missing, straight after the war. Hasn't been seen for decades. Vanished! No one knows if he's dead or alive or has kids of his own. Duncan stands to cop the title and most of the estate but in these circs, he can't inherit. Limbo land. He and brother Keith are Lady Jilly's sons, second brood, half-brothers to our hero. The dearly departed Andrew remarried during the war, almost sixty, the randy old bugger, when she was half his age. Raised a few eyebrows at the time, I'm told.'

Rosslie House had come into sight by then, silhouetted on a slight rise, backlit by the sun. It looked very fine, settled comfortably into the landscape, the red sandstone warmed by the sun's oblique rays, giving no hint of its current troubles. At its core was an ancient tower house, adapted as a shooting lodge in later times and altered over the years to reflect the fluctuating wealth and status of the baronetcy. 'They're stalled until the man's found or proven to be dead, and no one's got a clue where to start looking.'

Eva frowned. 'It was always going to be a problem, surely. They must have anticipated this.'

'They'd sent out feelers, I'm told, but drew a blank.' David went on to cheerfully disclose what Duncan Maxwell had confided in him. The Rosslie estate was in a financial mess, its twentieth-century decline held in check by a successful salmon farm, which Duncan had persuaded his father to allow him to establish in the estuary. But expansion was needed if they were to make serious money, and the estate had debts, lacked capital. 'I met him when I was doing a piece on fish farming for the paper and we've kept in touch.' Which probably meant that David, a shameless social climber, plagued the poor man to death. 'He's the brains behind the operation, brother Keith not being keen. Something of a prig,

I gather. Anyway, there's now concern that the fish farm'll have to be mothballed, or sold, as he can't compete now that others are springing up. Duncan says he had some big investors all lined up but they've gone coy until matters of title are resolved, so his hands are tied. Selling his mother's paintings seemed the only alternative.'

Until that plan had run spectacularly into the sand.

'When was Archibald Maxwell last heard from?' Eva asked now as they approached the outskirts of Glasgow.

David chuckled. 'Nineteen forty-five.'

She turned to stare at him. 'He's dead, then, surely?' She hung on, white-knuckled, biting back a protest as he took a corner with a squeal of tyres, narrowly missing a cyclist.

'They can't assume that – there're rules about this sort of thing. They've got to explore every lead and then wait God knows how long. He'll be in his early sixties now but I'm with you, and I reckon he's six feet under.'

CHAPTER 2

Rosslie, 1940

Archie

Archie switched on his bedside lamp and lay there sweating as the frights retreated. A glance at the clock showed it was barely two o'clock and he groaned at the hours which stretched before him. Cravenly he'd believed that being at home would help. On the train north, attended by a nurse paid for by his father, he'd salved his conscience by telling himself that he would mend faster at Rosslie, escape the frights, and be fit to return to the fray all the sooner.

Maybe then he would shed this burning sense of shame.

'*Shame*!' Andy had retorted when they had spoken briefly on the hospital telephone and Archie had tried to express to his brother how he felt. 'Christ, man! You *escaped*, you chump, against all the odds! You should be crowing that you got away. It's what you're supposed to do, *and* you got those others away too. Survival's what it's all about right now and frankly what you did was a triumph amidst this madness.'

Aye, but hundreds had died, he countered, left on the beach to be picked over by gulls and corrupted by flies, but his brother was having none of it. Archie tried to describe the desperate retreat and how he'd felt, knowing that the rest of the Highlanders had been led off, exhausted in defeat, compelled to accept humiliating terms of surrender. Men and boys from every household north of the border, forced to lay down their weapons and submit, condemned to spend their war in POW camps. God knows how they'd survive that!

'And you'll take that on yourself, will you? The whole bloody retreat, and the surrender? All on your account, eh?' But Archie sensed that his brother understood. 'Go home, Archie,' he said, 'get mended, get better, then come back and we'll give 'em hell, eh?' There was a pause on the line and a change of tone. 'And her ladyship'll be there to look after you . . . Give her my best, won't you?'

And so he arrived at the station, his brain a coiling mess of pain and anguish, not caring a scrap that his father's new wife was now installed as chatelaine in his boyhood home. It had been a shock to learn of the sudden marriage earlier that year but, with weightier matters to consider, he'd hardly thought about it since. Rosslie was still home after all and he knew his father well enough to know that nothing in the running of the estate would change. Rosslie was a sacred trust to Pa, and then it would be Andy's; no woman would alter that.

Heavily drugged and exhausted from the journey, he was only vaguely aware of her standing on the platform beside Roberts. Between them all, and painfully, they managed to get him into the back of the Bentley with Roberts and the nurse on either side of him, and then her ladyship had driven them home. He'd been in no mood for social niceties that day, but once the nurse had settled him in and departed, the woman had begun popping in, asking what she could do for him, until he made it clear that he preferred the attentions of Roberts. She stood at the door, contemplating him for a moment, then left without a word.

But she got the message, and stayed away.

Archie reached for his cigarettes and lit one, remembering that today was the day set for the great descent. Lady Maxwell, Roberts had told him, was away for a day or two, which suited Archie fine; he didn't need an audience. He drew on the cigarette remembering too that Selkirk was due this morning to see if he passed muster. The doctor was a local man who'd come out of retirement on account of the war and had known Archie since childhood. No *Captain Maxwell, sir*, from him, but robust encouragement. 'Need to keep exercising, lad,' he'd told him on his last visit. 'Muscles'll weaken if you don't and that's no good at all. A few steps a day, every day. Roberts will support you, eh?' Roberts had nodded gravely. 'Just in your room to start with and then up and down the corridor outside, and then the stairs. Take care on the stairs, Archie – last thing you need is a tumble.'

Archie had given a bleak smile, and had done his best.

Over the weeks he'd made progress, determined to get used to the crutches, gritting his teeth and pushing himself to transcend the pain. 'Nerve damage,' Selkirk had said, seeing his jaw tighten. 'But they'll heal in time. Might need further work once this craziness is over. You'll always limp, I imagine, but think yourself lucky you kept the leg.'

Lucky. Archie stubbed out his cigarette and pulled himself up, resting a moment against the bed head. He'd try and remember that! Using the hook of his stick, he managed to pull back the curtains and saw that dawn was breaking. A pale mist rose from the stand of ancient Scots pine on the hillside, etched dark and lovely against a lavender sky, and he had a sudden yearning to be out there and whole, his rod in his hand, settling down beside the chill river waiting for the trout to rise.

How strange it was to be here. How quiet, almost other-worldly. The nightmare he'd escaped from was still all too real in his head and yet here he was, at Rosslie, in some sort of mystical cocoon. Europe had been transformed into a version of hell where life and sanity were threatened by an apparently unstoppable foe, but Rosslie continued its charmed existence, unchanged except for the fact that his father was absent, in charge of a desk down in London, and Andy was somewhere on the south coast flying sorties to God knew where.

And an intruder now lived here, playing hostess. Disturbing the dust.

* * *

His progression that afternoon, along the corridor and down the stairs with Roberts at his elbow, was slow and excruciating, and did little to improve his mood. Selkirk proclaimed himself delighted, deposited Archie in the library where he promptly fell asleep and slept for a couple of hours until he was woken by noises in the hall. Roberts appeared at the door. 'Lady Maxwell has returned, rather sooner than expected, and has gone to take off her hat. I've laid two places in the dining room and she said she'll be down directly. Shall I help you through there now, sir? Dinner is ready.'

Damn, Archie thought as he struggled out of the chair. Polite chit-chat was the last thing he wanted, but he saw no way out. He'd stiffened while he slept so progress was slow and he arrived to find her ladyship already seated at one end of the table. 'Oh, well done, Archie!' she said as he lowered himself into a chair opposite her.

An expanse of polished mahogany stretched between them.

'All the way downstairs without a stumble, I hear. Some feat!' She raised a hand to her forehead and laughed. 'Oh God, sorry, feat–feet. Dreadful pun.'

'Except it's my leg.'

'Yes, of course.' She bit her lip and dropped her eyes to her soup. 'I won't ask if it was painful, as it obviously was.'

He felt childish then, and churlish. But found he had nothing to say . . . Until this moment he'd not really considered what his father's marriage would mean but now that the reality of it was sitting opposite him, looking very much at home, he found himself unreasonably nettled by her. It wasn't as if the woman had usurped his mother's place, as he could barely remember her, but she was another damned thing that required accommodating.

And she was so young! She made Pa look ridiculous, he thought, frowning down at his plate. Besotted old fool. Young enough to be his daughter. Glamorous too . . . Was Pa hedging his bets, he reflected grimly? With two sons in uniform, replacements might well be needed; the family, the baronetcy and succession, were an obsession with him.

Belatedly he realised she was speaking to him. 'Sorry? Forgive me.'

'I was just saying that Rosslie must have been a wonderful place to grow up. For you and Andy.'

'Yes, it was.'

'All this space.'

'Lots of space,' he agreed, and thought he caught a flash of wry amusement. He pulled himself together and made an effort, giving her a tight smile. 'We were very fortunate. Lacked for nothing.' Except a father who exhibited any sort of human trait. His mother, he sometimes thought, must have concluded that the fourth baronet would never change his autocratic ways and had given up trying to penetrate his thick hide, and had slipped quietly away, leaving him a vague memory of her as a sweet and gentle soul. Cancer of some sort had taken her off but sometimes, after one of his more painful confrontations with Pa, Archie decided it had been despair. He'd been eight at the time, Andy fourteen, and learned the hard way that his father was a cold man, aloof and domineering, devoid of empathy and humour with no interests beyond the estate, the army and his status in the county. He'd often wondered what sort of marriage theirs had been and once puberty had raised an interest in such matters he and Andy had speculated on the reason for the gap between their ages. 'Just twice, m' boy,' Andy had said, in accurate mimicry of his father. 'Once every six years is quite enough for that sort of thing.'

He raised his eyes and studied the new Lady Maxwell as she turned to address Roberts. The act of procreation between his father and this vivid creature was too ghastly to imagine . . .

He called his mind to order.

He was being rude, he knew he was, but his leg was paining him and he'd have preferred to eat alone in his room. The woman, however, seemed entirely unperturbed by his silence and had begun telling him about the old walled garden and the glasshouses that were under repair. His father had mentioned something about this the one time he'd come down to see Archie at the hospital in Kent. 'Working jolly hard on it, she is, and it needed doing,' he'd said, as if this somehow justified his extraordinary marriage. Archie had given no response; set beside the raw pain of seeing Scotland's manhood heading for defeat, the flourishing or otherwise of vegetables had seemed entirely inconsequential. His father had appeared uncomfortable and found nothing more to say beyond a gruff command to get better quickly and back to the field of conflict. Andy's telephone call a couple of days later, had been brief, but much more sustaining.

Across the table the woman was persevering and Archie half-listened, nodding occasionally as he continued to examine her. 'The glasshouses themselves weren't in bad shape, just needed a few panes replacing and the hinges oiling . . .' She was a looker, he'd give her that, sleek and well-groomed, but in her cream cashmere and narrow black skirt nothing less like a gardener could be imagined. Town clothes. She'd been away, of course . . . But surely she could have done rather better than Pa. Or was the title the attraction? And the prospect of wealth? *Ha!* She'd miscalculated there, and he doubted she'd money of her own, otherwise why choose Pa? He stretched his leg to relieve the pain and watched her paring an apple with a delicacy that grated. She must be what, thirty-ish? Did she intend to breed, he wondered, and produce little half-siblings twenty years his junior? Good God, what a thought. And if Andy married, as he surely would after the war, his children would be the same age as hers. His brother had a long-standing thing going with Fiona Brodie from the neighbouring estate, and they were expected to make a match of it once hostilities were over. Andy had confided that he couldn't take on the responsibility of a wife right now in case things went badly, and it had been Archie's turn to scoff. He was a survivor, was Andy, and he would come home, marry Fiona, spawn little Maxwells, and eventually inherit Rosslie, making a dowager of this newcomer.

Archie repositioned his leg. He rated his own chances of getting through the war pretty low; he'd used up his luck at St Valéry. The idea of dying didn't bother him all that much, as long as it was quick – not a death prolonged, alone, in darkness, like the poor bastards they'd left on the shore, too wounded to move, knowing that no one would come for them other than an unkind foe. His heart clenched at the thought as he reached for the bottle to refill his glass. Andy had damn well better survive, he thought, watching the firelight catch the crystal as he raised it. The prospect of surviving himself only to be burdened with the estate, the baronetcy and all the associated claptrap made death with his comrades a preferable option. Andy was born to it and would take it on with the cheerful self-assurance that defined him, with or without a stepmother his own age to deal with.

He became aware that she was watching him and made another effort. 'You've been away, I gather?'

'A friend was up from London, visiting in Glasgow.'

'Nice time?'

'Splendid, thank you.' But the smile she gave him was brittle.

They ate in silence for a while. 'Good food,' he said, though it was dull stuff.

'Rabbit,' she replied. 'Kenny shot him in the cabbages, so to speak. The vegetables are ours too. Nourishing, though hardly haute cuisine. Our own barley bread and butter too.' Why not eat better, he wondered. There were salmon in the river still, and deer multiplying in the hills, but perhaps austerity was what the servants would notice and report.

Good move, Lady Maxwell.

Did she know, he wondered, that he had been ruthlessly working through his father's wine cellar? His malts, too, bidding Roberts keep him supplied in his room. Pa wouldn't be amused when he discovered this but too bad . . . Another casualty of war. Tonight Archie had taken it upon himself to send Roberts for one of his father's finest clarets and the man finally baulked. 'A little heavy, perhaps, Mr Archie,' he'd remarked, glancing at his mistress, 'with the rabbit?'

But Jilly applauded his choice. 'Just the thing for the season,' she said. 'Lovely and mellow and warming.' He felt oafish then, realising belatedly that he should have consulted her since, like it or not, the cellar was more hers than his.

Raising his glass he studied her over the rim. It wasn't easy to come to terms with a stepmother who wore her glossy hair piled up on her head like a starlet and who'd found a source of bright red lipstick somewhere in wartime Argyll. Unless she'd had it sent up from London, which wouldn't surprise him; she looked the type. Perhaps her friend had brought it up with her . . . The claret did little to improve his mood as the meal progressed and he began to find her appearance (her very existence?) an increasing affront, so he rose as soon as they'd finished eating, making a brusque apology, and staggered off on his crutches to sit before a smouldering fire in the library and consume several glasses of his father's cognac. Where her ladyship spent the rest of the evening he neither knew nor cared.

And if she considered him a bore, so be it.

He felt vaguely ashamed of himself, though, as Roberts helped him up to bed, his head heavy with brandy and dark thoughts. Hardly a good start to the night and sure enough the frights soon penetrated his sleep. They arrived with the ghastly throb of the Stukas which had trailed them to the coast, followed by the dreaded high-pitched whine which presaged a cacophony of explosions and responding fire. He moaned as he endured again the sight of his comrades being flung into the air, jerking grotesquely to fall beside dead horses or lorries ablaze along the road, and smelled once more the blood and carnage.

Film-like, the nightmare then cut forward to the hours of darkness to the heart-pumping escape along the beach beneath the cliffs, pursued by flares and the beam of Very lights which illuminated with cruel clarity the living as they'd fled among the dead.

They had developed an almost choreographed routine to avoid its scrutiny: freeze, *run*; beam sweep, drop and freeze, *run* – hiding behind boulders or lying doggo beside the dying as the light passed over them.

Tonight the frights added a new twist, winding the reel back in time to when fragments of the ragged Highland Division had reached the cliffs above St Valéry, knowing that they were surrounded with nowhere left to go, the relieving ships fog-bound in the Channel. Archie had turned to his childhood comrade, Fergus Kincaird, and gestured to the cliff edge. 'We could do it!' he'd cried, the adrenaline pumping. 'Let's give it a go.' As boys they had scaled the rocky off-shore stacks together, raiding gulls' nests for the thrill of it. And Fergus had nodded, his eyes ablaze.

And so, using ropes recovered from an abandoned farmhouse, they'd rapidly instructed those men willing to make the attempt and several made it safely to the beach, slipping down the cliffs in the gathering darkness. Then snipers on the heights to the south saw what was happening and swung their lights on the spot, and started picking them off one by one. Archie and Fergus kept going amidst the hail of bullets, sending men over until the last one had gone and Fergus whooped in triumph. They grinned across at each other as the night clouds parted to reveal a crescent moon.

'Ready?' Fergus asked. 'Race you to the beach!' Archie seized the first rope and started backing over the cliff edge but to his horror he saw Fergus stumble, a loop of the other rope tightening around his ankle. He shouted a warning but too late, and in a frozen moment that would never leave him, he saw Fergus go over the edge to hang there suspended from above, a helpless target.

He'd had no choice but to continue his descent, Archie endlessly told himself, and Fergus was yelling at him to leave him and continue down. Miraculously he had made it to the beach unscathed to stand paralysed in the shadows, and watch in agony as the snipers found their aim. The scene was branded on his brain and he'd refused to move until his friend's body ceased to jerk before he let his men drag him away.

Tonight, however, the frights contrived that it was not Fergus but Andy who hung there, dangling by his ankle, and it was Andy's voice that was yelling at him to run. 'Save yourself, for God's sake! Survival is a triumph in this madness.' In his dream he turned back and tried to scramble up the crumbling chalk, slipping and falling back, shouting out to his brother to kick himself free, gasping and sobbing as his hands failed to find a grip. Then Andy's voice seemed to change and soften, he stopped yelling and began instead to reassure, as he did years back when thunderstorms brought childhood terror. 'Steady, Archie. It's all right . . . Shh, now. It's all right, I tell you. Honestly, it really is . . .' And, as the image faded, the frights retreated and he fell at last into a deep and dreamless sleep.

CHAPTER 3

Glasgow, 1980

Eva

'Fancy a pint?'

David had turned to her as they cut through Glasgow's rush hour traffic the day of the failed auction but Eva had had more than enough of him for one day and made an excuse. He'd shrugged and dropped her off at home and then went to ground for the next few days; it was what he did when there was something big on the cards. Nothing more had been said about a shared byline but that too was typical of the man. It didn't trouble her, though, as the auction wasn't the first time she'd wondered if this type of journalism was where she wanted her career to go, and was relieved to disassociate herself from events of that afternoon. It had unsettled her.

Selling off a few paintings hardly spelled hardship for the Maxwells, but she was intrigued by the idea of a missing man and how, even now, the war cast its shadow.

That, to her mind, was the story, not the calamitous auction.

When David was out of the office she went through back numbers of the paper and found the article he'd written some weeks ago about fish farms, and sat down with a coffee to read it. *Aquaculture is the farming of the future as far as coastal communities are concerned*, David had quoted Duncan Maxwell as saying. *It's no different from intensive pig farming or raising battery chickens, and fish provide a valuable source of protein. We're simply harnessing the resources of the ocean instead of the land.* For balance, David had quoted others who expressed concern about disease spreading from captive fish to wild ones, worries about the effects on the marine environment of faecal matter building up below the salmon cages, as well as the welfare of the salmon themselves concentrated in such large numbers losing the natural rhythms of the breeding cycle. A local group had formed to challenge the proposed expansion of the Maxwells' fish farm, calling itself Wild Seas, and there was a photograph of protesters holding banners displaying photographs of dead seals washed up on the shore, apparently shot by fish-farm workers.

It was a well-written article, but then David was an old hand, presenting both sides of the argument before coming down on the side of Duncan Maxwell, and doubtless taking his readers with him. *Norway has managed to control the size of individual fish farms and establish successful co-operatives,* he'd written, *and Maxwell insists that the initial planned expansion at Rosslie is modest. The sea lochs are, in many ways, ideal places for these sea-cages, which are naturally cleansed by the tides, and such initiatives might well provide a keystone in the regeneration of Scotland's coastal communities.*

But now, it would seem, all talk of expansion was on hold.

The following week, David's article for the supplement appeared. She'd half expected him to discuss it with her or at least show her a draft, but normal courtesies didn't apply to David and so it was there, on her desk, marked up ready for publication, a fait accompli, with a scrawled note paperclipped to the top. *What do you think?* Far too late to make a contribution, of course.

The article opened with a photograph of Rosslie House taken from the drive, the trees as now, resplendent in their autumn colours. Had he sent a photographer out there, she wondered, or had he driven back? The article began with a brief history of Rosslie's development from a hunting lodge on a ducal estate to the seat of a baronetcy and went on to describe the panelled hall with its portraits, the makeshift podium and the library where the drinks had been served. He discussed Lady Jillian Maxwell's lifelong devotion to the arts, the collection she had built up since the war, and then dealt surprisingly briskly with the failed auction, downplaying the whole question of ownership. Eva frowned, puzzled. Was that it? He had been so animated at the time, scenting blood . . . A simple misunderstanding over a single painting, the article concluded, and the auction would be rescheduled for the summer, by which time, it hinted, there would be exciting additions to the catalogue once certain paintings had been cleaned.

She lowered the pages. An accommodation had clearly been reached; a deal struck. Intriguing . . . and how very unlike David. Over the page, however, all became clear. The story, as her own instinct had told her, was no longer the auction, but had homed in on the missing heir. The Maxwell family had provided David not only with photographs but also exclusive personal insights, presumably in exchange for his forbearance regarding the auction. A classic David Mallory trade-off and a journalist's dream of a story: war hero, family row, missing heir, tangled inheritance and now a beautiful widow forced to sell her cherished paintings.

David had pursued this angle and laid it on with a trowel. The half-page spread was dominated by the photograph of a young man in the dress uniform of the Argyll Highlanders, together with a closer portrait of him wearing his beret and, inset in one corner, a medal awarded to him after the North African campaign. She glanced briefly at them and went on to read David's account of the man's courageous, if not reckless, wartime deeds. These had earned him the honour and helped not only to secure victory but to reassert the pride of the re-formed 51st Highland Division. David also recounted how, five years earlier, at St Valéry, Archibald Maxwell had gathered up a number of his men and escaped capture by abseiling down the cliffs, then tearing along the beach to reach a waiting fishing boat. Heroic indeed, she thought, and looked again at the photograph. A handsome young man, in his twenties perhaps, and the resemblance to his half-brother Duncan was unmistakable – that same high forehead, half-covered by his beret, and the same straight nose. He had been badly wounded at St Valéry and again at El Alamein, David had written, a bullet missed killing him by a fraction of an inch, grazing his left cheek.

Leaving a scar.

Something lurched inside her. A pulse began to throb in her head even before she could begin to reason why. She stared at the photograph and it felt as if the young man stared back, giving her a slightly quizzical look. She became utterly transfixed by his image then dragged her eyes away to study the medal itself.

The Victoria Cross. *For valour.*

She froze. She felt her face flame as her stomach began to churn and, in her mind's eye, as clear as day, she saw an identical medal lying among rusty fish hooks and lead weights, covered with dried fish scales, and heard her own childish question.

What does valour mean?

Trying to get your bloody head blown off and failing.

Her eyes went back to the photograph and the drumming in her head grew louder.

No.

Ridiculous!

But her mouth had gone dry and her heart began to pound as long-suppressed emotions swamped her. Remorse and guilt vied with confusion and a deep, almost childish, sense of having transgressed. She pulled out a magnifying glass and leaned over the grainy image, trying to imagine what twenty years and hard living might do to a man.

'So! What d'ya think?' David appeared at the door and she jumped as if scalded. 'Good, eh? I went back to Rosslie, you know, as I'd got thinking that the story wasn't really about the auction and dodgy title – great pun, by the way, I contemplated using it – it was about the missing hero and the mess they're in. Duncan opened up a bit once I put it to him that the publicity could help flush the guy out, and so they gave me permission to use those photos – so long as I downplayed the fiasco.' He winked at her, then paused, and frowned. 'What's up?'

'No, nothing . . .'

He perched on the edge of the desk and studied her. Too sharp by half. 'So what's with the red face and big wide eyes? And that—' He gestured to the magnifying glass.

She stared again at the picture. 'He reminds me of someone.'

'Who?'

'Someone I knew once.'

'*Who?*'

'As a child.'

'And you think it's him! The missing link?' He scoffed. 'Come on . . .' She looked away, thrown off-balance by the intensity of her feelings. She felt sick, transported back . . . And David went on looking at her. 'Those old wartime photographs all look the same. Besides, you told me you grew up in Canada?'

'It was there—'

'Where?'

'Newfoundland.'

'And you were how old?'

'Ten, eleven.' She found suddenly that she didn't want to say more.

'Yeah, right!' he mocked. 'Shall we go and tell Lady Jilly?'

His tone had an edge to it. Did he think she was trying to steal his story, make herself interesting? With an effort she pulled a face. 'You're right. War heroes in khaki? Ten a penny.'

David continued to contemplate her for a moment and then switched tack. 'How's the missing football-club cash coming on?' She pushed the article aside and showed him what she'd written but even as he read it her eyes were drawn back to the photograph. Archibald Maxwell had not been wearing a smart jacket with a strip of medals on his chest when she had known him, but a checked shirt, frayed and grubby at the neck, and the baggy trousers the fishermen wore. Worn boots and a slouch hat. And he had not been standing to attention but limping, often staggering, too inebriated to walk, for back in the little coastal outport of Heart's Repose he had not been Lt Colonel Archibald

Maxwell VC, heir to Rosslie, he had been Tam Nairn, the village drunk and troublemaker.

She used to feel anxious when he was drunk, and a little frightened too.

She felt the same now, and looking up she saw that David was watching her.

CHAPTER 4

Heart's Repose, Newfoundland, 1966

Eva

'Careful how you go, Eva, the path will be icy.' Miss Sinclair shut the door to keep in the warmth as Eva bounced down the wooden steps. Snow had fallen last night, and the temperature had plummeted. April's weak sun had melted the drifts through the day but now, sure enough, wet patches were freezing again. A biting wind nipped at Eva's face as she trotted along the path towards what was now home while overhead the clouds were dark with snow that had yet to fall. The schoolteacher had bookshelves in her front room, an informal lending library for those she considered responsible individuals. They were her *own* books, she endlessly explained, a collection lovingly curated to which she was slowly adding, at her own expense, by sending requests for what she deemed appropriate reading back to her brother in Scotland.

Eva, being the doctor's daughter, was one of the favoured few.

Having rounded the corner, and now out of sight of Miss Sinclair's house, she attempted a glide on the compacted snow. She often stood and watched the local children sliding for yards on the ice and here was a golden opportunity to practise away from their mockery. With spring just around the corner, people were emerging from their houses and if she improved her style perhaps she might fit in rather better. Establishing common ground had been hard since her family arrived here, from Scotland, six months ago, just as winter was setting in, and while her father encouraged her to make friends, her mother complained about the lack of suitable ones. 'They're ignorant and ill-mannered,' she said. 'Almost simple, some of them,' and had given her husband a baleful look. Eva hadn't thought so and wouldn't have minded anyway – she just wanted friends of any kind.

She went back to the start of the icy stretch and executed two or three successful glides before hitting a patch of grit scattered by a good neighbour. It stopped her in her tracks and she went down with a whoomph, sprawling her length in the snow, bruising her hands as Miss Sinclair's books flew from their grasp.

'Whoa there!' She looked up. A pair of worn-out boots had halted in front of her, one boot cocked at an angle. Their owner bent, not to help Eva to her feet as she expected, but to pick up the books and dust the snow from them. 'That's no way to treat books, young lady, you'll have the old besom after you.' The wearer of the boots squinted at the titles, apparently focusing with difficulty. '*Second Form at Malory Towers*. Good God. And another! *Third Year at Malory Towers*. Christ! Can't she do better than that?'

Were these remarks directed at her, Eva wondered, or at Miss Sinclair? Or at the author, perhaps? She got to her feet, examining her hands for injury and gave the man a stern look. She knew who he was, of course, everybody did, although she'd never spoken to him. And there was no requirement to be polite to Tam Nairn. 'The first one was *very* good,' she informed him, adding, 'and you shouldn't swear in front of children.'

His eyebrows shot up. 'Just at 'em, eh?' He grinned back at her. '*Very* good, was it? Let me guess, *First Year at Malory Towers*.'

'First *Term* actually,' she replied, pleased to have scored a point.

His eyes gleamed. 'So whadda they about?'

'Malory Towers is a school . . .'

'No!'

'A *boarding* school.' She scowled at him. 'It's in England, and a girl called Darrell goes there and—'

'You're Bayne's lass, aren't you? The doctor?'

'What if I am?'

He nodded, satisfied to have placed her. 'What's your name?'

'Eva, short for Evaline,' she replied, then wondered if she should have told him.

'So explain to me, Eva-short-for-Evaline, what's good about them? The books.'

Books had been her salvation over the winter and she liked talking about them, which was why a friend to share them with would have been nice. 'Darrell arrives at the school and has to try hard to make friends . . .'

'Have you?'

'Tried hard?'

'Made friends?'

She considered the question. 'The books make it sound quite easy but I'm not sure it is, at least . . . well, things are very different here.' She looked around at the haphazard scatter of wooden houses, jetties and fish stages clinging to the rocky shoreline, and tried to explain what she meant. 'They play games like netball and hockey at Malory Towers, you see . . . and have midnight feasts, stuff like that.'

'Sounds like pap to me.'

She didn't relish his tone, but was curious about the word. Words intrigued her and she collected them. Feral was one she'd recently acquired having asked her father about the dogs that lived in the woods and howled in a rather terrifying way during the night. They were once working dogs, he'd explained, or their offspring, which weren't needed so much these days but still roamed the margins of the community. 'Once domesticated but now living a wild state,' he'd said.

Looking at Tam Nairn with his unshaven face and worn boots, the word came to mind. He spoke just like her father, though his appearance belied the educated tone. 'What's pap?' she asked.

But the man was casting his arm in a wide arc and didn't answer. 'You're reading that stuff *here*, for God's sake, in *Newfoundland*! Where's the hockey pitch, and the other jolly schoolgirls, eh? How can it *mean* anything at all to you?' His speech was slightly slurred and she suspected he'd been drinking. Men drank a lot here, her father had told her, rather too much for their own good.

'They're just stories. They don't have to mean anything.'

He grabbed onto a small balsam growing beside the path and steadied himself. 'Forgive me. I thought they did.' Tam Nairn was a fellow Scot, she'd heard her father remark, which must be why he sounded like home. 'And a wastrel,' her mother had added.

The man was frowning now as if considering what Eva had said and she felt absurdly flattered. 'But maybe you're right, Miss Eva Bayne . . . Maybe nothing has to *mean* anything at all, and that's rather a consoling thought, don't you think?' But then he shook his head. 'I fear you're mistaken, though, as perhaps you'll discover one day.' She wasn't sure what to answer. 'But you're wasting your time on *Malory Towers*. There are better books and she has 'em, I know she has, I've seen 'em.' He handed her the books with a little bow and she caught a whiff of that sour smell the fishermen brought with them to the door of the medical station, unsteady on their feet, brandishing cuts or complaining of stomach pain. His eyes glinted at her. 'Ask her for them, young Eva, I dare you. Tell her you want something with teeth, something that'll make your soul sing and your spine tingle, something to make you weep. Then maybe you'll find they *do* mean something after all. Come and tell me if they do.' He straightened and belched before stepping past her and limping away in a lop-sided manner down the winding path towards the fishing stages. Snowflakes were in the air again, dancing around his head. She saw him stumble and heard him shout something as he passed the schoolteacher's house but the words themselves were lost.

After that encounter, for some reason, the exploits of Darrell Rivers and her classmates seemed less satisfying and her interest in them waned. Tam Nairn was right – the books were as far removed from life here as fairy stories, though she still longed for the sort of friendships she had found between their pages. Were there really other books with teeth, she wondered, ones which could make your soul sing? She didn't particularly want to weep, and wasn't exactly sure what the man had meant about her spine and she could hardly ask Miss Sinclair, who considered Malory Towers ideal reading for an eleven-year-old. The series had been sent out as part of her worthy campaign to get the local children reading. Some of them might themselves go on to board in St John's if they were to continue their education, she had told Eva's mother, and her father, when this remark was relayed to him had barked with laughter. 'Even Ada Sinclair must know that'd be a very different experience.'

Yes, Tam Nairn had a point, Eva decided, as she sat on her bed, having tossed the books aside. There were no hockey pitches or corridors of classrooms here, no school uniforms and chattering companions, just a sagging clapboard schoolhouse perched on a rock where the children gathered to glean what they could – or would tolerate – from the dutiful Miss Sinclair. And *any* sort of friendship remained elusive. After school most of the children had chores to do and her quest wasn't being helped by Miss Sinclair. Eva's previous education had already far outstripped that of her contemporaries and she was regularly held up as a shining example to the others. Every time she was summoned to the front of the class to read aloud she squirmed, her face burning, knowing that her hopes of acceptance among her contemporaries had not been well served.

Eva returned the books to the schoolteacher a few days later. 'I liked them well enough,' she said politely, then added, 'but I actually think they're pap, and I'd like something with teeth.' An appalled silence was swiftly followed by an interrogation as to the source of the word, but wild horses would not have got Eva to admit that she had been talking to Tam Nairn. He was a disgrace, someone you ignored, someone you never *ever* engaged in conversation but took steps to avoid. An outsider, an enigma, her father had said when her mother had decried him, and then explained the word for Eva. 'A person, or thing, that's puzzling,' he had said, 'or difficult to understand.'

'Something to tingle the spine,' Eva added hopefully as Miss Sinclair's interrogation ceased but she left, nonetheless, with *Upper Fourth at Malory Towers.*

She shoved it deep into her school bag, in case of another encounter with Tam Nairn.

But when they met again it was very much closer to home, and in circumstances that her parents had to admit were unavoidable, although regrettable, and her mother had been quick to instruct her how to handle such incidents should they occur in the future.

Her father's medical responsibilities covered a large stretch of coast and much of his time was spent attending patients in the scattered outports, most of them only reachable by boat. Heart's Repose was where he lived with Eva and her mother in a square clapboard building, its front room sub-divided so that half of it served as his consulting room. A second external door had been inserted so there were now two, side by side, one marked *Surgery* and the other *Private*, but patients simply banged on both doors until one or the other produced a response. It was established practice, her mother was told when her protests failed to persuade anyone to behave differently.

Eva was alone at home one afternoon when she heard a knock on the surgery door and waited for the inevitable second knock. When it came it was a loud and determined one, and she decided she'd better answer it. To her dismay she found a burly fisherman standing on the porch supporting Tam Nairn, who had one arm draped across the man's shoulders, his other held awkwardly, bandaged with a rag. Blood was seeping through the grubby fabric.

Both men smelt of drink. 'Yer dad home?' the fisherman asked.

'No—'

'Aha, the jolly hockey player.' Tam's eyes focused on her and he gave her a lop-sided grin.

She ignored him and addressed the fisherman. 'He's gone up to Mrs Baird. It's her time. Twins . . . ' There was surely nothing wrong in saying so, everyone knew everyone else's business here. 'Mummy's gone with him.'

'Open up next door den, an' we'll wait. Lizzy Baird's dropped a few so she'll not keep dem long.'

It seemed a reasonable suggestion so Eva took the key from behind the door, squeezed past them and unlocked the surgery. The man helped Tam over the threshold and was about to lower him into a chair when Eva stopped him. 'He'd be better there,' she said, indicating the worn examination couch. 'Then we can wash the cut. Dada always does that first.'

'Are *you* gonna wash it?' the fisherman asked, eyes widening.

That hadn't been what she'd meant but she caught a challenging gleam in Tam Nairn's eye and lifted her chin to show that she was a very capable person. 'I think we should. That rag's dirty and the cut might get infected.' Somewhat to her surprise the man did as she bid, helping Tam onto the couch, and then stood aside as Eva brought over a bowl of water and a flannel, rather enjoying herself. Close up, however, Tam's face with its stubbly chin and red-rimmed eyes was rather alarming, and the lines that fanned out from the corner of his eyes were ingrained with dirt and dried blood from a small cut above his eyebrow.

He was regarding her with amused curiosity.

But fresh blood was seeping through the grubby bandage on his arm so she ignored him and, steeling herself, began to remove the rag, revealing an ugly, jagged gash. She took a step back, gulping in dismay. 'I'm not quite sure what to do,' she admitted, looking up at the fisherman. 'Perhaps we should just put something clean on it, and wait until the doctor returns.' Mummy always referred to Dada as 'the doctor' when talking to villagers and Eva felt important saying it.

Hopefully he'd not be long.

'Right. You do dat, missee. Tell him it were glass but it broke clean.' The fisherman turned to leave.

'Oh, you should stay . . .' but the man was already out of the door. It slammed behind him and she turned back, gulping again as more blood welled up through the wound and began trickling down Tam's forearm. It was an awful sight, the wound edges were ragged, exposing raw, torn flesh. Lifting worried eyes to her patient she met an amused but gentle look.

'Just wash the dirt away from the edges, Eva, away from the open wound. That's all you need to do.' He was apparently sobering fast and his calmness steadied her. 'Then look around for some iodine; there'll be a bottle of it somewhere. Brown bottle, red label with *Tincture of Iodine* written on it. Good thing you can read, eh?'

She swallowed hard and began opening cupboards, hurriedly looking for the bottle he'd described, spotting it at last on a high shelf. She climbed up on a stool to reach it and read the rest of the label. 'But it says *Poison* on it.'

'Dab some on the cut using that flannel.'

She read carefully out loud: '*A p . . . potent and useful ger . . . germicide for—* What's germicide?'

'What I need on the cut. It's only poison if you drink it.' Even so he winced as she did his bidding and she stepped quickly back, eyes wide as the smell of iodine filled the room, masking the aroma of drink he'd brought in with him. 'It's supposed to sting,' he said. 'That's how it works. You're doing fine.' Reassured, she carried on, taking infinite care. 'Now, there'll be some lint or gauze somewhere,' he continued. 'Cloth that looks like wadding; white, thickish stuff. I'll hold the flannel while you have a hunt.' After pulling open several drawers she found what fitted this description and held it up to show him. 'That's the stuff. Cut a piece off, fold it over a couple of times and then press it on the cut. Firm but not too hard.'

'Have you done this before?' she asked.

'I have.' His eyes unfocused for a moment and he murmured, 'Red on white.'

She wasn't sure what he meant but did as he told her, her confidence returning as she followed further instructions and by the end was rather pleased with the job they'd managed between them. When she'd finished she remained standing there, beside the couch, and they looked at each other. 'Does it hurt a lot?'

He smiled a little. 'I've had worse.'

'Shall I wash the cut on your forehead too?'

'If you like.'

She fetched clean water and began dabbing gently at it. 'Were you fighting?' she asked. It was the usual reason for the fishermen and their cuts, she'd heard her father say.

'Others were. I got in the way.'

She wasn't sure she believed him. 'Had you been drinking?'

'I rather think I had.'

'Dada says if the fishermen didn't drink so much there'd be fewer fights.'

His eyes glinted again. 'He's absolutely right, but there's something to fight about at the moment.'

'Is there?' She wondered what that might be, but perhaps it wasn't her business.

His eyes remained fixed on hers in an amused but friendly way, and suddenly she felt the need to explain about the book in case he should somehow come to hear. 'She wouldn't give me anything else, you see. Miss Sinclair, I mean. I did ask. She just gave me the next Malory Towers one, even when I said the others were pap . . .' His body shook as he chuckled and his face creased in a grin. 'Keep still! You'll make it bleed again . . . You see, I didn't know what to ask for.'

'Stupid of me. Remind me what I said?' He had a nice voice, she decided, low and gentle, even though his breath was foul.

'You said I should read something that'd make my soul sing.' His face twisted oddly at that, which must hurt the cut but he didn't mention it. 'Or had teeth.'

'Not very helpful, was it? Not specific enough. What do you like to read?'

She shrugged, not daring to say she'd quite enjoyed Malory Towers until he'd made her question it. 'Adventures,' she said.

He considered her for a moment. 'Adventures, eh?' She nodded. 'Just in stories or real adventures?'

'I'm only eleven, I've not had much chance—'

But he wasn't listening, he was staring ahead in that same distant way. 'Be careful what you wish for, young lady.' Then, a moment later he refocused on her. 'Try Rider-Haggard or Stevenson, Arthur Ransome, even, or Jack London.' The names meant nothing to her and she'd never remember them. 'Aye, ask her for *The Call of the Wild*, that's got teeth, and she has that one, I know she has. No hockey sticks, though, just cudgels, poor Buck, and the law of club and fang. But he comes through in the end, finds his place in the world – which is all we can hope to do, eh? Or ask her for *Kidnapped*, or *Treasure Island*, she's got them too. You'll be told they're boys' books but never mind that.'

'Do you borrow books from Miss Sinclair too?' she asked, surprised but intrigued.

He pulled a face. 'Used to.'

'Why not now?'

'Never you mind.'

And so had begun their friendship. Her father was surprised to find her in the surgery when he returned later that day, standing sentinel over the village drunk who was snoring loudly on the examination couch, and her mother was horrified, especially when Eva told her how she'd found the man's conversation interesting.

'Would you like me to wash *all* your face for you?' she'd asked him when they'd run out of other things to say. 'You've still got some dirt in your eye corners.' And he smiled back at her, and then nodded, so she fetched clean warm water and another flannel, and very carefully wiped away the blood from his cheek. At her request he closed his eyes so she could wash the dirt from around them while he tried to think of other books she might like, poems she might read.

'You've a gentle touch, Eva Bayne,' he remarked, opening his eyes a crack as she stroked the flannel down the sides of his straight nose, and gingerly over the greying stubble of his chin, patting his skin dry with a small towel. She smiled, pleased by the compliment, and sensed him relaxing under her touch and so continued gently wiping away the dirt. The flannel was quite another colour when she finished and he seemed younger now, less alarming – less feral. It was a nice face, she decided, especially when he smiled and warmth lit his eyes. She'd uncovered other scars as she went along: there was a small one, an old one, shaped like an L high up on his hairline, and a deeper one along the edge of his cheekbone as if something had caught him as it sped past. She ran her finger lightly over the puckered skin, tracing the line of it and wondered at its cause, but didn't like to ask. His hands were scarred too, the knuckles skinned and red, but they were strong-looking and capable.

'I'll clean your hands too,' she offered. 'Might as well,' and she washed off the dirt, exposing more bruises, then turned them over, one at a time, exposing grubby palms and fingers that were nicotine yellow, and he watched her without speaking, his expression unreadable. She wanted to ask him what the men had been fighting about but he looked so peaceful now. 'Lift your chin, please,' she said, the hand cleaning finished, and he obeyed, revealing what her mother called a high-tide mark, a line of dirt where his frayed collar rubbed against his neck. He shut his eyes as the flannel completed its job. 'There, the dirt's all gone, and your hands are perfectly clean now,' she said, hoping for further compliments or another smile, but his eyes remained closed and to her acute dismay she saw tears escaping from under the lids and trickling towards his ears. He was crying!

'I've hurt you!' she whispered, horrified. 'I'm so sorry, I didn't mean to.'

His head gave a tiny shake but his eyes remained shut and the tears flowed unchecked. She watched him with deepening alarm, having never before seen a grown man cry, watching his Adam's apple move as he gulped. Impulsively she slipped her hand into his and felt his fingers curl around it in a little squeeze but he remained silent and lay there, quite still, until at last his jaw slackened. His breathing changed and he began to snore. Eva felt a great wave of relief; she *must* have hurt him and he was just being brave saying that she hadn't. There had been something dreadful about his face as he wept, something far beyond her understanding, something twisted and infinitely sad, beyond mere physical pain . . . Better that he slept, she told herself, carefully withdrawing her hand from his slackened grip.

But she remained standing there beside him, watching over him, until her father arrived.

After that day, by unspoken agreement, they became companions, conversing in snatched moments when their paths chanced to cross. 'I actually *liked* Long John Silver,' she said, falling back from a group of children when they encountered each other down by the fishing stages one day. 'Even though he was a very bad man.'

He cocked an eyebrow, 'Do you think maybe we're supposed to?' That hadn't occurred to her and she stopped to consider the matter. 'Folk are complicated, Eva Bayne. Run along now, keep up with your friends.' He nodded towards the girls who were leaving her behind.

'They aren't really my—'

'Off you go,' he said firmly and turned aside.

Could a bad man be likeable? she wondered as she caught up with the girls who were looking at her askance. Another time, when he sat smoking outside the general store, he spoke in a low voice as she dawdled while her mother dispensed advice to a local woman. 'Washed my own face today, young Eva. Am I no a bonny fighter now?'

She turned to him with a delighted grin. 'Alan Breck Stewart!'

'Terrible show-off, wasn't he?'

'Yes, but he looked after David when—'

'*Evaline!*' Her mother had turned and seen who her companion was.

Tam raised a knuckle to his forehead in a mock salute. 'Flawed, though, like the rest of us,' he hissed. 'Off you go.'

She caught up with her mother. 'He was only saying hello,' she said, in response to the sharp question. And then later, as they climbed back uphill to the house, she asked, 'What does "flawed" mean?'

'Faulty. Having a weakness,' came the tart reply. 'Like that man has for drink.'

CHAPTER 5

Rosslie, 1940

Archie

Archie woke and gingerly moved his injured leg, re-awakening the pain, and reminded himself to be grateful he still had it. It'd been shattered in two places, hit as he'd been pulled into the overloaded fishing boat that darkening evening when they'd made their escape along the beach. The little vessel had been tossing in the surf, close to the shore, its occupants shouting encouragement as the soldiers ran towards it, leaving the shadows of the ghost-white cliffs, half carrying those injured in the reckless descent. Gathering them at the water's edge, Archie had ordered them to shed outer layers and boots while bullets peppered the water around them. He'd hung back, driving the exhausted men forwards, determined that they'd make it, and then followed the last one off the beach. Within an arm's length of the boat a bullet had hit the lad's forehead and he'd disappeared beneath the waves and, as the sailors reached out to Archie, his own leg had exploded with pain. God knows how they'd managed to hang on to him.

Thanks to another miracle, an army doctor, grey with weariness, had later put him back together. 'You'll limp and it'll give you hell sometimes but you'll be glad of it, one day, for the dancing,' and he had moved on to the next bed. Pa had visited him just that once, interrogated him briefly, ascertained that he would survive and, as soon as he'd been fit to be moved, Archie had found himself being put on a train north.

Strings had been pulled.

He had not seen nor heard from Pa since, but his father was a busy man. A general in the Great War, he was considered too valuable to be sent abroad, or so he had implied when his determined efforts to get a command had failed, and he'd been given some sort of a role in the War Office. This tied him to London, though exactly what he was doing there remained unclear; requisitions came into it somewhere. Privately his sons wondered whether it was his age that had kept him away from the action, or his famously volatile temper. Harper's Duds was the unkind epithet applied to the Highland Division during the early part of the Great War, and Pa had had the misfortune to be in that part of the Division that had fired upon retreating Portuguese allies, mistaking them for Germans. He never mentioned it, of course, and no one else did. But for whatever reason, Pa had been given a desk in London rather than men to command and quite why his new wife had not stayed there to keep him company, Archie could not imagine.

He rose and dressed slowly, frustrated by his continuing fatigue, and accepted Roberts' assistance down the stairs to breakfast. He ate it alone and afterwards, balanced on his crutches, went outside and set off with grim determination towards the river. Ambition outstripped ability, though, and it was not long before his leg started sending impassioned messages to his brain, and he collapsed onto an old tree stump, swearing aloud and fighting back tears of vexation. After resting awhile, he clenched his jaw, gathered himself and went on, then sat again on a boulder and focused his attention on a kingfisher darting from twig to twig as it made its way along the riverbank. How calming it was here, how restorative to the soul! If someone were to carry a chair down another day, he could perhaps fish. Save him from going mad . . . And if he was physically tired at the end of the day then perhaps he would sleep more deeply and outwit the frights. It was damnable to be so helpless, and always so tired. He could no more ride a horse than walk and there was no solace to be had from books. He simply couldn't focus. Nor, he discovered, could he write; his brain was far too distracted, his thoughts ragged or raging. And anyway, what would he write? Should he describe the hell from which he had escaped, leaving others doomed, or whine about the frights when every man had his own? How crass that would be. A pitiful, self-serving indulgence for which he would rightly be despised. No, all that needed to be said about the futility of war had been said by the poets of a lost generation, a flowering of youth trampled into that same quagmire of mud from which the Division had just retreated. The old soldiers had stayed grimly silent about what they'd endured, dealing with the horrors as best they could, and he would do the same.

'Archie?' He turned his head. 'It *is* you – good heavens!' Jilly was approaching from the house. In tweedy trousers this morning with her dark hair tied back, she still managed to look stunning. 'Roberts said he saw you heading this way.' She explored his face as she drew near. 'You've overdone it, haven't you?'

'No.'

'You're very pale.'

'Too long indoors,' he replied, with a tight little smile. Damned if he'd accept her sympathy. 'I'm fine.'

'Liar,' she said, pushing aside a lock of escaping hair. He shrugged, thinking that it suited her much better tied back like that, rather than piled on top of her head in that ludicrous starlet style. 'And what a chump! Actually I was coming to find you to see if you were up to being useful. But if you're done in—'

'Useful?'

'I've some deliveries to make and I had thought you might drive me . . .' *Drive her?* '. . . easier that way as I can just hop on and off the cart and don't need to worry about Milly. She can be skittish, but I expect she'll behave better for you.'

Ah, she meant the old dog cart not the Bentley, and he felt a spurt of pleasure. Should have thought of it himself. 'Right now?'

'Are you up to it?'

'Of course.'

She gave him a slanting, speculative look then nodded. 'Kenny's loading up so why don't you wait here and I'll drive round. Easiest that way.'

He was being managed, spared the walk back to the house, but all right, fair enough, so he waited until she'd gone then rose to relieve himself against a tree; it would never do to be caught short while they were out. A few minutes later he heard the comforting clop of hooves and the old four-wheeled dog cart rounded the corner. He and Andy had used it as boys before they were allowed near the little Austin, but these last years it had stood neglected in the barn. And his spirits lifted as he saw Milly, an old friend who, despite her years, had a fair spring in her step. Jilly drew up in front of him and jumped down, and he saw that cushions had been placed on the seat, and another on the dash so he could rest his leg there.

The mare rewarded his attentions with a snicker while Jilly stood by, holding the reins, and watched as he pulled himself up, offering no assistance or banal words of caution. His opinion of her improved. 'All set?' she asked once he had settled himself, panting a little and gritting his teeth against the pain. He nodded and she sprang up beside him and handed him the reins. 'We can turn back when you've had enough. I got Kenny to replace the springs when we restored it and hopefully it won't jolt you too much.'

'We?'

'Me and Kenny. Well, Kenny, really – he did most of it; I just did what I was told.' She flashed him a smile. *Kenny!* If she'd managed to win over that old misery she must wield a formidable charm. 'With the Bentley out of bounds, except by order from the general,' she gave another quick smile, 'it seemed the obvious answer. I'm not a good rider but Kenny taught me how to handle this rig so it means I can get around. Milly's fuel isn't rationed, after all.'

He digested this information as he rearranged his leg to find a bearable position and, as they bowled down the drive, he spared a moment to note the autumn colours ablaze in the stand of oaks as they had been every year for as long as he could remember; the sight of the gnarled old trees was always a joy. And it was good to feel the reins in his hand, to be in control, not dependant on others. Almost normal.

Emboldened by this feeling, and after a long silence, he turned to her, going in fast and deep. 'So why are you here and not in London with Pa?'

She glanced at him and quickly away. 'Much better here, being useful. Safer too. And healthier – fresh air and all that.'

Fibber, he thought. 'You must find it very dull.'

'I don't imagine the war's a lark for anyone, is it?'

He decided not to push her, not now, at any rate. And as they drove along the narrow road he felt a pulse of pure delight. Home. Every inch of the estate was familiar, he thought, glancing up to see the rooks, like dark rags, circling the ancient rookery that swayed in the top branches of the oaks, cawing lustily as if the world was still sane.

'Actually, I don't find it dull,' she added, as they headed down a field track. 'In fact I've rather fallen in love with Rosslie, more than I imagined I would. I've become quite obsessed with the walled garden and the glasshouses, which is where some of this lot comes from.' She gestured into the back of the dog cart where a wooden crate full of vegetables had been stowed. Marrows and what looked like beetroot rested on top of potatoes and turnips like a harvest-festival offering.

'You sell them?'

'No, no. Cook and Kenny, or Roberts, tell me where things would be most appreciated and then I do a weekly round, dropping things off.'

'Ah, the Lady Bountiful.'

It came out as a sneer, which he'd not intended, and she shrugged. 'Perhaps, but it means I get to know the tenants and if they need stuff, then all well and good.'

'I'm sorry I said that.' God, he was becoming a bore.

But she simply gave him a smile. 'I often think it, and laugh at my London self.'

And that smile, he decided, went a long way to explaining why it was that his father had come to marry this particular woman. Maybe it also explained why he thought it safer to have her here, on the estate, rather than in London while he was so fully occupied.

'Leg doing all right?' she asked.

'Not bad,' he lied, but felt himself relaxing.

That evening, though, he paid for the day's exertions. The walk to the river, compounded by stiffness from sitting in the dog cart, had left him more exhausted than he was prepared to admit. At least he would sleep, he told himself as he slowly undressed, once the Scotch had taken the edge off the pain, and it had been good to get out. It helped rebalance him. And, as he sat on the edge of the bed, he found himself having to revise his opinion of his stepmother. She had been an easy companion, not afraid of silences but equally prepared to make remarks as they occurred to her, and had asked a great many questions about the estate with what appeared to be genuine interest.

'You love the place, don't you,' she had said, giving him another sideways glance.

He'd surprised himself by how much he knew about its management. 'I do, especially as I know it'll eventually be my brother Andy's job to take it on, whatever's left of it after the war. It was hard enough to make ends meet before.'

They tooled along in silence for a while. 'And he adores the place,' she remarked, almost to herself.

He looked across at her but her head was turned away. 'You've met Andy then?'

'Yes, of course. Here. Pull up. Old Mr McInnes is very partial to tomatoes and a few have already ripened.' She jumped down to deliver them and the moment had been lost. On the way back the pain in his leg took all his attention and conversation became thin as he gritted his teeth and focused on getting home. Perhaps she sensed this as she said very little.

Over dinner, however, something of the easy conversation of the afternoon resumed. 'So when did you last see Andy?' he asked.

'Oh, at some army bash or other, I forget. More vegetables?'

He shook his head. He'd not seen Andy since he got back from France; the phone call was all his brother had been able to manage. It was hard for him to get leave, he'd said, as he was kept very busy. Now an experienced pilot, when he wasn't flying sorties himself he was busy training raw would-be flyers, plugging the appalling gaps created by escalating losses. Recently he'd been seconded to Coastal Command in the north, so perhaps he'd get home on leave.

He went up to his room soon after, still wondering what Andy had made of Jilly. He sat on the edge of the bed and drained the whisky glass he'd brought up with him then lifted his injured leg onto the mattress before sliding, ungainly, between the cold sheets. He'd glimpsed another side to the woman today, he decided, but wasn't wholly convinced by the country-loving Lady Bountiful. Was her distribution of largess a natural impulse or a shrewd contrivance to win folk over?

He was still debating the matter when sleep overtook him.

And there the frights found him, hitting him hard and fast. Tonight they transported him back to the ruined French farmhouse where they'd sheltered en route to the coast and where the frights, in playful mood, contrived that he and his men were guarding a cache of vegetables. In his dream they were trapped there, the place surrounded by Germans with fixed bayonets who were shouting at them in broken English, demanding that they came out with hands raised. He was crouched in a corner, panting hard, seeing no way to escape. The enemy was advancing and, with the absurdity of the dreamworld, he became frantic lest the vegetables fall into enemy hands. 'Stay back,' he cried out. 'They're for civilians, for God's sake, the people are starving!' But still they came, closing in, and he could only wait, helpless and terrified, for them to arrive. He ran to a window, thinking to escape through it, but even as he reached it an enemy bayonet shattered the glass. He struck out and must have hit the bastard who gave a high-pitched shriek.

'I'm putting a light on. Shield your eyes.'

Abruptly he surfaced, gasping for breath and saw a figure standing beside the bed, a hand raised to its cheek. He stared out, wild-eyed and trembling, then threw an arm across his face. 'God. *Jilly* . . .' His heart was pumping hard, his mouth dry and whisky-foul. 'Was I shouting out?'

'Yes. You were.'

'And I hit you, I think.'

'It doesn't matter.'

He squeezed his eyes shut. 'You . . . you had a bayonet.'

She laughed. 'I'll be sure to bring one next time.'

'I'm dreadfully sorry.'

'Don't be silly. It was bad tonight, I gather. You usually settle earlier.'

He digested this, his arm still over his eyes. 'Usually? As in often?'

A slight hesitation. 'Quite often.'

'*Very* often?'

'Most nights, actually.'

His pulse began to steady but he didn't move his arm. 'How tiresome for you.'

'Don't be silly,' she repeated.

He remembered then how Andy's dream voice had altered that other night, softening and gentled. Had that been Jilly too?

'You're very kind,' he said stiffly.

'Aren't I just? I've brought you a cup of sweet tea, better than Scotch on this occasion, I think. And one for myself, for company, so sit up if you can.'

He removed his arm and squinted up at her. 'Some water too, perhaps, if you would. There's a glass—'

'Not now, there ain't. I'll fetch mine.' Slowly he pulled himself up, remembering the sound of smashing glass. She returned a moment later, stepping carefully to avoid the broken shards, and handed him a tumbler of water. 'I'll sweep up the bits in a minute, but be careful in the morning until Roberts checks.'

She was wearing a soft woollen dressing gown, pale blue in colour, and her hair was loose, her face devoid of make-up, which managed to make her look both younger and older all at once. Less glamorous, for sure. And oddly vulnerable. She sat herself in his armchair, tucking her legs up and sipped at her tea, watching him from over the rim. 'It must have been hell, Archie, no wonder it haunts you. But your father says that the 51st's rear guard action saved many lives.'

'And lost a lot too. Then surrendered.'

She took another sip, watching him. 'Tell me?'

He turned aside to pick up his own mug, saying nothing. He understood now why the old soldiers kept silent about the horror of the trenches, for how could he possibly convey to her the atrocities and the carnage and the fear and the sheer godawful relentless brutality of it? Besides, it was the last thing he wanted to do, drag it out into the open, especially not here in this room of his unsullied childhood, with its worn rugs and faded watercolours of cattle grazing beside still water. Far better that it stayed locked in his head.

'Dreams are funny things,' she went on when he said nothing. 'They scramble everything, and yet they've a strange sort of logic of their own.'

'I expect it was gibberish, whatever I said.'

'Yes, it was.'

He returned her a reluctant smile. 'Well, you'll be impressed to learn that I was defending a pile of vegetables from a group of storm troopers.'

'Well done, you!'

The atmosphere eased a little and they stayed quietly like that for several minutes sipping their tea, the lamp catching highlights in her hair while Archie sat, leaning back against the bedhead, staring ahead.

'We ask so much of our young men,' Jilly said at last. 'We ask them to fight and then to bear the pain and fear in silence, and send them back for more. God knows what that does to a man.'

'Leave it,' he said, feeling the tension return.

But she went on. 'You're what, Archie, twenty-one, twenty-two? You should be out there making hay, getting drunk, getting laid, having fun but instead—'

'I said leave it,' he repeated, frowning at her. 'There's a job to be done, and it comes at a cost.'

She said no more and then, a few minutes later. 'Andy said you wanted to be a writer, before the war.'

'In another life.'

'Will you write about—'

'No.' He put the mug down. 'Look, Jilly, thanks for the tea, and I hope I won't disturb you again. They'll be back, I daresay, but I'll ride 'em out as usual and they'll be gone by morning.'

'Who will?'

'The frights.' He gave her a twisted smile. 'Like the poor, they're always with us.'

CHAPTER 6

Heart's Repose, 1966

Eva

'He was talking to her again. I saw him.' Eva's mother spoke in that sharp tone she used these days. Eva had woken needing a wee and, in tiptoeing past her parents' door, she'd seen it was open a crack. Hearing Tam's name, she'd paused outside to listen. 'And she was paying very close attention to what he said, smiling at him and responding.'

'He's quite harmless, my dear,' her father's tone was weary. 'We've had several conversations and he's an educated, intelligent man.'

'He's a drunk! And just because he's well-spoken—'

'We can't know what brought him to his current state.' *An enigma*, Eva applied the word with quiet satisfaction. *A person that is hard to understand.* 'He clearly has a past but that's not our—'

Her mother scoffed. 'An unsavoury one, I expect. Why else would he bury himself in this godforsaken place.'

It had been a long winter and spring was slow in arriving. Eva was beginning to realise that her mother was unhappy at Heart's Repose, and wondered anxiously if this was somehow her fault. Nothing seemed to please her. But maybe her mother missed *her* friends as Eva did her own, and perhaps she missed the shops back home as well, since as she seemed to spend a great deal of time looking through the catalogues from which almost everything had to be ordered. She would wait with eagerness for the steamer to make its deliveries only to be invariably disappointed. 'The quality is *abysmal*,' she'd say, throwing some offending garment onto the table. 'But then what did I expect?' No, there were few things her mother liked about life here and Tam Nairn was not one of them. 'He's a drunk and wastrel. And it's not the past I'm concerned about, Rory, it's the present. Evaline has no common sense at all. She's always off by herself, in her own little world, and it's my opinion that he's noticed this and started singling her out. He targets her.'

'Rubbish, Mary, he's hardly a predator.'

Predator? She knew that one. It meant a fierce animal like a wolf. The image of Tam Nairn dressed as the wolf-granny in little red riding hood came to mind and she stifled a giggle.

'We don't know that, and why else would he keep speaking to her? And the silly girl encourages him! I've told her many times to ignore him, to walk past if she can't avoid him but instead she smiles and stops to say hello. Such a naïve child . . . And it all started that day we found him in the surgery, alone with her.'

'*Ach!* The man was asleep.'

'Drunk, you mean.'

'Either way he was hardly going to molest her!'

Molest? That word required investigation – it sounded bad. 'The poor man's wife's not been dead two months, so maybe being drunk helps a little.' Tam Nairn had a wife? 'And Eva did very well that day; I was proud of her.'

The praise did something to counterbalance the uneasy feeling in her tummy she always got when she heard her parents quarrel, but her mother was speaking again. 'You mean that slattern he lived with? No *wife* was she, from what I've heard! Besides, I'm told they were both drinking heavily long before she died.'

Her father's reply was weary and sad. 'Tuberculosis didn't care whether she was married or not, Mary, and she'd a terrible time of it, poor woman. Does it matter anyway? It was a dreadful blow for Tam, and for their boy.'

Their *boy*! Eva stared down the dark corridor, nonplussed by this news. Tam had a son too? He never came to school, she was sure of that. Her interest was now well and truly piqued and she strained to hear her father's words. 'And it does me no good, my dear, if you repeat that sort of tittle-tattle. We aren't here to judge these people. It's a hard life they live, and getting harder—'

'But they have a *solution*, offered on a plate, with money attached, if they'd only the sense to take it. I was explaining exactly that to Mrs Bradshaw, but she just stared back at me with that blank look they give you. You should grab the opportunity with both hands, I told her, instead of arguing, but they're an ignorant, uneducated . . .' The rest of her mother's words were lost and the conversation moved on.

Eva slipped past the door, went to the toilet, and got thoughtfully back into bed. They would have to be more careful, she thought, she and her unusual friend. But why was her mother so hostile? Tam Nairn was no wolf, for goodness sake. He offered her no harm; her father was right! They simply liked to talk. She found him interesting, he had time for her, answered her questions and they discussed all manner of things.

But she made a mental note not to smile at him if people were around.

She was very sorry indeed to hear about his wife, though, she thought as she rolled over in bed, how sad that was, and she felt sorry too for their son, losing his mother. Hers might be short-tempered and unhappy, but she couldn't imagine life without her. She must have seen him around, of course, and not known he was Tam's son; the shack where he lived was on the other side of the cove where she was forbidden to go. A mix of people lived there including those her mother scornfully referred to as drifters – fishermen without their own boats who came and went with the seasons, and men who spoke with thick foreign accents. Their clapboard houses were small and shabby, slipping on rotting foundations, their painted planks flaking and weather-worn. Tam's son perhaps stayed over there, and went to work on the boats. But her father had called him a *boy* so shouldn't he be at school? Tam had never mentioned having a son and she wondered if he'd mind her asking about him. She knew nothing at all about her friend, and could never tell which of her questions he would answer and which he'd pretend not to hear. His sudden silences made her a little wary of him, conscious of strange adult taboos.

It was true, though, she did look out for him.

Even so, their meetings were usually accidental. Sometimes, when he saw her coming towards him along one of the little tracks that bound the community together like the twine which was knotted into the fishing nets they used, he would swerve aside to avoid her. This had confused her at first and she'd been a little hurt, but recently she'd begun to think that those were the times when he'd had too much to drink and so would have very little to say to her.

But what did 'molest' mean? she wondered as she lay there. Doubtless Tam would know.

Heart's Repose had grown up in a disorderly, haphazard way. It had begun life centuries ago as one of several seasonal outports for fishermen sent out by merchants from Poole, Miss Sinclair had explained to her largely disinterested class, but gradually the men had stayed on through the winter, women had come out to join them and it had become a permanent settlement. The outport's core was reached from the sea down a short, hook-shaped inlet, which provided a sheltered south-facing cove. Over the years its shoreline had filled up with wharfs and fishing stages, gutting sheds and salting rooms, with twine and sail lofts above. Young spruce trees had been felled to build broad flakes, the platforms on which the salted fish were dried, positioned high to gain best advantage of the sun and the wind. Square clapboard dwellings stood on patches of flat ground between the boulders or sat astride rocks with logs or wooden piles to level them.

Away from the rocky shore, land had been cleared for a church and nearby a graveyard with white marble gravestones was demarcated by a fence of palings. Beyond were hay meadows that held the stunted forest at bay. Hardy vegetables grew on patches of manured land and were stored in root cellars built into the slope, while goats roamed on long tethers, pigs rooted in small enclosures and hens ran free. There was a school, and a general store that also served as a post office, while down beside the stages a cooper had once made barrels, although he, along with the blacksmith, had left some years ago.

Eva and her family had arrived last year just in time for the last of the crowberries and partridge berries. 'Careful,' her mother had said. 'They could be poison,' but in the warm buzz of late summer, she had watched the other children gorge upon them and noted which they took. There had been no planning to the outport's growth so there was no coherence to its appearance. There were no streets such as Eva had known back home in Scotland, no pavements, no solid stone buildings; only the shallow-roofed wooden houses perched precariously on their rocky platforms, looking as if a strong gale might carry them off.

And sometimes did.

Reaching Heart's Repose by land was barely possible for its folk looked seaward, not to the wooded interior. A rough track linked the little outports but it was a trek to reach the larger road that connected them to the rest of the vast island. The sea was their highway, their life-blood; a bond that gave them their living even if it sometimes took their lives. Every man had a fishing boat or a share in one and boys who yawned over their alphabet were quick to read the wind and the weather. For centuries, like the seabirds that came ashore to rear their young on cliff ledges and in rocky crevices, Heart's Repose men had done the same to rest, to marry and raise their sons, before taking them onto the water and schooling them in the ways of the sea. Their women remained ashore to gut, split, salt and dry the fish that the boats brought back, their hands red and raw with tasks that bound them to the place, and they taught their daughters to do the same.

The other side of the inlet faced north and enjoyed little shelter from the blast of winter gales. Icebergs brought south on the currents occasionally grounded at the mouth of the inlet and could take weeks to melt. If there was a risk they'd prevent the bait fish entering the inlet these Arctic giants were dynamited or towed back out to sea. Jetties and stages had been built during the boom years until every strip of shoreline was occupied but these days many had been abandoned, the wooden dwellings and sheds stood empty, bleached bare by the weather, housing only nets or crab pots. A few that straggled along the opposite shore gave shelter to those disadvantaged by circumstances, men who were sick or injured, whose boats had been lost or whose catches had been light for too long.

Or who drank too much and worked too little.

Tam Nairn lived among them and so, Eva had just learned, did his son.

As sleep began to overtake her she remembered she'd once seen a boy helping Tam into a boat before rowing him across the bay. A barefooted, dark-haired boy with a dog at his heels, a mongrel, half husky. Perhaps that had been him. Did he not go to school at all, she wondered, or did his father teach him at home? Tam seemed to know plenty, after all, and he liked to tell stories. And when he did his eyes would light up and he had the sort of smile that crinkled at their corners. He would tease her too, calling out 'Jolly hockey stick!' to no one in particular if she passed him when she was with other children. They simply giggled, imagining him to be drunk or raving, but she knew better and would drop her eyes to hide a smile, recognising it for a greeting. But if no one was around when they met she would stop to chat. 'Here again, are you, bane of my life?' he would say, but always with a twinkle.

One fine day she decided she'd go out to the little square wooden lighthouse at the end of the headland, where she liked to watch the seals basking on the rocks below. Sometimes there were icebergs too, far out to sea, drifting south towards oblivion. Once she'd been almost certain she'd spotted the blow from a spouting whale and had waited, breathless with excitement, to see if it would rise to the surface and show its tail like she had seen them do in pictures. It hadn't, but ever since that day she had been obsessed with the idea that she might see another.

It was Saturday, not a school day, and one of those rare and wonderful days when the sky was a deep blue with great billowing clouds sweeping across it like ships in full sail. She ran through the hay meadow, her curls bouncing, breathing in the sweet heady smell coming off the high-summer grasses that moved in silky waves before her. As she ran, her eyes fixed on the ocean, she suddenly tripped on something hidden by the tall grasses and sprawled her length.

'Jesus *Christ*! What the—' It was Tam. He rolled over, scowling furiously, then saw who it was and laughed. 'You all right, young hockey stick?'

She sat up, a little shaken, and dusted her hands, alarmed to find her face so close to his. 'I tripped over you.'

'You did!'

'Were you sleeping? But why here?'

He rubbed his eyes and yawned. 'As good a place as any.'

'Are you drunk?' Best to establish this, she decided.

'I was,' he admitted. 'But maybe not so much now.' He sat up and grinned at her. Reassured, she smiled back. 'Where are you off to?'

'I'm looking for whales,' she explained. His eyebrows shot up and he scanned the hay meadow through narrowed eyes, shading them with his hand. 'In the *sea*.' She laughed. 'I know a good spot down among the rocks at the end of the headland. Have you ever seen them?'

'Aye, I have.'

'Then you could come too! No one will know—'

But he was already shaking his head. 'Off you go, bane of my life. I've still got some sleeping to do.' He gave another yawn and scratched at his chest. 'But if I'm found in the sweet-smelling hay with a little lass like you, I'll be strung up. On your way, girl, but go steady, the cliffs are crumbly since the rain, and the whales'll have you for breakfast.'

'They won't! They only eat krill, and they're really very gentle.'

He squinted at her. 'Oh, aye?' His voice sank to a low rumble. '*The most dreaded creatures glide . . . treacherously hidden beneath . . . tints of azure*. Read *Moby Dick* and then decide; heavy going in places but skip those bits, it's a cracking yarn. She's got it in that little library of hers.'

Treacherously hidden . . . What splendid words. 'Do come and help me look,' she pleaded, wanting to prolong this interesting topic, but he waved her away.

'Leave a man in peace.'

Tints of azure, she thought, as she continued on her way, her mind refocusing on her mission. She must write that down. 'Azure' was another word for blue, she knew that one, but she'd forgotten to ask him about 'molest'.

Mossy heathers and juniper made for a soft and springy trail as she ran through the stunted, wind-blasted trees, which the locals called tuckamores, another lovely word. Salty gales had stripped them bare, leaving a tangle of silvery branches along the clifftop, but she soon reached a opening where she could see the ocean spread out before her, a blue-black canvas of possibilities. She loved the sea and the stories Tam had told her to read and she stood there a moment, wondering why Miss Sinclair had been so disapproving of her recent requests.

'But those are boys' books,' she'd said, just as Tam Nairn had predicted. 'Is it your father who's suggesting them?' and Eva had avoided a fib with a mumbled reply. 'Well, I'm surprised at him.'

Her father too had been a little nonplussed by her choices, but he'd approved. '*Call of the Wild*, eh? Better than that other rubbish you were bringing home.'

'Pap,' she'd agreed, trying the word for a second time. He'd spluttered into his teacup but there had been a gleam in his eye as he'd suggested she avoid using the word in her mother's hearing. A mental note had been made to learn the meaning of the words Tam used before trying them out.

She left the track before reaching the squat little lighthouse with its red-painted trim and balustraded walkway and found a rock at the edge of the cliff to sit on. The lighthouse keeper had an alarming way of appearing and shouting at the outport children if they strayed out to the end of the headland and although he was probably asleep now it was best to stay hidden.

So she sat on her rock, swinging her head from side to side, searching the wide expanse of ocean for the telltale spout of a whale, watching a gentle swell breaking against the off-shore stacks. What had Tam meant by 'strung up', she wondered. Like strings on a fiddle, or a split cod hung to dry? She would ask him next time . . . He'd told her once that Newfoundland used to be joined to Scotland, laughing at her frank disbelief. 'Same rocks, same fossils. Then they split and Newfoundland drifted off. So I stepped aboard and came along for the ride.' His eyes had glinted at her and she'd returned him a scornful look. 'How else d'ya think I got here?' he asked, and she'd spent time in class next day cricking her neck, squinting at the map of the world that hung there and saw that, while Africa and South America seemed to fit together, Newfoundland and Scotland didn't. 'Well, things sort of twisted and turned a while before Newfoundland hit Canada,' he admitted. 'I remember it well.'

Below her the seals were basking on their low-tide rock, sliding in and out of the water, and their mournful song was borne back to her on the wind. She watched them for a while but grew restless as a regular sweep of the ocean revealed no surfacing whales. It was a pity Tam hadn't come because no one would have known and tittle-tattled back to her mother and they could have chatted for longer. And two sets of eyes were better than one.

She set off back and just beyond the point where she re-joined the main track, she encountered Tam Nairn again. He was sitting on a boulder, and looked up as she approached. 'Any luck?' he asked. It felt almost as if he'd been waiting for her.

'No, and you're too late now, I'm afraid,' she said. 'It's gone choppy – you wouldn't be able to see them.'

He nodded. 'Not quite the season, maybe. Stick to the path as you go, wind's getting up.'

'Are you going back too?'

He nodded. 'You run on ahead, though.' He had a limp, she remembered, and this seemed a good time to ask about it. 'Pirates,' he replied, with the twinkle in his eye that convinced her that he was nowhere near as bad as people said.

'I don't believe you.'

'Fought off half a dozen of them, I did. Folk round here forget that, you know. But it was before you came.'

She pursed her lips at him. 'Like when you drifted here from Scotland?' He laughed. 'And there've never been pirates around here.'

'Wrong again, young lady. A very successful one used to live down on the Avalon Peninsula. Peter Easton. Sensible fellow, avoided both the rope and a watery grave and retired to the south of France, with all his loot.'

'You're making it up,' she protested, but he shook his head.

'God's truth. Lived happy ever after and not many of us can say that. Now off you go home.'

'I'll walk with you,' she said, wanting to hear more about this pirate. 'I don't mind going slow.'

He scanned the trail ahead and got to his feet. 'Just for a bit then. But tell me what you saw from the rocks.' So they discussed the seals and wondered between them how far a seabird might glide without flapping its wings, and whether whales preferred stormy seas to calm ones or if they cared at all, or even noticed . . . and eventually their conversation drifted back to stories, and from stories arrived at poetry.

'I've not read many poems,' she admitted. 'I prefer stories, or songs.'

'Aye, well, poems are somewhere between the two. Shorter. Tighter than stories. Words have to work hard in poems because there aren't so many of them, and rhythm matters so they're a bit like a song. Try writing them; you'll soon see.'

'Do you?' she asked, intrigued. 'Write poems?'

'Only bad ones.'

'I'd like to hear them.'

He shook his head. 'I've a book I'll let you have. Much better ones in there.'

'Your own book?' she asked, thrilled at the thought.

He smiled, an odd little smile that pulled down one corner of his mouth. 'Borrowed. Overdue, you might say.'

'Can I come now and get it?'

'No, you can't. I'll give it to you sometime.' She tried to conceal her disappointment; *sometime* was a put-off.

As they continued along the path, engrossed in conversation they failed to notice a figure coming towards them until he was almost upon them. The lighthouse keeper had not been asleep after all but visiting the village. 'Damn,' she heard Tam mutter. 'Run along now, Eva,' he ordered. 'I'll get you that book.'

She trotted ahead, saying hello as she passed the keeper but he returned only an odd, scowling look. And when she looked back, Tam Nairn had disappeared.

CHAPTER 7

Rosslie, 1940

Archie

Archie slept through the rest of that night, and if he dreamed again then the dreams were forgotten by morning. When he woke he lay a while, watching the sunlight pooling on the eider-down remembering the events of the night.

It was mortifying to think he cried out in the darkness, flinging his arms about and smashing things. He hated to think of Jilly, just across the landing, listening to his bleating or whatever it was that he did when the frights besieged him. Perhaps he should move to the end of the corridor where he wouldn't disturb anyone; he preferred his own room but she was bound to hear him.

He'd give the matter some thought.

And he wondered what she might be telling his father . . . The general was hewn from granite and would have little sympathy for a son who cried out in his sleep. He reached for his cigarettes and lit one, lying down again to smoke it, and stared up at the ceiling as he tried to remember if he had ever seen his father express emotion of any sort, other than some version of fury or contempt. When their mother died, he'd simply told his sons not to disappoint her but to carry on and make her proud, and so it had been Andy who'd held him in the night while he wept for her, and Andy who'd watched him in the days and weeks that followed, bearing the pain for them both.

He lay there, savouring the tobacco. How was Andy faring now, he wondered, it would be good if could get leave and come home.

Later, as he shaved, he considered how he ought to greet Jilly this morning. Should he thank her, or simply ignore the whole business? He was still considering this as he made his way downstairs only to learn from Roberts that her ladyship was already out working in the walled garden so at least that problem was solved. 'She's taking advantage of the fine morning,' he remarked as he poured Archie's tea, 'though heavy rain is expected later. Do bear that in mind, sir, as it could be slippery in places.'

Archie thanked him meekly, and dawdled over his toast.

Later, drawn outdoors by the continuing sunshine, he made his way to the walled garden, curious to see what was going on there. He pushed open the door and stood a moment, leaning hard against the frame, taking in the scene.

The place was transformed. He remembered it as a neglected relic of former days, overgrown with brambles and largely abandoned. Now, however, he saw that areas had been cleared, the raised beds repaired and that the fruits of these labours were ripening in the summer sun. The little orchard in one corner was no longer a knee-high thicket of nettles and bracken with plums and apples unpicked or fallen, a fermenting feast for the wasps, but the grasses had been scythed and the trees were fruiting. Cabbages and turnips grew in neat rows, runner beans clung to tall frames, raspberries had been netted and what looked like potatoes, half of them already harvested, had been neatly divided into beds separated by what appeared to be newly-planted espaliered pear trees.

There was no sign of Jilly, however, so he went further in, moving slowly on his sticks, and then he glimpsed the bright red of her jumper through the glass of the hothouse. She must have seen him as she appeared at the open door. 'Come in and admire,' she called. 'I thrive on appreciation.'

That was very likely true, he thought, and as he entered the glasshouse he was assailed by a wonderful, warm, humic smell redolent of lost summers, and felt absurdly comforted. One half of the place still stood empty but the remainder had been restored, the glass cleaned of dirt and algae and he was, despite himself, impressed. 'I found a stack of replacement panes,' Jilly told him when he said as much. 'And Kenny produced some putty from somewhere, so we did it between us.' Tables lined one side loaded with old clay pots, mossy and grey with age, planted out with ripening tomatoes.

'You've been working very hard,' he remarked.

'I jolly well have! Kenny did the lion's share, of course, as well as being a mine of information. I was starting from scratch, I'm afraid, but I'd no idea this sort of work could be so satisfying. I thought I was a city girl through and through but somewhere, lying dormant all this time, there was a more earthy me.' She gave him that smile again and held up soil-stained gloves.

Kenny appeared from behind her and nodded a greeting at Archie. 'Aye, she's a natural.' Good God, Archie thought, she really *had* won him over. Once the head gardener but now retired, Kenny was a dour soul, ever ready with a clout when stray cricket balls smashed panes in the abandoned glasshouse. He was even more gnarled now and stooping, but doubtless he'd relish the role of advisor to a lovely woman.

'By which I believe he means a simpleton.' She smiled, and Archie caught an appreciative gleam in the old man's eye.

'And if you've nothing better to do, Mr Archie,' Kenny said, the gleam fading as he turned to him. 'You can make yourself useful.'

'Twice, in two days!' Jilly murmured, her eyes laughing at him.

'I hardly dare refuse.'

The old gardener dragged over an empty tea chest, turned it upside down, and swept it briefly with his hat. 'Sit yerself down and you can dust aphids off these tomato plants. It'll no strain ye.' And Archie saw Jilly turn away to hide a smile.

'Will they fight back?'

'We'll have to see, won't we?' The old man fired him a look that made Archie regret his quip; he'd forgotten that a nephew of his had been in the Seaforth's. Had he got away, he wondered, or was he now a prisoner with the rest of them. He wanted to ask but felt that he couldn't . . . *Every household felt the shame*, some wretched news hack had written, having no concept of what it had meant for the Highlanders to lay down their arms.

And here he was, at home, tending tomato plants. He stared grimly through the newly cleaned panes and wondered if the others who had made it back felt as he did, if they too bore an overwhelming sense of guilt. Yesterday he'd thought that one or two of the tenants had greeted him stiffly, asking themselves perhaps how it was that he, an officer of the landed classes, was here, recuperating at home, delivering vegetables while their menfolk were languishing in some unholy POW camp.

Or lying dead along that road to perdition.

When Kenny had gone, Jilly looked across at him. 'Our hoary-handed son of the soil doesn't understand sympathy.'

He bridled, resisting her again. 'Why would he? I doubt he's ever encountered it himself. His sister's son, did he say what happened to him? He was with us at Veules.'

'They're waiting to hear,' she replied, moving some of the tomato plants to where Archie could reach them. 'Worrying for them, of course. And now he's become obsessed by these little white flies, sees them as a personal afront. Dusts or wipes the plants every day, but it seems to me they just keep coming.' Like pursuing panzer divisions, he thought, staring into the void, increasing in numbers as each new day dawned, pressing forwards, pushing them inexorably towards the coast, boxing them in.

He pulled a plant towards him and began wiping away the white and pink aphids with the soapy cloth Jilly had given him. He found a strange satisfaction in destroying so weak an enemy even if it didn't stop him remembering how the weather had turned against them, the ceaseless rain bogging them down as they floundered, divided and in confusion striving desperately for the little seaside town that offered their only chance of escape.

He finished the first tray and Jilly, wordlessly, replaced it with another.

And the enemy hard on their heels, taking their time, knowing that they could afford to wait until that final night when they had encircled St Valéry with their tanks and their mortars, a still and silent presence as menacing as the attack that would surely follow if terms were not agreed. Stalker and prey both knew by then what must happen when the sun rose over St Valéry en Caux.

Lost in his bitter thoughts, Archie was barely aware of Jilly moving around the glasshouse until he heard the sound of a kettle beginning to boil and saw that she had lit a Primus stove. 'We usually have a cup of tea about now,' she said. 'You're tearing through those trays. Kenny'll be delighted.'

They waited for him but Kenny never came and Jilly shrugged, clasping her own mug with two hands. 'He'll please himself,' she said, with a wry smile, 'as always.'

'When did you last see Pa?' Archie asked after they had sat in silence for several minutes.

'Oh, golly. Early June, I suppose. I'd already been here a while when he phoned to say he was sending you up.'

'I hope you're not still here because of me. I'll be fine if you want to get back.'

She shook her head. 'Your father thinks I'm safer here especially now the evacuations have begun. He wanted me to come as soon as it was clear that France and the Netherlands would be overrun.' Archie nodded, remembering how it had become inevitable that their forward line would crumble. And it did make a sort of sense for her to be here, he thought, although it was children who were being sent out of London as the threat of bombing raids grew. He wondered fleetingly if she was pregnant but couldn't tell under that baggy jumper.

'When exactly did you get married? I've rather forgotten in the midst of everything.'

'April the ninth.'

'Just as things were starting to hot up,' he remarked, then added, to provoke, 'An odd time to choose.'

'Perhaps, but there was a strange sort of defiance in the air.'

'Defiance? Or impulse?'

She gave him a sharp look. 'One breeds the other, to my way of thinking.'

'Where did you meet?'

She contemplated him a moment, her own face unreadable. 'At a memorial service for my fiancé who was killed on reconnaissance in advance of the Norwegian initiative. Your father discovered me crying in a cloakroom.'

He began to stammer something that might have been an apology had Kenny not chosen that moment to reappear. and she turned aside to make him some tea. Afterwards she went with the old man out into the walled garden and did not return.

That evening, however, he tried to offer an olive branch, an expression of sympathy. 'Oh, I don't need your compassion,' she said, cutting him off, but speaking lightly. 'I only told you to stop you asking impertinent questions. I quite understand that you must see me as some dreadful opportunist, a gold-digger even.' Her directness unbalanced him but since this was very close to the truth he said nothing, focusing on the stew. Bloody rabbit again. 'The word congratulations, I notice, hasn't passed your lips. Nor welcome to the family or any of the other common niceties.' She gave him a glittering smile but her tone was thin. 'I don't mind, you know. I didn't really expect it, but we might as well have it out once and for all rather than let it lurk there.' He said nothing, completely wrong-footed and embarrassed. 'I intend to make your father an excellent wife.'

'I'm glad to hear it.'

'And, as you see, I'm busy restoring your brother's inheritance, not frittering it away, if that's what's eating you.'

It wasn't, and he had never even considered the matter. And unless his father had undergone a metamorphosis it was unlikely that Jilly would have a chance to fritter any of the family funds, such as they were. He kept a tight hold on the strings of the diminishing purse, did Pa. 'Glad to hear that too.'

'So there's really no need for you to be disagreeable, or at least there's no need for you to be disagreeable to *me*, but I expect your leg's giving you hell so a little general grumpiness is forgivable.' He was treated to the smile again, and reduced to schoolboy status.

'Ought I to apologise?'

She twirled her wrist in graceful dismissal. 'Only if you want to – I'm entirely indifferent. I've a hide like an elephant, and couldn't care less what anyone thinks of me – you included.' A little tremor in her voice belied the words.

'Perhaps I will, just the same. I'm sorry.'

'Jolly good,' she replied, and the rest of that evening passed without incident.

That night, however, the frights returned and, cynically they took on aphid form. Aphids, grown large and woolly, had somehow infested the barrels of his company's rifles, rendering them useless. Separated from most of their regiment, as in reality they had been after crossing the Béthune, his small band made what progress they could along a narrow road crowded with refugees. There were French troops among them and others who had become lost all joining the slow line of retreat, diverting past lorries aflame, dodging for cover as the Stukas took their toll. In his dream, the men with him were unable to defend themselves until they had rid their weapons of the aphids, and were forced to halt and address the problem. Even the small mortars they found abandoned on the roadside were infested with the pests, grown as large as cotton-wool balls. And somehow Kenny was there, berating him. 'Saving yourself, then, are you? Where are the rest of them? Where are your men? Left to the ravens, eh?' and he was torn between turning back to refute this slur and pressing on. He chose the latter course, leaving Kenny shouting abuse after him, while his men were picked off one by one by unseen snipers, unable to return fire. Then the scene switched again to that ghastly moment on the cliff edge when he and Fergus had grinned across at each other, sharing the memory of another place where turquoise seas crashed below them and gulls wheeled above, screaming fury at their thievery. When Fergus stumbled Archie screamed, watching him, helpless, as the beam of a Very lamp found him—

The room flooded with light and he felt his shoulder being shaken. 'Wake up, Archie! You're at Rosslie. You're at *home*.'

Jilly's face was close to his and he stared back at her, wild-eyed and sweating. 'I . . . I cried out again?'

'Yes, but it's all right.'

His heart was pumping hard. 'We did all we could . . .'

'Of course you did.'

'It was chaos – we got dispersed, they had us trapped . . .'

'I can't begin to imagine.'

He felt a sudden compulsion to explain. 'Our only chance was over the cliffs, those of us who could . . .'

'You went over the cliffs!'

'On ropes.' And he lay there, staring up at the ceiling, as the awful reality flooded back. 'Some tried rifle-slings linked together,' but these had tended to break or came undone and he could still hear the men screaming as they fell. 'They weren't used to it, you see, hadn't done it before, but Fergus and I had—' And so he told the story, babbling uncontrollably, because it was suddenly essential that he explained. 'We'd got a dozen or more down and then it was just me and Fergus left on the clifftop, and we were laughing, *laughing*, I tell you, with a mad sort of relief. I went over, then he . . .' Jilly had perched on the edge of his bed and unconsciously he gripped the edge of her dressing gown, imagining it was the bedclothes and by the time he'd finished he was gasping for breath with such a pain behind his eyes. 'And . . . and I had to leave him . . . just *dangling* there!'

She gave him a few moments, then spoke softly. 'But you managed to reach the beach.'

He gulped. It was like spewing bile, painful but unstoppable. 'We saw boats loaded with men blown out of the water by the mortars on the cliffs . . . men staggering, crying out . . . a transport towing empty boats sank just yards from the shore and we had to watch the boats, still strung together, drifting away, into the fog . . .' Jilly moved, settling herself against the wooden foot of the bed, her legs curled up under her, looking back at him, saying nothing. 'We managed to reach a fishing smack that had come in close . . .'

'You did well.'

He bit back a sob. 'Then why does it feel like the very worst sort of betrayal? Pa thinks it was – I know he does.' *Damn*, he'd not meant to say that.

'He doesn't, you know.'

He reached shakily for the glass of water on the bedside table, leaned back against the pillows and shut his eyes, his head clearing as he drank. Bloody woman had got him to talk after all. 'I woke you again,' he said, looking at her, and tried for a smile, which came out crooked. 'Blame Kenny's aphids. I dreamed that they were clogging up the rifles so we couldn't fire.'

She smiled a little in return.

'I'll shift rooms,' he said, 'into the box room.'

'Don't be ridiculous.'

It became a sort of pattern after that, not quite every night but most of them. Some nights he either slept untroubled by the frights or else he bore their onslaught silently and did not call out and disturb her. But when he did, she would come, bringing tea or cigarettes, and so little by little he told her the story of the retreat, that long hellish journey, and she listened as he told her the things he had seen, or some of them anyway, perhaps not in a way that made any sense but she never said so, but just listened and encouraged him to talk.

CHAPTER 8

Glasgow, 1980

Eva

David gave Eva a long, speculative look when he left the office that day, sticking his head back round the door to remind her to send in the copy about the football-club scandal before she went home.

It was Friday, and David always left early on Fridays. The article he'd written still lay on her desk and, when he'd gone, she pulled it towards her and stared for a long time at the photograph. Could she be wrong? Was it really credible that Archibald Maxwell and Tam Nairn were one and the same man, transformed by time and circumstance? Deep down, though, she felt certain it was him. That scar on his cheek had been more prominent in 1945 when the photograph was taken, but she remembered quite clearly sponging away the dirt and tracing the puckered skin with her childish finger, wondering at the cause of it. And she recognised too the strange intensity in his eyes, which could gleam with humour one minute before darkening, for reasons she could only imagine, the next.

An enigma indeed.

They had been friends, of a sort, but it was a friendship that had cost him dearly. She sat for a moment considering the fog of confusion that still surrounded the events of that fateful day that she had tried so hard to forget. Confusion was tinged with guilt although the reasons for that were lost. And yet now, years later, she experienced again that sick feeling of having somehow transgressed.

But what ought she to do? She should tell someone, but who? Not David, the world's least sensitive journalist, but perhaps someone in authority? Or should she go, privately, and talk to Duncan Maxwell and his mother and put the matter in their hands?

They would think it a strange tale. Quite probably they'd not believe her. There'd been hundreds of crackpot sightings of Lord Lucan, after all. She gave the picture one last long look, filed her copy then gathered her belongings and left. But over the weekend, Tam Nairn's craggy face continued to haunt her. She wished she could've consulted her father, he would have known what to do, but he had been dead for five years. It was now too late to demand an explanation about Tam Nairn and the events of that night at Heart's Repose.

Asking her mother about it was unthinkable.

Eva had been ill immediately afterwards, that much she knew, and she remembered hearing her parents arguing as she lay in bed, failing to focus on *In the Fifth at Malory Towers*, which had been supplied by Miss Sinclair to aid her recovery. 'You think it'll be forgotten, Rory, but it won't! Every time folk look at Eva, they'll remember and gossip among themselves. You know what they're like . . . And this place is finished now.'

Eva had lain there consumed by shame, bewildered to learn that, in some obscure way, she was responsible for the fate of Heart's Repose. Her parents' quarrels had worsened and that too seemed to be because of her, because of what had happened that night. Gradually she began to understand that her mother was demanding that they leave the outport and return to Scotland and Eva had twisted her fingers in the bedclothes, wondering why, and if there was any way she could put things right. If only someone would explain what had happened! All they would say was that she should forget the whole business.

Eventually, out of weariness perhaps, her father had given in and sent Eva and her mother home to Scotland, following them a little later. He returned to Newfoundland in the years that followed, though, travelling between the remaining outports every summer, until his own health began to fail.

She stood at the kitchen window of her flat and stared out at the ceaseless rain, reliving the pain of those years knowing that somehow it all tied back to whatever had happened that night at Heart's Repose. As a child she'd been told nothing and had not understood, but as an adult she could imagine adult concerns. She remembered hearing the word abduction but back then, outside the context of storybook knights and stolen maidens, it had made no sense to her. It had not been an abduction, that she knew for sure. Tam *had* taken her to his cabin but that was because she was wet and cold and frightened . . . From the point where she had heard his voice calling out to her and felt his arms encircle her, though, until the moment she surfaced in her own bed, recovering from pneumonia, her mind remained a blank.

What had become of Tam Nairn and his son after she'd left Heart's Repose, she could only imagine.

Looking back now she realised that it was at this point that her parents' marriage, already strained, had broken. She'd hoped they would stop quarrelling once they'd returned to Scotland, but the arguments had intensified and the silences lengthened. Appearances were kept up for a number of years as her father travelled backwards and forwards to Canada, but she'd seen little of him during that time and had missed him dreadfully. Even when he *was* at home, from autumn to spring, she was away at boarding school. Malory Towers, at last, she had thought with a little buzz of excitement when she'd learned she was to go, but soon discovered that hockey was only one of the vicious games played at a school where she fitted in no better than she had in Miss Sinclair's schoolroom. Present troubles had banished past ones and neither parent had seemed aware of her unhappiness, being engulfed by their own. And, as she grew older, she had buried it all, leaving it behind, and set herself to build a life of her own. Her father had died and her mother had remarried and moved south, leaving her to do just that.

But now the photograph of Archie Maxwell brought it all back, and here she was with the wound exposed and painful, conscious once more of a troubling sense of wrongdoing and shame.

And Tam Nairn had been someone else entirely!

Over the weekend she remembered more about their curious friendship. 'What's a vagabond?' she'd asked one day, coming across him as he sat smoking on an upturned boat.

'Someone bonded to vaguery,' he replied, then laughed at her expression. She hoped the wry look in his eyes didn't mean he'd guessed the origin of her question. 'What rubbish, eh? No, it means, in the literal sense, one that wanders.' She considered the answer; it didn't sound too bad . . . Her mother's description of Tam as a useless vagabond had implied something much worse.

Even as a child, Eva had recognised that he too was out of place in Heart's Repose. He was like a character from a book, an outlaw or heroic fugitive, and as he fed her quickening appetite for stories, she imagined what his past might have been. She wondered now if the man he'd described, who'd once got lost in the northern forests, driven mad by mosquitoes and blackfly, had in fact been Tam himself. And had it been him who had hunted whales until the sight of the creatures being slaughtered had driven him ashore, repelled by it all? There had been many other stories and Eva smiled as she put away the dishes, remembering how she'd learned down by the fishing rooms of a monstrous menace, which had awoken under the sea, pulling ships down to their doom, dragging folk from coastal settlements, remembering too how he had chuckled as her eyes had fixed uneasily on the water swirling around the mussel-encrusted jetty.

Perhaps he had sensed that she too was an outsider and lived in her imagination.

One of her favourite stories had been Jack London's classic tale of Buck, the dog taken from domesticated comfort to be brutalised and beaten in the harsh northern lands, scarred for life but endlessly resilient. Tam's son, she'd learned, had named his dog Buck so he must have been told the story too . . . Even now when she heard dogs bark in the night she thought back to Heart's Repose.

'What's your son's name?' she'd asked, and learned that it was Ross. 'How old is he?'

'Depends on the day,' came the unhelpful answer. 'Anywhere between a troublesome five and a reliable forty, but close on fifteen most of the time.'

She'd started looking out for Ross too, but soon discovered she was beneath his notice. She'd see him heading out to sea, a lean and fit youth, tall for his age, working alongside the fishermen, spreading nets to dry on the net gallows or helping fix damaged boats that had been winched ashore, far more industrious than his father. Once, however, she'd caught him watching as she and Tam were chatting in the shadow of a broad flake where salted fish were drying. He'd scowled at her, then disappeared.

His hostility was something she'd not understood back then but now she wondered a little . . . Had he sensed, even then, how things might develop?

'What does molest mean?' she had finally remembered to ask.

An eyebrow was raised and Tam drew on his cigarette before answering. 'It's from a Latin verb *molestare*, which means to annoy, or cause trouble.' The answer was a surprise. Tam never annoyed her, quite the opposite, though she gathered he sometimes caused trouble. 'Why do you ask?'

'I . . . I read it somewhere,' she replied, dodging eyes which had darkened.

'Yeah, where?'

Her face burned under his scrutiny. 'I can't remember.'

'Right,' he'd said, then stubbed out the cigarette, rose and walked swiftly away.

These and other memories came to Eva as she lay awake that night considering what she ought to do, and by morning she'd arrived at a decision. If he was still living, Tam Nairn had a right to know that his father was dead and that he need no longer struggle, living under a shadow, perhaps in poverty, he must be told, and then it was up to him what he did – the choice would be his. She would write to him that evening, trusting that there was someone left at Heart's Repose who might know where he'd gone. But what about his family? Did they also have the right to know where he was? Perhaps, after all those years of uncertainty, they did, but she'd wait to see if she heard back from Tam before talking to them.

And even then, she needn't tell them everything.

But events next morning derailed her plan. She arrived at the office and had hardly taken off her coat when the phone rang. One of those days, she thought, reaching across to it. 'Eva Bayne speaking. Can I help you?'

'Miss Bayne? This is Duncan Maxwell from Rosslie.' She let the coat fall onto the chair. 'You came with David Mallory last week, to the auction . . .'

'I did.'

'He rang me over the weekend and told me a rather odd tale.'

'I—'

'Said he didn't believe a word of it, mind you, and only told me as a sort of joke.' Duncan Maxwell's tone was devoid of humour. 'Is there any truth in what you told him? That you recognised the photograph of Archibald?'

Caught off guard she could hardly deny it. 'Perhaps. At least, I think I do.'

'Think? Only *think*?' His response was sharp. 'Look. This isn't some sort of put-up job is it, on behalf of your paper?'

She took a moment. 'No.'

'I'd not put it past David Mallory. He's your boss, I gather.'

'My manager.' Her sympathy for the man began ebbing away.

'Right. Well, look, I'm tied up today but I want to hear what you've got to say. How about tomorrow evening. Can you do that?' Too late to draw back now so she said she could. 'Right. I'll meet you at The Central, in the bar. Eight o'clock. And do me a favour, would you – say nothing about this to Mallory. It's a family matter, a *private* family matter, and I'm asking you to respect that. Understood? Until tomorrow then.' He rang off, leaving her holding the receiver, once more the grubby hack.

David didn't make an appearance in the office that morning. He'd apparently leaped on an early train to Edinburgh, chasing some story of an MP accused of financial irregularity, so she was left alone to consider Duncan Maxwell's phone call.

It had unsettled her.

And it complicated things.

Twelve o'clock rolled around and she was pulling on her coat intending to nip out and get a sandwich when Janine, the general secretary with whom she was friendly, rang through to say that her mother was in the café across the street. 'Said to come and join her.'

'My *mother*—?'

'Wanted to surprise you.'

'But my mother *never* comes to Glasgow . . .' She'd moved down to East Anglia when she re-married and more or less stayed put, other than annual trips to the Mediterranean. Eva tried to visit at least once a year but her mother never reciprocated.

Was she ill? Eva wondered as she crossed the road. Had she had some awful diagnosis? Or had this marriage also come unstuck? Lord, she hoped not, but there had been no suggestions of disharmony last time she was down there. Whatever could have brought her here? She dodged a speeding car and headed for the only café there was across the road – an unassuming place with plastic tablecloths and steamed-up windows, a place where her exacting parent wouldn't normally be caught dead.

A warm, greasy fug met her. The place was full of people and noise, the clientele were mainly men, construction workers from a nearby building site, and Eva could see no sign of her mother. At a table in the corner there was a woman on her own, wearing a stylish toque hat pulled well down. Definitely not her mother . . . But she glanced up as the door shut behind Eva and raised a hand, beckoning her over. 'Ah, yes, I remember you now,' she said as Eva approached her table. 'You were with that dreadful Mallory man.'

Eva gaped. Lady Jillian Maxwell.

'Forgive the deception, won't you, my dear. I took a gamble that your mother wasn't dead or anything awful, and that you'd come. I didn't want your office to know I'd contacted you, you see, and this seemed the easiest way. And here you are.' She gestured to the chair opposite her and, after a moment's hesitation, Eva pulled it out and sat. 'Do you have a mother? Still living, I mean.'

'Yes.'

'And is she well?'

'Yes . . .'

'Thank goodness for that. I should hate to have upset you. We'll order some lunch, shall we, and then we can talk. I've decided on the sausage and chips on the recommendation of those gentlemen over there.' Two burly workmen turned at her words and grinned, giving Eva a thumbs up. 'Will you have the same? Or something else? Anything you like, in fact. And tea? Or coffee? They don't have a license, I'm afraid, so I can't offer anything stronger.'

Which was a pity as a stiff drink might have anchored her. The woman raised an imperious finger, bringing a waitress to their table.

'You've been speaking to your son,' Eva said, once the order was placed, feeling the need to take back the initiative.

'I have. Though I've not told him I've stolen a march on him by meeting you first, and I'd rather you didn't either.'

And Duncan hadn't wanted her to tell David of their meeting. Such secrecy. 'Why not?'

'I'll explain. But let's cut to the chase, my dear, and you start by telling me about this man you believe to be my stepson. Where did you know him and when was this?'

Eva paused a moment, still hesitant, but could see no way to refuse. 'In Canada, just over fifteen years ago.'

The woman's eyebrows arched. 'And you're how old now? Twenty something?'

'Twenty-five.'

'So you were ten.'

'Ten – eleven. Yes.'

'Hmm.' Lady Maxwell contemplated her and might have said more but the waitress returned with cutlery and sauce bottles. 'I doubt I could remember a single thing at twenty-five that happened when I was ten. But never mind that. Describe this man to me.'

There was something peremptory in the woman's manner and Eva found herself resisting. It had just occurred to her, suddenly and belatedly, that Tam Nairn might have very good reasons not to be found and she grew cautious. 'The man I'm thinking of was living in a small community on the east coast of Canada,' she answered carefully. 'I thought I recognised him from the photograph, older when I knew him, of course, but—'

'Thought? Only thought?' she interjected, echoing her son. 'And what were you doing on the east coast of Canada, aged ten – eleven.'

'My father was the doctor there.'

An eyebrow arched. 'And you remember this one man, out of all his patients? It's rather important that we find him, you know, so I hope you aren't wasting my time. *Was* he a patient? Was he ill?'

'He had a cut arm on one occasion and came to the surgery.'

'And you remembered that single incident?'

'It wasn't a large community—'

But Lady Maxwell was pressing on. 'Did he have a job, a profession?'

'He helped on the fishing boats sometimes. And . . . and I think he wrote a little.' The woman looked up from her plate. Eva had forgotten that until just now – it had come to her suddenly. 'Poetry, he wrote poems . . . but he had no steady job when I knew him.'

'And how *did* you come to know him? How does a part-time fisherman-poet impress a doctor's eleven-year-old daughter so greatly that she remembers him fifteen years later?'

Eva looked towards the steamed-up window and took a moment before replying. 'He taught me to read,' she said, turning back to Lady Maxwell. 'Not literally, of course, but we used to talk about books.'

Lady Maxwell looked steadily back at her, her eyes sharply intelligent, summing her up, then she lowered her gaze and loaded her fork again. 'Did he have any physical features that you remember?'

'He limped.'

'Which leg?'

Eva paused, unsure, and shut her eyes trying to remember how he walked. 'He favoured his left leg, I think, so it must have been his right one that was injured.'

'Did he say how he got the injury?'

Eva smiled. 'Pirates, he said,' and Lady Maxwell laughed in a way which changed her face entirely. Eva felt herself relax a little.

'Anything else?'

'He had a scar on his cheek.'

The laugh faded. 'You can see that on the photograph; it adds nothing.'

'And another on his forehead, just below the hairline, shaped like an L.'

The woman stared at her and seemed to grow paler. 'How could you possibly know that?'

Eva felt herself blushing. 'I washed his face for him once,' she replied, and explained the circumstances.

Lady Maxwell said nothing, digesting this. 'Was he married when you knew him?'

Eva shook her head. 'No. He'd been living with a local woman but she'd died. I never knew her.'

'Did he have children?'

'He had a son.'

Lady Maxwell froze, her fork half raised. 'A son?'

'Yes.'

'With this woman?'

'Yes.'

'But they weren't married, you say? You're sure of that?'

'No . . .' Then the implication of the question hit her.

'As in no, not married, or no, not certain?'

Eva shrugged. 'It's what everyone said. And his son used his mother's surname, not his.' She wished then that she could disappear. Ross. *Ross!* The name suddenly shrieked at her and she clenched her hands under the table, feeling way out of her depth. Ross for Rosslie. She should have kept her mouth shut, thought things through much more before saying anything.

She'd kicked a hornets' nest.

'Which was what?'

'McLeod. A lot of the native women have Scottish names . . .' She hoped the woman would not ask for his forename and rapidly reviewed what she'd told her. Nothing much of any use . . . She'd not mentioned Tam Nairn by name, nor the community, not even the province. Had she? No . . .

Jillian Maxwell was looking at her with a thoughtful expression, her meal abandoned. 'You know what, Eva Bayne, I'm rather inclined to believe you,' she said, at last. 'But I shall say the opposite to my son. I shall tell him you're a foolish girl seeking attention and on the look-out for a story. I shall tell him you couldn't put together anything like a coherent description and fell apart upon questioning, and I'll recommend that he doesn't bother meeting you.'

Eva's jaw dropped. 'What—'

'And in the meantime I'll write to Archie and explain the situation and decide what to tell Duncan once I have a reply.'

'But why?'

The woman leaned forward and spoke quickly. 'Because, my dear child, if you decide to go and live in the back of beyond you must have a reason and perhaps that reason is that you don't want to be found. I rather doubt that Duncan has considered that, his only thought is of the estate and the financial mess we're in. We need to resolve matters, of course we do, but we can do that through lawyers once we've established whether Archie's still alive. You don't know that, I suppose?' Eva shook her head. 'It was, as you said, fifteen years ago, so anything could have happened to him since then. If you'll give me his last known address I can trace him through that and you can safely leave the matter in my hands. And I very much hope that I can trust you to keep this whole conversation to yourself.' The woman's tone had changed completely and her hand was shaking slightly as she pulled a notebook and silver pen from her bag.

It was rarely a good idea to annoy the person you wanted to help you, Eva thought, keeping her temper in check and, besides, she had a question of her own. 'Why did he leave, all those years ago? And not come back—'

'So you *are* looking for a story!' Jillian Maxwell's face hardened.

'I'm just curious.'

'Well, you would be – you're a journalist, after all. Now, are you going to give me that address or do you hope to strike some sort of deal with me, because I'll tell you bluntly that I don't play games.'

Eva returned her glare steadily, and came to a sudden and determined decision. She took the pen and notebook and wrote: *c/o The General Store. Heart's Repose, Newfoundland*, then got to her feet.

'That's *it*?'

'It was a small place. And he was well known.' She needed to reach the door before the obvious question occurred to Lady Maxwell.

'Wait, Miss Bayne, hang on . . .' She put out a hand.

Too late. 'Got to go.' Eva pulled on her coat. 'They're very strict on lunch breaks at the office.'

'Well, I know where to find you, I suppose. And I only hope you're not spinning me a tale.'

Eva made for the door, her pulse racing as she crossed the road, not daring to look back. How long, she wondered, would it take an intelligent woman to realise that a man who wanted to remain missing would not be using his own name.

CHAPTER 9

Rosslie, 1940

Archie

They were finishing their meal when the news reached them. They were laughing, Archie was later to remember, easy now in each other's company, filling their glasses with his father's best port, nibbling on a soft cheese that Jilly had made herself. Archie had just declared it to be without taste or texture or any other redeeming feature, smirking at her outrage, before squinting to light an expensive Cuban cigar he'd found in a box on the mantelpiece. He was savouring the taste of it and watching the flickering reflection of the fire on the brass fender, feeling relaxed for the first time in months.

Roberts appeared at the door. 'Telephone, sir. Your father is on the line.'

Archie groaned and carefully placed the cigar on the side of his plate. 'He's bloody well smelled it! D'you think he was saving it for special?' He topped up his port glass and rose, balancing precariously with one stick, the glass in his other hand, and followed Roberts into the hall.

He put the receiver to his ear. 'Pa,' he said, and a moment later he cared not at all that the port had spilled, leaving a blood-red stain down the wallpaper, nor that the glass lay in fragments at his feet as he toppled against the wall, his eyes screwed tight in denial, shutting out the words, the phone receiver swinging on its cord, his father's voice reduced to a distant barked repetition of his name.

Roberts, summoned by the crash, stared at him in horror, then picked up the receiver. He spoke to the general, stiffened as he listened, then murmured something and returned the instrument to the cradle before bending to Archie who had slid to the floor, his head bowed over a bent knee, his injured leg stretched out before him.

Jilly appeared at the dining-room door. 'What . . . ? Oh God, Archie!' She came over quickly and crouched down beside him, the broken glass crunching under her heels. She looked up at Roberts in enquiry.

'It's . . . I believe it's Mr Andy, madam.'

Archie began to shake as the spoken words made it real. And from the place he was inhabiting on the floor, amidst the shattered glass and spilled port, he sensed Jilly freeze.

His father's voice had, for just a brief moment, quavered as if some human emotion had broken through the iron pan of self-control. 'Bad news, son,' he'd said, the line crackling as if in sympathy. 'No easy way to say it, no easy words. They saw him go down, the other pilots, they saw him, you see, flying like a madman, they said. He'd shot down three of the Hun and was on the tail of a fourth when he got hit. No chance of survival, they saw him go down in flames, my poor lad.' It had been then, that telltale gulp followed by a clearing of the throat as the general got a grip on himself. 'We should be proud, Archie, tremendously proud—' and the phone receiver had slipped from Archie's grasp.

He watched blood ooze out from under his palm as he sat, sprawled on the floor, just as he'd been on the deck of the ship on which he had escaped from the French coast, and remembered how they'd seen a plane engulfed in flames glide past them and seen the pilot beating furiously at the cockpit window, his gloves on fire. And all they could do, those who watched beside him, was pray that the burning plane fell faster.

He felt Roberts slide an arm around him. 'Let's get you into the library, Mr Archie. There's a fire in there.' Then he saw the blood. 'Ah! You've cut your hand, sir. Madam, if you would—'

From somewhere he heard Jilly say. 'Yes, of course.' She left and then she was back, crouching beside him again, binding his hand with a table napkin, her hair falling forward, covering her face. 'Shall we need help?'

The latter must have been addressed to Roberts who calmly replied, 'Between us I think we can manage to get him up, madam. Come now, Mr Archie, let's make you more comfortable.'

Archie put his bound hand to the floor and gritted his teeth as he tried to stand. Dear God. There would be no comfort now; a part of himself had died, perishing in flames beside his brother. Somehow they managed to get him on his feet and he allowed Roberts to support him into the library where he sat heavily, registering as he did that this worn old armchair was the one that Andy always preferred. The thought overwhelmed him, it felt as if his whole world was in tatters, and suddenly he was sobbing at the sheer bloody pointless waste of it all, facing a future that was unimaginable because his brother was not part of it. The manner of his death was something he was quite unable to confront, all he could do was put his face in his hands and weep. Roberts, whose touch was probably the only one he would have tolerated, placed a hand on his shoulder and stood silently beside the chair and let him sob, knowing with the wisdom of the elderly that no mere words could bring comfort.

It was only when he moved away and went to build up the fire that Archie was able to regain a little control. He dashed an arm across his forehead, using his bound hand to wipe his eyes and, as he lowered it, he saw how blood had seeped through the linen.

Red on white.

He lifted his head and looked across to where Jilly sat, motionless, staring into the fire, her face drained of colour. Roberts went to the sideboard, poured a drink and brought him the tumbler. 'Drink this, sir. It will help, if only briefly. And for you, madam?'

'Yes . . . Please.'

He returned to the sideboard and brought her a smaller measure. 'I'll leave you now. You'll ring if there is anything else, won't you, madam. Might I tell the staff, sir?'

Archie nodded. Roberts would do it right. He'd give Andy the dignity he deserved, and which his father would expect; Archie would make a terrible mess of it himself.

When Roberts had gone, they sat there, he and Jilly, in their separate silences like patients catastrophically injured, placed there by a benevolent nurse who could not save them. Archie was only dimly aware of her presence on the fringes of his consciousness, grateful that she did not speak or offer facile sympathy, and it was only as the minutes ticked by that he realised that she was as detached from him as he was from her, staring fixedly into the fire.

He felt a flicker of annoyance. Was this some sort of act? A pretence at grief, a crass faux empathy? She had hardly known Andy! Or was she concerned at his father's anguish? The spurt of anger brought a strange sort of relief; he'd identified a target and he was about to challenge her when he remembered the dead fiancé and realised what it must be that she was reliving and held back.

Roberts re-appeared at the door. 'I've lit a fire in your room, sir; the bed's aired and is warm. I'll take the decanter up, if you like, in case you wake in the night. Perhaps you'll allow me to help you up there now.' His tone was firm and fatherly. 'It really would be for the best.'

'I'll stay here a little longer, I think,' he replied, not out of perversity but because he was not yet ready to be alone, and at the mercy of the frights.

Roberts turned to Jilly. 'There's a fire in your room as well, madam, and there's a hot water bottle in your bed.'

She seemed to jerk awake. 'Thank you, Roberts. Yes . . . I will retire, I think,' she looked over at Archie, 'unless you want company?' He did, but he was damned if he'd admit it so he shook his head. When she'd gone, however, the silence became unbearable and so he downed his drink and rang the bell.

Roberts helped him upstairs but he dismissed him when they reached the landing. 'Thank you, Roberts. I'll be fine from here.' Last thing he wanted was the man hovering, putting him to bed as if he was a child. But as he crossed to his room, he paused for a moment to regain balance and heard a strange muffled sound coming from Jilly's room. He went to stand outside her door and listened to the strangled gasps and realised that she was crying, making an awful keening sound. He raised a hand to knock, and then let it fall.

His own grief was for Andy and he'd no comfort to give her for another.

Once in his room he poured himself a large measure from the decanter Roberts had provided, drained it, undressed and poured another then sat on the edge of the bed feeling hollowed out by the pain of overwhelming loss. Andy's credo had been that survival was paramount but his blind faith in himself had failed him in the end, and if Andy failed then what hope was there for the rest of them? Archie had seen how men died. He'd watched wounded men crawling away as if they could escape death, men weeping as they died, others drowning silently. Fergus had been grinning at him on the clifftop one minute and riddled with bullets the next. He'd seen death in all its guises – floating cadavers, bloated bodies, fly-infested wounds, gull-pecked eyes, the whole hideous panoply begat of conflict. If death could take Andy, it could surely take him too, find him as the frights did nightly, and finish him.

So what point was there in prolonging life?

He raised his head. That dart of poisoned reasoning became lodged in his brain. Why *not* cheat death then and seize oblivion? On his own terms. *Right now*. Why not simply load his revolver and finish things, spare himself further pain and grief? If Andy could bail out, then so could he. He drained the glass, poured another and as he sat there the poison worked its devilry. Life without his brother was unimaginable, a yawning, unbreachable gap, and beneath the grief was the burden of knowing that he was now his father's heir. He was caught, trapped by the tyranny of inheritance, and would be obliged to shoulder a responsibility he'd spent a lifetime rejoicing in having escaped. His father's shadow loomed large and uncompromising and he felt physically sick . . . So why *not* simply put an end to it all and leave the matter in Jilly's hands? She was young enough to produce heirs aplenty. Pa would consider it the coward's way out, but bravery didn't save you, Pa.

It got you killed.

He sat there a while longer, gulping at his drink, and the plan became a chilling compulsion. He rose and staggered across the floor to the chest of drawers, pulling open the top one where Roberts had put his service revolver. He picked it up, weighing the cold steel in his hands . . . In the temple or through the mouth, which was more certain? His heart began racing with a sudden desperate determination to carry the matter through before he changed his mind, quickly before he thought too much about it, before the image of Roberts running upstairs at the sound of a shot, of Jilly crossing the landing . . . He clenched his jaw and cracked open the revolver. The cylinder was empty and he cursed and began scrabbling around inside the drawer for cartridges. Gone. He pulled out the other drawers, emptying the contents on the floor, but found nothing and banged the drawers shut, swearing viciously. They had been there, with the revolver – he'd watched Roberts unpack. Must be somewhere . . . He wrenched open the wardrobe, the gun still in his hand, and began going through the pockets of his uniform, cursing Roberts, cursing his father, cursing Andy, cursing . . .

The door opened and Jilly stood there, her face ravaged and pulled, her eyes fixed on the gun in his hand. 'You won't find any. I made Roberts remove any ammunition when you first arrived.'

He swung round, almost losing his balance. '*Damn* you, what right—'

'Even then I thought you capable of damaging yourself.' She made no move to come closer but just stood there, looking back at him.

He was breathing hard now and if he could have reached her, he'd have throttled her. 'You can't stop me, you know.'

'I can try.'

Panting, he squeezed his eyes shut, swaying on his feet, then he hurled the gun into the open drawer, grabbing at the side of the wardrobe for support. 'Why the devil would you?'

'Because you're twenty-two and one day you'll thank me.'

Still she didn't move and the situation was suddenly absurd. 'So you're going to stand there all night, are you, in case I try to string myself up?'

'You'll find it difficult, I think, with that leg of yours.' She came into the room and calmly shut the wardrobe door and closed the open drawers. Pouring a tumbler of whisky, she held it out to him. 'You could drink yourself to death, of course, but it'll take a little longer.'

He was definitely unsteady now and the room was undulating horribly but he worked his way back across it, grabbing at whatever he could for support, cursing her as he went. Reaching the bed, he slumped onto the mattress, took the glass and downed the contents in one go. He felt weak and hopeless then, emasculated, drained of any sort of resolution and with difficulty he swung his legs onto the bed where he hunched up like a wounded animal, his back turned to her. His leg was throbbing and his head was about to split open and he found himself sobbing again, no longer caring that she saw him like this, a pitiful, pathetic excuse for a man. *Go, woman, for God's sake, go!*

And yet she still stood there.

At last there was a click and the room went dark. He heard the door close and squeezed his eyes shut, suppressing a moan, terrified now of being alone. The frights would find him on his knees with no defences left, they would annihilate him . . .

He sensed movement beside him, then felt cool air down his flank as the corner of the covers was turned back. A chill body slid in beside him and he stiffened in astonishment as her arm came around him. He lay there, too shocked to move, as she pressed her cheek against his back and clung to him. She was crying, her whole body shaking with silent sobs. He turned awkwardly in her arms. 'Jilly?' he whispered.

Her response was inaudible and so he said no more. For what could he possibly say? Silently he wrapped his arms around her and held her, and they remained like that, neither of them speaking.

And in a little while, they slept.

CHAPTER 10

He woke next morning alone and disorientated. He blinked, conscious of a thundering head as he tried to get his brain to focus. The world was feeling more than usually oppressive . . . How much had he drunk last night? And then recall kicked him hard in the pit of his stomach. *Andy!* He rolled over, staring up at the ceiling, rigid with horror.

Last night—

He pulled himself up and sat, staring at the dented pillow beside him, his head pounding hard, his mouth foul, while confused images began to swim into focus. A whisky tumbler lay on the floor beside the bed, an empty decanter beside it. He'd drunk too much, far too much . . . he felt like hell. Gradually the night's chaotic mess came together in his head. Jilly . . . ? Surely *that* never happened! And yet he could still feel the slimness of her encircling arm, her damp cheek against his skin, and he frowned at the pillow, picked it up and held it to his face, breathing in the unmistakable scent of her. He looked over at the chest of drawers from which he had hurled the contents, frantically searching for something. And then that too came into focus. Bullets. He had been searching for bullets . . . He went cold. Clutching the pillow to him he began to shake. He'd actually held his revolver in his hand with deadly intent; he looked down at his palm in horror. He'd have done it too, he'd have followed through and, but for Jilly, his body would be lying beside the bed, sprawled out there, brains and blood soaking the worn rug.

He lifted a shaking hand to his forehead. Poor Roberts . . .

And thank God for Jilly.

Would he *really* have done it? The cynic in him jeered: he'd not have found the courage! But after considering the matter dispassionately for a moment, he concluded that the sober truth was that he would. In that moment of bleak, drunken despair he'd been perfectly capable of pulling the trigger, and ignominiously departing this world.

He continued to sit there and contemplate the thought.

Then he looked again at the chest of drawers and saw that the clothes he'd dragged from them were gone. He rose, his head and stomach protesting as he crossed the room, and pulled the drawers open to find the clothes neatly folded back where they'd been and the revolver gone. Roberts?

No, not Roberts.

Jilly. Covering his tracks.

He sat on the edge of the bed, clutching the pillow again, and remembered the comfort of her presence and the deep, healing sleep that had followed. No frights had come. And while nothing could begin to heal the wound of Andy's loss, he knew that the thing he might have done last night he would never attempt again. No matter what. A worthless, spineless act that Andy himself would have despised.

He must find Jilly and tell her.

But his mind chose instead to linger on the feeling of her body against his, distracting him, and he tried to remember the last time he'd lain beside a woman. It must have been in Bailleul, back in early April, in a brothel, immediately after France and Britain had declared their common purpose and unity. They'd just relieved the French troops defending the line and he remembered how, drunk and outrageous, he had tried to explain to some thin and desperate girl how their coupling would honour that greater alliance. Neither pairing had proved long lasting, or in any way satisfactory.

Downstairs, Roberts, looking old and drawn, informed him that her ladyship was already out in the walled garden and, having gulped down two cups of strong coffee, Archie went looking for her.

He saw her from the gate, at the far end of the garden watering the runner beans and talking to a young man who was unloading what looked like manure from a handcart, creating a steaming pile beside the potting shed. She raised a hand when she saw Archie making his way towards them. 'Kenny was looking for you,' she called out, in a falsely bright voice. 'Seems the aphids are back.' Her face was pale and taut, her hair pulled back in a simple ponytail, and she lowered the watering can as he approached, subjecting him to an intense, unreadable scrutiny before turning back to the stranger.

'Would you finish the watering when you've unloaded the cart, please, John, while I set Captain Maxwell up in the glasshouse.' The young man agreed, and nodded at Archie.

Jilly set off and Archie followed. 'Who's that?'

'John McAdam.'

'Who's John McAdam, and why's he not in uniform?'

'He's a conchie.' Archie stared at her and looked back over his shoulder at him. 'With rather radical views about war and society.'

He frowned at her. 'And so, on that basis, you employed him?' This was not how he had intended their conversation to go but he was momentarily deflected. They reached the glasshouses and Jilly held the door while Archie manoeuvred himself in with his sticks. 'You took my gun,' he said.

'Yes.'

'It won't happen again, Jilly.' It wasn't the apology he had rehearsed either but the appearance of a conscientious objector, on this of all days, had thrown him, and his throbbing head made him abrupt.

'That's good,' she said, setting a tray of tomato plants in front of him.

'So you can put it back. And the ammo too.'

'All in good time.'

He scowled at her. 'It was a mad fleeting moment, the shock of—'

'You don't need a revolver here, nor do you need to explain.' She busied herself with another tray. 'If I see storm troopers coming up the drive, I'll let you have it back. Bullets too.'

He would have continued to protest but Kenny appeared and looked across at him. 'Morning, sir,' he said. Kenny never called him sir, but it was the old man's way of saying so much more. A veteran of the last war, he had returned to join the ranks of the silent and his eyes were red and rheumy as they held Archie's. 'He'll be missed, sir, will Mr Andy.'

'He will, Kenny.'

It was as much as either of them could manage. The old man turned away to set the kettle on the Primus and proceeded silently to make tea while Jilly called from the door to the young man, who set down the watering can and came towards them. Kenny looked up and muttered something inaudible. Jilly gave him a frown, which the old gardener ignored and, as the newcomer approached, Kenny turned to address Archie. 'Have you met Mr John McAdam?'

'After a fashion.'

The young man knocked the mud off his boots and came inside. 'McAdam, this is Captain Maxwell,' Kenny continued. 'Almost lost a leg in the service of the King, and has just lost his brother.' The old man was eyeing McAdam like an angry bull. 'And this, sir, is John McAdam, whose conscience keeps him safe.'

The newcomer was probably about Archie's age and gave him a grave but direct look from strikingly blue eyes. 'How d'ye do?' he said. 'And . . . and may I say how dreadfully sorry I am to hear your news. He was a good man, your brother, and I liked him very much.'

Archie took a mug of tea from Kenny. 'You knew him?'

But Kenny was not done. 'They say that the valiant taste death only once. The same's not said of cowards, as I recall.'

'Kenny! That's enough,' Jilly said

'I'll take my tea outside, if you prefer,' said John McAdam, addressing Archie.

'I'd prefer you to stay and tell me how you know my brother. I don't remember seeing you on the estate.'

'You wouldn't. I usually stay with my father in Glasgow, although my mother moved back some years ago to be near her family.'

'But still you knew my brother?'

McAdam nodded. 'My mother wrote and asked him to attend my tribunal, and he did, for which I'm grateful. I spoke to him for a while afterwards, and he was good enough to listen.'

Kenny hawked and spat.

Archie was baffled. He wanted to know more, but was not prepared to ask his questions under Kenny's hostile eye. 'Well, maybe there'll be a chance for us to speak as well,' he said.

The newcomer had an open, intelligent face, and absorbed Kenny's ire with unruffled calm. 'I'd like that.'

The four of them drank their tea in a chilly silence that even Jilly made no attempt to break. McAdam was the first to go back to work, rinsing his mug under a tap and nodding his thanks. Kenny watched him go, muttering still, and after a moment he too left.

Leaving Archie alone with Jilly.

'Have you spoken again to Pa?' he asked.

'Just briefly, this morning. He's being very stoic, as you can imagine, and burying himself in work.' She glanced at him, and away. 'He asked after you.'

Archie nodded, wondering what she'd told him. 'Will he come up?'

'He says not. Too much going on. He hopes you're getting on all right. Sends his love.' He doubted that very much, but he nodded, resuming his task with the tomato plants. Covertly he watched her busying herself filling pots with soil, pushing seeds into the earth, watering them carefully from a long-spouted copper can. Believing in a future in which they might flourish.

'You were very kind,' he said, having carefully weighed his words. 'Last night.'

She didn't look up, nor did she answer at once as if she was doing the same. 'The moment seemed to call for comfort.'

'And I'm very glad you'd removed the cartridges.'

She looked across at him then and there was a nakedness in her eyes. 'I'd never have been able to forgive myself . . . We *have* to survive, Archie, and we do it as best we can, even when it seems impossible. We give and take as the moment requires and last night we did a bit of both, you and I.' He digested this, wondering a little what she meant. 'It was a dreadful blow to absorb. How are you now?'

'I'm fine.'

'Fine?'

'Yes, fine.'

'Stupid word,' she said, giving him a twisted smile, her eyes filling again. 'There's nothing *fine* about any of it, is there?'

He shook his head and pulled another tray towards him, remembering how she had put her arms around him, and then clung to him. Giving and taking. Had that been fine in her book? He doubted his father would have agreed. Her presence had been wonderfully comforting but where were the limits of *fine*? 'I've seen men with their legs blown off lying there in stunned disbelief, telling me they're fine. Fine, sir, dying perhaps, but *absolutely* fine.'

She smiled a little, that same wry smile. 'It's a word that buys a little time, and distance, while we figure out how to carry on.'

They worked together in silence. It would take more than a little time to come to terms with Andy's loss, but with each passing day he was discovering that Jilly was not what he had initially thought her. Intrigued, he took a risk. 'Why *did* you marry Pa?'

Jilly's smile became ironic. 'You've wanted to ask that question ever since you arrived, haven't you?'

'Perhaps.'

'And it's a very impertinent one.'

'Yes, I know.'

She pulled a packet of cigarettes from her pocket and offered him one. He shook his head so she lit her own and continued to wave the match long after the flame had gone out. 'Because he asked me. Will that do?'

'Not really.' If he was ever to know, he must push the point.

She gave a short laugh. 'No?' and took a drag on the cigarette. 'Then rather than let your imagination run wild, I'll tell you, and then you'll know the worst of me. I was very much in love with a married man; I was his bit on the side for several years. When he decided to divorce his wife, we lived openly together, and the world we inhabited condemned us. We didn't give a damn, though, and last year Jack asked me to marry him when the divorce came through and I said yes, but then the war came and he was sent to Norway on reconnaissance and never returned. Simple as that. His father was an old friend of your father's and we met at Jack's memorial service. He found me sobbing in a cloakroom having been roundly abused by Jack's mother who told me that I had no business to be there, I'd ruined her son's life and destroyed his wife's chance of happiness. She was in great pain, of course, and perhaps she was right. If she could have found a way of blaming me for Jack's death, she would have thrown that at me too. I became the focus for her anger and her grief. It hurt, it was humiliating, but I could understand . . .' She took another long drag. 'Your father was kind, he let me sob and then he took me away and gave me tea and toast, and told me about you and Andy, his fears for you both, and how he'd lost his wife and how devastating it had been.' Archie looked across at her, astounded. Never once had his father expressed such sentiments in his hearing, never once shown anything resembling compassion, or grief. But Jilly, he was finding, had a way of drawing out a man . . . 'And then a couple of days later he asked me out for dinner, asked how I was getting on, said he was concerned about me, took an interest, and it went rather fast from there. Is that enough?'

'Do you love him?'

She narrowed her eyes against the smoke. 'You don't know when to stop, do you?'

'Simple question.'

'I told you once before that I'll be a good wife to him.'

'That's not an answer.'

'It's all you're going to get. I'm thirty-two years old, written off as a thoroughly bad lot, a marriage wrecker, and was offered a chance of security, a kind husband and . . .'

'A title and decent amount of pin money.'

He regretted the words as soon as they were out and she continued to consider him, her cigarette held at an angle. It made her appear hard, harder than he knew her to be. 'You'll be apologising for that remark in due course, I imagine. Your brother asked me the same question, and I gave him the exact same answer.'

She'd met Andy at some bash in London, she'd said, hardly the obvious place for such intimate discourse. He pulled the cigarettes towards him and lit one.

'Tell me about your brother,' Jilly said, before he had a chance to further question her, but he shook his head. It was impossible to convey what Andy had meant to him: hero and champion, friend and mentor, shielding him from his father's exasperation, covering for him, teasing him, encouraging him. If he attempted to express these things he'd be sunk. 'He told me you wanted to be a writer,' she said, dropping her cigarette and stamping on it.

'I did.'

'He said you're very good.'

He shrugged. 'Partisan.'

She smiled and shook her head. 'When the war's over you must get back to it. You owe it to yourself.'

'Pa'll have other ideas.'

'If you can escape from mortars and machine guns you can surely escape from your father for a few years.'

'Before I'm reeled back in, you mean, and trained to be a baronet?' The bitterness and pain churned inside him again, corroding his gut. 'Knocked into shape, a second-rate Andy. God, Jilly, give him sons, dozens of them! Then he can disown me and leave me in peace. I never wanted any of this.'

She put her head on one side, contemplating him. 'You don't *have* to have any of it. You can make your own choices, Archie, as long as you're prepared to accept the consequences. If this war has taught us anything it's to seize our chances when they come.'

CHAPTER 11

Next morning, at breakfast: 'D'you think Kenny would take a chair down to the river and set me up?' Archie asked. 'I could dig out a rod and some flies and see how I get on. Rods still kept in the backroom, Roberts?' He had risen early, determined to demonstrate to Jilly, and to himself, that he would find a way of coping.

'I'll look one out for you, sir.' Roberts too looked a little better than yesterday.

'And I'll ask John to set you up, not Kenny,' said Jilly. 'It'd be good to get them away from each other for a while. Maybe pack a flask, Roberts, and some sandwiches. And I'll find a rug.'

'Yes, madam.'

'I'm not an invalid, you know,' Archie remarked when he'd gone.

'Isn't that exactly what you are?' She gave a smile over her shoulder as she left. 'But we'll expect trout for supper nonetheless.'

As he made slow progress towards the river he noted how the summer was already melting into a golden autumn. The sun had lit the hillside against a sky that was a cool and restful blue and already there was a mellowness in the air.

And thanks to Jilly's foresight he was alive to appreciate it.

But which reality would he inhabit today? The one where his brother was dead and only carnage and further grief awaited him, or the one in which his father's wife had slipped between his sheets and they had clung together like frightened children, or would he simply bask in the idyllic scene before him now? Was he allowed to choose? Dappled light had set the river a-sparkle and a pair of ducks floated serenely downstream beneath a cloud of insects dancing in the sun. Perhaps, just for this morning, he would allow himself the balm this small corner of sanity was offering him and put the rest aside. Until the guilt kicked in again.

John McAdam had already set up a chair on a pebbly strip of land. A good spot; Archie had often fished from there. He quickened his step and, unthinking, caught one of his sticks on a tree root and tripped, falling heavily on the sward.

McAdam was beside him in an instant. 'Wait! Don't move,' he said. 'Catch your breath.' Archie cursed volubly instead and the man smiled a little. 'Right!' he said when Archie had finished. 'Can you roll over? Easy . . . Good. Now let me help you.' With his leg protesting violently Archie managed to get upright again, leaning hard on the man's shoulder. McAdam helped him to the chair and lowered him in, lifting his injured leg onto the fishing basket and Archie thanked him through gritted teeth. 'Stupid of me. Blame the trout – I got excited.'

'I've seen a few jumping, big ones too.'

'Then let me at them.' McAdam considered him a moment, then went back to pick up the rod, which Archie had dropped.

A favourite fly was already in place and his grip tightened on the rod, an old friend, but now he faced the dilemma of how the hell he was to cast from this position. Wincing a little he lowered his leg. 'Keep clear, this could go anywhere,' he said, and it did, snagging the brambles behind him. After two or three further attempts he gave up in disgust and looked at McAdam. 'Can you cast a fly?' Wordlessly the man took the rod and cast a flawless line that uncoiled gracefully, catching the sunlight, to land upstream from them in exactly the right spot, sending ripples circling out. Archie grunted and took back the rod. 'Seems you can.'

'I'd a good teacher.'

A sweet breeze ruffled the surface of the water and there was another silence as Archie reeled in, keeping tension on the line. 'Who was that?'

'My grandfather. Poaching on the Avon.'

Archie glanced at the man and saw that he was smiling, a quiet smile. 'Then cast again, would you.' They continued in this way for a while, neither finding the need to speak. They had one or two bites but each time the fish escaped and eventually, tiring a little, Archie reeled in and set the rod aside. 'So,' he demanded. 'Is it religion or politics that keeps you out of uniform?'

McAdam was crouched a yard or so away, balancing on his heels. 'Not religion, that's for sure. No, I was weaned on pacifism.'

Archie frowned at him. 'And that's it?'

'My father was a conchie in the Great War, so there was never any question of what I would do.'

'Except think for yourself,' Archie snapped.

'I always do.'

The man's cool demeanour irritated him. 'Signed the Peace Pledge, have you?'

'Years ago. My mother was as ardent a pacifist as my father. Began protesting before I could walk.' He faced Archie with a calm expression. 'And I'm not ashamed of it, you know, or of them.'

Archie considered him, the firm jaw and resolute eyes. 'I see that. But don't you find it hard, standing on your soapbox, hugging your conscience, while others die to preserve us all?'

The question was doubtless a familiar one and the man answered it evenly. 'It was much harder for my father, first time round. They were treated very badly, cruelly even, and quite unnecessarily so. He was imprisoned then sent to Dyce Camp where they starved the poor buggers. Caught pneumonia there and was never healthy again, but his experience simply strengthened his determination. It was a pointless war, utterly futile, so resisting conscription was easy. It's harder this time.'

'Harder than fighting?' Archie asked, the throbbing pain in his leg making him sour.

'No.'

He'd not meant to shut down the conversation. 'Cast again, will you?' They continued fishing in silence, McAdam casting, Archie reeling in, but nothing much was biting. Should have got out here earlier, he thought, or waited until evening when the light began to fall.

He glanced at his companion, and was about to ask about his encounter with Andy when the man spoke again. 'It's easy to be a pacifist in peacetime, easy to avow the wrongness of killing and denounce war. But then war comes and you're faced with having to make a decision . . . Perhaps if I'd not been in Spain it would've been different, but I saw for myself how war destroys our very humanity—'

'You fought in Spain?'

'I drove ambulances, and patched up those who saw no solution other than war.'

Idealistic fool. 'How would you stop the fascists then? With sweet reason?'

McAdam looked back at him. 'We should never have arrived at this point. If we'd made more of a stand, more of us—'

'What d'you think we're doing, for God's sake!'

'Earlier, I mean, much earlier. Politicians didn't seem to mind Hitler so much until he got expansionist ambitions, turned aside with a complacent eye and now . . . now we're back where we were twenty-five years ago, grieving for wasted lives.' He gave Archie an unflinching look. 'Your brother might still be here if the politicians had been more astute and seen where Hitler was heading.'

The bitter words struck a deep chord. 'How did you know my brother?' They seemed unlikely companions.

'I hardly did, but once I was given Category B status, farm work became an option. When he came to the tribunal he said the estate could do with a hand, if I'd agree to come.'

'*Agree*? Kenny might have you shovelling shit but it's pretty cushy work.'

McAdam gave him a quizzical look. 'My father was at the tribunal too.'

'Meaning what?' There was something here he didn't understand.

'Meaning that he was old enough to remember the evictions.' Archie looked blank. 'From Aber Rosslie.' The ducks lifted off the river and flew upstream, low against the current, and McAdam's eyes followed them. 'Coming here wasn't a straightforward decision for me, you see, and one he too wrestled with.'

Aber Rosslie. Archie knew where he meant. Down by the estuary there were the remains of houses, some now used as lambing sheds and fodder stores while the roofless walls served as sheep dips and fanks while others were left open to the sky, crumbling away to become heaps of moss-covered stones. It was years since he had thought of them at all.

'But you're here nonetheless,' he said.

'My mother is ill so your brother's offer was welcome. Glasgow air doesn't suit her so she stays here with her sister.'

'And your father is in Glasgow?'

'Aye, he'll never move back.'

Archie gave him a sour look. 'So his convictions keep you out of uniform and himself apart from his wife.'

McAdam returned the look squarely. 'They'd still be at Aber Rosslie if they'd had the choice. What happened there made him what he is, what he's been all his life. It was inhuman what was done to them. He was only a bairn and it left a deep scar. Eight families were thrown off on a single day, close-knit families, fishing folk who farmed a field or two, bound to each other and to the land, driven off so that the estate could run sheep there. And now sheep are barely profitable and the houses stand empty. Where was the sense in it?'

Archie had no answer.

The ruins stood on a little headland, out of sight of the hall, and he remembered seeing the remains of a slipway down to the sea, and there were traces of old lazy beds covered in daisies set back from the shore. He'd never once considered them as anything other than places to play or watch the shearing, never thought about the displaced lives and broken threads. 'He says he only had to remember the sight of his home being torched to harden his resolve. Why should he fight for a government that would allow such a thing?'

'You've hardly the same excuse!'

McAdam lifted his gaze and scanned the river and the amphitheatre of purple hills that framed the valley. 'Maybe not, though were it not for the evictions, I might have grown up here rather than in the Gorbals in a place where no child can thrive. My mother might not cough her lungs out every night and be here with her family, where they belong. My parents shaped my thinking but my reasons not to fight are entirely my own.' He paused. 'My father shook your brother's hand, though, when he spoke for me at the tribunal, and that was a big step for him.'

Archie struggled to find a response, and returned instead to McAdam's earlier point. 'Since the politicians *have* failed, and your pacificists and socialists haven't prevented this second conflict, what are we supposed to do? Let Hitler overrun us all?'

'That's the problem.'

'Aye, John McAdam, it is! Cast again.'

He cast, handing the rod back to Archie, and almost straight away there was a tug on the line and then the two men were bound in common purpose, their differences put aside. Archie rose, braced his back against a tree trunk and played his fish, relentlessly bringing it in, seeing sinuous silver beneath the surface while John stood poised with the net in the shallows and a few moments later, breathless and triumphant, they landed not a trout but a fine salmon.

It lay on the grassy sward, glistening, iridescent in the sunlight, an old warrior by the size of it. McAdam despatched it quickly, glancing up at Archie with the glint of a smile.

'The king of fish.' Archie found himself responding to the smile. 'Gut the brute, and take half home to your mother.'

They had the other half for supper at the hall.

Jilly had changed out of her gardening clothes and her hair looked newly washed and glossy. She congratulated Archie on the catch. 'Such a treat!' she said. 'Just what's needed after a day shifting muck. I ached in every muscle but a hot bath has put all to rights. And to honour your salmon I got Roberts to plunder the cellars.' She nodded towards a bottle on the sideboard. A Rhenish wine, he noted – a fine vintage. He picked it up to study the label, which depicted a terrace of vineyards and a distant castle, bordered by fiercely Teutonic crests and seals, complete with helmets and sabres.

'You chose *this*?' he asked her, gesturing to it. 'Must have been in the cellar for years. Oughtn't we to pour the contents down the sink and hurl the bottle into the hearth.'

She smiled. 'I'd rather pour the contents down my throat, drink damnation to the Fatherland and *then* smash the bottle.'

Another of Jilly's accommodations, he thought as he poured the amber liquid. 'You should have got John McAdam to shift manure rather than indulging me.'

'He deserved a day off.' And, when Roberts had left them, added, 'What did you make of him?'

Archie sat back, savouring the wine, the taste of an older, more civilised Germany. 'I liked him, though I utterly dispute the stance he's taken. Head-in-the-clouds idealist. There's a history, I gather, of family defiance—'

'What do you mean?'

'The Aber Rosslie evictions.'

'Ah. Andy mentioned them when he wrote, said we owed them something.'

Archie considered her. 'He wrote to you, not Pa?'

'Mmm. He knew I was here and asked me to find work for John,' she pulled a face, 'and suggested hiding the man if your father ever came up from London. I like John. He works very hard and puts up with Kenny, who is absolutely foul to him. He actually asked me not to reprimand Kenny, you know, as he reckons being nasty to him helps the old man bear things.

He gives John the very worst of the jobs and rides him hard.' Quite right, Archie thought. 'But he clearly doesn't care a fig what other people think, he has his own principles and he sticks to them. I rather admire that.'

CHAPTER 12

Archie lay awake that night wondering what would happen now if the frights returned. Would she come if he cried out or would there be constraint between them? Lying there, between the sheets, he could still feel the touch of her, the warmth of her skin through her thin nightdress, the smell of her . . .

Those incautious thoughts carried him into a deep sleep and he woke feeling better than he'd done for months. Had Jilly's presence vanquished the frights? he wondered as he dressed. What a thought! Going down to breakfast seemed less painful too, his leg less stiff and awkward. And yet this strange euphoria seemed entirely at odds with the news of Andy's death still so fresh.

That thought sobered him.

Jilly was just finishing breakfast when he appeared at the door. 'Good morning,' she said, surveying him. 'No frights last night?'

'Not one.'

'Excellent.' She poured a cup of tea and pushed it towards him. 'You look better. So what's today's plan? More aphid slaughter?'

'God, no. I can only take so much of Kenny. Have you deliveries to make?'

'Not today. Tomorrow, perhaps.'

'I'll come with you.'

She glanced at him. 'Very well.'

He passed a desultory day doing not much of anything, resenting a little that Jilly chose to spend it among the vegetables where she'd provided neutral territory, she told him at dinner, between

Kenny and John McAdam. 'No matter what Kenny threw at him, the man simply absorbed it! I was almost ready to punch Kenny myself.'

Archie grunted in reply.

After dinner she went straight up to bed, claiming that she was worn out, and he felt resentful again when she left the room; he had wanted to build on their companionship and to talk to her, learn more about her. He'd *wanted* to talk about Andy now, to keep him alive. It felt as if, at last, he was emerging from his own cocoon of pain and guilt and found that he craved company and so, having moodily finished off the wine and not wanting to drink port or whisky on his own, there seemed no point in staying up. He made his way stiffly upstairs, noting a strip of light under Jilly's door as he crossed the landing and he hesitated a moment, emboldened by the wine. On balance, though, the lipstick and the black dress had hardly been for his benefit, but for herself after a day shifting horse shit.

She must miss her London life . . .

He fell asleep at once only to discover that the frights, far from vanquished, returned with renewed vitality. This time they came at him from a castle, which strongly resembled the wine-bottle label. Stukas appeared, driving him towards the river and he was running ahead of them, breathless, hobbled by his injured leg, signalling desperately to John McAdam who, all unaware of the pursuit, was midstream in a small boat, fishing. Archie reached the bank and shouted out to him but McAdam, taking in the situation, shook his head. 'I'd be aiding the war effort,' he called back. The Stukas dipped, peppering the riverbank, bullets missing him by a whisker, but McAdam remained implacable. 'Must stay neutral.' Archie started to wade towards him, shouting furiously, struggling against the flow, but the man simply rowed further into the current. 'Your brother was a good man, but what's been gained by his death? Tell me that!' And suddenly it was McAdam's fault that Andy was dead, and Archie drew his pistol only to find it empty, but in hurling it at the man he unbalanced himself and fell into the flow of the river, cracking his head on a rock—

And woke, in pain, on the bedroom floor.

A moment later the door opened and Jilly flicked on the light. 'Oh, Lord.'

He put his hand up to his head and found it sticky. 'Bloody frights,' he muttered and tried to get up.

'Wait! Stay still, you'll only go over again.' She came over to him and disentangled his feet from the sheets, lifting his damaged leg with cool and gentle hands. Fortunately he'd fallen on the other side, but even so he was in pain. 'Pushed you out of bed, did they? I thought I heard you but I'd no idea you were tying yourself in knots!'

'You heard me, but didn't come.'

She paused, her face close to his and frowned at him. 'Is that why you fell out of bed?'

'Cracking my head on the table for good measure?'

She raised her gaze to his forehead. 'It's bleeding.'

'I know.'

'But only a little.'

'Still needs attention.'

Their eyes held for a moment and she left the room, returning a moment later with a small towel. She ran water into Archie's sink, wet the towel and returned to where he still sat on the floor beside the tangle of sheets. She knelt beside him, focusing her attention on the cut.

Her breast was at eye level, the nipple a dark shadow beneath her nightdress, pushing out the flimsy silk. It was all he could do not to reach out and cup the roundness of her in his hand. He exhaled noisily and she looked down at him. 'Compared to your other wounds, Captain Maxwell, this one is trivial.' She made a bandage of a sort and sat back on her heels. 'Now, can you get up or do I fetch Roberts?' In answer he braced his back against the bed frame and struggled up onto the mattress, where he sat and their eyes met again. 'And you wonder why I didn't come,' she remarked before reaching out to turn off the lamp.

Next morning Archie looked in the shaving mirror and was momentarily surprised to see dried blood streaking his forehead; Jilly's makeshift bandage had come off in the night, exposing a nasty bruise. He wiped the blood away with his flannel and revealed a small right angle of a cut; it formed a perfect L just below the hairline. He stood there, looking himself in the eye, not quite accepting that when Jilly had turned off the lamp last night he had held his breath, wondering if she would slip into bed beside him, only to be crushed with disappointment when she hadn't.

Quite what that said about him, he didn't choose to examine.

He went carefully downstairs, noting a new pain in his leg. Roberts was at the sideboard when he entered the dining room, and Jilly was tucking into a bowl of porridge. She looked up at him and pulled a face. 'Did you hear the rumpus last night, Roberts? Mr Archie fell out of bed and banged his head. I couldn't imagine what the noise was.'

Roberts came over and examined him. 'Dear me! Are you quite all right, sir?'

Archie nodded, pulling out a chair. 'Just felt bloody silly. Hope I didn't wake the household.'

'Well, you couldn't really, sir, not from there.' Archie filed that away. 'Perhaps I should move into the dressing room, in case you need help in the night?'

Definitely not. 'Thank you, but I can always ring, or holler, though I doubt it'll happen again.'

He glanced at Jilly who betrayed not a flicker. 'It's to be hoped not,' she said. 'Such a thump – I thought the Germans had arrived.'

'And your leg, sir? I heard you fell by the river too. Perhaps you are being a little unwise, taking rather too much on—'

Jilly rose. 'I think you're absolutely right, Roberts. But today he'll be under my eye as he's driving me on my rounds. I'll see that he doesn't overdo things.'

Archie felt absurdly happy as he climbed into the dog cart while the vegetable boxes were being loaded into the back of it, and resolutely pushed aside the thought of his father. No reason to consider him; after all, there was no harm in this. He would live for the moment, he told himself, and be grateful he was alive to enjoy the late summer sunshine, the cool sweet air and the companionship of Jilly beside him.

No harm at all.

They understood each other, he and Jilly.

John McAdam was helping Kenny load up the dog cart, silently obeying barked instructions, but he took a moment to ask Archie if he'd suffered any ill-effects from the previous day. 'Thank you, no. Good salmon, eh? A mighty beast. Did your mother enjoy it?'

'She did, yes, and sent her thanks.'

Archie caught a startled look from Kenny as Jilly hopped up beside him. 'Right, off we go,' she said, adding when they were out of earshot, 'Shouldn't have mentioned the salmon, Archie. Kenny will be twice as hard on him now. He wasn't going to take any but I insisted that he should.'

Archie was bewildered. 'But I told him to take half of it!'

'Did you? Well, he wasn't going to, you know, but I wrapped up a chunk of it and put it in his pocket.'

'Stupid fellow. Does he wear a hair shirt too?'

'He's not a prig, just very aware of offending sensibilities. Mindful of his mother's position too, and his aunt. His uncle won't have him staying with them, you know.'

'So where does he sleep?'

'Above the tack room where the grooms used to live. Says he's happy there. There's a fireplace so he's warm and he has his books and claims he enjoys his solitude. Not sure he can spend the winter there though.'

Jilly's accommodations were everywhere. 'And when Pa comes home, what then?'

'Who knows. I can always hide him, I suppose, although if I tell your father it was Andy's idea, he might just accept it. Anyway, he's no plans to come, as far as I know. Far too busy.' Her tone had changed. He looked across at her but she had turned away.

CHAPTER 13

Heart's Repose, 1966

Eva

Both her parents were waiting for Eva when she returned from school the day after her visit to the headland and her stomach did a flip when she saw their faces. Her mother wore that pinched look that meant she was angry, or had been thwarted, and her father's expression was grave. The kitchen table, scrubbed to within an inch of its life, stood between them. 'So will *you* say something, or will I?' her mother said, frowning at her husband.

Eva looked from one to the other. Whatever had she done?

'How was school?' Her father pulled out a chair and sat, gesturing for her to join him and she did, tucking her schoolbag under the chair, wondering if they could possibly know what was contained within it.

'Fine.'

'Old Jacob said he saw you out on the headland yesterday.'

Ah, was that it? She relaxed a little and nodded. 'I was looking out for whales.'

'See any?' Her father cocked his eyebrow in a friendly way. Whatever this was about, he'd been put up to it.

'Only seals, and then it got windy and the waves had crests so I wouldn't see them spouting, and I got stiff and came back.'

'Anyone out there with you?'

'No . . .' which was true.

'No one?'

She shook her head, pleased that she could meet his eyes. 'I met Tam Nairn on the way back, though, and I saw the—'

'Did he speak to you?' Her mother stood with her arms folded across her chest.

'Just said to be careful cos the cliffs were crumbly after the rain.' That was earlier, but true, as far as it went.

'Anything else?'

She gave a little white-lie shrug. 'And I *am* always careful, and where I was wasn't crumbly at all.' A sulky tone might deflect them onto more general grown-up concerns but she sensed there was something else here, something unspoken and beyond her understanding. Her mother was always telling her that she shouldn't speak to Tam Nairn but never explaining why. Miss Sinclair too had taken her to one side and said much the same, probably put up to it by her mother. Eva had resented both as interference. She *liked* talking to Tam and looked forward to their conversations, which started in one place and took extraordinary twists and turns before arriving in quite another.

'Jacob said he saw you walking with Tam Nairn, talking to him, along the trail.'

She pulled a face. 'I just asked him if he'd ever seen whales.'

'I've told you times many—'

'And had he?'

Eva nodded at her father. 'But not that day. He said this maybe wasn't the best season and that it wasn't a good idea to stay out on the headland when the wind was getting up.' How easy it was to tell adults the things they wanted to hear.

'And he's absolutely right. Stay away from the headland and the clifftops, Eva. Jacob was complaining that you children have no understanding of how loose those shale rocks can be, especially after winter frosts. One slip and you're done. And in a high wind . . . You're not a gull, you know!'

She smiled back at him, sensing the interrogation was coming to an end.

Not quite; her mother wasn't done. 'And keep *away* from Tam Nairn. He's got no business speaking to you, a child on your own. There's a lot of ill-feeling building against him.'

'But for an entirely different reason, my dear, and Tam's not a *bad* man,' her father said, then added, 'It's quite true, of course, that he's not a suitable friend for a young girl, although Jacob can be a bit too—'

'Too *what*?'

Sensing that she was no longer at the centre of the storm, Eva began slowly pushing back the chair, taking up the strap of her bag. Seemed they *didn't* know, after all.

'Too quick to judge. There're plenty in the village with views about Tam Nairn at the moment, but he was giving Eva good advice.' He turned back to her. 'Does he ever bother you at all, Eva, or . . . or annoy you?' Annoy? As in *molestare*? She shook her head. 'Or follow you?' She gave her best surprised-and-bewildered look, which came easily, for why on earth would he?

'Or ask you to do anything?' her mother asked.

She considered a moment, not understanding. 'Like what?'

'Or give you sweets, or other things?'

Guilt flooded her. They did know! But it was a loan, not a gift . . . And then, miraculously her father rescued her. 'That's all just fine, then. And you can say hello if you see him, like you would to anyone else.' Her mother snorted. 'Now, away with you and get started on your homework.'

Eva clutched her bag to her and slipped past them, head down. Once inside her room she shut the door, threw the bag on her bed and, with a final glance over her shoulder, pulled out her trophy.

Collected Poems.

He'd remembered! He'd been waiting for her as she came out of school that afternoon, leaning against a rock near the school-house, apparently asleep. When the children had piled out, he'd stood up, stretched elaborately and yawned. She'd slowed a little as she came towards him and he'd first cast her an indifferent glance, and then given a wink. 'Behind the rock,' he'd muttered.

'Go get it, girl,' and he'd limped away. She bent to adjust her shoe and, when the others had gone, looked and found a package wrapped in an oilskin cloth.

She opened her bedroom door a crack, and listened to the argument which was continuing in the kitchen 'They must all *surely* see . . .' her mother's voice was strident '. . . but the wretched man has persuaded at least three families to stand against it, while all the sensible, right-thinking ones . . .'

And then her father's measured tones. 'I know, I know, but he makes some good points . . .' The discussion had moved on and so she'd be safe for a while so she sat on the edge of her bed and opened the book. On the flyleaf she saw *Miss Ada Sinclair* written in black ink. It wasn't his book at all!

Overdue, he'd said . . .

Tucked inside, she found a sheet of paper, a hand-written list of poems with comments or thoughts pencilled in beside them, and this she knew was for her.

The book fell open at a page with a poem called *Sea-Fever*. It was a short one and she saw that he had underlined one line, half way down. She began reading and when she reached that line, she learned what he'd meant about spine-tingling. And that night she lay in bed, saying the line over and over to herself, rocked to sleep by its rhythm.

To the gull's way and the whale's way where the wind's like a whetted knife.

Her next encounter with Tam Nairn, however, turned out to be an opening salvo for what was later to come.

As Eva became more accepted by the children of the outport, two of the younger boys took it upon themselves to teach her to fish and she was sitting with them on one of the jetties, her legs dangling, a baited line over the side when the row broke out. They were just across from one of the larger salting and splitting rooms, which stood, straddling shore and sea, on sturdy wooden posts with a gutting room perched at the end of its wooden stage. Upon arrival she had puzzled as to why these sheds were called rooms until Tam explained the process to her. Fish were gutted and split in the small room at the end, the entrails dumped through a hole in the floor, then the split cod were salted and packed into barrels in the larger room where they would stay until deemed ready to be laid on the broad flakes to dry in the sun and the wind. The fish would last for weeks, he told her, if the process went well, and doing things well was what the outport depended upon, because times were hard and change was in the air.

Rooms and stages were clustered close together here at the heart of the outport and the older boys would dare each other to leap between them. Not wanting to push her luck with her young mentors, Eva sat slightly apart from them in the shadow of the salting room and listened uneasily to raised voices coming from within. Some sort of a meeting was going on but it was not until she heard Tam's distinctive tones that she paid it any attention.

'The Icelanders convinced *their* government—'

His voice was drowned out by the angry responses. 'Fishin's done here . . . any eejit can see—'

'No one wants salt cod now . . .'

'Who'll listen to us in Ottawa—'

Tam tried again, raising his voice. 'An exclusion zone, like Iceland's, would—'

'. . . stocks are too low. Fished out . . .'

She saw that the boys were listening too.

'. . . stocks *bounced* back during the war when there was no fishing . . .'

'There's fish off the rocks still, if yous know where to look . . .'

Tam again. 'Aye, but if you move to new places, you *won't* know where—'

'Me, I'm done with d'fishin' anyway. Der's money in lumber, I'm told.'

'You don't get to choose where you go, Burt, if you want the handout.'

Up until then the argument had been reasoned but suddenly the mood changed. 'Think we don't know that, b'y?'

Tam was undeterred. 'Read the fine print, Bob. You'll have burned your boats, my friend, quite literally.'

The same voice continued. 'And who's you to be tellin' us anyt'ing? Ya not from yer.' There was a threatening groundswell of agreement. The boys exchanged looks, their eyes widening.

'No, but I know you're being gulled,' Tam retorted. 'Bribed. Conned. And what happens when the money runs out, eh? What then?'

'It's a t'ousand bucks!'

'Thirty pieces of silver,' Tam replied. 'Only it's yourselves you'll be betraying. Measure it against what you'll lose, Joe Morris, and set that in the balance? Have you actually *thought*—'

'So ya'll not be signing?'

A loaded silence fell.

'That's right, I'll not.'

'And ya'll stop d'rest o' us—' The next words were drowned in a tumult of angry voices. She glanced across to the two boys who had ceased to fish. Scott was Joe Morris's son and his expression was fearful.

'What are they arguing about, Scott?' she hissed across to him.

'Resettlement.'

'What's that?'

The boys exchanged manly, contemptuous glances. 'Government'll give us money to move.'

'Move where?' she asked and Scott shrugged. 'And why?'

'Cos dey want us to go.'

Bill's contribution confused her more. 'Cos of d'fish and d'steamer having to come, 'nd all that. But I don't *wanna* go.'

'Me neither,' said Scott.

She recalled then the scraps of conversation she'd heard between her parents and the argument the other night; she should have listened more closely. She opened her mouth to ask another question but paused as Tam raised his voice again.

'An exclusion zone banning foreign trawlers and draggers would allow stocks to recover while fishing is modernised. It *can* be done! If money went into building a refrigeration plant, refrigeration ships, even, instead of giving these handouts and setting up new industries which could fail. When fish stocks *do* recover we've an economy that's viable, a way of life worth preserving. Believe me, you'll lose more than you can begin to imagine—'

'Believe *you*, Tam Nairn! When ya can't stand up fer five minutes.' The laughter that followed had a hard edge. 'Four more signatures, dat's all we needs. Rob Collins signed this morning . . .'

'Ach, no, did you, Rob?'

'So just you and t'ree more. T'ink *haard* about dat, Tam Nairn . . .'

Another hush fell and it was as if the sun had gone behind the clouds.

Eva shivered.

'Or what, Walter?' she heard Tam ask.

A deep-throated rumbling grew, like thunder far out at sea, and then there was the sound of boots on the wooden planks, jostling and scuffling inside the room. 'Stow it! Keep things civil!' someone said. 'But you've gotta sign in the end, Tam, stands to reason.'

'*Reason!*' Tam's voice came again as she had never before heard it, filled with an angry passion. 'I'll give you reason. Broken promises, broken lives. Folk sitting it out on welfare. Lost! *Nothing* folk can do for themselves anymore. Where's the dignity in that, eh? Handouts. Is that what you *want*?' The gutting shed had gone quiet. They were listening again. 'No money to rebuild. Plots too small to grow anything on. I've seen it up the coast. And what of the old folk, taken from the only place—'

An angry voice gave a counter view and shouting broke out again and there were more scuffling sounds, louder now. Eva looked across at the two boys and, from the corner of her eye, saw that a dory had set out from the other side of the bay with a slight figure pulling hard at the oars, rowing swiftly towards them. The two boys had seen it too, exchanging looks as it approached the jetty. Bill went forward to catch a thrown line.

Tam's son. Ross McLeod.

'Where is he?' the youth demanded, glancing at Eva but addressing her companions who were eyeing him with what appeared to be respect.

Bill gestured towards the salting room. 'Folk are gettin' mad in der, Ross.'

Ross made no response but strode down the stage and pushed open the door. The shouting died down and the shuffling stopped. In the little silence that followed she heard Tam say, 'Go home, Ross.'

'I'm stayin'.'

Her two companions pulled in their lines and crossed over to the stage and went to stand at the open door. Eva got to her feet but stayed where she was. 'Christ,' she heard a man say. 'More kids!'

'You too, Bill, away wit' ya!'

'Do we *gotta* leave, Dad?'

The tumult of argument resumed and Eva only caught snatches '. . . for your future, b'y . . . place is done . . . fished out . . . need more schooling,' and then Tam's voice rising above the others.

'You'll lose them to the cities, man, I've seen it happen. They'll head for St John's if you're lucky; Toronto, if you're not, or way out west. But if we stand firm . . .' This time the response was a shout, a curse and then a thump of something falling heavily followed by more tussling. Eva began pulling in her line.

'Watchit, Bob. The kid's pulled a knife.'

'*Jesus*, Ross, put it away!'

'Scott, away home wit' ya, out of it! Go.'

Then a furious, youthful voice. 'Leave my dad alone and I'll put it away.'

'*Ross—*'

'I say we finish dis now, b'ys. Get d'signings we need.' Roar and counter-roar came from within.

Finish it?

Eva felt suddenly sick. Something bad was about to happen . . . The image of Tam with his bloody arm came back to her. Red on white. Was this what he'd meant by getting in the way? If only her father was here, she thought, hopping from foot to foot, he'd a way of calming folk, but he was away up the coast. Looking up she saw some women were coming down from the houses, word of the row was spreading, but they'd be too late! The danger was real and now.

In desperation she did the only thing she could think of and took a deep breath. She let it out in a piercing scream, shut her eyes, pinched her nose, and hurled herself off the jetty, making as loud a splash as possible. She'd learned to swim back in Scotland and had been astonished to discover that many of the outport children didn't, but as she hit the piercing cold she understood why. She surfaced, spluttering and gasping at the shock of it, tried to yell again but found she couldn't.

The door to the salting room was flung open and men came tumbling out. 'Doctor's lass,' one shouted. 'Throw her a line! She's going down.'

'Help!' she gasped, in earnest now for her legs were cramping in the cold.

'Hang on, girl!' A rope was thrown that she grabbed at and missed. Someone began hurriedly untying Ross's boat while others reached down to her but were pushed aside by a slim figure who darted through the group and leaped into the water beside her. Eva felt her hair being grabbed, then her arm, and she was dragged, gulping and gagging, towards outstretched hands.

They pulled her onto the boards where she stood shivering uncontrollably. The women had run down and gathered round her, wrapping her in stripped-off cardigans, clucking in distress and from under an encircling arm she saw Ross McLeod climb back onto the stage, water pouring off him. One man clapped him on the back as he nodded acceptance of a coat which another draped over his shoulders.

Tam came over to him and stood looking sternly across at her, while on his son's face Eva saw a puzzled scowl.

CHAPTER 14

Glasgow, 1980

Eva

David's eyebrows shot up at her sudden request. '*Ten days!* Where're you off to?'

'A friend's taken a gîte in Provence and asked me to come. Someone pulled out, last minute.'

He adopted a mulish expression. Theirs was an uneasy working relationship. She'd been grateful for the opportunity to work with him as David Mallory, with his bloodhound nose for a story, had a fearsome reputation and jobs like this were rare, especially for women with little or no experience. But he was not an easy boss. It had been soon after she'd started work that he'd begun making half-hearted, clumsy advances until she'd made it clear that gratitude had very defined limits. He still tried it on whenever he could and took an intrusive interest in her personal life. 'House party?' he asked. 'Or just you and your pal.'

'I'll know when I get there.'

He smirked, preparing to be awkward. 'I'm not sure I can spare you.'

'And I'm sure you can, David. I've loads of leave owing.'

'How will you get there?'

'I'll fly.'

He whistled. 'Come into money?'

'I can get a cheap ticket.'

The cost of a flight to St John's in Newfoundland, however, turned out to be anything but cheap. And, as she boarded the plane two days later, she questioned, and not for the first time, whether she had gone quite mad.

But she had to do it, though. She had to know if Tam Nairn was still alive and what had become of him. She'd had sleepless nights since seeing his image in David's article and, if she found him, she might finally begin to understand what had happened that night all those years ago. No one had told her anything beyond her father saying, 'It wasn't your fault, Eva, forget about it. You've your new school to think about, a new beginning. Lock it all in a box inside your head, and throw away the key.'

But the lock had sprung and the lid was off.

She was worried too that Jillian Maxwell, or her son, would get back in touch with her and she would be dragged further into the complexities of the situation without understanding Tam's position. A phone call had come through to her office in the afternoon after her odd lunch with Lady Maxwell, cancelling the meeting with Duncan, and she was left wondering exactly what the woman had told him. She'd heard no more from either of them since then and David's fickle attention had moved on as the financial scandal in the government spilled into new salacious areas.

As she sat waiting to board the plane she thought again of Lady Maxwell. Another enigma, she decided. Behind the sleek persona Eva had glimpsed a sharp mind and a great deal that had been left unsaid. She must know why her stepson had vanished from Rosslie all those years ago, and her whole demeanour had changed when she'd learned he had a son. Was she concerned that in these more liberated times Ross might one day lay claim to the estate? Eva smiled a little, thinking that the wild boy she remembered might have trouble convincing *anyone* that he should.

Had she written her letter? Eva wondered, and rather doubted that she had.

She also considered, as she boarded the plane, whether she was required by law to disclose what she knew about the missing man.

Perhaps not, but this too had made her uneasy. Quite when she'd decided that she was honour-bound to try and find Tam Nairn herself and speak to him, she wasn't sure, but the idea, once born, had come to obsess her. He might, of course, be long dead; his lifestyle had hardly been conducive to longevity, and that thought brought more guilt. He'd had little enough to his name when she'd known him and she feared that because of her he'd been left with less. As the plane took off, she drew a deep breath, letting it out slowly and closing her eyes as the tension of departure left her. But how would it all play out? Had she any chance of finding him? Considering what had happened in 1966 it was unlikely that he would still be in Heart's Repose and she could only hope that someone knew where he'd gone.

Before she'd left, David mentioned in passing that the office had been inundated with reports of sightings of Archibald Maxwell, all in unlikely situations, including two hopeful claimants to the title. 'Attention seekers, eh? Looking for a stage.' He'd watched for her reaction, and probed her again about her fictitious companion in the make-believe French gîte, obviously piqued by her skimpy responses.

But, as the plane rose through that nebulous zone and into the blue infinity, she shrugged and let it go, and thought instead of the last time she had seen Tam Nairn and Ross McLeod. It had been on the day of her family's departure from Heart's Repose when she had stood with her parents on the windy wharf beside suitcases and boxes, still weak from almost a month spent in bed. Her mind had been in a turmoil, hating the thought of leaving Heart's Repose, sensing that something special was going out of her life. Her father was well respected and folk had gathered to wish the departing family well and waited with them, watching as the launch leaving the steamer came down the inlet towards them.

As it grew closer she saw that there were two disembarking passengers aboard. A murmur rippled through the gathering as they recognised Tam and his son and, as the boat came alongside, her mother made a strange, strangled sound. Where had they been, she wondered, sensing the sudden tension, and she felt her father's hand drop gently onto her shoulder. Ross stepped onto the wharf and stood there, chin up as he scanned the assembled group, his dark eyes defiant as they skidded past her. 'Lousy timing,' she heard the storekeeper mutter. Then Tam himself rose, a little stiffly as if his bad leg was troubling him, and came ashore.

Her stomach had lurched at the sight of him. He looked pale and haggard, world weary and grim. Unconsciously, she strained forward and her father's grip on her shoulder tightened. 'Be still,' he said, but softly. Ross saw her move and stepped forward, scowling, ready to repel her, but Tam said something to him and briefly his eyes met Eva's in a little glint of greeting. He looked away at once and gave a nod to her father. It was a fleeting moment, lost to most as men began loading their possessions onto the boat, following her mother's shrill commands. Then Tam turned very deliberately and surveyed a hard core of men who stood blocking his way. A stand-off! He gave them something of his old ironic smile, draped an arm casually over his son's shoulder and murmured in his ear. They remained standing there, giving look for look, apparently prepared to wait all day.

But Tam, she sensed, was restraining Ross as her father had her.

And then, in an extraordinary development, Miss Sinclair, the schoolteacher, pushed through the group of men and came forward, holding out her hand. Tam shook it and the old woman turned, out-staring those who gawped, and the group finally parted. The schoolteacher then fell into step beside Tam and Ross, flanking Tam's other side, and the oddly assorted trio continued up the hill, not once looking back.

Eva turned her head in enquiry to her father but he simply urged her towards the launch that was now making ready to return to the steamer. There was no time then for questions or protest and her mother remained tight-lipped as she stepped off the wharf. And, as they'd pulled away, Eva had looked back, watching miserably as the waving hands had grown smaller and her life at Heart's Repose had come to an end.

In packing for her quest to rediscover that life, there had been an oddly prescient moment. As she'd retrieved her suitcase from a top shelf of a cupboard, a book had fallen at her feet. *Collected Poems*. She stared at it, having long forgotten that she'd smuggled it out among her possessions when they'd left, wanting to retain some connection to Tam. She bent to pick it up and from it fell not only the list he had made for her, but another sheet, which must have been tucked inside the jacket. It was a handwritten poem.

<u>Heart's Repose</u>

Repose for the Heart?
A beacon beckoning
Or a false wreckers' light?
Or a name, just a name, named to claim
Just rewards?
Or in hope, perhaps,
If one dared to hope.
Or is the risk of hope too great?
The risk of falling foul,
And the fall itself too far.
Too far for a Heart
Already fallen far too far
From grace
For Repose.

CHAPTER 15

Newfoundland, 1980

Eva

St John's, Newfoundland enjoyed a mixed reputation, her father used to say. People either loved its quirky character or they despaired of it and fled west to improve their chances in life. Eva could barely remember anything about the city other than the sheltered harbour reached through The Narrows, flanked by Fort Amherst on one side and Signal Hill on the other. She spent her first night in a soulless motel near the airport, gathering herself and studying an old map of her father's that she'd found, preparing to collect the hire car next morning. She'd never driven on the other side of the road before, nor handled an automatic, and would have to swiftly master both.

These were just two of the things concerning her next morning when she went to collect the vehicle. Having gone through the hire policy and the controls, the young man handed her a company map.

'You know where you're heading?' he asked.

'Sort of,' she replied and opened the map. 'It's north, then east and along the coast here . . .' But it wasn't, they couldn't find it and so she pulled out her father's old map and showed him. 'There. Heart's Repose.'

He peered at it and shrugged, but by matching the coastline on the two maps they were able to establish her route. 'Just a small place, I guess,' he said with a shrug and set her on her way. It was hardly an encouraging start.

But as she set off north, leaving the sprawl of the city behind her, she felt both nervous and exhilarated. She'd never done anything like this before! It felt quite unreal but after a while her confidence grew. There were few cars on the road and, as the miles passed, she felt able to relax her focus on the driving and look about her. She'd not remembered so many trees! Spruce for the most part but tamarack and balsam among them, low-growing in a watery landscape. Where the trees thinned she decided it was an almost Hebridean landscape, with patches of bare, barren rock and peaty soil, which, now, in April, bore a muted palette of russet and gold. In some places the forest opened up to reveal hidden ponds, small lakes with their edges fringed by marshy land. No wonder the Scots and the Irish had felt so much at home here. And she smiled, remembering Tam telling her how the landmasses had once been joined, and how he'd arrived there.

After a couple of hours of driving, a road sign indicated her turning and she branched off onto a smaller road, which took her eastwards. She now made slower progress on increasingly poor surfaces and struggled to pinpoint exactly where she was. Some of the small communities she'd passed through had been signposted, but others marked on her father's map had not materialised. Like them, Heart's Repose had faced the sea with its back to the forest and it felt strange to be arriving now from the land. She drove on through an unchanging landscape, catching glimpses of a broken coastline, of headlands and inlets. They too reminded her of Scotland, except for the wooden houses along the shore, which struck deeper chords within her memory. The road weaved and twisted, running beside the coast in places before turning inland again to be shadowed by the trees, and as she drove it became narrower and the potholes deeper, then it became gravel and the empty stretches between settlements stretched out. Very few vehicles passed her now and, as the light began to fail, she started to worry about finding a bed for the night.

But should she go on, or turn back?

She pulled up at a place where the road widened, got out and stretched, breathing in the forgotten smell of juniper and balsam on salt-laden air, conscious of the evening chill. Decision time . . . She picked up the map again and studied it. The last large settlement she'd driven through had had motel units behind a gas station and there had been a convenience store. But to backtrack all that way seemed a pity . . . She was on the point of deciding to press on for another half an hour when a battered pickup appeared from around the bend and braked beside her, sending up a dust cloud and blocking the empty road.

The window was wound down. 'Now if ever a soul looked lost, darlin' . . .' A woman with a round face and silver hair scraped back into a ponytail contemplated her through the open window. 'Where're ya headin'?'

'Heart's Repose. Do you know it?'

The woman stared at her a moment and then her shoulders shook with laughter. 'You looking fer ghosts, girl? Heart's Repose's long gone.'

Eva went across to the pickup. 'Gone! Completely *gone*?'

'You're more'n ten years too late, darl. But why d'ya want to go der?' The woman's accent and intonation brought back a life Eva had all but forgotten.

'I . . . I'm trying to trace someone.'

'Well, they ain't der now, dat's for sure.' The woman laughed again, displaying gaps in her mouth where teeth had once been, and she gave Eva a curious look. 'You got a place to stay?'

'I passed a motel a few miles back. The Bayview, do you know it?'

The woman chuckled again. 'I know the Bay. And bed bugs is d'best you'll find there, creeping in between d'sheets.' She looked Eva up and down, openly appraising her. 'You don't want to be out here in the dark on these roads. Wind's getting' up too. You come home with me, eh, while we work something out. And dere's no call to look worried! It's a quiet place, I live alone and I'll see ya safe. You jest turn yourself around and follow me.' The window was wound back up and the pickup pulled forward to allow Eva to turn in the road.

Dark clouds had crept over the sky, bringing forward the night, and the suggestion was a welcome one. This was, despite her memories, an unfamiliar land and she was a stranger here. The woman might know where a room could be had, so she turned as instructed and tucked herself in behind the pickup, accelerating rapidly as it sped away. They drove back a mile or so until, without warning, her guide turned off the road and headed down a rough track in the direction of the coast, bouncing ahead of Eva, avoiding yawning holes in the road and swerving past rocks that protruded onto its narrow course.

Eva followed as best she could.

After two or three miles of this, the low spruce forest opened up to reveal a vista of cleared land where, set back from the track, there stood a small salt-box house, facing a rocky cove. More houses and sheds were dotted around the bay and, but for the fact that the houses were built of wood, this too could have been somewhere along Scotland's west coast or off-shore islands. In the low evening light there was a strange stillness about the place. No lights showed in the blackened windows and there was no one about, no dogs, no boats, although she could see jetties and stages in the fading light. Rusting machinery and detritus were strewn among lichen-covered boulders and scrubby grass, and close to the first house she'd seen chickens scratching inside a wired enclosure beside a sturdy hen house. An old-fashioned root cellar was set back into the hillside and down by the shore a wooden dock sat askew on rotting timber posts; a solitary boat with an upturned bow and outboard motor was moored there.

How strangely empty the place was, and silent.

The pickup had come to a halt outside the first house and the woman got out, revealing herself to be short of stature and wide of girth. She came towards Eva with a smile. 'Welcome to Doyle's Point. I'm Shelagh Doyle, sole resident, which I reckon that makes me mayor, fireman, police and d'whole population all rolled into one.' Again that laugh which made her whole body shake. 'And you've no call to be t'inking you're doing just what your mammy told you never to do, latchin' onto strangers.'

Eva smiled. 'I'm Eva Bayne,' she said, and shook the outstretched hand.

'Come on in, Eva Bayne, and welcome, I'm always glad fer company as der ain't much around here now. I'll make us some tea, and you can tell me who yous lookin' fer, in a place most folk've forgotten.'

Sole resident? Eva looked back down the cove at the unlit houses. Were they empty then? The stillness was explained.

The house Shelagh Doyle led her too, however, was not. From the outside it was a typical east-coast clapboard building, two storeys at the front with a steep-pitched roof sloping down over a single storey at the back, but it had seen better times. Once painted with red ochre, the boards were now bleached and both ends of the house sagged as if discouraged about its future. Shelagh beckoned her into what must be the parlour and Eva stopped in the doorway to stare in astonishment at the sheer quantity of *stuff* that had been crammed into every available space. Battered furniture lined the walls, groaning under the weight of items piled high. One table had three old wooden radio consoles stashed beneath it and a Bakelite one on top. A treadle sewing machine occupied a corner of the room beside a glass-fronted cabinet crammed full of cheap crockery and glass preserving jars. A set of shelves held everything from an old egg-whisk to a collection of clay pipe bowls and what looked like porcelain ointment jars, while any remaining wall space was covered by foxed old prints or faded samplers lovingly embroidered in an era before even wirelesses provided entertainment. Yellowing newspaper clippings had been nailed into the spaces in between.

On a rocking chair a black cat snoozed on a shawl of crocheted squares and in front of the hearth, layer upon layer of ancient rag rugs, one on top of another, covered a painted wooden floor. 'Sit you down,' her hostess said, and disappeared into what must be the kitchen. Eva perched on the edge of a horsehair day bed and surveyed the room, half junk shop, half museum, while a clock ticked softly on the mantelpiece resetting the pace, redolent of another time. She was still puzzling over the extraordinary collection when Shelagh Doyle kicked open the door and entered, puffing mightily and carrying a tray full of bone china.

She set it down and mopped her brow. 'Timed your visit just right, Eva,' she said as if she was a regular guest. 'I baked dis morning so dere's scones.'

'You're very kind.'

'And we'll use Ma's china cups. First time since d'funeral.' The cat made no protest as the woman picked her up and kissed her. 'And here's Puss. Never did get round to deciding on a name. She'd one of her own once, I guess, but she's never said.' Again came the fat chuckle as tea was poured and a saucer of milk placed in the hearth. 'Help yerself, and tell me who yer looking fer?'

Eva took a plate and scone. 'A man called Tam Nairn. A Scotsman, or at least he was.' At what point did your adopted country subsume you, she wondered fleetingly, providing a new identity. 'He must be in his sixties now.'

The woman shook her head. 'Don't know him. Though we'd all sorts here in the old days. Folk call themselves Irish or English or Scots, generations on, and speak of d'old country like dey only just left.'

Eva shook her head. 'Tam Nairn wasn't one of those. He came out from Scotland after the war and was living in Heart's Repose in 1966, which was when I knew him.'

Shelagh Doyle looked up at her. 'Why you'd be just a nipper.'

'I was, my father was a doctor, based there, and he used to go out to . . . '

The woman sat forward. 'Whaddya say ya name was?' Eva told her. 'You Doc Bayne's girl?' Tea slopped into the saucer as Shelagh shook with excitement. The fact that her father was remembered made Eva's throat suddenly tighten and she nodded, not trusting herself to speak. 'Well, I'll be *damned.* Now dat was one foine man. Delivered my Shona, he did – breeched she were but he turned her round neat as anyt'ing and out she popped. Well, well, well.' She stopped a moment, the tea dripping, unheeded, onto the layers of rag rug. 'It was around sixty-five he left, wasn't it?'

'It was. Though he came back in the summers for a few years after that.'

Shelagh nodded as if remembering this, watching the cat, which was now sat at her feet, washing its paws. 'Some say him leaving was the final straw, and the schoolteacher soon after.'

The schoolteacher. 'Miss Sinclair?' So she was remembered too.

Shelagh nodded. 'Was that her name? Hung on a while, she did, but dey'd never get another schoolteacher once that shiny new school got built in Port Bradshaw. Hardly any kids by dat point, so no reason to hang on . . . Not *viable*, the government said. How they did love dat word! Doyle's Point was another. Not *viable*. Used to be a couple of dozen families livin' here, schoolhouse and store, back when I was a kid, when there was fish to catch and seals to hunt. We was viable then.'

So were *all* those silent houses empty, their windows forever dark, monuments to another time? How strange it was. The woman's blue eyes seemed to fade a little more as she continued. 'But dat was way back, before d'war.' She spoke with that curious blend of Irish, Scots and West Country. 'Who'd you say you're lookin' fer?'

'Tam Nairn.'

'Fisherman, was he?'

'Sort of. He didn't have a proper job.'

Shelagh snorted. 'Fishin' was a proper job once. Not'ing to do '*cept* fish – and drink. Did he drink, this Tam Nairn?'

'Yes, I think he did.'

Shelagh nodded. 'All d'men was drinking in sixty-five, and d'women too. Downing hooch, drownin' despair. No future, see? That's why dey went in the end, took d'money and left. And they'd the young 'uns to t'ink of.' The old woman's mind had wandered off again but Eva let her talk. And, as she spoke of the government scheme Eva had so little understood at the time, things began to make a sort of sense. 'Bringin' folk in from the outports was the big new idea, resettle dem, the government said, once everyone agreed to go, or most everyone anyway.' Snatches of conversation came back to Eva: the angry gatherings down by the stages, fingers jabbed into chests, choleric faces within spitting range, fists clenching. And Tam Nairn in the midst of them, arguing. 'Divided communities it did, though, families who'd been tight bound for generations. T'ings got downright nasty in some places.' And Eva remembered suddenly how she'd thrown herself off the jetty in an absurd attempt to defuse a dangerous moment . . . It was years since she'd thought of it. 'Promised dem d'world they did! New pulp mills, cement factories, textile plants, good jobs for everyone, a better life for all but der was only the welfare for most. Kids grew up, moved away, left to find work out west.' She stared down into the fire. 'And den folk were left with not'ing. Fish was all these folk knew! Old timers could find the fishing grounds by smell, for God's sake, except the smell had gone. All fished out by draggers and trawlers. And foreigners.' She rubbed her nose again, more vigorously, and lifted watery eyes to Eva. 'Some choice, eh? Stay and starve or take d'money and go. And once dey'd gone the names of places were wiped off the map, hopin' folk would forget.'

Wiped off the map. 'And that's what happened at Heart's Repose?'

She nodded. 'And Doyle's Point. Folk crawled away like hermit crabs, pulling d'houses behind dem while d'rest just up and went, leaving everything.' Eva looked again at the cluttered shelves and crammed-in furniture. And so Shelagh Doyle had become a one-woman salvage operation, clinging on.

'Bin Doyles here for as long as anyone can remember. First to come, last to go, dat's how I see it.' She was well away now. 'Houses closest to the shore were dragged down to the water, fixed to rafts made o' empty oil drums and floated to new places. Others were taken apart and shifted, the rest just left to fall apart.' The cat jumped up onto her lap as if sensing her need for comfort, and the woman's veined old hand began to stroke it. 'It were hardest on d'old folk. Lost everything, they did. They'd a purpose before, see, mending nets or minding kids.' The cat began to purr, eyes closed, soothing them both. 'I've never even seen half my grandchildren, 'cept in photographs. My kids went west to Toronto and some on to Winnipeg. I've only Shona close by, and she's in Trinity.'

And Eva saw again the cluster of men down at the harbour in Heart's Repose, smoking and talking, the angry words, and Tam Nairn trying to make himself heard.

'Who d'you say it was, d'man you're lookin' fer?'

'Tam Nairn,' Eva repeated, seeing that the old woman was tiring. Outside it was dark now, no lights would show in the abandoned houses and the old house was creaking as it absorbed the gusts of the rising wind.

She should make a move.

Shelagh Doyle was shaking her head. 'Coulda gone anywhere. Folk scattered, see; the young ones left and folk just drifted apart. Fifteen years is a long time, girl. Some old 'uns went to rest homes in St John's where dey stick 'em in front of the TV and wait for 'em to die.'

Eva couldn't imagine Tam in such a place. 'He had a son!' Why hadn't she mentioned that before. 'Ross McLeod. He'd be about thirty now.'

But Shelagh shook her head again. 'Don't know 'em.'

Eva looked out of the window thinking she'd little choice now but to head back to the Bayview and take her chances with whatever might crawl between the sheets, but her hostess noticed the glance and picked up on her thought. 'You stay here, darl. It'll be an honour to have Doc Bayne's girl under my roof; no one had a bad word for him. And in the morning, I'll take you down the coast to Heart's Repose so you can see fer yourself, eh?'

CHAPTER 16

That night Eva lay awake for a long time, going over all Shelagh had said and listening to the creaking of the old house. She could hear dogs howling in the forest, maddened by the wind, and thought again of Buck – and Tam. Was he out there somewhere, watching this same moon? Through thin curtains she could see a sky darker than any she had seen since leaving, bejewelled by countless stars, and the air that gusted through the ill-fitting window brought with it the smell of sea salt and rockweed. Rockweed . . . She paused on the word. Back home she would automatically have said seaweed but the local word had risen from the recess of her mind.

Eventually she slept but was woken early by ravens on the roof, and lay listening to the gulls far out at sea, asking perhaps where the fishing boats had gone. And the fish. She went to the window and looked down towards the sagging little dock, held in place by wooden piles. What anchored her these days, she wondered, and what had anchored Tam?

In the kitchen Shelagh greeted her with a broad smile. 'I heard you moving about. Eggs do fer you?' Eva nodded her thanks. 'And then we'll head on out.'

Shelagh, for all her years, proved to be an impressive mariner. Refusing any help she humped an old metal gas can down to the jetty, puffing under its weight, pausing only to point out rotten planks for Eva to avoid, hooked up the hoses, and soon the outboard motor roared into life. They set off down the inlet, leaving a wide curved wake behind them, passing the remains of dilapidated stages and collapsing fish-drying flakes. Weathered boards showed where houses had once stood, imploded by time, piled up beside others that still stood, leaning drunkenly on rotting foundations. Her hostess bawled above the roar of the outboard, pointing things out, but Eva could catch only snatches of what she said '. . . Dad's old rooms . . . me first kiss beside the . . .' she gave a wink and a chuckle, followed swiftly by a sober expression '. . . lost years back . . . mighty gales . . . just a pile o' boards . . . and old Jock in 'is filthy long johns . . .' She gave another great laugh and Eva smiled her appreciation, seeing the delight Shelagh took in telling the stories – what a treasure trove they were!

Rounding the headland a moment later, the wind from the open ocean hit them and the old woman let out the throttle, her hair blowing wildly around her head in a mad halo of white. She handled the boat as one born to it, her face as alive as a young girl's, gesturing occasionally to where gannets were diving out at sea and where waves pounded the rocky coast sending spray high into the sky while the gulls circled above. Everywhere there was a sense of movement, of life, in stark counterpoint to the stillness of the abandoned outport they had left behind them. The swell lifted the boat and Eva gripped the seat, feeling an exhilaration so alien to her that it took her breath away. She had forgotten the sheer beauty of the place! And while the people might be gone, the land had a resilience of its own.

Heart's Repose.

Or Heart Break, Eva thought as they turned down the inlet towards what had once been home; Doyle's Point had prepared her for what she saw but it was still a shock. She spotted the lighthouse first, up on the headland, and as they passed under the cliffs she remembered old Jacob's scowl that day. Would coming back here fill other gaps?

A few houses were still standing, on both sides of the cove, and yet it looked quite different, so much smaller, and somehow *less* than she remembered it. There were no boats, for one thing, they should have been everywhere, tied up at the stages or winched onto slipways, but the only ones she could see were pulled up high above the shoreline, like fish dragged from their element, rotting amidst grasses and willow shrub.

And the people, they were missing too.

Shelagh throttled back and Eva became aware that the woman was watching her. 'Spooky, ain't it?' she said. 'Feels like it's waiting for folk to come back, same as Doyle's Point.' Eva nodded and looked across to the exposed side of the bay, trying to identify Tam Nairn's house. It had stood away from the others, isolated, closest to the sea, but she couldn't place it.

And then she did and her heart lurched.

A pile of charred boards marked the spot, overgrown now with scrubby grasses, and she stared at the place, not daring to imagine what had happened there. They continued up the inlet, slowing the engine, and she found herself suddenly overwhelmed by a sense of loss. She could see now that the remaining houses had holes in their roofs, few windows still had glass, doors were missing or standing wide open. Somewhere a shutter was banging. 'Snoopers and vandals,' Shelagh said, guessing her thoughts. 'Taking what they fancy. Same happened at Doyle's Point. That's why I've collected stuff in case folk come back for it.' Had anyone ever done that? Eva wondered, doubting that they had. 'But word got out I'd a shotgun and that stopped it.' She grinned at Eva.

A one-woman security force, guarding the past.

Eva looked up to the hill to where she'd lived with her parents and saw that it too had gone; all that remained were the foundation blocks. The house next door had been burned out, quite recently, it would seem, the surrounding ground was still blackened. 'Kids. Forgive dem, Lord, dey know not what dey do.'

What a desperately forlorn place it was, Eva thought, as the memories flooded in. She could almost see herself, a small child running between the broad flakes, oblivious to the rising tensions, looking out for her unusual friend, never guessing that time was running out for the centuries-old outport, nor how soon and swiftly the end would come. But what a struggle it must have been, even then; what relentless bone-wearying lives people must have led until the offer came that was to divide them. Which was harder, she wondered, to stay or to go?

And then had come a day when fog had rolled in from the sea and the balance had tipped, sealing the fate of Heart's Repose. The thought that *she* might have been the catalyst drove the breath from her, and suddenly she wanted to leave, wanted never to have come. Better that she remembered it as she had last seen it, watching the waving hands as the boat took her out to the steamer. She wanted to go no closer, to not land there and not tread those paths that wound through vegetable patches long gone, past root cellars with doors wrenched off, but to leave, get her car and head for the airport, turn her back on it again. The quest to find Tam Nairn had begun in a moment of madness but she would give it up, go home and leave the man in peace. Or in his grave.

But it was too late. Shelagh had already swung the boat around the hooked curve of the bay and was pointing. 'Why, lookee der! We ain't alone.' Eva followed the pointing figure and saw that moored along the wharf from where she had departed all those years ago there was a boat very much like their own. An old man sat on a folding stool beside it, fishing and looking entirely at his ease, as if it was in no way extraordinary that he should be doing so, here, in this abandoned place.

He raised a hand as the boat approached and called out a greeting.

'Can ya catch a line?' Shelagh shouted back.

'Sure can.' He rose heavily and came to the edge of the jetty.

Eva tugged at Shelagh's sleeve. 'Don't . . . please, don't tell him who I am,' she whispered. She didn't recognise the man, but if he was from here he would know . . .

Shelagh gave her a quick glance and nodded. 'Anything bitin'?' she asked, as she made fast and hauled herself onto the jetty.

The man gestured to a keep net hung over the jetty's side where silvery forms moved just beneath the surface. 'Pretty good,' he replied. 'So, where you folk from?' Shelagh told him and he nodded. 'I'd cousins there once.'

'You from yer, I guess?' Shelagh said as Eva joined them on the stage and the old man nodded a greeting.

'Man and boy, generations back. Don Morris.'

'But you ain't living here now, surely, Don?'

The man shook his head. 'Parked my car at Rawlin's Head and brought the boat round. I come by most years and stay a while, fishin'. Can't seem to keep away.' He gestured towards a house set back from the shore. 'That's my place there. Sometimes I stay over.'

'Vandals left it alone, eh?'

He shrugged. 'Nothing worth taking. I bring what I need when I come and put things right if I have to. We ain't supposed to repair the old places, but I do anyways, gotta keep the weather out.' He and Shelagh continued to swap stories about how long folk had stood against moving, who took what with them, where they ended up . . . 'My boy Joe went out west but Scott never settled. That's my grandson, Scott, he came back.' Scott Morris! The name leaped out at Eva. 'I don't *wanna* go,' the boy had said that afternoon as angry words were exchanged in the salting room.

The past came closer, fusing with the present, and she knew then that there could be no turning back. She had to see this through. 'What does he do now?' Eva asked. 'Your grandson.' Perhaps he would know what had happened to Tam Nairn.

'Got a hardware shop in Trinity. He's doing all right, Scott is.'

Eva nodded. Should be easy enough to find.

Shelagh picked up on her thought. 'I'd someone come by askin' about a fella who used to live here. Name of Nairn, Tam Nairn.'

'Ha!' The old man's reaction was immediate. 'Now there's a name! Folk shoulda listened to Tam Nairn. Right all along, he was. Some of us thought so at the time, but the young ones didn't want to listen. We shoulda made more demands, shoulda took on the government and fought to stay – but we didn't.'

There was a little silence, with only the lapping of the water round the jetty to fill it. It hadn't been sea monsters that had dragged the people away in the end, but government paperwork and promises.

'D'ya know where he went, Tam Nairn?'

The old man shook his head. 'He'd a spell in jail over some funny business with a kid . . .' Eva felt Shelagh shoot her a glance and knew her face had registered the shock. *Jail!* '. . . and folk who'd held out gave in and signed while he was away. Shame on them . . . But then the rules changed and we were sunk, sold down the river. I came close to blows with my boy Joe over it. He said we *had* to go, he'd the young 'uns to think of, but Tam Nairn was right, I tell you, and Scott came straight back here soon as he could.'

'And what happened to Tam Nairn?' Eva prompted, hardly daring to ask.

'Someone burned him out while he was away, goddam 'em,' he nodded towards the pile of charred boards on the opposite shore, confirming Eva's worst fears, 'but the schoolteacher took him in, and he stayed on a while. His boy took off and then they closed the school so the old woman had to go and Tam left too.' And Eva saw again the three of them, Tam, Ross and the schoolteacher heading off up the hill. His house must have already been burned by then, and Eva hadn't known . . . 'I'd left by then, it was jest what folks told me.'

Shelagh pressed him again but the old man's interest was waning. Instead he reeled in his line and insisted on taking them up to the old churchyard and Eva saw for the first time the state of the wooden church. Its roof had slid to one side, knocking the tower askew, giving it an oddly raffish appearance, a cruel sort of mockery. The graveyard was much as she remembered, demarcated by a simple fence of palings that had been recently repaired, the encroaching trees cut back. Plastic flowers adorning some of the graves looked brash against the mellow red-and-gold vegetation but plastic, she supposed, would last between visits.

'I lost count of the generations we got in there,' Don was telling Shelagh, 'but see that one? "Seventeen twenty-two, Douglas Morris, born in Tarbet, Scotland". Some go back even earlier. We'd grown roots, see, and had to pull them up. That's my wife, Mona, over there. I come to visit her, see?'

Back at the jetty the boat sat lower on the ebbing tide. They took their leave of Don who raised a hand in farewell. 'Try asking Billy Norton at the Pondside gas station – seems like Billy knows everything round here. And if you find Tam Nairn tell him from me that he was right, we should've made a stand, but I reckon he knows that.'

Eva pulled out her camera as they left the wharf, her journalist's instinct not quite dead as a sense of outrage grew within her. Jagged fragments of memory had begun flickering through her mind: the close smell of cigarettes and sweat, a panting next to her ear and the feel of cold clothes being pulled off her. And yet these memories brought with them no sense of wrongness; Tam had saved her life that night, of that she was certain, but he'd been pilloried for it – sent to *jail*, his home destroyed and she had been told *nothing* of this! It became imperative that she found him, even if only to discover that he was dead, but she'd not rest now until she knew the facts. When she returned home her mother *must* be made to tell her!

But she would rather hear it from Tam himself.

'The old man's right,' Shelagh said as they reached the mouth of the inlet where the steamer had waited that day to take her away from the outport. 'Billy Norton has a handle on everyt'ing round here so we'll swing by the gas station on our way home. He's got a boat dock and I can fill the can while we're talkin'.' She gave Eva a curious look. 'Seems your man's one worth findin'.'

Eva nodded grimly as once more she left Heart's Repose in her wake.

Billy Norton recognised the name immediately. 'Tam Nairn? Sure I heard of Tam Nairn. Folk still talk about him, though I never met him myself. Too young.' He grinned at Eva, eyeing her with interest.

'Do you know where he went?' she asked.

'St John's, I guess. That's where everyone was headin', back then. Why d'you want to know?'

'I want to speak to him.'

'You a journalist or something?'

She began to see why Billy Norton knew everything. 'Why would you think so?'

'Cos of what happened, way back.'

Way back, but not forgotten. The man took his time filling the can, watching her as he chewed, waiting to see if she would take the bait.

She disappointed him. 'No. I'm not a journalist.'

At least not right now.

He shrugged and took the money Shelagh gave him, counted it and stuck it in his pocket, making change slowly.

'He had a son. Ross McLeod,' Eva said. It was a long shot but worth a try.

Billy seemed to consider this, staring down at the ground. 'There's a Ross McLeod down on the Avalon, making a name fer himself building boats. Old-time boats, like they used to be. Got a boatyard at Severn, south side of Trinity Bay. He's the only one I know. Could that be him?'

'Maybe.' She turned to help Shelagh lower the full gas can into the boat.

'Yer carrying some baggage, I reckon,' Shelagh said once Billy went out of earshot. 'Best shed it, girl. You know this Ross McLeod?'

'Yes. If it is him.'

'And he'll remember you?'

'Oh, yes.' She paused, recalling the dark resentment in Ross's eyes the day that they had departed. 'He blamed me, I think, for what happened that night.'

CHAPTER 17

Heart's Repose, 1966

Eva

Tam was proving difficult to find, and Eva was worried. She wanted to know more about the angry words in the salting room, much more, but in the days that followed her dramatic leap from the stage she'd seen neither him nor Ross. She'd tried asking her mother to explain about the resettlement programme but her answers were unsatisfactory. 'They've no ambition, these people, no gumption, no drive to better themselves. Although those with any sort of initiative will leave anyway.'

Eva considered this, trying to fill in the gaps. 'Wouldn't that be all right then?'

'And leave the no-hopers? Hardly! But you're too young to understand.' And that had been the end of it so if Eva couldn't find Tam to ask him, she'd have to wait until her father got back. Her mother was simmering with ill-temper these days and her father was never here – he'd no sooner return than he was off again, a pattern which fuelled her mother's discontent – although Eva was beginning to suspect that her mother's sharp tongue and her father's absences were directly connected. Their quarrels left her feeling increasingly unsettled, and with neither her father nor Tam around to reassure her, the questions were multiplying.

She began looking out for Tam. After school she dawdled on the way home, hanging around the stages and the store where he was sometimes to be found but failed to see either him or Ross.

Men often gathered there in close clusters these days and again she heard raised voices but Tam's was never among them. She grew more and more uneasy.

Had they driven Tam away? Or locked him up somewhere? Or . . . or worse? The thought of foul play took root in her head where it spread like a malign creeper and she convinced herself that he'd come to harm.

She *must* find out!

And so she formed a plan. Leaving for school next morning she headed up the hill instead of going down towards the schoolhouse and then took a wide sweep inland through the trees, following the footpath that linked the string of little outports, crossing the stream where it narrowed, and then made her way back along the other side of the bay. She'd never been over there on her own and was torn between thrilling at the adventure and a nagging anxiety about Tam. She mustn't be seen – folk would ask why she wasn't at school – so she kept to the high ground where she was hidden in the woods, praying she wouldn't meet anyone on the path. Emerging at last on a rocky ridge above the little cluster of shabby houses, she found a place where she could look down on the cabin where Tam and Ross lived.

She crouched among a low growth of spruce, glad to rest a while for it had been a long walk and from here she could keep watch. Tam's house was near the shore. It stood apart from the others, a couple of hundred yards from the nearest, and to her surprise she saw that the door stood open. Was that a good sign or a bad one? Had Tam been dragged from the house, or . . . Her mind rehearsed a range of possible, increasingly desperate scenarios drawn from her recent reading. Perhaps he was lying inside, bloodied and beaten, unable to summon help? Or had they taken him to the cliffs? It was only a short way . . . The image this conjured up terrified her, but the angry men had seemed capable of anything that day.

Even as she watched, though, a figure appeared at the door. Ross! He called something back into the house before making off towards the cove, leaving the door behind him open. This gave her pause. So was Tam simply inside, at home? She felt deflated. Then she saw Ross sling a shotgun across his shoulder and her eyes widened . . . But he was sauntering, kicking at a loose stone, and she had to concede that he looked not at all like a boy bent on an act of vengeance, or whose father had been beaten up, or kidnapped.

Or worse.

Relief was tempered by an odd sort of disappointment. She felt foolish now and unsure what her next step ought to be. It'd be awkward to simply return home and she'd not yet fixed upon the story she'd eventually have to tell her mother, and Miss Sinclair. Rather belatedly, she realised she'd been relying on the fact that she'd uncover some violent misadventure that would deflect everyone's attention from her absence, and cast her in an honourable, if not heroic, light. But there again, she'd only *assumed* it was Tam that Ross had called back to – she'd not actually *seen* him so perhaps she should wait a little longer.

Her eyes followed Ross's progress away from the cabin until he disappeared among the trees and she continued to wait, increasingly unsure of herself. Some instinct told her that her mother would be horrified if she simply went down there and knocked on the door, and she suspected that even her father would disapprove. Tam, too, she reckoned, might not like it. Which meant the only thing she could do was go back home and think of a plausible excuse for not appearing at school, and face the inevitable consequences.

A rather poor end to her adventure.

She straightened and was dusting off her hands when, to her delight, Tam himself appeared at the door, carrying a fishing rod and tackle box. He looked fit and well and it was all she could do to stop herself from leaping up and calling out to him, but the same instinct told her that he'd not like that either.

Adults were unpredictable. Especially these days.

She hunkered down again and watched to see where he went. He appeared to be headed towards the rocks, going in the opposite direction to his son and, without thinking, she began to follow him. Her relief at finding him unharmed, and with nothing more serious on his mind than fishing, led to the happy idea of stalking him and she began dodging behind rocks and shrubs as David Balfour and Alan Breck Stewart had done, evading the soldiers on the hills of Morven. It became a game; he'd no idea he was being followed! Once he'd found somewhere to fish, well out of sight of people and houses, she would reveal herself and they could settle down and have a long and satisfying chat.

And all her questions would be answered.

It was a wobbly stone that betrayed her. She'd watched him disappear among the rocks as he headed down towards the open ocean and she'd followed, anxious not to lose sight of him. Carefully she made her way over surfaces slick with rockweed, telling herself it wouldn't do to twist an ankle here. Once she thought she'd lost him but then she saw the tip of his rod and smiled to herself. So close! She crept nearer but a careless step set a loose stone rolling and Tam swung round.

'Eva! Christ, what the . . . what are you doing out here?'

She bounced over the last few rocks towards him, laughing. 'I've been following you for ages.'

She saw him glance swiftly back up behind her before returning her a frown. 'Why?' He didn't seem pleased to see her.

'Because I hadn't seen you for days, and I was worried?' His eyebrows raised. 'After the shouting in the salting room that day . . . I hadn't seen you. Or Ross.'

He considered her, an odd expression in his eyes that wasn't quite a smile. 'And so you were worried. Why aren't you at school?'

She slid past that one. 'Did Ross really have a knife?' The fun of the game faded and the fear that had come to her that day returned. 'Everyone seemed so angry.' He gave her a wry look, ignoring the matter of the knife.

'Some folk like shouting and talking big. There was no need to be worried, although I'm touched by your concern.' His look got drier. 'And you know what, young Eva, in my experience, when someone falls off a jetty they yell *as* they fall, not a second or two before. More of a yelp too rather than a full-throated scream, though I must say it was a good loud one.' She turned away, making a play of choosing a rock to sit on beside his tackle box. It was open and she peered inside it, letting her hair fall forward to cover her blushes. 'And I don't know why you're sitting down, young hockey stick, because you aren't staying.'

She looked up. 'Why were those men so angry with you?'

'Because I was telling them what they didn't want to hear.'

'About leaving? Why do people have to go?'

'They don't. That's the point. Now, off you . . .'

'What did you mean about thirty pieces of silver?'

'You go to church, don't you?'

She found a stick and began rooting through the tackle, careful to avoid the barbed hooks, and his eyes. 'You mean like Judas?'

'Aye.' She risked a glance at him and saw that his face had gone serious again.

'Scott Morris and Bill Bennet don't want to leave but if their dads say they must, they'll have to.'

'I know.'

'Why can't those who want to stay, stay, and those who want to go, go? I don't understand that and when I asked my mother she said I was too young to—'

'Then ask your dad, and be off with you.'

Having come all this way, she wasn't planning to leave without answers. 'He's away, up the coast.'

She saw him glance again at the rocks behind them and then he reeled in his line. 'Bane of my bloody life,' he muttered but in a way that was more like his old self, and he sat down on a rock opposite her. 'Right, then, listen hard and then off you go. Deal?'

'Deal.'

'And don't you go throwing yourself off jetties or worrying about me and Ross. We'll manage without heroics.'

'Ross had a gun with him just now.' There was still drama to be milked from this adventure.

His eyebrows raised again. 'Have you been spying on us?'

'Why'd he have a gun?'

'Rabbiting. No more questions. Pin back your ears and then off you go home or the deal's off. Understood?'

She nodded and then sat and listened as he explained about the scheme being offered, the conflict it had set up in the community and how only a few thought they should hang on. 'There's twenty-three households here and twenty of them have to agree to resettlement. Right now eighteen want to go and five want to stay so eighteen households are angry with five households and five households are feeling bullied.' She continued to poke about in the tackle box as she listened, separating the colourful jiggers from the silvery minnow-shaped lures, the floats from the weights.

She looked up. 'And you're one of the five, you and Ross?'

He nodded. 'Aye. Once I might have sided with the others but not now. I knew a man a long time ago who described to me what happens when a tight-knit community gets broken up and people scatter.'

'What?' He was gazing out over the waves and no longer seemed to be addressing her. 'What happens?'

'A bond is lost and all the strength it had to hold lives together. That bond is precious, he made me realise, I'd never even thought of it before.' She wasn't quite sure what he meant. 'In his case the families hadn't any choice but these folk . . . they'll lose more than they'll gain. They'll regret it. The world has surely moved on and they should make a stand, demand the changes which would make it possible for them to stay.'

'Is that what he did? This man?'

Tam didn't answer, but continued staring out to sea. And, as the silence lengthened, it seemed he had forgotten to insist she went home; in fact he seemed to have forgotten all about her. She carried on rootling in his tackle box until something caught her eye in the bottom, something which was neither hook nor lure. She pulled it out and saw it was a metal cross with splayed arms and it had a design on it – a lion and a crown and some words.

She rubbed it on her trouser leg and looked again. '"For val . . . valour",' she read, but Tam's gaze was still fixed on the horizon and he made no response. 'What does valour mean?'

'Hmm?' He turned back to her, saw what she was holding and she knew at once that she'd done wrong.

'I . . . I'm sorry. I'll put it back. But what does valour mean?'

His face was as grim as she'd ever seen it and he reached across, taking it from her. 'It means trying to get your bloody head blown off and failing. Aye, even at that! Now, be off with you. I mean it, Eva. Go home. Take care on the rocks but go home. Now!' He flicked the cross into a rock pool where it made a tiny splash, and the look on his face was enough to send her scuttling back up the rocks, her heart thumping.

She'd almost reached the top, head down, when she heard a voice above her. 'What the . . . ? Whadd'ya doin' here?' It was Ross McLeod and his angry expression was a mirror of his father's.

'Nothing. I'm going home.' She tried to evade him but he grabbed her arm and pulled her round. 'I'm *going*, I said.'

'Whadd'ya want with my dad?'

'Nothing! Let me go!'

The gun and a dead rabbit lay on the ground beside him. The rabbit's fur was red and its eye dull, and she was frightened now. Ross was glaring at her and seemed about to say more but released her and gave her a shove. 'Go then. And you leave him alone, you hear me? Just stay away.'

It was left to the schoolteacher to offer an alternative meaning for the word valour at the lunchtime next day, after what had been a difficult interrogation. 'You've a note from your mother, I expect, for yesterday?'

'Must have lost it,' Eva mumbled, and made a play of looking in her schoolbag.

'Were you ill?' This was awkward as Miss Sinclair would doubtless check.

'I felt sick.'

'Did your father say you were sick?'

'He's away.'

'But your mother thought you too sick to come to school?'

Eva made a non-committal sound but, on a sudden initiative, asked. 'Please, Miss, what does valour mean?'

It did the trick, hooking the pedagogue's interest. 'It means outstanding courage. From the Latin *valere*, to be strong, to have worth. Words like value and valiant come from the same root. Why do you ask?'

'I read it somewhere.'

'It often refers to a soldier's conduct on the battlefield, selfless courage, extreme bravery in the face of danger.'

'Oh!'

'Bring a note tomorrow, Eva, and don't you forget.'

So why had Tam thrown it away? Eva thought furiously as she ran, gasping for breath, re-tracing her footsteps from the previous day and trying hard to understand. It took courage to stand up for what you believed was right. It took bravery to defend your principles. The books he'd told her to read made this very point. Buck, David Balfour, Jim Hawkins . . . If you were courageous and stood firm, then, in the end, that courage was rewarded. She'd be in trouble when she got back, she knew that, but this was much more important than missing an afternoon at school. The future of Heart's Repose depended on this! To be one of five against eighteen was hard; to stand firm needed strength. She'd heard the bitterness in Tam's voice, the resignation, but he should *not* have thrown away the cross thing. He must have been given it in the war, which was a long time ago but even so . . . He'd seemed out of sorts yesterday, not all that pleased to see her, and he'd regret throwing it away, she was sure he would, so if she could find it and show it to him again then perhaps he'd find the courage to go on resisting. The thought made her feel rather noble and, as she crossed the little bridge, pausing to catch her breath, she rehearsed what she would say to him.

First though, she must retrieve the cross. She ran on, keeping her head down, watching her step on the uneven ground as she left the forest and approached the rocks. A rising on-shore wind blew in her face and had she lifted her head she would have seen that the horizon had become blurred.

A moment later it disappeared.

She ran on, heedless, down towards the shore but having got there found it harder than she'd imagined to discover the place where Tam had gone down through the rocks the day before, and harder still to find exactly where they'd sat. Half of her hoped he'd be there again and she'd prepared a rather stirring speech but there was no sign of life, other than a cormorant standing sentinel on the rocks. It flew off as she appeared and she stood a moment looking about her, trying to remember which rock Tam had sat on. It must have been that one, the rounded boulder, and she moved to sit there, pantomiming how he had flicked the little cross away. So it was *that* pool it fell in . . . She wriggled onto her front and stared down into the dark water. It was deeper than it had been the day before, refilled by the incoming tide, and the weeds swayed with every pulse, which made it very hard to see.

She picked up a stick and gently stirred the fronds, looking out for a glint of metal. Had the tide moved it? She'd not considered that. Once she thought she glimpsed it and pushed up her sleeve, reaching an arm into the pool, but the water was freezing cold so she pulled back, tucking her hair behind her ears and stirred the pool again. No luck. She'd not anticipated this much trouble and sat a moment considering whether it really had been this pool, and decided it must have been – she'd seen it splash right into the middle where, unfortunately, the water was deepest. But having come to find it she wasn't going until she had. She pushed her sleeve up higher and plunged her arm in again, the cold was numbingly painful but she mustn't give up. There were hours yet until sunset but the pool seemed to be getting darker by the minute. Carefully moving a weed aside she again thought she spotted a glint of metal. There, yes, just out of reach. Determination had won the day! Unable to bear another moment of the icy water she pulled out her arm and rubbed it briskly, grimacing as she flexed her fingers back to life. The very air felt colder now but she kept her eyes fixed on the point where she'd seen that shimmering through the water, holding the weeds aside with her stick. It was there all right, gleaming against the dark of the rockweed in the deepest part. She wriggled further forward and stretched her arm as far as she could.

Got it!

But that final lurch was her undoing. She unbalanced, losing grip with her other hand and fell forwards, banging her face on the rock and cutting her chin as the whole top half of her went under. Gasping and appalled she struggled to grasp the slippery weeds, her other hand holding tight to her trophy seeing red drops diffuse into the pool beneath her as she did. She was bleeding! She cried out as she struggled, grazing knuckles and elbows on the sharp rocks, hair dripping into her eyes, and wailed in fear and frustration. Eventually, awkwardly and painfully, she managed to wriggle backwards, scraping knees and shins, until at last she was able to sit up, her chin still bleeding, now shivering with the cold.

She began to cry.

And it was only then that she realised that the world around her had changed. It had grown still. The wind had dropped and she found herself in a cocoon of damp whiteness. Sea fog . . . The muffled sound of the foghorn reached her and she realised then it'd been sounding for a while – she'd been too absorbed to notice. All the time she'd been bent over the rock pool the fog must have been moving in, like a phantom army rising silently from the sea to assault the land and it now covered the whole shoreline in a great blanket, thickening fast.

The damp chill soon sapped her remaining warmth. And courage.

She stood up, feeling utterly miserable, her wet clothes clinging to her frame, and began to shudder with the cold. Quick.

Think! Must keep moving. Must get home. Slipping the cross into her trouser pocket she lurched forwards, looking for the way she'd taken coming down, but all seemed altered now and she'd only the sound of the sea to guide her. Must keep heading up, though, through the rocks, but she mistook her way and found her route blocked by a boulder too large to climb. She turned back, her heart pounding, and began to whimper. She tried a different route. Same thing. She was truly frightened now. Her next attempt seemed more hopeful – she'd have to scramble over one of the boulders but it looked manageable and it would have been but for a patch of dark weed. As she stepped onto it her foot shot from under her and she fell with a cry, tearing her trousers and ramming her foot down between two rocks.

Where it stuck fast.

Later, much later, when asked how long she'd lain there in that other-world, entombed in the cold dense fog, she'd no idea. It had seemed like forever, the distant sound of the foghorn her only link with the world, her ankle throbbing as it swelled. She'd called for help for as long as she could and then stopped, and sobbed instead, growing so tired and wretched that she'd given up and curled up like a wounded creature, waiting to be found. With the fog had come a strange half-light but soon true darkness fell and Eva stopped crying, feeling drowsy, discovering to her mild surprise that the rocks were actually not that hard after all; they were soft, almost pillow soft, and she was floating away, the foghorn growing faint.

And then, from out of the darkness, she heard a voice calling her name. The sound came closer, then stopped. It came again, and she roused, knowing that she must answer. She tried to stand, forgetting her ankle, and cried out in pain, and then there was a quick rattle of stones and a light was shone in her face, and there was Tam's voice, close by, and then suddenly he was there beside her, holding her close. She sobbed with relief, clinging to him, and then screamed as he tried to move her. 'It's her foot, it's stuck.' Another voice? Ross. Together they struggled for what seemed like forever, heaving aside the smaller rocks and pulling painfully at her leg, twisting it to free her.

Then nothing.

Dimly she remembered surfacing and realising that she was being carried, her ear pressed close to Tam's chest, an arm slung around his shoulder, her head resting there. She could hear him panting, feel his heart pounding and smelt cigarettes on his clothes. Through half-closed eyes she saw a cabin ahead, and a door which Tam kicked open. 'Make up the fire, son, quick as you can,' she heard him say. 'And turn your back.' She was held drooping in front of the stove, unable to stand unaided while her wet clothes were peeled off her. She'd no more agency over what was happening than a rag doll. 'Fetch a towel and a blanket. Hold the blanket to the fire.' He took the towel and briskly rubbed her shuddering body until she whimpered, begging him to stop, but he carried on, and all the time his voice was calming her. 'Need to get you warm, lass. Need to get the blood flowing again. Shh, now. You're all right, you know. I'll stop in a moment. You're doing fine. Safe now, I promise. That blanket warm yet, Ross? Good. Let me have it.' And she was wrapped tight in a cocoon of warmth and held. A strange lassitude came over her and the voices began to fade.

'Right, she'll do,' he heard Tam say. 'Now go and tell her mother where she is.'

'I'll stay with her, you go.'

'Off with you, Ross, quick as you can.'

CHAPTER 18

Newfoundland, 1980

Eva

The more she spoke, the more it all came back to her and the scraps of memory began to fit together to make a whole. They were sitting beside Shelagh's fireside and the woman had listened without interruption. 'And you've carried this wid you ever since?'

She had, but what had happened next was a blank, except for what she'd learned today. 'You heard what Don Morris said. Tam went to jail because of me!'

'You didn't know?'

Eva shook her head. 'I'd been told to forget about it and . . . and so I did.'

'Course you did! You were a child and you'd bin taken away, to another country, another life.'

'It became like a bad dream.' She'd known that Tam had been accused of something, though. Her father had been sent for and once the fever had left her, she'd explained to him what happened on the rocks and he'd disappeared for a while. Her mother had kept her confined to the house, away from people, and so she'd known nothing of what was being said.

Next thing she'd known they'd been all packed up, ready to leave.

'You need to be on yer way, girl,' Shelagh said. 'Find yer man and lay yer ghosts.'

And so next morning, she'd hugged Shelagh, promising to return one day. She'd fill the car up at Billy's garage, and then go on to see if this Ross McLeod was indeed the boy who had warned her off years ago, telling her to leave his dad alone, to stay away.

'It'll be like havin' a tooth out,' the old woman said as Eva got into the car. 'Nags away at ya, painful gettin' sorted, but soon heals over.'

Just *how* painful, Eva wondered.

Billy recognised her straight away. And as he stood there in his oily dungarees, filling up the gas tank, he resumed his questioning. 'You headin' down to Severn now?'

'I'm going that way, yes.' She'd found Severn on the map and worked out how long it would take her. Several hours she reckoned.

'So how d'ya know Ross McLeod?' His eyes dwelt on her in a way she didn't quite like.

'I hardly do.'

'Heart's Repose's mighty popular all of a sudden,' he said, taking his time, 'for a place that don't exist.'

'Is it?'

'I'd a guy come through earlier asking about someone he'd been told used to live there.'

She turned back to him. 'But not Tam Nairn?'

'Nah, some other name. And I said same as I said to you – everyone's about forgotten d'place then suddenly two comes along askin'. He was a Brit, too.'

Something clutched at her heart. 'You told him I'd been asking?' He nodded, shaking the last of the gas off the nozzle and wiping his hands on his overalls, still watching her. 'Did you say who I was looking for?'

He shrugged, his expression growing ever more curious. 'Shouldn't I?'

Her hand wasn't quite steady as she pulled out her wallet. 'Do you remember who he said he wanted to find?'

'Nah, but there's no one round here with the name.'

Her mouth had gone dry. 'It wasn't Maxwell, was it?'

Billy looked up. 'Yeh! Dat was it. So maybe yous know each other, eh?'

Maybe they did! 'What did he look like?' David, it had to be David Mallory, on the trail of a red-hot scoop. *Damn him!* But how had he found her? 'And did you tell him what you'd told me?'

Billy was scratching his head, doing a yokel impression but his eyes remained shrewd. 'He'd be fortyish, talked like you do. In a hire car, same rental place as this one.' He kicked the car's rear tyre. 'Said this guy Maxwell was at Heart's Repose in the sixties, and he needed to find him. Told him to ask at Trinity. Before my time, I said, but it wasn't a name—'

'And what did you say about me?'

'Just that it was a strange t'ing, the two o' yous coming in two days. And you stayin' with Shelagh Doyle and all.'

Somehow she managed to get away from the man and back on the road. Even David with his legendary snooping skills would be hard pressed to find the track down to Doyle's Point should he try to find her there, and Shelagh she trusted to keep her counsel if he did. Oh God, what had she done! And if Ross McLeod *was* Tam's son she'd have to come clean and warn him that David was hot on his trail.

She drove fast, juddering over the broken road surface, swerving around potholes, constantly checking her rear-view mirror and blessing the empty road. She followed the route she'd taken on the way up, and eventually re-joined the larger road down the narrow isthmus where there was more traffic for her to disappear among then continued south until at last she was back on the Avalon peninsula, where she turned east again following the south shore of Trinity Bay. The road hugged the coast and she was so focused on the drive that she almost drove straight past the sign to Severn Seas Boatyard.

She braked, turning off as indicated, and parked down by the shore where at last she could draw breath. If this Ross *was* Tam's son he was never going to be pleased to see her and she must be prepared for a difficult interview but, at the very least, he could get a message to his father, explain the situation at Rosslie, and warn him that the hunt was on.

Ahead of her was what looked like an old salting room that had been repaired, repainted and made into an office. She tried the door but it was locked. No bell, no one around. She went down to the water's edge where some traditional wooden boats had been pulled up, their weathered ribs exposed like the bleached carcasses of sea creatures. Beside them on the slipway were two dories, newly painted. An image of Ross helping the men repair boats at Heart's Repose flashed into her mind. Had that wild, dark-browed boy become a craftsman? She swung round as the phone started ringing in the salting-room office and waited for someone to appear, but it just rang and rang until the caller gave up. There was a pickup truck only a little less battered than Shelagh's parked in the shadow of the building so someone must be around.

Then she caught the sound of rock music on the breeze and lifted her head to listen. It was coming from round the bay where there was a large boatshed, and the sound grew louder as she approached. Large seaward doors led onto a timber slipway with iron rails down to the water. The doors stood open so she stuck her head inside and called out. No response. The sleek hull of a large vessel occupied most of the interior but there was just enough room for her to squeeze down the side of it. 'Hello!' Still no response. The music was coming from a radio at the far end where she could see an overhead light. She called out more loudly, feeling like a trespasser as she moved along the hull towards the bow.

Beneath the light she could see a man crouched down by the hull, planing the wooden planks, totally focused on the job. Was this the Ross she had known, grown to manhood? 'Hello!' she said again, stooping to get his attention.

He didn't move. 'Sure, I heard you. Just gimme a minute.'

She straightened, and stood there while whatever it was that he was doing was finished to his satisfaction. Then he rose. And it was

Ross all right. He was tall, as his father had been, and he looked lean and fit as one might expect of a man in his line of work. He put down the plane, flicked off the radio and stood, dusting off his hands as he contemplated her with no hint of recognition.

'Hi,' he said.

'Ross McLeod?' she asked, her courage ebbing away.

'That's me.' And suddenly it seemed quite impossible to ask him about his father, impossible to say who she was and why she'd come but he was continuing to look at her, a little puzzled when she said nothing more. 'You wanting a dory?' he asked, quizzing her. 'Or a schooner?' He gestured to the half-built ship behind him. 'Takes longer, costs more.'

There was humour in his eyes and the smile he gave her was his father's, one-sided and ironic. It didn't make things easier. 'Neither, although both are very fine. I . . . I saw the dories at the jetty. No, in fact, I'm looking for your father.'

The humour vanished. 'Yeah?'

'Can you tell me where I can find him.'

'I can.' He leaned against the hull, still wiping his hands, and looked steadily back at her. 'What d'ya want with him?'

'I want to talk to him. To ask him something, and . . . and to tell him something.'

'Tell me first.'

'I really can't.'

'You a journalist or something?'

'No! At least, well, I *am* a journalist but I'm not here as . . .' He pushed himself off the hull then and moved towards her, making shooing gestures with his hands. The smile had gone and his eyes were flinty. She stood her ground. 'It's a personal matter, and I really need to speak to him.'

'Nah. We're all done here. Time to go, Miss Whatever-your-name—'

'Bayne. Eva Bayne.'

He froze, his hands mid-air, and he gaped at her. Then his brows snapped together and he took a step closer and peered down at her. '*Christ*, it damn well is,' he said and his eyes sparked, 'so we really *are* all done here.'

'Wait, Ross. Listen—'

'No, you leave, Eva Bayne, and you don't come back. Not *ever*. Got that?'

He'd used almost the same words once before and had given her a shove, but he was older now and looked much more dangerous. It was all she could do not to turn and run as she had done that day above the rocks. But she too was an adult now and answered with a firmness she was far from feeling. 'I *will* leave, Ross, but first I need to know where I can find Tam. I have to speak to him.' She raised her chin, determined that she'd not leave without an address.

She'd expected a rebuttal, after all, she'd expected this hostility, and she'd been prepared for a tough conversation – she had even been prepared to be told that Tam was dead – but what she *hadn't* been prepared for was that a shadow would lengthen along the schooner's hull, taking the light from the entrance to the boatshed, and that out of the shadow a familiar voice would ask, 'Must you, Eva? I can't imagine why.'

CHAPTER 19

She swung round and there he was, backlit by the sun, no more than a silhouetted shape. He moved forwards, his face still half in shadow, half in light. She'd have known him anywhere; that slightly uneven stance, that low, cultured voice. 'Tam . . . !'

Ross's reaction to his appearance was explosive, but his father simply raised a hand to silence him. 'Hang on, Ross—'

'*No*, she leaves.' Ross made a cutting gesture with his hand, and attempted again to drive Eva towards the open boatshed door, but Tam was now blocking her retreat. 'What's she gotta say that you need to hear?'

'We won't know unless—'

'We don't *need* to know. Eva Bayne only ever brought trouble.'

'That's hardly fair, son. It's a surprise, I grant you—'

'Tam, I . . . I really must speak to you.'

'Yes, you said. So let's you and I go up to the house—'

Ross swore. 'Not on your own, you're not. I need to hear this.'

But Tam shook his head. 'I'll tell you, Ross, afterwards. I'll tell you every word, I promise, but I imagine Eva's come a long way to say whatever it is, and so I'll hear her out.'

'She's a fuckin' journalist!'

Tam's eyebrows raised. 'Is that so?'

'Yes.' Eva was still recovering from the shock of seeing him. He was so close that if she reached out, she could touch him. 'But that has absolutely nothing to do with why I'm here.' Which wasn't entirely true but she'd no intention of trying to explain matters with Ross McLeod standing by, ready to choke the life out of her.

Tam considered her coolly. 'A hack, eh? Well, I'm duly warned, I suppose. Come along anyway.'

'Wait!' Ross put out a hand. 'Give me your bag.'

'My bag?'

'Tape recorder.' Silently she handed it to him and he peered inside, stirred the contents and returned it without apology. 'Right. Half an hour, then she leaves. Got it?'

'Thank you, Ross,' said his father, his eyes faintly amused.

In a daze she followed Tam across the yard, feeling Ross's eyes burning into her back. He led her towards a square clapboard house, its planks a faded yellow ochre like the other buildings scattered around the bay. 'I'd not have known you, Eva,' he said as he ushered her into a tidy kitchen, then went across the room to put a kettle on the hob. 'Your hair has darkened, and the freckles have gone. Wait while I make us some tea.' He gestured her to a chair at the table and she sat, watching him assemble mugs, a teapot and milk. To an eleven-year-old he had always seemed old but he could only have been in his forties then, and strangely he seemed little changed. In fact he looked better than he had back then – perhaps he'd given up the drink. His hair, which had been greying, was now almost white, and it suited him. His face was craggier, weather-beaten and lined, but he was still a good-looking man.

As he stood with his back to her, she pulled the pages of the magazine article from her bag, unfolded them and laid them on the table. They did, after all, make matters clear.

'This is most unexpected, Eva,' he said, turning to the table with a mug in each hand. 'Whatever brings you—' His eye fell on the pages and he stopped, set down the mugs and then leaned forwards, straight arms supported on knuckles, and stared down at the image of his younger self.

For a long time he said nothing.

Then said, 'Dammit,' and lifted his eyes to her. 'Who have you told?'

How she would have loved to be able to tell him that she'd kept her suspicions to herself, her mouth firmly shut. Then she'd not have felt like this. A hack, he had called her, a grubby hack tracking him to his refuge.

'It's not quite that simple.'

His eyes were as hard as Ross's now, any trace of humour gone. 'My family knows?'

'Lady Maxwell a little, and perhaps her sons too, but I'm not sure what she told them. And . . . and my boss, the man who wrote this. He's guessed, I think.' Tam sat down, pulled spectacles from a top pocket and read the article through without another word.

'So Pa's dead,' he said at last, laying down the pages. He stared at the table, saying nothing more before coming back into the moment. 'And Rosslie's in a mess.' He removed the glasses, sat back and contemplated her. 'They should've had me certified dead years ago.' His expression was unreadable, the shutters pulled well down. 'But how on earth did you get involved with all this?' Briefly she told him and he nodded. 'And so you've told them where to find me.'

She shook her head. 'I mentioned Heart's Repose to Lady Maxwell, but not your name, not Tam Nairn.'

'Ah. So maybe there's hope for me yet.'

Oh God. But there was no escaping it. 'I'm not sure there is,' she said, and told him about Billy and the man who had come asking questions. 'I think it's my boss,' she concluded, gesturing to the article. 'When he wrote this, he showed me, and I . . . I said I thought I recognised you, and he didn't believe me but he must have, and then he was suspicious of where I was going, coming here. He . . . he must have worked it out and I think he's followed me, hoping for a scoop.'

It all tumbled out and she burned with shame as she saw a look of profound weariness pass over his features. 'Explain from the beginning, if you would, Eva, then I'll know what to expect.'

And so she told him everything, as coherently as she was able. He said nothing but his eyes never left her face. He looked briefly amused at the story of the old gentleman sabotaging the auction, frowned a little at Duncan Maxwell's phone call and grew still as she told him about her strange lunch with Jillian Maxwell. 'It was only then that it occurred to me that you might not want to be found.'

'Only then, eh? You didn't use to be stupid.' The words were lightly spoken but they stung and she stuttered to a halt, finding herself unable to tell him what had caused Lady Maxwell to alter her tone and position. 'And how is Jillian?'

'I hardly know. I only spoke to her that once.'

'And she has sons, you said. More than one?'

'Two. Keith is the other, younger, one.'

'And how well do you know them?'

'Not at all. I saw them at the auction but only spoke to Duncan on the phone. Keith, I've never met.'

'Tell me about Duncan.'

'I hardly—'

She broke off as she heard boots on the steps and the door to the kitchen was flung open. Ross McLeod came in with a face like thunder and fixed her with a glare. 'What the hell's going on here? First you turn up, and now I've had a fella asking for Archibald Maxwell or Tam Nairn. This is all down to you, isn't it?'

Billy. *Damn* Billy! And damn David . . . He must have gone back and pressed the man then followed hard upon her heels.

Tam gave her a chilly look. 'He's good, your boss.'

'Oh God, I'm sorry.'

But Ross's eyes were flicking between them. 'Yer *boss*?'

'What did he look like?' Eva asked but Ross's eye had been caught by the photograph on the open page. He spun it round and stared at it a moment, then looked up at his father in bewilderment and jabbed the image with his finger.

'Like him.'

CHAPTER 20

There was silence in the room. Oh God. Not David. Duncan Maxwell.

It had to be.

Eva looked across at Tam and saw that his face had drained of colour and he suddenly looked very much his age. Ross was scowling, his eyes flicking between the two of them, and the photograph on the table. 'What's going on?' he demanded again.

'What did you say to him?' Tam asked.

'That I'd not heard either name. He wouldn't leave so I told him to clear off or I'd set the dogs on him.'

Tam gave a thin smile. 'Ah.'

'He'd see my car,' Eva said.

'So?'

'It has the same St John's rental sticker on it. He'll guess.'

Ross frowned. 'Guess what?'

'That I'm here.'

'And so he'll be back. He's followed Eva here, you see,' Tam explained coldly. 'And anyone he asks in Severn will tell him that your father is living here, with you.' He turned to Eva. 'Where are you staying?'

'I was going to find somewhere—'

'Edith'll have you. She takes paying guests in the summer.' He got to his feet, looking like a man badly needing to escape. 'I'll go now and ask her. You must stay while we work this out. Don't leave.' And he was gone.

The door slammed behind him and Ross bent over the article, reading it with a fierce intensity, and when he'd finished he sat, turned back the pages and read it again more slowly before pushing it aside and staring at the door through which Tam had left.

'You didn't know?' Eva said, feeling the need to break the silence.

His shoulder was all the answer that she got.

Not for a moment had she considered what Ross did or didn't know of his father's past, and the article spread out on the table must have sent his world into a tailspin. How naïve she'd been, coming here, blundering in, how thoughtless! But things had moved too fast, slipping from her control and now anything could happen. The eyes of Archibald Maxwell's photograph stared up at her, no longer ironic but distant, blanking her.

Ross turned back and looked at her with the same coldness. 'So who is he, this guy following you?'

'His brother, I think. Duncan Maxwell. Half-brother.'

He absorbed that silently. 'And you say he followed you? Looking for Tam.' She nodded. 'So what happens now?'

'I . . . I'm not sure.'

He grunted and pulled the article back to read again. 'You know him, this brother?' he asked, not looking up.

'No.'

'Yet he followed you.' She explained as briefly as she could and he listened, expressionless.

'So if you'd not seen this,' he pointed to the photograph, 'they'd have gone on lookin' for him, then given up, and things could have carried on as they were?' It was true and they both knew it so she said nothing. 'Why d'ya come?'

'To ask him if he wanted to be found.'

He regarded her, his lips a thin line of anger. 'The answer was staring you in the face, woman! If he'd wanted to go back, he'd have gone.'

'He didn't know that his father had died.' It was a poor defence.

Ross snorted. 'Probably thought him long dead. He was ninety-six, for Christ's sake, and if they'd wanted to make up, they'd had

God knows how many years to do it.' He folded his arms and rocked the chair back, still contemplating her, his jaw set. 'You've no idea, have you? Not a clue! We *really* don't need you, comin' here makin' trouble again. It's only been these last few years—' He broke off.

Making trouble. 'I didn't mean to—'

'And that makes it OK? Not meaning to? You, of all people. *Jeez.*'

'Look, I'm sorry—'

He'd turned away again but now he swung back, gesturing again to the paper. 'Why d'he leave then, all those years ago?'

'I don't know.'

'Guess.'

'Really, I've no idea.'

He considered her, assessing the truth of her denial. 'That family of his didn't say? Those brothers?'

'I've hardly spoken to Duncan, and not at all to Keith.'

'The press'll go wild over this, piling in, diggin' up the dirt again.' He was right, they would. 'God knows what it'll do to him. Why couldn't ya just leave us be?'

'I wish I had.' So very much . . .

He glared at her, got up and stood looking out of the window, his back to her, hands deep in his pockets.

The silence became unbearable. 'I'd no idea, Ross. About Tam going to jail, about you being burned out, or any of it. I only heard yesterday.'

He didn't move. 'Yesterday? So it's not forgotten, eh? Even now.'

'No one ever told me what happened. My parents never would. The last thing I remember was being out on the rocks when the fog rolled in, my foot stuck between two boulders, and being terrified and cold, shaking so hard and then Tam's voice and yours . . . and then warmth.' She began trembling as she spoke, the shreds of memory reforming in her mind. 'Next thing, I woke up and people kept on and on at me, asking me questions I didn't understand . . .'

Ross turned back to look at her, unmoved. 'But you can guess, right? You're an adult now and you know what some men do to little girls. Well, that's what he was accused of, the story they decided to tell.' He had gone white around the lips, his anger palpable. 'They said he'd lured you to the cabin, that you weren't lost at all, you'd been there all the time. Said I'd covered for him and was just backing up his story. You were bruised all over, on your legs and arms, and they said that was him, or me, or both of us, restraining you.' Her hands went to her burning cheeks but she was unable to look away. 'Your face was cut about, your hands all torn – trying to escape him, they said.'

'I fell! On the rocks—'

'We knew that and I reckon they did too. But his story didn't play so well when they came and found you in his bed, naked and wrapped in a blanket looking like a battered child, your clothes all over the floor.' She saw him swallow, the muscles in his cheeks tightening. 'I think he guessed what might happen; he wouldn't let me stay but sent me to tell them you'd been found. Like he knew . . . I went to the first house across the bay then headed back so I was there when yer mother arrived. She went mental when she saw you.' Eva could well imagine. 'You were running a fever and out of it by then, muttering and delirious, tossing about crying *stop, Tam, stop*, which made her flip.' Eva felt sick. 'He tried to tell her what had happened and then just stood there and took it, all the crap she kept throwin' at him. She was way past listening by then and it was only when Ada Sinclair arrived and slapped her face that she quit her hollerin', accusing us of all sorts. *Jeez.*' He fairly spat the word. 'Then others started piling in and she went crazy again, and the bastards latched on to what she said, had him dragged off, and . . . and I did a runner.' She glimpsed guilt, recognising its stain, and she could only listen in dismay. It was worse, much worse than she'd imagined.

'I'd have died on the rocks that night if he'd not found me,' she managed to say. 'Did *no one* believe him?'

Ross snorted again. 'Suited them better to bring him down. Ada Sinclair said it was a load of rubbish but no one was going to listen to her; she was holding out against signing too.'

'Was that what it was about?'

'Course it was.'

'And then what?'

His eyes sparked again. 'He was charged with abducting and abusing you, Eva Bayne, that's what. He was taken to St John's and held there pending trial, and you can guess how that was for him! It was only when your dad got back from the Labrador, heard what had happened and headed down there that it got sorted. *He* knew no one had done you any harm – he recognised opportunism when he saw it and got all charges dropped. But while Tam was inside, Morris and Bennet put pressure on the doubters and got 'em to sign and that was it. Resettlement happened. Burned us out for good measure.'

She was reeling. He might as well have struck her. 'And Tam, and you . . . What did you do?'

But he was finished. 'We got by.' He scowled at her. 'And now you turn up *again*, and we're back in the shit.' He scowled at the magazine. 'He doesn't need this.'

'Ross, I'll do—' She broke off as the kitchen door opened. Tam walked in and she looked up at him, stricken with remorse, but he appeared not to notice and spoke briskly.

'Edith has a room for you, Eva. Just follow the track round. Red house, yellow door, she's expecting you and she'll feed you. You'll be fine there.' She shook her head; she wanted to leave, find her own place, regain some control, she needed to absorb what Ross had told her and started to say so, but Tam raised a hand. 'Stay close. No slipping away. We'll speak in the morning but right now I need to talk to Ross.' He held open the door, courteous but cool, and escorted her out onto the raised porch where he pointed out Edith's house and the track she needed to take. 'Come back after breakfast. I've told her you're the daughter of a friend of mine and I suggest you stick with that.' He gave a wry smile. 'It's true, after all. Is your father well?'

'He died, five years ago.'

'I'm sorry. He was a fine man. Goodnight, Eva.'

CHAPTER 21

There was a car parked outside Tam's house the next morning and Eva's stomach lurched at the sight of the St John's rental sticker in the back of it. Duncan Maxwell had wasted no time in returning.

He must have made enquiries in Severn last night, she thought, as she drew up beside the car, and she was swamped again by a sense of having betrayed Tam. Having virtually ruined him fifteen years ago she'd returned only to destroy the man's peace. *He doesn't need this*, Ross had said . . . She'd lain awake much of the night, conscious of Tam just around the bay, lying there probably thinking much the same. Things were happening too fast; there had been no opportunity to explain – or to understand.

And now, when she was so ill-prepared, there was Duncan Maxwell to be faced as well. All three Maxwell men had reasons to despise her, which was hardly a good place to start the day.

Tam must have heard her arrive as he came out onto the porch. He looked haggard, confirming a sleepless night. 'Eva. You were comfortable at Edith's, I hope,' he said. 'She's a good sort. Come inside, Duncan's just arrived.' He spoke calmly as if this was a casual gathering of well-acquainted friends, but the tension in him was plain to see. He ushered her into the kitchen where Ross was seated in the same place as yesterday; he glanced up as she entered but gave no greeting. Duncan Maxwell was sitting opposite him, a mirror image as far as appearance and expression went, but different in every other way. A waxed jacket had been slung over the back of his chair and he was dressed as if for a day on the grouse moor. He looked out of place and wary, and gave her only the merest nod.

The atmosphere was already combustible, needing only a spark to ignite a conflagration. Perhaps Tam thought the same for he addressed her in a mild, easy tone. 'Have a seat, Eva. You and Duncan know each other, I gather.'

Eva shook her head. 'We spoke once on the phone.'

'And then you met my mother.'

She held Duncan's look and sat. 'I did. And between the two of you, and David Mallory, you contrived to follow me, although I can't quite see how you managed it.' She was, however, determined to find out; Tam and Ross were watching her and somehow she must gain their trust.

Close up the physical resemblance between the three men was startling. Ross had his mother's dark colouring but they all had the long nose and high forehead of the Maxwells, and right now their faces bore the same look of strain. She could only imagine what was going through Duncan Maxwell's mind as he sat opposite his older brother's son.

'This business needed resolving, Miss Bayne,' he said, addressing her in icy tones. 'There's a great deal at stake! Mallory had his suspicions about your sudden request for leave, given what you'd told him, and you'd no right to withhold what you knew, while my mother—' He broke off. 'No matter. It was my decision to come after you. We needed to find . . . Archie, and we have, and so there's an end to it. The matter is concluded.'

The tension in the room gave his words the lie.

Tam's eyes had been fixed unwaveringly on Duncan as he spoke but his expression gave nothing away. A little silence followed his words, then Tam remarked, 'I was about to suggest to Duncan, just before you arrived, Eva, that he should explore the delights of Newfoundland for a week or so and then return to Scotland and declare it to have been a wild goose chase. Forget we ever met. The success of that approach, however, rather depends on you.'

Duncan stared at him and his face darkened. 'You can't possibly be serious.'

'Never more so, I assure you. Ross and I discussed it last night and want no part in it. It's all yours, Duncan. Either pretend you never found me or give me something to sign and I'll renounce the lot.'

'You must know it won't be that simple. We'll need legal advice—'

'Then get legal advice, charge it to the estate and send the papers for me to sign.'

Duncan's jaw tightened. 'Forgive me, but what you suggest is absurd. You've no choice but to return to Scotland so that things can be properly sorted out – and I imagine it'll take months.'

Tam shook his head. 'I won't do that.'

'You must!'

'Tell them I'm dead.'

Duncan glared at him. 'You place me in an impossible position. If I have to I'll send lawyers out to you here but that'll simply drag out the process and raise the costs enormously. The press will follow them and I doubt you'll relish the attention.' Ross flicked a look at Eva, who quailed at the thought. Oh God, if Duncan only knew! But he was right and she could imagine the headlines: *Rosslie heir found!* An attention grabber followed swiftly by *War Hero: The Missing Years?* or some such, before, and with an awful inevitability: *The baronet's secrets laid bare.* David would be like a pig in muck, well ahead of the pack using the leads he had. But Duncan was continuing. 'They're already comparing your disappearance to Lord Lucan's. Ask Miss Bayne how they behave, – she's one of them, and doubtless delighted she's managed to steal a march on the others, and can break the story.'

Tam lit another cigarette, considering her. 'Came looking for a scoop, eh?'

'No.' Oh God, that he could even think it! She dug her nails into her palms, desperately wanting to speak to him alone, to explain matters and to understand the whole of it – and to warn him of how it would be if Duncan did unleash the press. She'd not wish that sort of hell on anyone.

'Tam goes nowhere he doesn't want to,' Ross said, addressing Duncan. 'Do like he says. You found no sign of him. False lead.'

Duncan had begun an angry riposte when footsteps sounded on the porch outside. A young man opened the door and stuck his head in. 'Deliveries, Ross. Need ya to check 'nd sign.'

Ross swore under his breath and rose, fixing his father with a glare. 'Agree to nothing while I'm gone.'

Tam gave a slight smile. 'I won't.'

The door closed and Duncan turned to him. 'This obviously concerns him too.'

Tam shook his head. 'It doesn't.'

'He's your *son*.'

The terse words failed to disguise the emotion behind them and Eva saw a curious look flit across Tam's face. 'The estate is yours, Duncan, or however you plan to share it with your brother Keith. I make no claim and Ross *has* no claim.'

Duncan absorbed this, his jaw tightening again. He clearly wanted to ask the obvious question but was unable to bring himself to do so. 'The lawyers will need convincing.'

'The absence of documents will be trying for them, I'm sure, but Ross and I discussed all this and his life is here, and so is mine. We'll not make trouble for you and I'll sign anything you come up with, more or less, and not interfere. How is your mother?'

The abrupt change of topic made Duncan frown. 'Concerned to have things settled.'

'She's what, almost seventy, I suppose. Staying fit, is she? Wearing well? I can't imagine her any other way.' Eva was watching Duncan as Tam spoke and saw a light flare in his eyes. It was so quickly gone that she doubted what she'd seen. 'And you must be almost forty yourself, Duncan,' Tam continued. 'My God, is it really that long ago?' He gestured to the article which lay, folded now, on the kitchen table. 'You're struggling at Rosslie, I gather.'

'The estate needs investment and this legal limbo makes that impossible. My father didn't like change so things have atrophied.'

Tam nodded. 'I always thought Pa stalled somewhere around nineteen twenty, so I can imagine your difficulty. You have plans though; I read of salmon farms.'

Duncan Maxwell seemed to thaw, just a little. 'That's the idea. We started with hatcheries and moved on to sea-cages but we need to expand. Aquaculture has proved profitable in Norway and we'll follow their model.'

'Aquaculture! Now there's a word. Very enterprising of you, Duncan. And where are these cages?'

'In the estuary.'

Tam nodded. 'Deep water there.'

'It's ideal.'

'I wish you every success. But the world's come to a pretty pass, hasn't it, if we have to farm *fish*! Having raped the oceans we now keep the poor creatures in cages. Good God! Why salmon, though – their natural instinct is to migrate?'

Duncan, neatly distracted by Tam, had begun to explain the reasons when Ross returned and restored attention to the matter in hand. 'I thought you'd be done here,' he said. 'Tam's made his position clear enough.'

'Duncan is concerned to know *your* position on the matter, Ross.'

'Is he? And you told him I'm a bastard?' Ross grinned across at his father.

Tam smiled back. 'Not in so many words.'

'Well, I am. Does that answer things for you?'

'Lawyers will require some proof,' Duncan replied.

Ross leaned against the kitchen counter, his arms folded across his chest. 'Proof that I'm a bastard?' He gave a short laugh. 'Ask the fellas that work for me – they'll vouch for me on that one. I meant it about the dogs, you know.'

Duncan gave a dry smile in return. 'I never doubted it,' but it seemed to Eva that he relaxed again and she wondered if some sort of truce had been reached.

Tam must have thought the same and was quick to take advantage of the moment. 'On that conciliatory note I suggest we leave matters for now and go about our various businesses. Ross has a ship to build, Eva and I have some catching up to do and you, Duncan, I suggest that you consider ways of getting us out of this jam that don't involve me returning to Scotland or being hounded by the press.'

'I can't see any.'

'Look harder.' He turned to his son. 'Ross, take the man and show him the schooner, get his mind off his troubles. Who knows, he might order one if the salmon farms turn profitable. What a sight that would be in the estuary! Eva, walk with me a while and explain how you ended up in the gutter. There'll be a way out of this for all of us, I'm quite certain of it.'

CHAPTER 22

Ross and Duncan set off across the yard while Tam led Eva down to the water's edge, walking quickly, his limp still evident. He glanced back as the two men disappeared into the boatshed. 'If one murders the other, would that simplify matters?' he asked and gave her his familiar slanting smile.

'Hardly.'

'I'd put my money on Ross, wouldn't you?'

'They'll find they have little in common, I think.'

'Except blood.' He went and sat on an upturned boat and gestured for her to join him. 'Which we must avoid getting spilt.' A chilly breeze was coming off the water. 'What a business, eh?' She started to apologise but he cut her short. 'Oh, don't say sorry, for pity's sake. The fates had a hand in this, I reckon. They cast you in the role of Nemesis many years back; retribution has just been a long time coming.' He lifted his eyes to follow the flight of a gull overhead. 'I'd *like* to blame you, of course, and had I realised the gods had thrown an avenging angel at my feet that day I'd never have picked you up.'

He spoke in the dry quixotic tone she remembered. 'You picked up the books, not me.'

'So I did. Perhaps that was my mistake.'

'You make light of it all, Tam, but I couldn't be more sorry—'

'I brought it on myself, my dear, years ago and perhaps I always knew there'd be a reckoning. The fates have simply been biding their time, awaiting the moment.' He turned back to her. 'But tell me, how did you come to take up such a sordid profession? I'd hoped for better things for you.'

'I have to make a living.'

'How dreary.' He reached down and picked up a handful of shingle and began aiming the pebbles at a post supporting the jetty. 'And how is Scotland these days?'

'Come and see for yourself. I think you're going to have to.'

He grimaced. 'Duncan is a determined soul, isn't he? Single-minded, it would appear, like my father. You know he has the exact same look in his eye – it's most unnerving. Makes me feel like a schoolboy caught in sin. An oddly familiar, and rather unwelcome, sensation.'

'It'll get sorted much quicker if you're there, and Duncan was in earnest about the press.'

'So was Ross, about the dogs.'

She smiled. 'You must take this seriously, you know. They'd make your life hell, you can't begin to imagine.'

'Oh, I can! And while I could remark that I'm quite familiar with hell it would sound poor-spirited and I want you to think well of me.' Another pebble was flung and missed its target. He seemed determined to be flippant and yet behind this front she sensed an inner turmoil. What a shock her arrival must have been, shattering his quiet existence, upsetting the balance.

Then his brother appearing, hard on her heels. A brother he had never known.

And how extraordinary it was to be sitting beside him like this, an adult now, with the passage of fifteen years lying so lightly between them, and how quickly that odd sense of comradeship had rekindled, lifted now to another plane. She'd have done anything to spare him this new ordeal but saw no reason to spare herself. 'Ross said you'd been to jail.'

'Just the once.'

'Because of me, I mean, because of that night?'

Her voice must have betrayed her and he turned his head, searching her face. 'Have you been carrying a burden, Eva?'

'I . . . I didn't know. I was never told what happened, you see, after you found me. No one would ever say.'

He started tossing pebbles again. 'You caught pneumonia and were poorly for a while, then your mother took you away.'

'I meant what happened to *you*. But Ross just told me.'

'Ah.'

'To accuse you of such things!' Her face flamed again with shame.

But Tam simply shrugged. 'It was almost poetic, you know, the liturgy of my crimes.'

'I can't begin—'

'They heaped on me a veritable Child Ballad of misdemeanours. I'd every vice imaginable: drunkard, wastrel, trouble-maker, child-stealer, child-molester and consummate rogue. I'd rather hoped to be memorialised in legend and scare babies for centuries to come; I even thought up a rhyme while awaiting trial, to spare them the trouble. Now, how did it go . . . ? "Go to sleep, my little . . ." That's it: "Go to sleep, my little bairn, or who will come but old Tam Nairn." Not brilliant, and barely scans but you get the gist. Admirable opportunism by my disingenuous neighbours, of course, getting me out of the way, leaving them free to do some arm twisting, although the vote'd gone through anyway as things turned out. Out gunned we were, and sunk.'

He grabbed another handful of pebbles and began tossing them aimlessly into the water. She sat silently beside him, trying to imagine him in jail, remembering things she had read about how child-abusers were treated there. And it was, at the heart of it, her fault. She had been a child, a silly, thoughtless child—

'I'd have died out there, on the rocks, but for you.'

He nodded. 'Damn fool place to go with a sea fog moving in. Whatever were you thinking? The whole village was out searching for you, but no one was looking on the bad side of the bay. I've often wondered what you were up to.' He half turned to her, raising a quizzical eyebrow.

'I was looking for you.'

He gave a mirthless laugh. 'That revelation would *not* have helped my case!' It had a bitter edge. 'They accused me of luring you to the cabin, you see, following a pattern of coercive behaviour with wickedness in mind. Your mother considered me the devil incarnate.' Eva bit her lip; that she could well imagine. 'We only found you because Ross'd seen you heading for the rocks as he left to go rabbiting. The fog drove him back home and I told him about the search, and that's when he said he'd spotted you earlier. And there we found you, wet and frozen, half dead with your foot jammed between two rocks. Idiot child! Surely you'd seen the fog rolling in.'

'I hadn't. I was looking in a rock pool.'

He shook his head in bewilderment. 'There always was something rather fey about you. It set you apart.'

'I was looking for your medal. You'd flicked it into the pool the day before and I thought you shouldn't have . . . I'd asked Miss Sinclair what valour really meant, you see, and so I went to retrieve it – and it took me a while.'

He stopped tossing pebbles and stared at her, then flung his head back and shouted, 'Jesus *Christ*, girl! Was *that* what it was? Idiot doesn't come anywhere close! But . . . oh God, Eva! Bane of my bloody life!' And to her astonishment he pulled her to him, holding her tight, almost crushing the breath from her. 'And you were going to pin it to my chest, were you, and remind me to be a man?'

'Something like that,' she said, muffled by his jacket.

She remembered again how he had wrapped her in a warm blanket that night and held her as he held her now and, absurdly, she found herself weeping. 'Stuck your nose in too many story books, you did. My own bloody fault, I should never have encouraged you.' He released her, looked at her face with wry compassion and pulled out a handkerchief. 'Blow your nose, there's nothing to cry about.'

She did, but found herself shaking.

'Tam?' Unnoticed Ross had come up behind them, halted, and was watching them.

Tam looked over his shoulder. 'Gone already, has he?'

Ross remained on the track, his eyes sliding between them, a frown on his brow. 'Says he'll be back later for an answer.'

'Doesn't like the one he's had, eh? Couldn't you have charmed him, son?' Did charm figure in Ross McLeod's repertoire? Eva wondered, pulling herself together.

'We need to talk.'

'Is there anything left to say?'

Apparently there wasn't as no one spoke and Eva stayed where she was, sitting beside Tam on the upturned hull, his handkerchief balled in her hand. Something had shifted a little, though, changed shape, and she felt a sense of lightening. She'd learned the worst of it now and seemed to have Tam's forgiveness, or at least his understanding. Ross, however, was another matter. He stood there on the track above them, tense as a wolfhound, his donkey jacket blown open by the strengthening wind, his gaze still switching between them.

But Tam was staring out to sea. 'It's not going to go away, is it?' he said at last. 'This business.'

Ross remained silent, leaving Eva to answer. 'I don't think it will.' And even if he did return to Scotland the press would pursue him for as long as there was a whiff of a mystery. The Maxwells might close the gates to Rosslie House but rumours would fester and spread, poisoning the air. David Mallory, thwarted and angry, would give neither Tam nor her a moment's peace, and she didn't like to think where his digging would take him.

'How long would it take you?' Ross asked.

Tam blew out his cheeks. 'Lawyers like to spin things out. Several weeks, I imagine.'

At least that, Eva thought, looking out over the sparkling water where boats bobbed at anchor and gulls hung on the wind. He'd have to leave all this and confront whatever it was that had driven him away all those years ago. And was it possible to simply renounce an estate and a title and give it to someone else? She wasn't sure but it was unlikely to happen fast. 'Perhaps you could go and set things in motion and then come back while they sort it out.'

'Perhaps.'

'You're not going on your own,' Ross said, his expression mulish.

'Why not? And you can't leave the yard right now, with the schooner half built and your customers on your back. You've just agreed a new schedule, haven't you?'

Ross scowled. 'Like I said, we need to talk. But it doesn't involve Miss Bayne.'

Tam chuckled. 'Why, Ross, you've not called a woman Miss since the day you slammed out of school and swore at poor old Ada Sinclair. Her name is Eva, my son, and none of this is her fault so you can stop being fierce.'

Ross's expression didn't change. She reckoned if he could have his time again he'd let her drown that afternoon at the salting room, or forget he'd seen her running for the rocks that fateful day when the sea fog rolled in. She got to her feet. 'He's right, though, you two need to talk.'

Tam caught at her hand. 'But you don't leave here. You don't go sneaking off. You stay at Edith's and wait to hear what's been decided. Understood?'

She nodded, having no intention of deserting him. 'Understood.'

CHAPTER 23

Eva walked back up the track towards Edith's house, sensing Ross McLeod's eyes following her. She didn't go inside, though, but continued on past, following the edge of the shore away from the boatyard. She needed time to think, and it was the sort of thinking best done out of doors. Above the tideline the ground was littered with broken crab pots and rusting scrap metal together with fraying rope ends and the broken shells of sea urchins. Beer bottles nestled in the long grass beside abandoned fish crates. She passed an old winch used to bring the fishing boats ashore and saw it had recently been cleaned and oiled and brought back into service. Was this all part of Ross's enterprise? He had built himself a life here.

She looked back and saw that he'd taken her place on the upturned boat beside his father. Both men had lit cigarettes and were deep in conversation.

Her sense of lightening began to fade as she walked. Tam might demand that she stay until decisions were made but she'd no reason to delay her return now that he'd been found. She had no place here, she was not part of the discussion, she was done; Ross had made that very clear. If there was anything she could do to ease Tam's present difficulties she would do it like a shot, settle her account and make amends, but she could think of nothing that would make a difference.

And if David Mallory decided to probe . . .

The thought of David sent her stomach to her boots; she still had him to face upon her return. On past form he would either turn on the charm and try pumping her for everything she knew, or he'd be livid and make her life hell, believing she'd tried to upstage him. The first approach would probably evolve into the second anyway for David was a vengeful soul, and whichever way she came at it, returning to the office was going to be tough. And if he required her to work on the Rosslie story, she couldn't – she'd have to leave. Maybe she should do that anyway . . . David was very good at what he did and she could learn a lot from him, but was that really what she wanted to do, become as 'good' as David? That said, though, she'd a living to make, her rent to pay, and jobs in her profession weren't that easy to find.

I'd hoped for better for you, Tam had said and, frankly, she'd hoped for better herself.

She climbed the low hill that overlooked the bay and glanced back again. The upturned boat was empty now; the men had gone. What conclusion had they reached, she wondered, and what would happen now? Tam had called her his Nemesis, the bringer of divine retribution. Perhaps it was true, for if you followed the thread back it was that encounter, when she'd fallen on the ice, that had set in train the slow twisting course of events that had brought them all to this point. How strange life could be.

As a child she had been naïve, ignorant of the reasons why such friendships as theirs were forbidden. Fey, he had called her. *It set you apart.* Had he, a virtual outcast, recognised the loneliness she had felt and was it that which had drawn them together? Looking back, though, it had been she who had pursued him, seeking him out, demanding answers to her endless questions. For his part, he'd tolerated rather than encouraged her, more attuned than she to the dangers of matters being misconstrued, tactfully steering her away from them, preserving her innocence.

Had Nemesis herself ever regretted the role she'd been given, she wondered bitterly, and wished it had been otherwise?

On this occasion, however, Nemesis had been manipulated; a malign force had been working backstage. She wondered again how it was that Duncan Maxwell had discovered, apparently effortlessly, where she'd gone and been able to pick up her trail.

She'd told his mother the name of the outport but had given no one Tam's alias – although she had Billy Norton to blame for letting that connection be known. David had dismissed her recognition of the photograph, pretending to believe she was heading for France, and Duncan had cancelled their meeting having been told by his mother that she was a fraud. None of them, even pooling their knowledge, had had enough to piece together the whole. But it had to have been David at the root of it, he of the bloodhound nose.

As she sat in the shelter of the rocks watching the waves breaking at the base of the distant stacks she allowed herself to imagine that her life in Scotland didn't exist and that she need not return there and face him and the inevitable furore. All around her were the familiar smells and sounds of her childhood and she closed her eyes, leaning back against the rocks, and let the years evaporate.

Rockweed or seaweed, which was she?

The afternoon passed, she dosed a while in the sunshine, making up for lost sleep, but eventually she rose and strolled back towards Tam's house wondering if any sort of resolution had been reached. As she drew closer, she saw that Duncan's car was turning into the boatyard again. He must have spotted her on the track as he drove on past the house, and pulled up in front of her. He got out and came towards her. 'Where is he?'

His resemblance to Tam was quite extraordinary. 'In the house, I assume. I've been walking.'

He glanced down the way she'd come then fixed her with a cold expression. 'He'll have to come back, you know – there's no other way to sort things out. He needs to be made to understand that. If he'll not listen to me, will he heed you?' Duncan must be about the age that Tam had been when she first knew him, she thought, as she looked back at him. But what a contrast! Duncan was smart and purposeful with an air of entitled self-interest, in every way unlike the vagabond Tam whose life had, for whatever reason, taken a very different course.

'I've not spoken a word to him for fifteen years,' she replied, bringing her mind to order, 'but he'll make his own decisions whatever I might say. I suppose it depends a little on why he left in the first place . . .' Duncan scowled but let her words hang there. If he knew, he was clearly not for telling. 'How did you know I'd come here, to Newfoundland?' she continued when he made no response.

'Mallory, of course.'

'I told him I was going to France.'

'He didn't believe you.'

But somehow he'd found out . . . She thought back: she'd made no phone calls from the office, booked her flight and car in person at the travel agent, collected the documents herself a couple of days before departure. There was no way he could have found out unless . . . 'He went through my handbag.'

'Probably.'

Almost certainly. She remembered popping out at lunchtime to collect the papers and, like a fool, she'd told him where she was going, hoping to cement her French holiday story never once thinking . . . He must have waited until she'd returned with them, watched for an opportune moment, and seized it.

'I've promised the man an exclusive in return.' He looked back at her, challenging her to object. Not a flicker of shame.

'Does Tam know this?'

'He will do shortly. Mallory's my ace, you see.' Duncan was eyeing her speculatively. 'I'm not sure what it is between the two of you, but if you can persuade him to do the sensible thing and come back with me, I'll agree to call off Mallory. That's the trade-off. Better all round if this is done in a private, civilised manner.'

Civilised? 'You're a well-matched pair, you and David Mallory.'

His expression hardened. 'This isn't a game, you know. I don't give a damn whether you're outraged by my following you here or by how it was achieved. Land and livelihoods are at stake, as well as a great deal of money.' He paused. 'Tell me, what did you talk about with my mother at that odd little lunch you had?'

'She surely filled you in. I told no one else about Heart's Repose.'

'She said you were a fraud. Why would she do that?'

'You must ask her.'

'She wrote a letter.'

So she had done, after all. 'And you saw it.'

'It was in the postbag in the hall. And yet, when I looked the place up on a map, I couldn't find it. Luckily the man at the car rental remembered you coming, asking to be put on the right road for Heart's Repose. You'd an old map with you, he said, and so he was able to direct me. It was only as I got closer that the locals told me the place no longer existed.' And then Billy Norton had done the rest. Duncan was looking slightly amused now, enjoying her consternation. 'It would've been easier all round if you and Ma hadn't agreed some weird pact to throw sand in everyone's eyes. Why would you do that?'

Here was a revelation: a split in the Maxwell ranks. No reason to tell him there was no such pact, better to keep him uneasy. 'Ask your mother.' She made to move past him but he put out an arm to stop her.

'My mother manipulates the world to suit herself, she always has. I know perfectly well how she operates, even if her motivations aren't always obvious, but I'm more interested in yours, Miss Bayne. I can find no reason for your involvement in all this, though I wonder what a little digging would uncover.'

She shook off his arm. 'You even *sound* like Mallory—'

'Eva?' Lifting her head she saw that Ross had come out onto Tam's porch. 'Everything all right?'

Duncan released her with a wry smile. 'The rottweiler. Though I've not actually seen any dogs, have you?'

'Will you risk it, though?' she asked. 'Such a long way from home,' and she called back to Ross, 'Be there in a minute.'

Her spirits lifted a little; he'd called her Eva, which was an improvement after all.

Back in the kitchen the three of them took the same places as before, perhaps signalling that their positions were unchanged.

Before Eva could sit, though, Tam caught her attention. 'Eva, would you make us some tea, please? You'll find things in the obvious places.' She paused, surprised; Ross and Duncan both looked up. Was he deliberately excluding her from the discussion? Fair enough, she thought, she'd no place in it, though his manner was far from subtle. 'There should be just enough milk, I think. Must get more.' A glint in his eye encouraged her to go along with him and so, wordlessly, she went to fill the kettle.

'Gentlemen, we resume,' Tam continued, offering cigarettes, which were refused. He took one himself and put it into the corner of his mouth then patted his various pockets. 'Eva, matches, please, can you see them?' She found them over by the stove and silently passed them to him. What was his game? 'Good. Now then, I repeat that I wish this whole wretched business to the devil but—'

'Duncan has promised my boss, Mallory, an exclusive,' she interrupted him, lifting mugs down from the cupboard as the kettle began to hiss. Whatever the game was, she wasn't prepared to be entirely side-lined. 'In return for him discovering where I'd gone. Mallory went through my handbag in my office, and found my plane ticket and car rental documents and passed the information to Duncan.' She could at least make it clear to Tam and Ross where her loyalties lay. 'That's how he found me.'

Tam bent his head over a cupped hand to light his cigarette before blowing smoke up to the ceiling. 'I told you yours was a sordid profession,' he remarked then narrowed his eyes against the smoke and looked across at Duncan. 'An exclusive, eh?'

Duncan's face darkened as he glared at her.

'I was obviously going to tell him, wasn't I?' Eva said, pushing a mug across the table and returning the look. 'David Mallory is your ace, you said.'

'Ah! Shouldn't show your hand, lad.' Tam gave him a slanting, wicked grin. 'Besides, I reckon I'll have played meaner poker games than you have in my time.'

Duncan had stiffened at the 'lad' but now he simply shrugged. 'I've nothing to lose by going to the press and everything to gain.'

'Quite possibly, but there's really no need to bandy threats about in this crude manner. We have, after all, the same objectives, you and I – you want matters resolved at Rosslie and I want to be left alone; we just need to find the swiftest way to achieve these goals.' Eva filled and distributed the other mugs, intrigued by the change in Tam. He was sitting tall, shoulders straight, and seemed to have come alive. She glimpsed a younger man. 'So, Duncan, it appears I must return to Scotland and cut the Gordian knots, set us free of each other once and for all. Then I can return here to live out my years and leave you to your caged fish. I'll come back . . .' Duncan raised his mug in a mock toast '. . . on three conditions.'

'Which are?'

'Nothing is said to the press about my return except by me. *Exclusively*. I've already heard more than I want to about this Mallory character. You get him off my back. Is that clear?'

Duncan nodded. 'It is. And the second condition?'

'Eva resigns her job the instant she gets home . . .' she froze mid sip '. . . and accepts the position as my private secretary for as long as it takes to sort all this out. That's the third condition.'

She stared back at him and the two men looked dumbfounded. Ross clamped his jaw shut but Duncan recovered quickly. 'The estate office can support your secretarial needs, and Miss Bayne is hardly qualified for the role.'

Tam smoked on, apparently amused by the reaction around the table. 'On the contrary, Miss Bayne has, quite unwittingly, just passed the interview. She can make tea and find matches, both invaluable services although she will, in due course, have other duties. We must discuss salary, Eva, and you can advise me, Duncan.'

'The estate can't bear unnecessary expense.'

'So what if she resigns, she's still a journalist,' Ross said, breaking his silence, 'and it was her got us into this mess.'

Tam rested his cigarette in the ashtray and picked up his mug. 'Do you accept the role, Eva?' he asked, ignoring them both and contemplating her over the rim. 'Subject to agreement over pay, of course, and whatever else we have to establish these days.'

Her interest was piqued, and she had the sudden thought that if she resigned, she'd not have to deal with David Mallory. 'Perhaps we can discuss—'

'Agree in principle, at least.' Again she glimpsed that conspiratorial glint. He wasn't excluding her, quite the opposite, he was bringing her into his camp. But why?

'In principle, yes. Although—'

'Splendid. We progress. Now Duncan, have you a flight booked home? What day do you go?'

Eva sat back and watched as Tam took control. He was barely recognisable as the man she'd first known, bleeding and filthy in her father's surgery, reeking of drink and despair. She was seeing a different man altogether, a man who had been too long in hiding, a man who used to give orders, and expect them to be obeyed. It was fascinating to watch.

Later, after a discussion regarding flights and after Duncan had been despatched to make the necessary arrangements, and after Ross, who'd remained strangely silent after his outburst, had gone back to the boatshed, Eva cleared away the mugs. Would washing-up be one of her new duties? she wondered. Only for Tam would she have considered such a step into the unknown.

'Do you mind?' he asked her, sitting back and lighting another cigarette. 'About the job?'

'You took me by surprise.'

He regarded her. 'Yes, I rather wanted to. But do you mind?'

'You'll need to explain.'

He smiled at her, that familiar enigmatic smile. 'Keep your friends close, they say, and your enemies closer.'

'And which am I?'

'Somewhere in between, I reckon. I don't doubt you mean well, but you have the unhappy knack of landing me in trouble. I'd like you where I can see you.'

'You can't possibly think—'

'I don't. I'm teasing. No, Eva, I want you to be my buffer, my talisman, if you like – you can be my eyes and ears. You were a sharp little thing once and returning to Rosslie without an ally would be unimaginable. I'll write you a marvellous reference at the end of it all. Jilly won't know what to make of you – it'll drive her nuts trying to work it out – and you'll serve to keep Duncan at arm's length while I get the measure of things.'

'And you trust me?'

'It goes without saying, my dear.'

'Ross doesn't.'

'No—'

'And you trust Duncan not to go to the press?'

'Not for an instant. But he's forgotten a rather significant advantage I have over him, over all of them, in fact.' He smiled a little. 'He'll no doubt remember as he drives back to his hotel.'

'Which is what?'

'Don't disappoint me, Eva.' He drew on his cigarette, watching her. 'Must I spell it out? The advantage, my dear girl, is that as of the day Pa died, the Rosslie estate became mine. Duncan and the rest of them remain there only as long as it suits me. There are benefits, you see, to being a baronet if it comes to a fight.'

CHAPTER 24

Eva travelled back to Scotland three days later, alone. And as the plane lifted off from St John's airport she wondered whether Duncan really would stick to his side of the bargain once he'd got home or would Tam be greeted by a hoard of baying jackals upon his return. The thought conjured up an appalling image.

Duncan had left two days earlier. To his intense frustration, it transpired that Tam's passport, when found, was years out of date but Tam had assured him he had the documents required to apply for a renewal and agreed to push the application through by attending the consulate in St John's in person. 'I'll come as soon as it's processed, don't you worry. I'll keep my side of the deal, Duncan, I promise you.' Duncan had looked annoyed but agreed that there was nothing to be done other than begin the bureaucratic process and had risen to go. 'At least I know where to find you now. Unless you have other alias's?' Tam had smiled and shaken his head. 'Too old to do another runner, I've not got it in me.'

They had all accompanied Duncan to his car. 'And so, next time in Rosslie, then?' Tam offered him his hand and their eyes had held for a moment, and then Duncan had left, not once looking back. Tam had watched him drive away with a curiously sad expression then turned to Eva. 'Will you have to work out notice?'

'I expect so.'

'I recommend you just resign and leave. What can the man do, after all? Buy your way out if you have to and send the estate the bill. I'll employ you from the day you do, so don't be concerned that there'll be a gap.' They went back inside the house where he instructed her to find him a hotel in Glasgow for a couple of days before heading to Rosslie. 'I imagine Glasgow tailors will have a rather wider repertoire than those in St Johns and I'll need to look the part if I'm to hold my own with lawyers and their ilk. The estate can at least clothe me decently whilst it's mine. You'll be living at Rosslie, by the way, I should have made that clear. Is there a young man who'll be cursing me because of that?' She shook her head and his eyebrows arched. 'No? Whatever's wrong with the young men of Argyll?'

She'd stayed another night at Edith's and Tam invited her to share their meal, but it had been a strained occasion. He'd kept the conversation going with accounts of childhood battles with Rosslie's head gardener, his exploits with an older brother who'd been killed in the war, their techniques of remaining beneath their father's radar but he'd said nothing of the war years themselves and gave no hint of family discord or the reasons for leaving. Ross had said little but had listened closely, his face expressionless, and once or twice she'd caught him watching her.

He'd hardly addressed a remark to her since Duncan left, but as she went to say her goodbyes the next morning, he'd surprised her.

'Come and see the schooner before you go.'

Tam had turned away, his eyes alight with amusement. 'An excellent idea, son. I should have suggested it myself. Off you go, Eva.'

They'd walked towards the boatshed in silence but once inside Ross turned to her. 'Tam says he's employing you to watch his back. Make damn sure that you do.'

'I will.'

His dark eyes searched her face for a moment. 'And you get in touch with me right away if there's any funny business going on.'

'I will.'

'He's been through a lot, even if I didn't know the half of it. But he said some things last night—' He broke off and she waited for him to continue.

'Things?' she prompted.

He shook his head. 'Just get him back here as soon as possible. He's good here. It suits him. He can work here, and he needs to work.' Work? What work did he do? It hadn't been the time to ask. Ross had leaned against the schooner, regarding her with a strange expression. 'He trusts you, says you're sharp. And there's something about that brother of his I don't get, so first sign of trouble, you get in touch. Got that?'

'I've said I will.' She hesitated, then took a risk. 'Did he tell you why he left?'

She'd expected a sharp rebuttal but Ross had simply shaken his head. 'Said blame the war, that was all, couldn't get more out of him. But I reckon that brother of his knows, he'd a weird, angry look in his eye.'

Eva waited for more then turned to go. 'I'll watch his back, Ross, I promise.'

'See that you do.'

Tam had been standing by her car when she returned and amusement was lingering in his eyes. 'So what do you think, my dear?'

'She's a very fine ship,' she replied, remembering just in time.

He smiled. 'Well done. You're still sharp, that's encouraging. Ross was rather ham-fisted, didn't you think? Never was a subtle man. Was he instructing you to keep me out of trouble?'

'Do you think I could?'

He'd smiled again and opened the car door. 'Drive safely, won't you, my dear. And yes, I'm rather depending on it.'

It might prove to be a tall order, she thought, as the plane reached cruising height. This business would hardly have a quick fix or be an easy ride for either of them. Duncan's attitude towards her had remained chilly to the end and he was unlikely to welcome her appearance at Rosslie. Jillian Maxwell's reaction to her new position she couldn't begin to imagine. 'It'll drive her nuts . . .' Tam had said, which was not encouraging either. But the next weeks would be an adventure if nothing else and if Tam could face down the Maxwells, then so could she.

She owed him that much.

CHAPTER 25

Glasgow, 1980

Eva

First day back, Eva stood outside the office building, letting the swish of rush hour traffic speed past her, and took a deep breath. Last chance to draw back from this crazy business. Her head said one thing, but heart and guts were united on the opposite and those, she decided, counted more.

She pushed open the outer door, signed in with a nod to reception and steeled herself to walk calmly into the office she shared with David. He looked up at once and an electric charge seemed to go through him. He put aside the copy he was working on, his eyes alive and dancing. 'Eva, darling!' He foot-peddled his swivel chair to the edge of the desk, smiling broadly. The charm offensive. 'You *found* him, eh? Clever girl.'

'Who?'

'Come *on*,' he growled, still smiling. 'Don't be shy with Uncle David.'

She put her bag on her desk, pulled open the drawer and began sorting through private as opposed to company possessions, separating the two. 'I'm not sure what you mean.'

'Eva! Hel*lo*. Are we playing games then? You've not been to France, have you, darling, you've been somewhere else entirely.'

'What makes you say that?' The stapler was theirs but the coloured paper clips were hers; she liked cheerful stationery.

He looked less amused. 'You winding me up? I *know* where you've been – Newfoundland, eh, hunting heroes. So did you find him?'

'Who?' The Sellotape was almost done, the end all ragged, but she'd take the glue stick; keeping her hands occupied meant that she didn't need to meet his eyes.

He sat back and slapped the desk with an open palm. 'OK, what's going on here? Maxwell's back and won't take my calls, Rosslie's gate's closed and all locked up . . .' Duncan sticking to the deal so far, she noted '. . . and now here's you, playing hard to get. Remember who you work for, sweetie.'

'Ah, that's the thing, David. I'm resigning, as of now. I'm owed holiday and whatever else we can settle by—'

'Whoa. Stop right there.' David raised a hand, his expression turning ugly. 'Think you've got yourself a scoop, eh? Made some deal with Maxwell, have you?' And now the vitriol. 'You ain't dealing with some greenhorn, sweetie, I've been round the block a few times. Maxwell has a deal with *me* and he's damn well sticking to it.'

'And what deal was that?'

'I discover where you're heading and in return—'

'Discover, how?'

He saw where she was going and snorted. 'So what? I'm an investigative journalist, it's what I do, I take my chances when they come.'

'And I was a colleague, and you rifled through my handbag, read personal documents and disclosed their content to a third party.' No hint of shame from David, just an indifferent shrug. 'And so let's count that in lieu of notice, shall we? Or do I take the matter higher up?'

He swore, as only David could swear, which gave her the excuse she needed to go. She pushed the drawer closed. Anything else of hers in there they could have; all she wanted now was to get out and away from a big, angry David. 'Walk through that door, Eva,' he said, 'and you'll never work again. Better believe it.'

'It's OK. I have a job. Starts today.' It was oh so tempting to tell him who her new employer was but she'd give him no more fuel. He'd not let this go – she knew him well enough to know that – but he'd get nothing more from her. She hitched her bag onto her shoulder. 'No need for a farewell-good-luck-missing-you-already card, David. The moment has passed.'

From a café, she wrote, as instructed, to tell Tam that she had resigned and, despite her show of confidence, her heart was racing as she sealed the letter. It had been scary, antagonising a man known for his ruthlessness and spite, but continuing to work with him would have been impossible. What if Tam changed his mind about the job, though? She'd be screwed . . . Anxious days passed before she had the relief of a phone call from someone at Rosslie wanting information to put her on the payroll.

No word came from Duncan Maxwell, but perhaps that was to be expected.

Tam had told her to stay put in Glasgow until he knew when he'd be arriving, telling her that once he'd seen a tailor and done whatever else he planned to do in the city, they would travel up to Rosslie and arrive together. *Do you have a car?* he asked in one letter. *Or should we ask Duncan to make one available?* When she replied that her rather battered red Fiat 126 was at his service, *unless it's beneath your dignity, of course*, she could almost hear his laughter.

It was exhilarating, she decided, this strange new job that wasn't a job. Almost daily thin blue aerograms covered with Tam's elegant scrawl arrived, often with bizarre instructions; they kept her interested, and amused, and she certainly couldn't claim to be over-worked. She was impatient now for him to arrive and for things to start moving, and sensed between the lines his own growing excitement at the thought of returning home. On one occasion he sent her out to see if a pub called His Lordship's Larder still stood on St Enoch Square, as he rather thought he'd like to take a drink there in recognition of his new status.

Gone more than twenty years ago, I'm afraid, replaced by a department store, she'd reported back.

Damn them, he replied next time. *Withstood the bombings only to fall to the axe of commerce.*

When she was given the job of assessing the different qualities of available shoe polish for the baronial boots, she decided that he was simply amusing himself at her expense and countered by fulfilling this and other such tasks with aplomb, and giving earnest lengthy reports. He mentioned Ross occasionally, usually in reference to progress on the schooner, and she wondered how his son was reconciling himself to the changes in his father's fortunes. Did he resent it, she wondered, and the circumstances which excluded him?

And then a telegram arrived announcing Tam's arrival in Glasgow the following day, propelling her swiftly into action. He was here! She was instructed to meet him off the London train as he had changed his plans and arrived at Heathrow Airport three days before. He gave the time of arrival, adding: CANCEL HOTELS TAILORS ETC. STOP. KITTED OUT. STOP. ON TO ROSSLIE. STOP. PACK. The fact that he had used a telegram, that fast-dying stalwart of the post-war years, showed how much catching up he had to do, and she wondered with some trepidation what *kitted out* might mean.

She need not have worried. Arriving on the platform, she walked straight past an elegantly dressed man as she searched for his face among the disembarking passengers, and it was only when he said her name that she looked back and realised that the distinguished figure in a Savile Row coat was Tam Nairn, the one-time village drunk. The garment hung perfectly from his broad shoulders and was worn over an equally well-cut suit. On his head was a trilby set at a rakish angle, pulled aslant his eyes. Beneath it she could see that his hair had been cut, his beard trimmed and he looked extremely dapper standing there on the dirty platform, a smart leather valise in hand. Handsome, even, and it was only because his eyes laughed into hers from under the pulled-down brim that she knew for certain it was him.

It wasn't only women, apparently, who dressed to impress.

'Eva, my dear,' he said, touching the hat rim with old-fashioned courtesy. 'How charming you look,' and she was pleased then that some instinct had prompted her to choose a simple dark dress and jacket and low black pumps, appropriate for the private secretary to a man of standing. 'And will you just look at the two of us! Fine as fivepence and not a whiff of salt cod. What a lark.' Her rain-spattered Fiat now seemed an absurd conveyance for such sartorial elegance. 'Good God,' he remarked, when he saw it. 'A toy fire engine! Do we wind it up?'

He spoke very little as they manoeuvred their way through the streets but kept his eyes glued to the window, occasionally commenting on the changes, the missing landmarks, the brash new buildings, and she realised that he was seeing in his mind's eye a very different, vanished, Glasgow. 'Almost forty years,' she reminded him.

'Which is a very long time.' They continued in silence and, as they left the city behind them, he sighed. 'Makes me feel old, Eva. A rusting relic,' and he was silent for much of the remaining journey. But as they approached Rosslie he sat forward and looked keenly ahead. 'Some things, though, are timeless and I hope that the . . . yes! The oaks. And the rooks, still there too! How splendid. Great-grand offspring of those I last saw, but thank God for that stand of trees. My lodestone! I always knew we were close once that copse came into view. Step on it, Eva, the adventure begins.'

She glanced sideways at him, wondering how this enthusiasm for his erstwhile home squared with his previous disavowal of the place. It was certainly not in Duncan's plan that Tam should decide to stay . . . Perhaps he'd have done well to follow Tam's initial advice to explore Newfoundland and return empty-handed, claiming his quarry had eluded him. Bespoke suits and trilbies had little place in a life based in Severn, so what exactly was Tam planning?

She had rung ahead to Rosslie to tell the household to expect them and so the gates stood open for the Fiat to swing through and onto the drive up to the house. It seemed a thousand years since the day of the auction. 'It's the same!' Tam exclaimed, looking from left to right as they approached the house. 'It's all the bloody same, and that's almost as disconcerting as driving through an unfamiliar Glasgow. The trees have grown but *nothing's* changed! Forty years or forty winks . . . Well done, Duncan, although I imagine it was the iron grip of Pa that froze it. He said as much, didn't he, but three cheers for atrophy, I say.'

'Which implies degeneration from lack of use.'

'Indeed it does, my little wordsmith. Like my sense of responsibility . . . and my conscience.' The last was muttered in a low tone as he looked out of the window.

'So not a good thing.'

'Not a good thing at all, Eva. Duncan's absolutely right to push for change.'

What a capricious, confusing man he was. Beside her he fell silent again. They reached the house at the end of the drive and she pulled up at the bottom of the steps that led to the main entrance. No one seemed to notice them, perhaps not expecting that the long-lost heir to Rosslie would arrive in a battered red Fiat. 'What am I to call you?' she asked, having meant to enquire earlier. 'Sir Archibald doesn't come easily.'

'I'd sack you on the spot.' He unwound his legs and got out of the car, limping a little with the stiffness. 'They'll know me as Archie here, which'll take a bit of getting used to again, but I remain Tam at heart, and always for you, my dear. Ring the bell, will you, and see if they'll let us in.'

She went up the steps and he followed more slowly and, as she listened to the sound of the bell echoing in the hall, she turned to see him standing quite still at the top of the steps, his hands in his coat pockets, a silhouette of trilby and Savile Row elegance, staring out over the acreage that now was his.

It was an image that would remain with her.

The calm before the storm.

CHAPTER 26

Rosslie

It was Lady Maxwell herself who opened the door. 'Archie!' she said and he half turned to look at her. It was a loaded moment, and seemed to hang there, suspended in time. There might have been just the two of them standing at the entrance, looking back at each other.

Lady Maxwell put out her hand. 'Welcome home.'

Tam stepped forwards and briefly took the proffered hand. 'Hello, Jilly,' he said. 'You've met Eva, of course. Shall we go in? Lead on, my dear.'

It seemed to Eva that he'd quite deliberately killed the moment, robbing it of drama and establishing control. She stepped into the hall where Duncan stood waiting. He acknowledged her briefly then looked past her to Tam, and she saw him take in his brother's altered appearance. They stood there, an awkward quartet, she and Tam facing the portrait of the late Sir Andrew opposite Duncan and his mother, who had positioned themselves as if harnessing the deceased baronet to their cause. Introductions being unnecessary, no one seemed to know quite what to say . . .

Then Lady Maxwell went as far as noting her presence. 'Miss Bayne,' she said with a tight little smile before turning back to Tam. 'And Archie! At last.' Her gaze lingered on him with an expression that was impossible to define. 'Good God, how like your father you are.'

Tam raised an eyebrow. 'Hardly an original remark, Jilly, nor an altogether welcome one.'

'But the likeness is quite uncanny. You look like he did when we first met. He was much the same age as you are now, or perhaps a little younger.' And Jillian Maxwell, Eva calculated, must then have been only a few years older than she was herself. *She won't know what to make of you,* Tam had said, and she began to glimpse his intentions.

He spun his hat onto the hall table as if he had done it a hundred times, which he probably had. 'You'll be telling me I've grown next. But you look well, Jilly. Silver hair becomes you. Very chic, very polished, very suave. Why don't we repair to the library, the hall's always was draughty.' He pulled open the door and held it, ushering them through and once again there was no mistaking the message. 'If we ring for tea will anybody come or do we do our own these days?' If he was at all apprehensive about his reception he showed no sign and took a seat beside the fire as if he had vacated it only a moment before. He glanced at the hearth where logs were smouldering listlessly. 'Never did draw well, that fire,' he remarked.

Lady Jillian took the chair opposite him and looked across at Eva with something that somehow failed to be a smile. 'I'm told tea-making is one of your duties, Miss Bayne. That and supplying matches.'

'That was just for the interview,' Tam assured her before Eva could respond. 'She supplies much more than that now.'

Eva bit back a smile as the innuendo arrested Jillian for a moment before she stretched out a languid arm and rang a bell beside the fireplace. 'Let's see what happens, shall we?'

'And I'm sure she'd rather be known as Eva, wouldn't you, my dear. So let's make her feel at home.'

The old rogue! Eva thought as the awkward scene unfolded; he'd given her no warning. 'How was your journey, Archie?' Lady Maxwell asked and a somewhat stilted conversation ensued; only Tam seemed at ease, although Eva suspected that was a sham. Banalities were exchanged about the flights they had variously taken, the delays getting baggage, London prices, and the shabbiness of the trains, all ignoring the elephant in the room. At least two of them – Tam and Lady Maxwell – must know what had prompted Tam's departure all those years ago and be navigating around it. But was Duncan also in the know, Eva wondered, or was he, like her, observing and speculating? She glanced at him and saw that he was in fact studying her, but he looked away as the door opened and a young girl came in carrying a tea tray, her attention divided between getting it successfully onto the table and obtaining a description of the new boss to take back to the kitchen. Eva rose, as befitted her new role, and gave the girl a hand.

'Thank you, Morag, that will be—'

The door opened again and the young man David had pointed out at the auction bounded into the room. 'I'm late. Missed your arrival, Archie. Terribly sorry. I'm Keith.' He gave a laugh. 'Junior half-brother, as it were.'

Tam got to his feet and took the young man's outstretched hand, smiling as he studied him. 'As it were, as you say. How d'you do,' he said, and turned to look across at Lady Jillian, his eyes glinting. 'How like your mother you are, Keith. And how very fortunate that is.'

Lady Jillian met his look and gave her wrist an elegant dismissive twist. 'Were you always so gallant, Archie? I don't recall. Or perhaps these are Newfoundland manners. Bring another cup, please, Morag. Keith, I don't think you've met Eva Bayne, Archie's private secretary. We've to call her Eva, and make her feel at home.' There was innuendo in her tone too and Eva saw a smile tug at the corner of Tam's mouth as Keith put out his hand. What exactly had Tam meant by her being a buffer?

'Eva. Yes! The key that unlocked the mystery. Hello! We're terribly grateful to you, you know. And all because of that ghastly auction. You were here, I gather, and witnessed the wretched shambles that ensued. Old Ferguson routed us good and proper that day.'

'Not *Sandy* Ferguson?' Tam exclaimed. 'I heard the story but Eva didn't know names. It was him! Good God. He must be knocking on his century.'

'He is,' said Keith. 'You must go and see him. He fought your corner hard and—'

'He'll be pleased to see Archie, I'm sure.' Duncan interrupted from where he sat observing proceedings. 'But bear in mind I've set up a series of meetings with various lawyers, starting tomorrow morning.' There would be little time, his tone implied, for pleasantries.

'Splendid. Getting things moving, eh?' Tam replied. 'And then in the afternoon you can explain to me all about fish farms, and take me down to see these cages. I'm intrigued. Meanwhile, Eva and I should settle in. Where've you put us, Jilly?'

Lady Jillian's eyes slid between the two of them. 'Not being quite sure . . . I put you in your old room, Archie, but I can move out of the master suite any time you like . . .'

'Wouldn't dream of it.'

'And I've put Eva in the room next door.'

'Excellent. I imagine I can remember the way so I'll take Eva up when she's drunk her tea.' After further desultory conversation he brought the tea ritual to a close and rose. 'Let's go, shall we, Eva? Perhaps someone would be good enough to follow with the suitcases – they're in the boot of Eva's car.'

Eva followed him out of the library, leaving silence behind them, and he led the way across the hall, pointing out the various portraits as they mounted the stairs, speaking loudly, as he described his ancestry. Once they were on the landing, however, he turned to grin at her and lowered his voice. 'How am I doing?'

'You've made it very clear who's in charge.'

'Good. And you don't mind my teasing Jilly, do you?'

'You might have warned me, but I'll tell you if you overstep the mark.'

He smiled. 'You need have no fear of that. I'd just like to keep her guessing.'

'Why?'

'Self-defence, to use her own words. Or just badness, who knows . . . This is me here, my boyhood room.' He opened the door and then halted. 'Good God. Split and gutted. A wasteland . . .' She looked past him and saw an austere room with just a bed, a chair, empty bookshelves and bare walls. He looked stricken for a moment then shrugged. 'But what did I expect, a shrine?' He stepped quickly down the corridor. 'I hope you've done rather better,' he said and opened the door to the next room. 'Ah, yes. Jilly's had a go at things in here, and there's a fire laid so that'll take off the chill. Light it early and ask for a hot-water bottle. I shall.' He turned at a sound in the corridor. 'Keith, thank you. Yes, that one's mine, and that's Eva's. I'll leave you to unpack, my dear. Come down when you're ready or simply go and explore.'

Eva took her suitcase from Keith with a smile of thanks, closed the door behind him and let out a long breath. First hurdle passed, but this job was going to keep her on her toes! The tension in the air had been palpable, although it was fascinating watching Tam deftly manoeuvre himself into position. Lady Maxwell was the one to watch, she decided, with Duncan a close second. Keith she needed to get to know but on first encounter, he seemed amiable and disinterested . . . She went across to the window and sat on the casement seat and looked about her. The furniture was old-fashioned but good quality, the bed was high off the floor and looked marvellously comfortable, as did the worn armchair which stood beside the hearth. She ran her fingers along the bookcase, examining its contents: old-fashioned gardening books and novels for the most part. She lifted her suitcase onto the bed and shook out the few clothes she'd brought with her, hanging them in the wardrobe, wondering exactly what Tam had meant by self-defence. Nothing had been said about days off but presumably she could go back to her flat at some point and get more clothes if needed. Nothing had been said about her duties either, but she was beginning to understand why Tam had felt the need for an ally.

She wasn't ready to go down again straight away so went back to the window and looked out over the parkland and fields, beyond which she caught a glimpse of the sea. A dramatic group of Scots pine stood on top of a knoll, their branches aglow in the evening light. Tam must have much the same outlook from his room and she tried to imagine him here, as a boy in the years before the war, returning wounded, and then . . . A blank. The trajectory of his life between 1945 and 1966 remained a mystery. She was no wiser than before. *An enigma*, her father had said. *Someone who is puzzling, difficult to understand.*

The enigma, however, soon showed that he knew how to get down to business. It was agreed that evening, during a rather stilted dinner in a chilly dining room, that Jillian Maxwell would join in the initial discussion with the lawyers. This had been her ladyship's own idea; Duncan had shrugged indifferently at the suggestion and Tam had not demurred.

'And will your private secretary be joining us?' she asked with that not-quite-smile at Eva.

'Not for openers. It'll be a tedious business, I expect, bringing me up to speed. Death duties to tear our hair out over, you said, even before we look at the question of succession? Then the lawyers'll go to their club and confer over brandy and cigars, at our expense, and doubtless return with grim tidings. Or at least that's how things used to work. But we'll have fired an initial salvo, got things moving and can start racking our brains over how to scrape the necessary together.' He nodded in the direction of the McTaggart landscape, which had been rehung over the sideboard. 'That'll have to go, I expect, despite old Sandy's protests.' All eyes went to it and Tam turned to Eva. 'I suggest you take the morning to acquaint yourself with the place. You won't get too badly lost so feel free to explore and get to know where things are. Settle yourself in.'

Eva caught a quick exchange of looks between Duncan and his mother, which Tam probably noticed too. 'Or I could show you round,' Keith offered. 'I'm no good with lawyers and accountants. I lose interest, switch off.'

'Lucky you,' his brother muttered.

David Mallory had described Keith Maxwell as something of a prig. He was certainly very different from his brother, and the differences appeared to be more than skin deep, but he had an open, friendly face and probably a sunnier disposition, although, as Duncan's remark implied, he didn't carry the responsibility for Rosslie's future on his shoulders.

Although neither did Duncan, she thought. That honour went to the baronet and Duncan was addressing him again. Single-minded, as Tam had remarked. 'Since Pa died I've been looking at options that allow us to pay the taxes and move forward, taking into account—'

'Not at dinner, darling,' his mother said. 'Let's keep it until the morning.'

Her son looked annoyed, as well he might, but Tam reached for the wine bottle and re-filled Duncan's glass. 'Good to hear you've been doing some thinking. Gives us a head start and I'll apply my full attention to it all tomorrow. This is a good wine, Jilly. You must have replenished the cellars. I remember doing them considerable damage when I was last here. Do you hunt, either of you? Are there deer still in the hills or has Pa shot them all?'

'I don't hunt,' Keith said.

'There's a reason for that,' said his brother, 'beyond the moral high ground. You can't hit a barn door at ten paces.'

'I see no reason to try.' Jillian Maxwell rolled her eyes and Eva saw Tam taking it all in, the personalities and the tensions, filing it away. Briefly he caught her eye.

Keith appeared the next morning as Eva was eating a solitary breakfast. 'Oh, thank goodness,' she said. 'I thought I was the last one down. I slept so well; that bed's a dream.' She'd been cold, though, and the dining room was even chillier than it had been the night before.

'You are, actually, unless you count Ma who has hers taken up on a tray, but I wouldn't worry.'

'You've eaten?'

'Mmm.' He pulled up a chair, reached for a piece of toast and began to butter it. 'I don't live in the house, you see. I have my own place. Former gardener's cottage. Suits everyone better that way. I just pop in around this time and see what's going, have a bit of a graze, so to speak.' He gave her a grin, helping to confirm her opinion of him. 'I couldn't inflict the family on poor Susie every night. A little of the Maxwells goes a very long way.'

'Susie?'

'My girlfriend. She's away at the moment but I hope you'll meet her. You'll get on. She's a sweetie. Still up for me showing you round?'

The house, he explained once breakfast was finished, was very much the product of its history with various modifications resulting in rooms being divided then reconfigured, and later opened up again and rearranged, leaving the place as something of a hotchpotch. It was hard to imagine Tam growing up here in this place of mellow charm only to end up, years later, two thousand miles away, bloody from fights with fishermen, sleeping off his drink in a hay meadow before returning to a sagging wooden shanty. His boyhood home had everything a gentleman's residence should have: a billiard room, a small smoking room (now Duncan's office) and a library, and below stairs there was a labyrinth of former stillrooms, game larders, stores and pantries. Since its heyday, however, the world had moved on, leaving it behind, and as Keith escorted her round Eva took in the threadbare carpets and faded curtains in rooms where the sunlight caught dust motes in the air. It had once housed much larger families, he explained, serviced by a full staff and regularly entertained neighbours and house guests. But now it was home for just Duncan and his mother, and Keith when he came to graze. Besides Morag, there was a cook who no longer lived in, and occasional dailies who couldn't possibly be expected to keep things up to scratch. Duncan had a part-time secretary, Keith said, but no longer employed an estate manager, doing the work himself. 'Belt-tightening time,' he said with a grimace. Only a few of the bedrooms were used these days, he explained as they passed closed doors along the upper corridors. 'Pa got too old to entertain and most of his cronies popped off long before he did. Mama does her socialising in London or Edinburgh. Whole place is a bit of an anachronism, really, and needs a shedload of money spending on it.' And a good clean, Eva thought, seeing cobwebs hanging in swags from coving in the high-ceilinged rooms and corridors. A dark stain at the top of the stairwell suggested recent roof problems. It was a beautiful house and had some very fine furnishings, but everywhere there was evidence of neglect. Tam's father, having lived there for almost a century, had either failed to notice its decline, or had not the means to halt it. No wonder Duncan went about the place grim-faced.

Or that his mother fled to the city to escape.

Keith took her down to the kitchen where she was drawn to the warmth of a large range. There were modern appliances too, below shelves of dusty copper saucepans, awaiting dinner parties that no longer happened. 'A long way to carry food to the dining room,' she remarked, trying to imagine the kitchen full of staff.

'Stone cold when it arrived too. Ridiculous arrangement, even then,' Keith agreed, as they left by the back door. This took them into a cobbled courtyard flanked by stables, half of which had been converted into garaging and where Eva's little Fiat sat incongruously parked between a dark, sinuous Jaguar and a business-like Land Rover. The Jag, she imagined, must be Duncan's rather than Keith's, unless it was Lady Jillian's. Both vehicles were elderly.

The other half of the old stabling had been converted into what Keith told her was his workshop. 'I make furniture, you see, using timber we fell on the estate, small scale stuff but it keeps me out of trouble – and out of everyone's way.' He pulled a wry face and Eva decided that she liked the man. He led her across the courtyard, indicating a cottage that stood a little apart. 'That's my place. Same reason. It'll be forever known as Kenny's cottage but I look on it as mine and we've made it very snug. You must come for tea when Susie gets back. What exactly will you be doing for Archie?'

The sudden question gave her a moment's pause. Not entirely disinterested, after all, she noted. 'Whatever he asks me to, I suppose, once he has the measure of things.'

'I need to talk to him about the wretched salmon farm before things go too far.'

She acknowledged the words with a nod and they left it at that.

He took her next through a gate and into a well-kept walled garden with old glasshouses along one side. 'This is Mama's domain. She started putting things to rights during the war and it went from there. Susie helps her and it's about the one place where they actually manage to get on. A meeting of minds over the raised beds if nowhere else. Rather different women, you see, different temperaments. Susie's an artist and my mother thinks she's feckless and shambolic. She thinks I am too, of course, but actually I'm just lazy.' He grinned at her again. 'Duncan likes being in charge and I could never be bothered to compete.' He paused, frowning a little, as if choosing his words. 'But it'll be different now, I suppose . . . Will he really just hand it all over? Archie, I mean. Was he serious, what he told Duncan in Canada?'

'You'll have to ask him.'

'Yes, of course. Didn't mean to put you on the spot.'

'About what?' Unbeknownst to either of them Tam had come through the open gate and was standing behind them, looking around the walled garden. 'Are you brow-beating my private secretary?'

The words were lightly spoken but Keith flushed. 'I hope not. I . . . I was simply wondering how you felt, now you're back here, seeing it all again. And whether it would make you reconsider what you said in Canada, about handing it over?'

Tam regarded him, amused. 'You're direct, I'll give you that, and I like that in a man. But tell me, is yours the Jag or the Land Rover?' The question, direct or otherwise, was left unanswered.

'Neither. I've a rather dodgy Ford but my girlfriend has it at the moment up in Inverness.' Keith explained about the painting course she was running up there but Eva saw that Tam wasn't listening, he was letting his gaze wander over the raised borders and glasshouses.

'Much troubled by aphids?' he asked, when Keith stopped talking.

'What?'

'Aphids. On the tomato plants?'

Keith laughed but looked bewildered. 'Actually, we are, yes. Why?'

'I was given the job of killing them once. I could sit, you see and do it with my leg stretched out. Meanwhile another man shovelled shit over there by the potting shed. There was a hierarchy, you see, even here, but I thought one of those men had principles.' Eva and Keith exchanged puzzled glances, something which did not escape Tam because he laughed. 'The mind wanders,' he said and together they strolled back through the courtyard.

'Your meeting went well?' Eva asked.

Tam groaned. 'It *went*, which in itself is well, but I fear there'll be many more of 'em. How those men can talk! But they've gone for now with their bundles of papers and will no doubt produce many more such bundles they'll expect me to read and absorb. Give me aphids to slaughter any day.'

Keith had been walking beside him but he halted now. 'You're going to the estuary this afternoon, you said.' Tam stopped too. 'With Duncan.'

'I am.'

'I'd like a word about the project, if you will, I usually try not to interfere but there are aspects of what's planned there that—'

Tam put up his hand. 'You can have your say, Keith, but not yet, I'll go there this afternoon with an open mind. When I wasn't being measured for suits I spent some time in London libraries getting myself up to speed on the subject of fish farms, but I'll see it for myself before I'll listen to lobbying.'

CHAPTER 27

When Tam left for the fish farm, Eva decided she would explore the grounds and following lunch she went up to her room to fetch a jacket. She was just leaving with it when Lady Maxwell passed her open door and stopped. 'You've settled in, I hope. Found all you need?'

'I have, yes. Thank you.'

'Do let me know if there is anything you require.' She was moving off again when she paused and stepped inside instead. 'You know, Eva, I have to say I find it very odd of you to have told me only half a story when we met that time. You obviously knew exactly where to find Archie.'

The directness took Eva by surprise. 'Actually I didn't. Not then. I simply followed what leads I had, and got lucky.' She resisted remarking that it had been odd of her ladyship to impersonate her mother.

'But you chose not to share that information, those leads. Why was that?'

'I wanted to find Tam . . . Archie first, and speak to him.'

'Oh?'

Clearly more was expected and the woman was between her and the door. 'You said yourself, if you remember, that someone who chose to live in the back of beyond might not want to be found. I wanted to ask him if that was so, but then Duncan turned up and I didn't get the chance.'

Lady Maxwell considered. 'I did say that, didn't I. But was that *your* reason? Duncan believed you were trying to steal a march on that dreadful Mallory man.'

There was no hostility in her tone, simply puzzlement. 'Mallory would have told him that.' Eva replied. 'But I wasn't.'

'I don't blame you for going solo, Eva, it was a bold move. Wholly admirable and no doubt a career-making coup, but if getting your hands on the story first *wasn't* the reason for heading off so abruptly, what was?'

'I wanted to speak to T . . . Archie,' she repeated.

But Jillian Maxwell was not so easily deflected and she came further into the room. 'You were only ten or eleven, you said, when you last saw him. And while *he* might have made an impression on *you*, it would hardly be the same for him.'

Eva smiled a little at that. 'I felt it might be.'

The woman showed no sign of leaving and Eva was trapped. 'How very odd,' she repeated. 'And now here you are! In this new role . . .'

'And proving to be quite an asset.' Tam appeared in the doorway.

Lady Maxwell turned but was unruffled by his appearance. 'I don't doubt it, Archie, but perhaps one day you'll explain.'

Tam held her look and nodded. 'Perhaps I will, but not right now.' He turned to Eva. 'Good, you have your jacket. I'd like you to join Duncan and me down at the estuary, if you will, and we're ready for the off if you are. Excuse us, will you, Jilly. We *will* talk, of course we will, but later.'

Eva slipped past Jilly and followed Tam downstairs. 'Do you want me to take notes about the fish,' she murmured as he held the back door open for her, 'or were you rescuing me?'

'She had you cornered,' he replied, with a smile, 'and as I remember Jillian has a way of drawing people out. You're safer with me.'

How long had he been listening, she wondered, but Duncan was waiting beside the Land Rover in the courtyard and there was no time for more. If he was surprised when Eva climbed into the backseat he hid it well. 'The Bentley's long gone, I suppose?' Tam asked as he closed the passenger door.

'The Bentley?'

Tam smiled, dismissing the subject. 'Never mind. Too much to hope for. Right, Duncan, I'm all ears, fire away.' And so, as they drove, Eva listened while Duncan outlined his plans for expansion and Tam fired questions at him. They were sharp, astute questions, he had been doing his homework, and Eva was further intrigued by this man she realised now she barely knew. But she too had spent time in libraries, awaiting his arrival, not researching aquaculture but discovering what she could about Lt Colonel Archibald Maxwell VC. There were various military commendations related to the medal awarded after El Alamein and to his actions at St Valéry, but one account included tributes from his men, which mattered more. *He'd a reckless sort of courage and yet you knew every move was calculated, he'd weighed the risks. It made it terrifying sometimes but we'd faith in him, and would follow*, said one. *He wasn't a one-of-the-lads type of commander, he kept his distance, but he knew men's names, or took the trouble to learn them*, reported another. *A fair man, disciplined but fair. You knew where you were with him.* Unable to endorse that last sentiment Eva nevertheless observed him putting those same skills to good use in handling his half-brothers, and it pleased her to watch him. Tam needed no buffer, he need not have brought her, but she was glad that he had.

'We bring them in at the smolt stage, get them used to salt water . . .'

'You've your own hatcheries, you said.'

'Small ones; we need to expand, especially if we want to run a five-year cycle, but we can buy in for now. The costs are mainly in extending the shore base – that's where we need investment; we're just making do at the moment. It all costs money – bigger stores, a proper generator house, fuel tanks, icing equipment, boxing space, a fish-food silo . . .'

'What do you feed them?'

'Dry pellets. Nutrition is vital, of course, but we buy in commercial ones that have the right blend of protein, fats, minerals et cetera . . . there's been a lot of research done. We supplement it with white-fish offal and shrimp waste, which helps with the colour.'

'The *colour*?'

'Pink flesh brings higher prices, makes them look more like the wild fish. I'm also investigating the cost of artificial carotenoids, which produce colour more quickly, and there've been experiments with a type of red yeast, which is also a supplementary nutrient.'

Tam grunted. 'Go on about the infrastructure.'

'Where'd I got to . . .' Duncan's enthusiasm was palpable. 'We need better pumps, somewhere to store cables and hoses where they won't get nicked. And that's just the shore site. Expanding the marine site means more collars and working platforms, more cage nets, cover nets, predator nets – I'll show you all of it. We want to move to fully automated feeder units but they've not proved reliable so far so we have to employ labour.'

'No bad thing?'

'Adds to the costs though.'

'Of course. Explain collars.'

'Better wait until we get there, then you can see.'

'Right.'

It was all very amicable and business-like. Tam's attention seemed fully engaged and Duncan had dropped his default air of brooding resentment and was making his pitch with convincing passion and commitment. The man really cared.

They reached the coast on a narrow potholed road and ahead of them lay the ocean framed by stunning views of felt-green slopes, which swept down to the sea. Rocky headlands gave way to white beaches where a high-tide mark of seaweed was punctuated with the inevitable fish crates, net floats and driftwood. They jolted over a particularly large pothole and she bit her tongue. 'Road'll need upgrading too and that's a massive expense,' Duncan remarked.

'*This* road?' Tam looked at him, incredulous, and Duncan laughed.

'No. There's a back lane I have in mind, much more direct, just needs widening and strengthening for the construction equipment, and then the vans. I'll show you on the estate map once we're back at the house, explain how we can do it.' The road rose and they paused on the brow where they could see the other side with the estuary before them, a-sparkle with diamonds in the afternoon sunshine. It was a breathtaking sight as it widened out to the ocean. At the other end, where it narrowed, Eva could see another beach, sheltered by rising land behind it.

A perfect scene.

Ahead of them, out in the estuary, she spotted a series of circular pods with walkways between them. The fish-farm cages. 'And there it is,' said Duncan.

'So I see.'

Something off-key in Tam's tone ought to have warned Duncan but he was so caught up with enthusiasm for his project that he missed it. Tam had gone quiet. The questions had dried up. He was still listening but responding only with a nod or a grunt, and his gaze was fixed on the sheltered white beach; Eva saw from his profile that his jaw had tightened. They drove round, over a narrow bridge, and stopped outside a cluster of low ruined buildings, against which were stashed various plastic drums and hoses. Two small boats stood on trolleys high up on what looked like an old slipway.

'Aber Rosslie,' Tam said.

'That's right,' said Duncan, and pulled on the handbrake. 'Is Eva joining us out there?'

'Will you come, my dear?' Tam asked, but she declined. Better that the two of them focused on the matter in hand and started to build some form of accord. She was encouraged by what she'd heard as they'd driven down, and stood back, watching as together they pushed one of the boats down the cobbled slipway. Perhaps this would be a turning point with positive energies directed towards a common goal. She could only hope. She watched as Duncan rowed them out to the cages, breaking off now and then to point and gesticulate, then offered Tam a hand onto the floating walkway, and she stood a moment observing him on the pontoons, obviously explaining the processes, and she found herself hoping Tam *would* support the project. If this was to offer a route to an amicable settlement and a solution to vexing financial concerns then Tam could go home to Ross while the other issues ran their course. Tam appeared to be listening closely, asking the occasional question, his eyes fixed on the cages, nodding every now and then or looking out to sea.

Or over his shoulder, back at the little beach.

She left them to it and strolled along the shore, watching little clockwork birds running ahead of her, poking their beaks into the sand before lifting off in a flash of white wings to settle a little further on. It was a lovely spot, bathed in sunlight with a view of the far horizon. No wonder Tam had been keen to return home, but how hard it must have been to leave . . .

One of the old buildings, the most intact of them, had been patched up with a corrugated iron roof and given a new door, which was sporting a stout padlock. The other buildings were roofless, open to the elements, full of nettles, empty oil drums, broken creels, fishing floats and all manner of detritus, and Eva was reminded of Shelagh's extraordinary collection, the discarded husks of former lives. Their stories might differ, but the impact on individual lives had been the same. Aber Rosslie's inhabitants had been scattered a generation or two earlier than those from the outports and yet these stone walls would still be visible in the landscape long after all traces of jetties and stages had vanished. It would be harder, she imagined, to wipe Aber Rosslie from maps and memories.

She continued on. A strange odour assailed her; it became a bad smell as she walked on . . . and then suddenly she was upon it – a seal, its eye dulled in death, its body bloated and putrefying. A bullet hole in the side of its head, just above the ear hole was raw and red and shocking, dried blood surrounded the wound, staining the skin.

A salmon thief, presumably, brought to account.

She stared at it a moment, distressed by the sight, and then turned back to see the men were climbing back into the boat, so went down the slipway to meet them. She saw at once that Tam's face was grave and Duncan's a little puzzled, as if he realised that something had gone wrong but couldn't fathom what it was. Her heart sank. 'Thank you, Duncan,' Tam was saying. 'That was most informative and, as I said before, you've shown tremendous initiative getting all this started. Lots to think about. So much so,' he continued, as they reached Eva, 'that I believe I'll walk back. I can go over the fields, I remember the way. Take Eva home, will you?' With a brief nod he set off before either of them could respond.

'What the—?' Duncan watched him go. 'He seemed so interested and then—' He broke off, remembering his audience, and gave Eva a tight smile. 'Right, home, then. Let's hope fresh air clears the man's mind.'

His expression reverted to one of tense gravity on the drive back and he said barely a word but as they pulled into the cobbled courtyard he stopped and turned to her. 'Look, I'm really not sure why you're here at all but if you've any influence over Archie then please use it to convince him of the project. I've got investors lined up who'll put big money into it. Roadworks could start as soon as they know that it has his support. Sorting out the handover and succession, if that's what he still intends . . .' he paused, then continued when she said nothing '. . . that can all wait, but we need to get going before this consortium decides to put their money elsewhere. They won't wait for ever. You do understand how important this is, don't you?'

He looked so impassioned and frustrated that she couldn't help but feel sympathy for the man. 'I do, and can see what it means to you, Duncan, but I've no influence at all over . . . over Archie. I've no idea what's going through his head, really, I don't. I . . . I just think he wants to do the right thing.'

'And this is that!' Duncan banged a fist on the steering wheel. 'Rosslie needs investment. It's fifty years behind the time. Pa just carried on doing things the way they'd been done before the Great War, totally blinkered, simply refusing to accept change. Stubborn to the end. For years I had to do everything by subterfuge to get past him and we'll go under if we're not damned careful! Think of those abandoned places in Newfoundland, like the one where Archie used to live, where you were. I talked to people in the place I was staying and they described the endless struggle, the slow decline, clinging to old, outmoded ways – it should be a terrible warning. If new thinking isn't embraced then places vanish – they can't survive.'

What exactly did he mean? 'But that place, those houses down by the estuary, they're long gone,' she said. 'The salmon farm won't bring them back.'

'Of course not. That's not what I mean, but the estate still supports a lot of people so it has to be in good shape to do that. Good *financial* state, stable at the core, and this expansion will do that.' Stable at the core. Outmoded ways perhaps but not an outmoded hierarchy. The money would come to the estate, to him, and the profits too – he would take the risk and expect to reap the reward, which was fair enough, but funds would be allocated across the estate as he saw fit, keeping the old system going. He would call the shots.

Was that what was troubling Tam, or something else entirely?

'He just clammed up out there! God knows why. Get him to talk to me, will you – get him to *explain* what it is he doesn't like. He said he wouldn't interfere but by not agreeing he'll sabotage everything I've done so far.'

'I'll try. It's early days, Duncan. Give him time.'

But Duncan was shaking his head. 'There *isn't* time – that's the problem. The investors are already cooling off, I can sense it, so we need to move fast to secure the deal. Early days or not, Archie needs to understand how important this is. I've kept them on the hook and did all I could to convince the man just now . . .' There might be passion in his voice but there was little warmth.

He held the door open for Eva and they went through to find the house in uproar.

'Thank God you're back.' Lady Jillian met them in the hall. 'The place has gone *mad*! The press have got hold of the story of Archie being back and everyone, I mean everyone, wants an interview. We had to take the phone off the hook; it just never stopped ringing! Where is he? They're like piranhas, circling, all wanting a bite. He'll have to call the police, you know. Morag said there are vans and cars parked outside the gates when she came, men with great long lenses taking pictures. She could hardly get through! We've had to put a chain across. Madness, absolute madness. Where's Archie? He was with you, wasn't he? Eva, where's he gone?'

'He said he'd walk back, across the fields.'

'Oh, good Lord! Why choose now? I hope he stays below the hedgerows or they'll be onto him. Duncan, call the police – get them to move those people on.'

Duncan was shrugging out of his waxed jacket while she spoke and he tossed it onto a chair. 'They won't unless an offence is committed.'

'But they're blocking access. We're virtual prisoners! It's quite appalling. Eva, you know these people – can't you just tell them to go away?'

'Oh, they'd love that. There's a headline right there.'

'So what do we do?'

'I expect they'll get bored eventually and leave.' As long as Tam's return remained the only story . . .

'Well, as soon as Archie gets back he must deal with them. If you won't call the police, Duncan, *he'll* have to. Might be better coming from him anyway; now he's in charge of things, he can complain about invasion of his personal privacy, his position, et cetera – all that must count for something.'

Duncan gave her a dark look, turned on his heel and left.

CHAPTER 28

Archie walked swiftly down the track until he heard the Land Rover start up and drive off in the other direction, and then slowed his pace. Once it was out of sight he went and sat on a low wall and looked bleakly back at the sea cages and saw again the writhing, seething mass of silvery distress. Dear God! It'd been all he could do to keep his tongue between his teeth as Duncan spewed information at him. Likely profits, risks, loans, investments, expected losses – fifty per cent was acceptable, apparently – while at his feet, round and round they swam, the king of fish held captive, driven to madness. He could have wept! Salmon were fighters, explorers and wanderers, driven by a deep-seated primeval purpose, an innate compulsion to find their way home, even as he had done, surviving storm and predator to reach their ancient spawning grounds and there, in the dappled shadows of overhanging branches, begin the next generation.

And what had *he* spawned?

Shrimp waste, Duncan had said, *for colour*, to create counterfeits of their wild cousins who leaped up salmon ladders, straining muscle to defy gravity, breaching crystal-clear waterfalls to find their way home. God, what had the world come to? He watched the Land Rover disappear over the rise and then crossed the little bridge over the river, which, by late October, would receive the first of the returning exiles harkening to the clarion call of home. The very idea of fish cages was anathema to him, but having watched the trawlers and deep-sea draggers rape Newfoundland's fishing grounds, decimating the cod, it was hardly surprising that they now had to farm their wretched brethren, leaving them bewildered, circling the wire of the cages and gazing out at a watery freedom that would be forever denied them.

'Saithe can be a problem,' Duncan had explained. 'They congregate around the cages, mopping up stray food. One got in once and it grew colossal, putting the salmon under stress, but we managed to shoot it.' He'd told the story with a smile but Tam managed only a grunt by way of response. 'Seals are a menace too, so we have to be vigilant, they spook the fish just being around.' He had studiously ignored several silvery bodies that floated on the surface in one of the cages. Collateral damage, no doubt, part of the fifty per cent. Accounted for. Morts were inevitable, he'd read in the London library, registering the starkness of their naming. 'Diving ducks and cormorants will have a go as well, hence the predator nets. They get torn in entanglements, which brings more cost as we have to repair or replace them.' The nets, presumably, not the birds. What price a cormorant, after all? No mention had been made of the proliferations of lice he had read about, nor the polluting antibiotics and unregulated chemicals, the long-term impact of escapees breeding with wild fish. Born in hatcheries, freedom without a compass pointing home would ultimately destroy the whole precious cycle.

Duncan could not be in ignorance of these concerns.

Or did he hope that *he* was?

He paused a moment to steady himself. He was being unreasonable. Too impassioned. And it was, he reminded himself, no longer his concern and Duncan was doing his best, doing what he believed he must to keep things going, embracing new thinking, exploring ways to survive in an increasingly challenging world. And who was he to judge him, after all? It was Pa who had allowed the place to fall into a lethargy from which it must now be rescued, as Duncan was trying to do, tossed in the torrid current of progress, trying to stay afloat.

Or was Duncan, like his wretched fish, entirely caged by circumstance, entangled in the mesh? If so, that mess was of his and Jilly's making, and he'd give anything to have it otherwise.

He carried on walking.

At last he reached the overhang of turf above the little beach and he stood there, breathless and despairing, looking down at the white sand. He could no longer remember exactly where they had sat that day eating sandwiches – salmon sandwiches, made from the great warrior he and John McAdam had hooked, and fought, in the upper reaches of the river. His mind dwelt on John McAdam with puzzlement for a moment, then he looked back down the estuary.

No confining cages then.

On that day it had been wild salmon the gulls had dipped and swooped upon, chased by seals in a fair contest, and their flesh had been flushed pink not by prawn carcasses but by the sheer joy of living.

And on that day, his course had been set.

As he stood there, looking down on the pristine sand, he could almost hear her voice. 'Bring the towel to the water's edge, will you. I shan't stay in long.'

1940

The heat that day was extraordinary. Sweltering and sticky with a heaviness about it, awaiting the coming storm to break it . . . They finished delivering the vegetables and were pulling away from the last cottage when Jilly announced that she'd brought a picnic.

Archie glanced at her and his spirits lifted. Today, more than on other days, he'd been conscious of a questioning behind the respectful enquiries about his recovery. Why was he still here, they seemed to ask, why hadn't he reported back? 'Shall I show them the scars?' he'd remarked with irritation as Jilly had leaped up beside him after the last call. 'Or climb down so they can watch me limp? Fat lot of good I'd be leading my men, unless I could persuade them to carry me!' Even so, he knew that the time was fast approaching for his return and the thought depressed him beyond reason.

It was then she'd told him about the picnic. 'And I need a swim. What about you?'

'*Swim!* I can't bloody swim.'

'Maybe not, but I can.' She gave him that marvellous smile of hers and his spirits rose further. 'Look, there's a nice spot just over there.' She'd been strangely distant until then, quieter than usual, distracted and thoughtful, avoiding his eyes. He'd wondered a little at the cause as he watched her, acutely aware of her there beside him, almost touching. He too had things on his mind, and he wondered, a little hopefully, whether their thoughts might be converging . . .

'There's a better one just beyond,' he said, thinking rapidly. A startled Milly was persuaded to a trot and they bowled briskly along in the sunshine towards the head of the estuary to a little beach he remembered. Just the place. They'd played there as children, he and Andy, and his father used to keep the skiff moored just offshore.

Beside him Jilly twisted on the seat. 'Here's fine, really, Archie. Do we need to go further?'

'Yes.' Because suddenly he wanted very much to take her there and show her, not acknowledging, even to himself, what it was he actually hoped might happen when they reached it.

And so they arrived at the place.

The edge of the shoreline was fringed with pebbles relinquished by the tide, worn smooth in the same maelstrom of storm and current that had sculptured the edge of the sand dunes, leaving it with a ragged overhang of turf above a white-sand beach. They'd be out of sight there, Archie decided, and there were sand walls against which to lean their backs.

'But you'll never get down there with your sticks,' Jilly protested. 'Let's go back.'

'I'll come along the stream bed. Wait for me there and then pass the basket down.'

He descended from the trap, pulled his sticks free and smiled up at her before setting off to hobble unsteadily through a shallow stream, the waters forming a shimmering delta spread across the sand. He lifted his face to the sun as he walked back along the beach to where Jilly was waiting. 'Can you scramble down?' he asked, looking up at her.

'Of course.'

She passed down a rug and the basket, and was sliding down before he had a chance to put out a hand to help her. She arrived beside him and stood dusting off her trousers, and he saw her brush an arm across her eyes. 'You're crying!'

'Sand. It blew into my eyes.' She gave him a quick, brittle smile.

But the silken dune grasses were barely stirring, the distant storm quiescent as it gathered strength. A rare windless day. She was lying, of course, but tears came easily these days and perhaps they were better shed than held back. And while the sheer beauty of the place raised emotions, heightening an appreciation of loveliness, it also intensified a sense of loss.

They had both, after all, lost loved ones.

He hesitated then. He'd badly wanted to show her this place, point to the view beyond the rocks where cormorants now stood, their wings outstretched to dry, and where the sea, yet untouched by the coming storm, rose and fell in gentle rhythmic swells. He noted, but disregarded, the darkening horizon. Later, tempest and tide would combine to bring waves thundering against the rocks, casting up walls of spray, but not now. Not yet. They had time. He'd wanted to come here before he went back to war, to store away the memory, but right now what he wanted most of all was to hold her again, here in this place, not in his bedroom, overshadowed by sorrow and fright-filled fear. They'd never mentioned again that night they had clung to each other in grief but it had forever changed his awareness of her. He could not forget it. It was in his head as they worked side by side in the glasshouse, or sat opposite each other of an evening idling over his father's wine, acutely so when she came to him in the night, bringing tea and reassurance, driving away the ever-present frights. He'd look at her, remembering, knowing now the feel of her and badly wanting her to slip in beside him again, but quite unable to tell her so. He probably owed her his life, and as God only knew, he owed her his sanity. *One day you'll thank me*, she'd said and he did, and he wanted to tell her that too. But not in words . . . He craved that closeness, that fleeting intimacy; he longed to hold her in his arms *here*, as a whole and sound man, not a broken creature who cried out in the night.

He saw then that she was looking at him, and saw too that she realised this, and turned his head away in sudden shame.

'It's all right, you know,' she said, in that slightly arch tone he had grown accustomed to. 'I quite understand but first—' Lifting her arms she pulled off her top then wriggled out of her trousers, discarding her knickers and bra, laughing at him. 'A swim . . .'

He gaped at her.

'Then sex.'

She blew him a kiss.

'Then food.'

'But . . . but, what—' Horrified, he scanned the area.

'What indeed, Captain Maxwell!'

He was stunned, utterly speechless. He'd half-expected that any advance he might make would receive a rebuttal, outrage even, or at least a token resistance and been prepared for that. But the sight of her standing unashamedly naked and smiling before him completely took his breath away..

Her eyes were glittering strangely, though.

'Jilly—'

'See the hordes gathering on the hillside, aghast and appalled?' she said, gesturing towards the empty landscape.

'Yes, but—'

'Bring the towel to the water's edge, will you. I shan't stay in long.'

She set off down the beach and he rapidly surveyed the area again, shocked and exhilarated in equal measure. The place was secluded, yes, but, dear God, the woman was mad! She was soon in the surf, walking, her arms lifted above the wave crests, but then he saw her take the plunge and begin swimming strongly towards the mouth of the estuary.

Oh Lord, though, what he wouldn't give to join her.

But it must be bloody cold. He saw a towel peeping out of the top of her duffel bag and he took it, tossing it over his shoulder, grabbed his sticks and hobbled down to the water's edge. It wasn't easy to keep his balance on the strip of pebbles. Or anywhere, in fact . . . He remembered that the beach shelved abruptly just off shore and reckoned she must have reached that spot for he could see only the top of her head and she was still swimming away, out towards the approaching bank of cloud.

But how on earth had they reached this point! And so suddenly . . .

It had happened by degrees, he decided, watching the frothy edges of waves pulsing up the beach, inch by inch, touch by touch. Perhaps there had been an inevitability about it. Over the weeks they had become easy with each other, familiar and companionable. He'd never known a woman like her, but . . . but whatever were they about? He felt confused and perversely shocked . . . He looked up again but couldn't see her, and raised a hand to shield his eyes, and then, between two waves, he glimpsed the top of her head. Far out, far too far . . . *Shit.* She should turn back, the currents would be too strong for her, he should have thought to say! He called out to her, knowing it was futile. 'For God's sake, woman!' he muttered, badly frightened now and yelled again. '*Turn back!*' but she kept swimming away from him . . . Then he remembered her tears and an appalling thought hit him. No . . . God, *no*! But even as the possibility overwhelmed him, he saw her twist in the water, raise an arm and start back to shore. He let out a long breath and his pulse steadied again as he watched her coming in with the waves. By the time she reached him he'd regained his composure, telling himself he'd been absurd to even consider such a thought. And when she emerged, pushing the hair from her face and smiling as she came towards him, he was able to quip, 'Like Botticelli's bloody Venus, except not half as modest.'

She laughed and reached for the towel, but he held on to it and tried to wrap it round her, to hold her there, then lost his balance and fell against her. 'Oops,' she said, still laughing, and propped him back up, covering herself quickly. Then she took his arm and draped it across her shoulder, supporting him, the other hand gripping her towel in place. 'Lean on me, that's it. Sticks in the other hand.' He cursed silently. This wasn't how he had planned it would be, but together they made it back up the beach, crossing the pebbled line. 'And don't kick sand on the rug. There's nothing worse when you're naked.'

'How d'you know?' he asked, his teeth clenched against the pain as he lowered himself down.

'Instinct,' she replied. 'Though shell sand is soft.'

'Ha! An expert on the differing qualities of sand upon the naked—'

'Shut up and dry me, for God's sake, and stop my teeth from chattering.'

He rubbed her briskly with the towel and then there was no more space for questions, and restraint was cast like blown spume to the strengthening wind. There was passion and urgency, yes, as she pulled off his shirt, but tenderness too, and later he would remember only the deep, deep solace of loving her in this peerless place. And he would remember too how the sand beneath the rug had moulded to their bodies and how her cold skin had warmed to his touch, and how, wordlessly, they had acknowledged and satisfied each other's need, finding the joy of losing themselves in the moment, in this place where war and its consequences had no substance.

Or so he had believed at the time.

Later, having dressed and recovered a little, she'd poured tea from the flask and unwrapped the sandwiches as if this was just an ordinary picnic on an ordinary day. 'Mmm, salmon,' she said, lifting an edge of bread before taking a bite. 'Well done, Roberts. I was dreading egg.'

'Jilly—'

'Don't speak. Eat your sandwich.' He gave her a frown and she mocked him with one of her own. 'There's nothing to be said, Archie, or at least not in that tone. It was lovely. The place, the swim and . . . and you—'

'But, Jilly—'

'No buts. A snatched moment, nothing more. Or less.'

'After the war—'

'Don't speak, I tell you.' Her hair was drying into mad curls that the wind blew across her face, obscuring it, but through it he saw again that strange glittering in her eyes. 'After the war, there'll be things we'll need to forget.'

'You want to forget this?'

She reached out a hand to him. 'Not for the world. But we'll keep it locked away and never mention it, even to each other, but take pleasure sometimes in remembering.'

It wasn't enough, not by a long shot. 'The thought of you with my father—'

'*No!* That I forbid.' Her composure was extraordinary as she sat there, her knees drawn up, one arm wrapped around them, eating her sandwich and squinting out to sea. 'Are you going to eat or not?' she asked, gesturing to the package.

'Damn it, Jilly—'

She groaned. 'Oh God. I thought we understood each other. It's only allowed, this once, because . . .'

'*Allowed?*'

'It's allowed because of this *bloody* war that you'll be going back to, and because we've already lost so much and stand to lose everything. We're surely allowed to grasp at *something*.'

She began crying, in fitful little sobs, and he thought his heart would break. But she was right! These were not sane times, and in the madness of it all perhaps those things that are forbidden might be defended if not excused, and he was upsetting her, spoiling the moment, spoiling the day.

'Yes, to a sandwich then,' he said.

'There's sand on it now, but that's your own fault. It'll be gritty.' She turned away to blow her nose.

'I didn't mean to make you cry, Jilly. Clumsy of me.'

'Must be the leg,' she said, 'unbalancing you.'

He reached out and took a sandwich with a slightly trembling hand. 'Stupid leg.'

CHAPTER 29

Archie continued to stare down at the vacant patch of sand, lost in that distant moment.

By what code had they convinced themselves – or each other – that it was *allowed*? In what world could it *ever* be allowable for a son to make love to his father's wife, and not expect a reckoning. It had been a moment of madness, of reckless folly . . . There was no excuse in that, of course, but it was hard now to remember the intensity of those far-off days, the all-pervasive fatalistic, doom-laden atmosphere and the desperate need to find solace and a reason to go on living. He'd behaved like a spoiled boy, infatuated by an older woman, absurdly obsessed with her, knowing full well that his feelings were not reciprocated.

And that she was his father's wife.

He began to recognise, as he had failed to do that day, what a desperate state Jilly must have been in to let it happen. Back then he'd been so bound up with his own wants, his own self-centred needs, that he'd not stopped to think what might have driven her to such wild recklessness. He remembered her crying in that wretched, hopeless way, insisting that there had to be *something* to grasp on to, but he'd not stopped to think from where the words had sprung. He had accepted what she had given him all those weeks of his convalescence, her kindness and her comfort, never really considering what emotions she had wrestled with herself. It must have been building in her as it had built in him, that desperate need for joy, for basic human connection, for physical intimacy. Grieving still for the lover lost in Norway, she had perhaps already realised that marriage to his father had been a mistake – as it surely was. As he stood there he felt a great wave of compassion for their younger selves, foolhardy and unthinking as they had been. Yes, they had transgressed, broken every code and taboo in trying to survive.

And by God they had paid a price for it.

Right now, though, it was Duncan who was being made to pay. His son. Ill-conceived, perhaps, but blameless. Archie looked bleakly at the salmon cages with their frantic prisoners and shared in their despair . . . He felt helpless to improve the situation. Duncan's very evident resentment of him was wholly understandable, and must be endured, but he'd also observed a coolness between Duncan and his mother; there were complex undercurrents here that he'd yet to fathom. He'd been naïve to think that his return would be an easy tying-up of loose ends, a quick fix and he found himself more emotionally drawn in than he'd expected. His beloved Rosslie was in a mess and Duncan was lost in some wilderness of his own, trying to hold things together but finding ways that were, in Archie's view, wholly unacceptable.

And yet, he was seeking his approval, *needing* his approval, for the whole thing to move forward. Christ, what a coil! And if not the fish farm then he must rapidly think of something else to reverse Rosslie's failing fortunes and set Duncan on the road to recovery. That was the best that could be salvaged from this sorry tale, and the very least he must do, and then he should leave, sever the link once and for all, and then cauterize the wound.

Duncan's needs were paramount.

Jilly he had yet to consider.

He turned his back on the estuary and set off towards the house. Whatever else, he told himself, he was honour-bound to stay until he could set matters right and must somehow persuade Duncan to work with him. It would mean breaking the assurances he'd given Ross if he stayed on longer and he stopped a moment, remembering how simple life had been in Severn, and how good. He'd once grieved for the loss of Rosslie but the thought of forfeiting his life *there* was unbearable.

At first his route home took him through the fields but now he re-joined the drive up to the house and, as he reached a slight rise, he looked back and saw sunlight glinting on the windscreens of cars parked outside the boundary wall. Hunt followers, perhaps, or spectators at some road event. He continued into the house, thinking no more about it, and it wasn't until he entered the library, rehearsing what he would say to Duncan, that he discovered his mistake.

Jilly rose as he entered. 'Thank God!' she said. 'This was *not* a good time to disappear, Archie. We're surrounded by the press – besieged! The estate office has had to keep taking the phone off the hook, it just rings and rings, the help are being accosted when they arrive at the gates, and Duncan won't call the police.'

'Where is Duncan?'

'He's gone off to Brodie's, on horseback across the fields to avoid the vultures.'

Damn. 'Why there?'

'He's got a thing going with Sarah Brodie. He'll have gone on to solace.'

As men do, he thought.

Eva was sitting by the window. 'What on earth is all the interest?' he asked her. 'Can't you somehow call them off?'

Jilly answered for her. 'I asked the same, and she said no.'

'Do you reckon it's Mallory's doing?'

'I wouldn't be surprised,' Eva replied.

He considered for a moment what the wretched man might have uncovered. 'Anything we can do?'

'I've been wondering. I suppose it might help if you released a brief press statement announcing that you're back, settling affairs, et cetera, saying as little as you can, using every cliché and platitude you can think of, and hope that some of the pack lose interest and drop away. The tenacious ones will hang on, I'm afraid.'

'Like Mallory?'

'Yes.'

'The phone has literally not stopped,' Jilly repeated. 'There've even been calls from Canada so the press have got hold of the story there too.'

Archie and Eva exchanged swift glances. 'So what do I say in this release?'

'I could draft it if you like.'

He nodded. 'Yes, do that, please. Could you make a start on it now? And send for some tea, if you would, for me and Jilly.'

Being a bright girl, she got the message and left.

Leaving him and Jilly alone together.

He looked across at her. 'Perhaps I should have stayed away.'

'You could have done, I suppose.'

'I suggested Duncan wrote me off as missing but he threatened to set the press on me unless I came back.' Jillian tutted dismissively and Archie shrugged. 'Seems to have happened anyway. And he was quite right to insist I returned. He's in an impossible position and matters need resolving.' He threw himself into an armchair opposite her. 'Caught in the coils, eh, Jilly?' She made no response. 'Does he know?'

'Of course he doesn't.'

He narrowed his eyes. 'You're quite sure?'

'Absolutely. How could he?'

'Pa?'

'He promised me he'd never tell him. It was in no one's interests that he should.' Archie raised an eyebrow and she shrugged. 'You frequently told me you wanted no part in running the estate.'

'I remember saying that.'

She frowned a little. 'Have things changed?'

'I'll not rob him of Rosslie. I owe him that much.'

They paused as Morag appeared with a tray of tea, then waited until she'd left and closed the door behind her.

'I can entirely understand his resenting me but I sense something else, a deeper anger. He's polite enough, and business-like, but the man's a coiled spring. How long has he been like this?' He rose and poured the tea.

Jilly shrugged. 'You said yourself he's in a difficult position, and he's not yet sure of you.'

Archie drank his tea, regarding her thoughtfully. 'Tell me about him. What was it like between him and Pa?'

She shrugged. 'Your father did all the right things, sent him to the right schools, made the right introductions but there was no real closeness.'

But then how could there be. 'Poor devil.'

She rose, and went to stand by the window, looking out. After a moment she spoke again. 'You never got to thinking what it was like for me, then? It was all right for you – you escaped.'

His eyes had followed her. *Escaped?* She was still a striking woman, erect and slim, but was she really so devoid of understanding? 'Maybe not as much as I should. You could, after all, have left Pa, taken Duncan.'

'It's easy for a man to say that.'

'Perhaps it is.' He paused. 'But you found consolation in other ways,' he said, and watched for her reaction.

She shot him a glance then looked away. 'It's not for you to judge me, Archie. After all, you hardly used your freedom wisely, from what I understand, and yet you always said you wanted only that.'

He stretched out his legs, wincing a little as his bad one still gave him pain after exercise and it had been a long walk home. 'Not wisely at all. I largely wasted it on remorse. After the war I had the romantic notion of joining a whaler out of Dundee, one of the last as it transpired, and slaughtered whales off the Labrador coast until I was sickened by it. Spent time with sealers there too but that was an even more hideous business. I drank a lot, picked fights with anyone who crossed me and pined for home and for a woman I thought I loved, a father who despised me and a son I'd never have a chance to know.'

She came back and sat again. 'And then what?'

No reaction? Fair enough. The compassion he had felt down at the beach curdled a little. Had she *really* become so hard or was this a front? 'Then I joined a lumber camp and cut down trees and drank and got into more fights and pined for home, cursed a woman I no longer thought I loved and tried to forget I had a son.'

'So nothing useful?'

God, she was a cool one. 'No, nothing like that.'

'A waste.'

'Yes, wasn't it?' He got up and refilled both their cups. 'I indulged myself in self-loathing and remorse for a few more years until I was drawn back to the sea and joined a fishing trawler. Then I met a woman who brought me solace and gave me a son I *could* get to know and things got better for a while. But she became ill, suffered terribly, and we spent what money we had getting her treated but she got worse, and so we both started drinking again, picked fights with each other, and our son ran himself ragged looking after us both, and then she died and I hit the bottle again . . .'

She shook her head at him. 'Archie—'

'Until one day, when I was at my lowest ebb, I met a little girl who looked at me very earnestly and told me I shouldn't swear in front of children and suggested I'd do better if I didn't drink so much. She offered to wash my face for me and was so gentle . . . so innocent—' He found his voice was cracking and stopped to clear it. 'And then, last month, she came to find me and bring me back to face the music.'

There was silence in the room. Then: 'Archie, don't.' Something in Jilly's tone, something sincere and stark, made him look up. Had he got through to her at last, penetrated the shell?

'Don't what?'

'Eva. Don't do it, Archie. I know you'll say I'm one to talk but if you love her at all, don't. It's unnatural, it's unkind. She might think she loves you now, I've seen the way she looks at you, but she'll meet someone else and then she'll have all the pain that I had to bear, and you'll have the pain of it all falling apart, and losing her. Learn from my mistakes if not your own, Archie, and let her go.'

He stared back at her. She was trembling, her hands gripping the arms of the chair, and there was such intensity in her voice that he felt rather ashamed of his teasing. Definitely cracked the shell, he thought, and he glimpsed the softer woman he had known forty years ago before life had toughened her. But he'd not let her off the hook. 'Jilly, while I very much hope Eva will remain part of my life forever, you really need not concern yourself.' And he had a question for her. 'She said you were planning to write to me. Did you?'

'I did.'

'What did you say?'

She shrugged. 'Simply that your father was dead. It seemed you'd a right to know.'

'It never reached me. We wondered if you'd send it, once you knew of Ross's existence.'

'We?'

'Eva and I.'

He saw her purse her lips as she absorbed that. 'I gather,' she said, at last, 'that his existence does *not*, in fact, complicate matters.'

'Were you concerned that it might?'

'You said yourself we couldn't deny Rosslie to Duncan.'

'I said *I* couldn't.'

'Are we going to quarrel after all these years?'

He smiled a little. 'I wonder if we will.' But perhaps, for now, enough had been said. He switched tack. 'Tell me about this woman of Duncan's. Is it serious?'

Jilly's grip on the chair arm slackened a little. 'On his part, yes. But her family are terrible snobs, and frankly so is she.'

'The Brodies always were. Andy was not-quite-engaged to Fiona Brodie before the war. I suppose this girl of Duncan's is her niece?'

'Quite possibly. She'd have him like a shot if he had the title and the estate, and our land marches with theirs so it makes perfect sense.' As it had done since days of yore, he thought – really nothing had changed at all! 'I think she's been biding her time, waiting to see whether or not you were found.'

'And doubtless she cursed when I was.' He switched tack again. 'This frisson I'm sensing between you and Duncan. If you're right and he has no reason to suspect his paternity, what's the reason for that?'

'Nonsense. There's no frisson! Duncan has just been very wound up with this whole business of the estate, ever since Andrew died, so the sooner it's all sorted out the better.' She hesitated. 'You told him you'd renounce the title and the estate.'

'I did.'

'And will you?'

'Didn't we just cover that? But frankly, Jilly, I'm not sure where *you* stand on all this. Never mind that the letter got lost, you still intended me to know that Pa had died. What did you expect me to do when I received it?'

She looked almost disconcerted and wouldn't meet his eye. 'I'm not really sure. I just felt I must and I'd no idea whether you were dead or alive. Nor did Eva, or so she claimed.'

'Tidier all round if I was dead, eh?'

She shrugged. 'I did the right thing for once in my life, Archie. I tried to make contact, belatedly I know, but at least my conscience is clear on that point.' So she claimed a conscience, did she? 'To be honest I didn't really expect that you *would* be found, and now that you're here, I'm not quite sure *what* I think—'

She broke off as Eva put her head around the door. 'It's done. I'll leave it with you. See what you think.'

'No, no. Bring it here. Let me see.' He took it from her and read, his eyebrows arching as he did. '*Much moved by the warm reception, after years in exile . . .*' He flicked a glance at Jilly. 'Much moved indeed. Will it do the trick?'

'Who knows, but a show of family unity might help to kill the story. I can phone it through to the few editors I know with any integrity.'

'Yes, do that if you will, my dear.'

* * *

Eva woke early next day and lay in bed considering what she had learned, or suspected about the complexities of Tam's past life. If her hunch about Duncan was correct then he had a *very* knotty problem to resolve. Would he bring her into his confidence, she wondered. It had also occurred to her that Jillian Maxwell might be contemplating a very different outcome to his reappearance than the one on which Duncan was depending, and that might account for yesterday's rather odd conversation. Tam's *self-defence* quip upon arrival began to make sense. What was it Duncan had said back in Severn? *My mother manipulates the world to suit herself . . .*

But Eva doubted she could manipulate Tam. He was tougher than that.

It was, of course, unthinkable to voice her suspicions, and Tam himself was impossible to read. He treated her much as he had when she was eleven, with that same half-mocking, half-serious manner, except that he no longer explained things but expected her to grasp them and understand the nuances – or chose to keep her guessing.

She rose and went to stand at the window. What was it, she wondered, that had got to him down at the salmon farm yesterday? Something had, but she was as much in the dark as Duncan on that one. She heard a sound below her and looked down to see that the door to the terrace was opening. Tam himself emerged, and she watched him stroll to the top of the steps and stand there, hands in pockets, gazing out across the old parkland as he had done on the day of his arrival. What was going through his mind, she wondered. Was he, after all, reconsidering his position now that he was here?

Perhaps he sensed her watching him because he turned and looked up at the window, saw her and beckoned her down, gesturing towards the river. She raised a hand in acknowledgement then dressed quickly and went to find him. It was one of those fresh, crisp mornings when it was a joy to be out with the sun half risen and the night's shadows still lingering. She came upon Tam standing on the riverbank, watching as ripples spread across the water from a surfacing fish. 'If you were a private secretary worth your salt,' he said, as she joined him, 'you'd have brought me a rod and a stool.'

'If you'd asked me, Sir Archibald, I would have. Shall I go back?'

'Not for the world.' He took her arm and tucked it companionably into the crook of his. 'What a morning, eh? We'll let the fish enjoy it too, though by God they've been taunting me. After yesterday, however, I'm not sure I'll ever go fishing again.'

'What happened down there? Duncan knew something had gone sour, and wasn't sure what.'

'Poor Duncan. I disappointed him.' But he said nothing more.

A heron lifted and flapped lazily away, legs dangling, as they approached the place where a moment before it had stood, sharp-eyed, in the shallows. 'So, my Nemesis,' he said, turning to her. 'I've watched you observing and considering, and I'm keen to hear your assessment of how matters stand. Having failed to anticipate my desire for a rod you must convince me that you're earning your keep.'

Behind the flippancy there was a serious request so she decided to be blunt. 'I think Lady Maxwell would like you to stay, and Duncan's worried that you will.'

'Very good. Anything else?'

'Keith will be content whatever happens.' She hesitated. 'He's very different to his brother.'

'Isn't he just! Go on.'

But how far should she go? She paused to consider, then continued. 'There's tension between Duncan and his mother. I think he senses her ambivalence towards you and he's worried she'll persuade you to stay, while she perhaps wonders how well he'll be able to run things on his own.'

'He's hardly had a chance to try, poor devil. I don't imagine Pa allowed him to shine and now here's me, wading in, spiking his guns; no wonder he always looks so sour. I must find a way through for him,' he paused, 'and you think Jilly wants me to stay?'

She tried a toe in the water. 'I . . . I think, maybe, she would like your company again.'

He gave her a slanting look. 'Go on.'

She swallowed, then cleared her throat. 'I think perhaps you got on well before and, in her old age, she would like—'

'Are you harbouring suspicions, young Eva.' She made to pull her arm away, but he tightened his grip. 'Spit it out.'

'Well, I wondered . . . it would explain why you left Rosslie, left Scotland if . . . if you were once in love with her.'

'It's worse than that.'

'Worse?'

'Much worse.'

She looked across at him and took the plunge. 'Duncan?'

He nodded. 'Duncan.'

It was one thing to have suspicions, quite another to have them confirmed. She glanced at him. What could she possibly say? 'Does he know?'

'Jilly says not, but I very much wonder. I've noticed something smouldering between them too, more on his part than hers – and wonder if he's guessed. There's a rage in his eyes.' They walked on. 'I must do right by him, but I have to do right by Rosslie too and expanding the salmon farm ain't right by Rosslie. He's in a godawful position, I understand that – he's as caged by the situation as his wretched fish, and I know he feels it. I really do want to help him and so I've got to clean up and clear out as fast as I can. It's just proving more difficult than I imagined it would be. I sense Duncan's made like Pa – and my brother Andy too – he needs to be the one calling the shots, can't tolerate being baulked, hates taking advice. Probably been chafing at the bit for years, poor devil, and it's scarred him.' He released her arm and turned away. 'I had forgotten just how much Rosslie once meant to me and so I'm torn. For Duncan's sake I cannot stay, and for Ross's sake I must go back to Severn. It sounds so easy but it's not because Rosslie must be considered too.'

'And Lady Maxwell?'

He did not reply at once. Then: 'Jilly and I must take equal blame for what happened. I thought I loved her once but I was mistaken. I'll do what I can for Rosslie so she will be safe here, and she has her sons.' He added in a murmur. 'As I have mine.'

It was the most revealing he had ever been, and she wished she had something to offer him in return. 'So what *can* you do? For Rosslie, I mean, and Duncan.'

'Sell some land, flog some paintings, find some other scheme he can get involved in so that Rosslie survives, then hope his sweetheart will have him and that I can go back to Severn. I don't yet know how I'll achieve this, and I worry that when I relinquish the reins, he'll run amok.'

A fallen tree lay parallel to the river and he gestured to her to sit there beside him. 'Are you terribly shocked?' he asked, pulling out a cigarette. She shook her head. 'Then you've very loose moral standards, Eva Bayne. You *should* be shocked – it was an abominable way to behave. People talk of the self-obsession of the elderly but the young are much worse. So wrapped up in their own wants and needs, they never consider the consequences, until they come back to bite.'

'It was during wartime.'

'Don't make excuses for me, Eva.'

'You were convalescing here?'

He nodded, blowing smoke to one side. 'But functioning on all cylinders by then.'

'You were what, twenty-two, twenty-three—'

'Old enough to know better.'

'Traumatised by St Valéry—'

'Like I said. No excuses.'

'And Jilly was thirty-something.'

He smoked jerkily, his jaw tense. 'It takes two, Eva. Jilly saved my sanity, you know, and perhaps my life. I'd have blown my brains out one dark night, had she not hidden the bullets for my revolver.'

She stared at him, appalled, but his profile gave nothing away. 'And yet, even so, knowing the state you were in, she seduced you.'

He shook his head. 'I was planning to seduce *her* if she hadn't, she was just quicker off the mark. Unbridled lust on my part. Not sure about her but we were seeking consolation, both of us, and a respite from reality, and strayed way beyond the boundaries.' He inhaled deeply, releasing the smoke though his nose almost angrily. 'Don't waste your sympathy on Jilly or me, Eva. Duncan's the victim here. And Pa too, I suppose.'

'Your father knew!'

'Oh, yes.' He bent to stub out the cigarette and lit another. 'Banished me beyond his kingdom like some storybook despot, and who could blame the man! Poor old Duncan must have been an affront every time he looked at him, and Jilly . . . well, Jilly . . . Pa was mad to have married her, of course, but he deserved better; between us we destroyed any chance he had of happiness. I can't put that right now, and it's a pain I have to bear.'

She could find nothing to say and so remained silent. The only sound was of the river, and the wind soughing gently through the trees along the banks. After a little while she said, 'If you find a way through for Rosslie, will you then be able to forgive yourself?'

'Who knows?'

'And return to Ross?'

His face lit up. 'God, I hope so. Ross has been my salvation.' He looked at her directly then, coming back into the moment, and gave a little smile. 'I once found that Jilly had a way of drawing out a man, but seems you have the same talent, my dear; I can think of no other person I could trust with all this.'

She felt absurdly flattered. 'I'm glad you did.'

'I don't *deserve* forgiveness, Eva, but I do need to find what redemption I can. Back then I believed I was in love with Jilly and that I despised my father – regular old Oedipus I became – I was wrong on both counts and I realise now that as much as anything I regretted forfeiting this.' The sweep of his arm included the river, the old parkland and the house, his cigarette leaving a little trail of smoke in the air. 'Not because I ever wanted to *possess* it, I'd always seen it as Andy's, but because it was part of my being and I wanted it to stay that way. And the devil is, I still do. It's in my blood. I'd forgotten . . .'

The heron chose that moment to fly back upstream, catching the morning sun on its light under-feathers, completing an already idyllic scene. 'You can keep coming back here, surely, even with Duncan in control.'

'I could, but I doubt he'd like that.' He paused a moment. 'I almost wish I could come clean with him and build things up from a point of honesty, but there's too great a risk of further harm.'

They sat in silence while he finished his smoke and then, just as he had done in Severn, he picked up a handful of pebbles and began tossing them into the river. 'I've been trying to come to terms with what happened here for years, you know, searching for lost time among the twists and turns of fortune. It's hardly a profitable pastime but perhaps you're unaware of the part you played in it.'

'The part *I* played?' She turned to him but he was focused on his pebble throwing.

'I used to watch you, the doctor's kid, fish out of water, never quite managing to fit in, and yet so self-contained and inquisitive. And when you found yourself alone one day with a very dubious character who was drunk and bleeding, potentially dangerous, you took it upon yourself to bind up his wounds and wash his face and hands, cleansing him of sin. I was at one of the lowest moments of my life that day – Ross's mother was dead, I was drinking far too much, Ross was grieving, I knew he was and could do nothing for him, the outport was tearing itself apart, everything was collapsing around me again. And then I got into a fight that day and was brought to the surgery . . .' He turned to her again. 'You might not even remember and couldn't possibly know what that moment meant to me – you were just a child, quite unaware that your innocent kindness had completely unmanned me . . .'

'I do remember.' The sight of his tears trickling down his haggard face was one that would never leave her.

'It felt like absolution. I was cleansed, you told me, and I began to hope then that redemption might just be possible.' Another pebble was tossed. 'When I woke and found you gone, replaced by your equally well-intentioned father who finished patching me up, I decided I would try and remain "clean" and see if I couldn't come about. It was too late, of course, in every way. By then I'd built myself a reputation that meant that no one would take anything I said seriously and resettlement was already a lost cause. Perhaps I was too . . .' He paused again and she thought that he would never continue. 'And then came the day when you were lost and I found you and they thought I'd *harmed* you . . . and it seemed then that the fates were laughing at me, conspiring, twisting the screw and showing me that redemption would never be mine. I was forever damned . . .' He paused again as if the unburdening had drained him. 'And then, damned if you didn't turn up *again*, bringing me another chance to put things right.' She hardly dared to breathe, not wanting to stop the flow. Nemesis, he had called her. 'I *have* to get things right this time, Eva, or I'll never know peace.'

CHAPTER 30

Tam appeared to have exhausted his confidences and after a moment he rose, offering Eva his arm again. She tucked her hand into the crook of his elbow and they walked back to the house, neither feeling the need to speak. It had been hard listening as he bared his soul, and she could find no words with which to respond – but she had been touched, and drawn closer to this troubled man.

They were met on the terrace by Jilly, who must have been watching out for them. 'Eva,' she said, in carefully neutral tones. 'A woman's been trying to reach you. Said her name was Janine and that she used to work with you, although apparently this is a personal matter. She'd like you to call her at home before she leaves for work. Use the phone in the office, if you like, it's quieter in there.'

Janine? Eva went hot.

Mallory.

She went at once, dialled the number on the pad, and listened. 'Look, I'm putting my job on the line for you here,' Janine said, as Eva sat there reeling when she'd finished. 'The man is pure poison. I saw the copy, all marked up, and I felt I had to warn you. Too late to stop it, I'm afraid – it'll be in the weekend supplement, front page and more inside.'

Eva's heart began to thud. She felt frantic, and sick.

The man had done his worst . . . It had taken an extraordinary bit of sleuthing to discover what had happened at Heart's Repose, but this was where David excelled. 'He must have started digging the day you walked out of the office and he's been on the phone ever since, firing up all his contacts, including some in Canada, and got them digging too.' The persistent Canadian was now explained, and from what Janine told her every salacious detail of Tam's life was to be laid bare. He was presented as an unstable maverick, a drunken, brawling troublemaker who had seduced a native woman and then lived with her in squalor. Gold-dust copy and the story would spread like wildfire! The existence of Ross – *the baronet's secret shame* – was gleefully revealed, provoking a wholly spurious debate over succession at Rosslie, which would be ruinous to Duncan's plans and destroy any hope Tam might have of establishing trust between them. But that was just the start: Janine outlined the lurid account of his arrest, describing how Eva had been found, bruised and feverish, naked in his bed.

Someone from Heart's Repose had been settling scores.

'When I read that part,' Janine said, 'I knew I had to tell you.'

'But all the charges were *dropped* – my father went—'

'That was mentioned, briefly,' and only, from what Janine described, after the whole business had been maliciously skewed to present Tam in the very worst of lights. 'And the fact that it was you who recognised the photograph and tracked him down has triggered speculation, which frankly beggars belief!'

Eva put down the receiver and sat frozen in a blind panic, quite unable to think. *Watch his back,* Ross McLeod had told her and she bit her lip remembering what else he said. *Eva Bayne only ever brought trouble.* If David had contacts in Canada, the press might well turn up at the boatyard asking questions. It would be the middle of the night in Newfoundland, but ought she to warn him?

Experience had taught her, though, that Ross McLeod could deal with intrusive hacks.

Besides, it was too late, there was nothing he could do, and she must focus her mind on Tam and how he could be protected. This would destroy him! Her press release looked pitiful now, a bent straw, and it would do more harm than good – they'd be forced onto the back foot, left to counter the trumped-up accusations of a howling pack. She shut her eyes, quailing at the thought. And in a moment she was going to have to go through to where Tam was eating his breakfast and tell him that Nemesis had shapeshifted into David Mallory, armed with whip and dagger, ready for the final reckoning.

And there was nothing she could do to prevent him—

Unless . . . She stopped, struck by a sudden thought. She dismissed it. But it returned, forcefully, and set her pulse racing again. She stared fixedly ahead, trying to get a grip and consider the idea dispassionately. But could she pull it off? And would it work? She drummed her fingers on the desk, thinking furiously. It might. Just possibly, it might . . . But was there time? She picked up a pen and began scribbling, jotting down thoughts, words, crossing them out, scribbling again, biting the end of the pen, her knee jigging up and down in sudden animation. Two days. Was there time? It was tight, but just, maybe just . . . She ripped the sheet off the pad, stuffed it into her pocket and made for the door, stopped, took a deep breath, then went to find Tam.

'Of course, you must go.' Sunlight was shafting through the windows onto the breakfast table where he sat, a newspaper spread in front of him, and he looked back at her with concern.

'She sounded terrible on the phone. I'd like to go at once if that's all right. I'll stay the night at the flat. I need to pick up some stuff anyway and I can circulate the press release from there.'

'Have some breakfast first.'

'I'll head off, I think.'

'Right.' He continued to study her. 'Sort yourself out and come back when you can.'

Keith was there too, finishing his second breakfast. 'You can avoid the press if you go through Carter's pig farm,' he said. 'It's a bad track but you can slip out that way and join the main road beyond where the mob's parked up. I'll come with you, if you like, and set you on the way.'

She nodded her thanks. Tam had put the newspaper aside and was looking at her in a disconcertingly sharp way. 'There's nothing else wrong, is there?'

'No, no. Just that. Janine. We . . . we're close, that's all.' She turned back to Keith, avoiding Tam's eyes. 'Could we leave at once?' She headed upstairs, scooped up her bag and coat, and came back down to find Tam waiting for her at the bottom of the stairs.

'Quite sure about that, Eva?' he said. 'Nothing else?'

'No! Really.'

She slipped past him. 'Not Mallory, is it?' he called after her. 'You worked with this woman, Jilly said?'

Oh Lord, he forgot nothing.

'I got to know her there, yes.'

Keith emerged from the library. 'Ready when you are.'

'Must go.' She turned and fled down the corridor, Keith on her heels, knowing that Tam's eyes, curious and unconvinced, were following her.

She drove through the pig farm and onto the main road without incident. Having dropped off Keith and waved her thanks, she then drove fast towards Glasgow, rehearsing in her mind the words she might use, the phrases, the angles, the story she would tell . . . Her experience in writing for the press was limited and this would be her biggest ever challenge, and never had the stakes been higher. A scoop? The thought made her stomach churn. Was that what Tam would think? *I can think of no other person I could trust with all this.* Just that morning he had used those words and she braked hard as a bus pulled out ahead of her, pushing them from her mind. So she *must* get this right; everything depended on that: right style, right tone, right message. It must be absolutely strictly truthful, but over the years she had learned that there were many ways of telling the truth and her goal must be to reverse Mallory's spin. It would take her all day to pull it together but first she had to convince the only editor she knew who would entertain her crazy idea.

She made the phone call from her flat, still wearing her coat.

'It can't be done,' he said, having heard her out. 'Not in that time frame.'

'It can. You know it can. If there was a bomb blast in Glasgow today, you'd make it happen. I'll start drafting it now and bring it round. Look, this is going to be big, Larry, really big. You don't want to miss it.'

'How do you know about Mallory's article?'

'A reliable source.' He gave a hollow laugh. 'A very reliable source – trust me, Larry. Look, he must be dropping hints, spreading it about, whipping them all up. Ask around. There's press lowlife camped outside the gates of Rosslie already – they must know something's about to break. I'm offering this to you on a plate, an exclusive, which has the added advantage of being the *truth*, not a pack of spiteful innuendo. I *know* the man, and it's my story too! Please, Larry, *please*. You'll absolutely kick yourself if you don't.'

There was silence on the other end of the line. Then, 'Stay there.' He hung up.

She paced the floor, coat still on, and it was ten agonising minutes before the phone rang. 'OK, Eva. Get yourself round here.'

They worked late into the night, coffee-fuelled and intense. Before leaving the flat she'd scooped up the photographs she'd taken of Heart's Repose: the solitary figure of Don Morris sat fishing on the sagging stage; the church with its roof sinking into the forest as the trees reclaimed the land; the pile of charred timbers where Tam's cabin once stood. He might not use them but at least he had the option. She made the medal her starting point, modifying Tam's cynical discard to one of loss (not quite true) a further tweak allowing her to grasp the significance of the medal having spoken to the schoolteacher (almost true) then followed events exactly as she knew them, with the gaps filled by what Ross and Tam had told her.

She moved next to the auction, David's article and her recognition of Tam as the missing war hero, and then on to the hunt to find him among the outports of Newfoundland. That part was pretty straightforward, the backstory less easy to convey, but the library research she had done before Tam had arrived from Canada was now invaluable and she summarised for Larry his clifftop heroics at St Valéry, the bullets that had shattered his leg as he'd been pulled off the beach, his recovery, his brother's heroic death and, finally, the deeds at El Alamein, which had earned him the VC – all of it achieved at a terrible personal cost.

'He was traumatised by conflict – that's why he vanished.' Or at least that was what they must tell the readers; revealing the real reason was unthinkable.

'Do you *know* that?' Larry asked.

She nodded. 'I saw what had become of him. He was drinking heavily when I met him, a real mess. Classic army-veteran stuff.'

'Wait.' He lifted his head to consider. 'It's topical. There was a splash in some recent psychiatry publication. Post-traumatic stress – I'll check it out. OK, good angle. Go on.'

'Then the woman he was living with got TB and—'

'His wife?'

'Not married.'

'Hmm. OK. You sure?'

'Yes, and any suggestion otherwise would be explosive.'

He considered again, then saw what she meant. 'Point taken. Just trying to keep the man respectable! Now, go back to his campaigning on this resettlement programme – that's topical too. Over-fishing, concerns about cod decline, community break-up and so forth.'

'Could we link it to old land evictions here? Bribing folk with promises instead of driving them off? Carrot versus stick.'

He listened to her argument. 'Complicated, but we could try. Cabin set fire to, you said, like the roofs burned off in the clearances. Maybe . . . And then we finish by curving back to little orphan Annie lost on the rocks, in the fog, foot stuck, wail, wail, wail, tide coming in, tug at heartstrings.'

She looked at him and swallowed hard, thinking how little suited she was to this profession. Why had it taken her this long to find out? 'But for Archie Maxwell I'd have died that night, Larry, and yet they *pilloried* him for it. And it was my *father*, a doctor, a well-respected man, who told them it was nonsense and got the charges dropped.'

Larry was scribbling as she spoke. 'Shook his hand, clasped him to his bosom, wept on his shoulder?'

She frowned at him. 'I wasn't there. I was recovering from pneumonia.'

They haggled over wording late into the night, then he went through her photographs, grimacing at the quality. 'Grainy images work well, though, they look intriguing. I'll see what the lads say. Soooo!' He twisted his shoulders, easing the tension from them. 'We done?'

She nodded. 'Can you do it in time?'

He grinned back at her. 'Oh yes. This'll be rolling off the presses right alongside Mallory's.' He gave her a shrewd look. 'It won't diffuse the situation, you know, if anything it'll whip up interest. You do realise this?'

She nodded, miserable to the core. 'I know. But he would never tell the real story himself. He's not that sort of man, and Mallory's article will crucify him if it stands alone. I *have* to tell it for him.'

'Would he do an interview?'

'Don't ask him! And I doubt that he would. But . . . but I don't expect to have a job after Sunday so you'll have to decide yourself whether to approach him.'

She went back to her flat and slept the sleep of the exhausted for a few hours, then rose feeling no better than before, resigned now to what would happen. There was little point in taking more clothes to Rosslie but she packed some anyway, had a shower and drove slowly back, feeling wretched to the core. He would see this as an unforgivable betrayal; but would he give her a chance to explain?

She returned to Rosslie through the pig farm, parked between the Jaguar and the Land Rover, and entered the house through the back door. It was only as she'd driven the last few miles that she'd put her mind to considering the other story she was going to have to tell. Would she give Janine some ghastly illness with a grim prognosis, or a relationship crisis? Or both? Perhaps an illness would be more convincing and she could quite reasonably be uncertain as to details. Hopefully she could avoid meeting Tam until she had it fine-tuned.

This, however, was not to be. He was crossing the hall as she came in from the back. 'Eva! Restored to us. How was your friend?'

'Not good.' She did her best, holding those intelligent eyes for as long as she could before turning away. 'The outlook for her could be grim.'

'How terribly worrying. You look as if you've not slept.'

'I hardly did. Just a few hours.'

He pulled a sympathetic face. 'And Janine? Did she sleep?'

He was blocking her way so she had no option but to respond. 'I'm not sure. I haven't spoken to her this morning. I believe she has quite a lot of pain . . .'

What an odd question, but he moved and fell into step beside her. 'And yet she made it into work, the brave soul, and I must say she sounded pretty chipper when I spoke to her.' Her stomach lurched and she shot him a glance. 'Painkillers doing their stuff, I expect.'

'Why . . . why did you want to speak to her?'

'Oh, I didn't, I just wanted to see if maybe you had gone into the office this morning. I didn't say who I was for obvious reasons but she just confirmed that you no longer worked there.'

'But why . . . why would I go into the office?' Desperately she tried to think, and normalise her responses.

He simply smiled by way of reply and headed off into the library, remarking, 'You've brought some more clothes, I see, which was wise as this could be a long siege.' He paused at the door. 'Press release went in all right?'

'What? Oh yes.'

'Tomorrow's papers?'

'Maybe, or could be early next week.'

'I'm sure you did your best.'

CHAPTER 31

She was lying, very obviously lying. And wasn't very good at it! Archie carried on into the library and threw himself into the armchair beside the fire. The question was why? She'd looked ghastly yesterday after that phone call, and even worse today, but she clearly wasn't going to confide in him. Perhaps, there was, after all, a young man backstage somewhere and things had taken a bad turn.

He rather hoped he was wrong, though, and that there wasn't.

She'd looked quite terrified just now, he thought, staring into the fire searching for a plausible explanation. The Janine connection brought this Mallory character into the frame and just for a moment he felt a flicker of unease. Was it possible the man had some sort of hold over her? Unburdening to Eva yesterday had been cathartic, but perhaps he'd said too much . . . And yet she was the one person he knew he could trust. Apart from Ross.

While she'd been away he'd bowed to pressure from Jilly and called the police to see if anything could be done to thin the ranks of photographers amassing at the gate, harassing staff and estate workers, and had been cynically amused by their deferential response. 'I'll send a couple of men round at once, Sir Archibald. Very tiresome for you, sir. We'll find some offence, I'm sure, even if it is only causing a hazard to traffic, and I'll arrange a regular patrol for a day or two, sir. I'm sorry you've been troubled.'

'There, I told you you'd got clout,' Jilly had said.

He smiled at the thought. Clout! A handle to his name and the obsequious still bowed and scraped. What a world! It was strange, though, this sudden gathering and perhaps he should be more worried, but he had more immediate and vexing concerns. Following a rather chilly exchange, he and Duncan had agreed to meet again to look at the route that the upgraded road might take, and talk about costs in the context of Duncan's wider business plan. And that meeting, Tam decided, was when he'd have to grasp the nettle and tell Duncan that he simply couldn't support the scheme. He wasn't looking forward to it one bit, and it would be hard for Duncan to accept but he must be told. There *must* be other ways to keep the estate viable and pay off the debts. He'd make it clear to Duncan that he'd work with him for as long as it took, and then return to Severn. And to Ross.

Keith had finally cornered him last night and not held back on his views of the whole enterprise which largely chimed with Archie's but he'd just listened and thanked him. For the time being Duncan was his main concern.

And Eva.

Eva could see no way of evading dinner that evening without fuelling Tam's suspicions. She sat opposite him, picking at her food, and was conscious of his frequent glances although no one else seemed to notice her silence. Jilly was still incensed about the siege they were under and informed the table that, following Tam's intervention, the police had promised to help clear the paparazzi. 'I knew they would if we asked. Things should be back to normal tomorrow—'

'That's not what they promised, Jilly.'

Jilly continued her complaint so Eva was able to let her mind go back over what she and Larry had written, hoping against hope that the plan didn't backfire. 'The phone had to be off the hook entirely today,' Jilly was saying. 'Such a ridiculous fuss! We had calls from Europe, from New York and more from Canada.' Had they overplayed the heroics? Eva wondered. 'Last night there was one from a phone box, would you believe, an extremely rude man who said he was coming over, determined to get an interview, but he ran out of change. It was almost laughable . . .' Or underplayed the false accusations? In the cold light of day she was beginning to lose her nerve.

'I hope they've all gone before Susie comes back,' Keith replied, spearing a potato. 'I don't want her driving straight into all that lot.'

'Tell her to use the Carter's route.'

'Not sure the Escort's suspension is up to it. Eva's Fiat nearly vanished down one of those potholes, didn't it?'

She failed to notice the ensuing silence.

'Eva?'

Tam's voice jolted her back to attention. 'Sorry. What did you say?'

'I didn't. But Keith remarked that the Fiat found the pig-farm route challenging.'

She gave a brittle smile. 'The Fiat finds most things challenging.'

Tam's gaze seemed to hover on her before he returned to his beef and the conversation moved on. She started to pay more attention and a moment later he addressed her again. 'Tomorrow morning I'd like you to be at the discussion Duncan and I are going to have about roads and so forth. I want you to take some notes.'

'Yes, of course.'

Duncan looked up. 'That sounds rather formal. I only want to show you the route and outline the costs.'

'Even so, a record of any decisions is always useful and if Eva makes notes I can focus on what you're telling me. We said nine, I think, in the estate office.' He picked up his glass and surveyed the table. 'And on the wider subject of salmon, I understand the sport of angling is now the preserve of the well-monied classes and read about the sums they'll pay for the privilege of standing up to their oxters in freezing water. Astonishing! Since we have an excellent trout stream running right through the estate I wondered if you've considered selling beats along its course?'

Duncan shook his head. 'Folk like that need somewhere decent to stay.'

'True.'

'And the hotels close by aren't up to much.'

Archie reached for the mustard. 'There's this place, of course.'

The Maxwells looked appalled; even the portraits seemed to stiffen. 'You can't be serious!' Jilly said.

Tam regarded her wryly. 'Where's that wartime spirit, eh, Jilly? You rose to the occasion once before.'

She put down her knife and fork. 'Are you telling me we're reduced to taking paying guests?'

'You're pretty damned close, I'd say, looking at the books.'

'Half the bedrooms are barely habitable. And where would people eat?'

'Here. You've a dozen or more chairs, a table the size of a rugby pitch, cupboards full of ancient dinner services and glasses for every sort of wine and spirit under the sun – unless you spent the last forty years smashing them – and there's more fancy paraphernalia gathering dust somewhere.' He paused. 'You've got all the props, you know – you just need to dress the set, bite your lip and swallow your pride. Ex-pats with Scottish heritage would pay a fortune to stay in a place like this, even in its faded glory.'

Eva watched Jilly's face. Her expression shifted from appalled to thoughtful as she raised her glass. 'They might, I suppose, if the baronet was their gracious host.'

He rumbled her straight away. 'Not part of the package, I'm afraid. They'll have to make do with the dowager, and her sons.'

Eva saw Duncan register that remark but he too shook his head. 'I doubt the income would offset the costs required to get things into shape.'

Tam took another mouthful and chewed, surveying his newfound family with an amused expression. 'Not right away, but you could build up the business and write off the losses while you did. And if you've not been out on the hills yourselves then a deer cull must be overdue, or take tweedy types onto the moors to bang away at game birds. You've lots to offer, you know.'

'Sounds horrendous,' Keith remarked and Tam gave him a dry look.

'Alternatively you could put up the rent from the cottages. How much are you currently paying for Kenny's cottage, Keith? You and your lady friend.'

Keith's jaw dropped. 'As in *rent*?' Tam nodded. 'We don't actually pay anything but we did the place up ourselves, Susie and me, and cover all the running costs. It was more or less derelict when we took over.'

'Excellent. Then a reduced rent seems appropriate, maybe taking into account the second breakfast and free dinners routine, or the two of you could put those same talents into restoring the bedrooms or the laundry buildings or other empty cottages around the estate. Rent them out to locals or advertise them as holiday cottages. There was a man living above the stables during the war – you'd have liked him, Keith – so presumably that could be made habitable again. Get ambitious, for God's sake, and restore Aber Rosslie. Now there's a thought! There must be five or six dwellings worth saving. Lovely spot, close to the water, slipway for boats, yacht moorings, even. Sea-angling. Run charters!' Eva looked across at Tam; he'd not been wasting his time while she had been away, he'd been thinking. 'Or take on an apprentice, Keith. You've a talent worth developing beyond salad bowls and stools. My son Ross built up his skills from nowhere and now has a profitable boat-building business.' Duncan seemed to stiffen at the mention of Ross. 'Talk to him, Keith – you're already ahead of the game. Put your talents to work! The salmon farm needn't be the only string to Rosslie's bow.'

Duncan's eyes had become fixed on Tam. 'It's the one that'll make us real money, though, and spare us hordes of Hooray Henrys cluttering up the place.'

Tam shrugged. 'Up to you, of course, once we've dug ourselves out of this hole. Maybe the land could be better used as well – you said Pa had let things atrophy. Talk to the tenants, Duncan. Get them on board – they might have ideas. Open a farm shop, sell produce from the walled garden – Jilly, you've got the magic touch and you can't possibly consume it all yourselves. Or supply the local shops. Go organic. Plant kale, ghastly stuff but I'm told it's the big thing.' Tam surveyed them again then turned back to Duncan. 'And on the subject of land, I dropped in at Kincaird's farm today. I'd never met Jim Kincaird but I knew his father very well. We lost him at St Valéry.' He stopped to clear his throat. 'Jim's a dead ringer of his father, it was quite unnerving, but he's under the impression that his tenancy is up for review? Some misunderstanding, I assured him.'

Duncan shook his head. 'No misunderstanding. It is.'

'Why so?'

'Yes, why?' Keith chimed in. 'Jim mentioned it to me the other day. He was fretting and I told him not to worry.'

'And what business of yours was it to tell him anything?' Duncan snapped.

'Quite right, none at all,' Tam interjected swiftly. 'What's the problem?'

Keith failed to take the hint. 'Duncan gave him a bollocking because he contacted Wild Seas about the salmon farm. He shares my views about it, but you can't throw him off because—'

Duncan's face went puce. 'I can, or at least I could until—' He broke off and Eva saw his jaw tense. 'But either way, you've no right to meddle whenever it suits your flaky principles.'

'For goodness' sake, you two,' Jilly protested, putting up her hands. 'Not this again! Keith, stop baiting your brother and, Duncan, you can surely leave all this to Archie to sort out now.'

Duncan went white and Eva saw Tam's face grow grim as the quarrel escalated. Jilly's contribution had hardly helped and Duncan's hand was visibly shaking as he put down his glass. 'I can, can I? Thank you, Mama. Let's see, shall we? Although Archie's right about one thing. Keith's a bloody freeloader and Wild Seas are a bunch of ignorant, pig-headed—'

'Hardly *ignorant*, there are several—'

'Enough!' Tam's voice silenced them. 'This is neither edifying nor useful. I know nothing of Wild Seas so I suspend judgement but what I do recognise is that Duncan's been doing a thankless job holding things together in very difficult circumstances. Stop sniping at each other, it's most unhelpful. The question of Kincaird's tenancy can wait until we meet tomorrow, Duncan. I'm sorry I raised it.' He gestured to the bottle. 'For God's sake fill up your glasses and cool your tempers. This is too good a wine to quarrel over.'

CHAPTER 32

Everyone dispersed as soon as dinner was finished and Eva crept away, not wanting to be waylaid by Tam, especially Tam in his current mood. She'd fall at the first assault if he cornered her. Later she glimpsed him from her window, strolling back towards the house, his limp more pronounced than usual; things were starting to take their toll. He'd clearly not enjoyed the quarrel at the dinner table and she'd seen him register how rapidly Duncan's temper had flared, and how his hand had shook. Matters were coming to a head.

She stood watching him, observing him unseen as he approached the house. A day ago she would have gone down to him and he might have felt able to share the load a little but that was out of the question now. She shrank back as he lifted his head but it was Jillian Maxwell who had caught his attention, and Eva watched as she came down the steps from the terrace and joined him. They stood there, talking, and their body language was clear. Tam was half turned away from Jillian, dismissing whatever it was she was saying. She was persistent, though, gesturing repeatedly back towards the house, trying to carry her point, but Tam kept shaking his head until she gave up and they walked slowly back to the house, still deep in conversation.

She crawled into bed and lay awake, a sickening anxiety growing in her. If the atmosphere was bad now, how much worse would it be when Mallory's article appeared? Would hers do anything to defuse it or had she been naïve to think it would? Perhaps she should have just told Tam and let him deal with it.

But there again, it was her story too.

★ ★ ★

She was in the estate office before the others next morning, clearing space for the estate maps to be spread out. The phone receiver was still off the hook and she decided to leave it that way for now. Given what was about to be unleashed on them, it would probably remain off for some time.

Tam and Duncan came in together at nine, chatting almost companionably. Duncan looked more in control today and had a rolled map under his arm, which he proceeded to spread out, weighting down the corners. 'It's actually a very direct route once you think about it, part of an old track to Aber Rosslie, I believe. Some trees will have to come down and the little bridge strengthened, but it's by far the least costly option. Starting here . . .' He picked up a pencil and began to trace the route.

'Which trees?'

'That stand of old oak. They're ready to be managed down anyway; they shed big branches with every storm, they'll hit someone one day.' Tam grunted and leaned closer, following the line of the pencil. 'And losing them allows us to continue along from the main access road straight down the slope, following what's now a track along the valley bottom, which bring us almost directly—'

'Hang on. Isn't that Kincaird's land?'

'It is. And that's part of the issue—'

'But surely that's the route up to their farm buildings?' He looked up at Duncan.

He nodded, tight-lipped. 'Just to expand on what was said last night and speaking frankly – and not for minuting.' Tam waved at Eva to desist. 'Kincaird's become something of a troublemaker. He's been against the salmon project from the start, encouraging dissent on the estate and feeding information to that wretched bunch of activists at Wild Seas. I had to give him a caution – *not* a bollocking – as he simply can't bad-mouth the project under the terms of the tenancy agreement. It's true that their lease comes up for renewal next year but we're not legally obliged to renew, we just have to give him statuary notice. I hinted to him that we're considering other options to give them a bit more time to plan a move, but the deadline for renewal is a fixed one and it's coming up. If we *don't* renew, that solves the question of access and the whole troublemaking issue in one go.' Eva was watching Tam's face and Duncan would have done well to do the same, but his eyes were fixed on the map and he pressed on, heedless of the brewing storm. 'And then, further down the line, when we have the expansion complete, those farm outbuildings could be transformed into a smokery and packing place, and we could rent the farmhouse to the fish-farm manager. It'd be ideal, right on this new route to the estuary and—'

'Duncan.' Tam's voice was hoarse as if he was straining to remain civil. 'I have to stop you there. We'll not be throwing the Kincairds off their farm – there need be no more discussion.' Duncan stared at him. 'Fergus Kincaird was my best friend. I left him dangling from his ankle on a rope off the cliffs at St Valéry, providing target practice by German snipers, shouting at me to run on. He died saving my life and countless others. You can't begin to understand, I know that, but what you suggest is absolutely and categorically out of the question.'

Duncan's face darkened. 'You said you wouldn't interfere.'

'On this I must. I'll sell land, *our* land, before—'

'You can't sell *land*, for God's sake!'

'Trust me, I can. I'll sell every damn painting, every stick of furniture before I evict anyone.' Eva saw Tam take a breath before weighing in. 'And I have to say, Duncan, I've concerns about the project myself. I feel—'

Duncan's temple began to pulse. 'I saw Keith bending your ear—'

'Keith has nothing whatsoever to do with my views. Look, let's put our heads together and explore some of those ideas I raised last night.'

'It's Kincaird then. He's been a pain in the arse from the start.'

'That's as maybe, but I told him yesterday his lease would be renewed, on the same terms as—'

Duncan went puce then white. 'You did *what*!'

'I said we'd get the papers signed as soon as could be arranged.'

And so the conflagration took off as conflagrations will when the fuel is tinder-dry. Duncan thumped the table, his eyes flashing with fury. 'You've no right—'

'I know this is hard for you, Duncan, but I've every right.' She saw him struggling to hold himself back. 'And in this case—'

Duncan was trembling, rapidly losing control. 'In *this* case, *and* in the case of the expansion I've worked on for months—'

'I really do understand but . . .' Tam seemed suddenly to recall her presence. 'Eva, give us ten minutes, would you? Make coffee, perhaps. Yes, bring us all coffee in ten minutes or so.'

She hurried away with the sound of the row intensifying behind her, Duncan's voice impassioned and furious, 'I *knew* this would happen once you got here,' and then Tam's more measured but implacable response.

She almost collided with Keith in the hall. 'What on earth's going on?'

'Don't ask,' she said, making for the kitchen, 'and don't go in there, whatever you do.'

He followed her downstairs. 'What sparked them off?'

'Roads and farms, I can't say more.'

'More than enough. And Duncan turns nasty if he's crossed. Pa was the same.'

'I don't think it'll come to blows.'

Keith leaned against the counter and blew out his cheeks. 'Let's hope not. He's been strung out like piano wire for weeks now, ever since he discovered that Archie was alive.' He grimaced at her expression. 'Sorry, but after all this time we'd rather assumed he wasn't. Delighted to be wrong, of course, and I must say I rather like him though I can see it's a bit of a blow for Duncan. He was pressing ahead with things, you see, until Pa died, and then the investors got queasy . . .' He opened the fridge, muttering, 'I do rather wonder where it'll end.' He took out a lump of cheese and cut himself a chunk. 'Apparently it *has* come to blows down at the gates, though. One dogged soul tried to scale the walls just as the police patrol was passing by. Carter saw him swing a punch at one of the constables who tried to pull him off. Got himself arrested and hauled off so that's one less to worry about! I've told Susie to stay away for a day or two until things have settled down.'

As if in mockery of that notion there was the sound of a door being slammed followed by heavy footfall across the hall. One of them had had enough, and Eva reckoned slamming doors wasn't Tam's style.

'Longer if necessary,' Keith added, raising his eyes.

They waited but there were no more sounds from above. 'He said ten minutes, then bring in coffee,' Eva said. 'Has it been ten minutes, do you think?'

'It hardly matters now.'

She waited a couple more then took up a tray with just two mugs as Tam must know that the slam had reverberated through the house. She tapped on the door and entered to find him sitting where she'd left him, his head in his hands, a picture of despair. He lifted it as she came in, and glanced at the tray.

'Eva. Quite right. Just thee and me. Duncan's gone.'

'I heard.' The map still occupied the table and she cleared a space beside it and set down the tray. She pulled up a chair and sat, looking at him with concern. 'It was bound to erupt, Tam, if not over this, then something else.'

'Things can't really get much worse, can they?' He sat back with a shaky laugh. 'I feel for him, I really do, but I could no more evict Fergus's son than fly. But how can he begin to understand the baggage I carry?' Silently she passed him a mug. 'Fergus was the very best of men, as much a brother to me as Andy.' He paused. 'You know about Andy, my older brother?' She nodded. 'He'd have been so very much better at all this than me, he'd know how to handle things. It brings it all back, the horror and the madness of it all, the godawful waste. But how can I explain that to Duncan and make him understand?'

He was looking all of his sixty-two years. 'I don't suppose you can.'

'As for this wretched fish farm of his, I can't *help* but interfere. Keith might be a tad self-righteous but he's right in what he says and I simply cannot support the idea. It's a damn shame there's animosity between Jim Kincaird and Duncan because the man had some sound ideas about land use when I spoke to him – he thinks the estate could be more profitable, says Pa let things slide. He claims that organic, sustainable farming is the way forward. I'd like to hear more, and I want Duncan to listen to him too, but what chance have I of getting those two in a room? I gather they've never got on. Fergus had a temper, I remember that, and I reckon Jim does too – and we've all had a taste of Duncan's.' He sighed, spinning his pen on the table. 'It's worth a try, I suppose. I'll call Jim and ask him to drop by because right now I can't see a way out of this wretched coil.'

Eva had begun to feel sick all over again as she sat there watching him, because things *were* about to become a great deal worse.

She came to a decision. 'Listen Tam, there's something—' But the phone chose that moment to ring and she jumped, staring at it in horror. 'Oh Lord, I did that! I put it back. Just now when I set down the tray. What should I do?'

'Answer the bloody thing!'

She reached for it. 'Rosslie House . . .' and listened. 'Yes, he's right here.' She mouthed 'police' as she passed it over and he raised an eyebrow. He listened, frowning, and then his eyes widened and, to her astonishment, his face split in a grin, that careless vagabond grin she remembered so well. 'Yes, Sergeant . . . Yes . . . I'm afraid he's absolutely right.' There was a glint in his eye though he managed to keep his tone serious. 'No . . . no, I understand. *Dreadful* way to behave . . . Can I stand bail? Well, that's very good of you but . . . Aye, well, give the officer my deepest apologies. Look, I'll come and talk to you about all this next week. No, no . . . absolutely not. I'll send a car . . . Where to?' He scribbled something on the edge of the map. 'Thank you, Sergeant. No, no apology required.'

He put down the phone, his hand resting on it a moment, then threw back his head and gave a great shout of laughter.

'Duncan?' she asked, fascinated.

She saw the tension draining from him as his eyes began to dance. 'No, no, my dear. It's the other one, the uncaged one.' He locked his hands behind his head and regarded her, the grin still hovering. 'Ross McLeod's arrival on Scottish soil has been signalled by his arrest attempting to scale the boundary wall, he punched a policeman for good measure and got himself carted off in handcuffs. Only Ross could manage such style! He's now cooling his heels in police custody but they seem prepared to let him go on account of his being my son – they wouldn't, mind you, if they knew his record! Go and collect the scoundrel, would you, Eva, and bring him home.' He pointed to the scribbled address. 'Keith will know where this is. Go now, if you will, while I find Duncan and try to calm the rage.'

CHAPTER 33

Eva left as instructed, but her heart was in her boots as she pulled into the little branch police station almost an hour later. Confronting Ross McLeod was the last thing she needed right now . . . His parting words were starkly clear in her mind: *first sign of trouble, you get in touch.* She hadn't, and she didn't imagine Ross was the sort of man to take prisoners.

She wasn't sure what to expect when she pushed open the door but it hadn't been to find him laughing and joking with an officer whose bruises suggested he'd come off the worst from their encounter. The man was sporting a black eye and a cut lip while Ross had only a bruised cheek, and laughter in his eyes.

His expression changed when he saw her, and the smile faded. 'OK. My ride's here,' he said, and another officer came out from behind the desk. Differences seemed to have been settled. Hands were shaken, apologies exchanged and airily dismissed. 'Come back and see us soon. Keep us on our toes!'

'I'll be sure to.'

'Did you have luggage?' Eva asked as they left the building together.

He slung a duffel bag over his shoulder. 'This.' They crossed to the car. 'You were supposed to keep me informed,' he said, giving her a dark look as he pulled open the door and folded himself into the front seat, tossing the bag in behind him. 'You were supposed to watch his back.'

She pulled out and joined the traffic. 'I've been doing just that, but things started moving rather fast.'

'So is that why I've had all sorts turning up at the boatyard asking questions I didn't want to answer?' She made no reply; doubtless it did. 'I tried ringing Rosslie – costing me a fortune every time – but whoever answered kept hanging up on me. I tried polite, I tried nasty, but no one would put me through to either Tam or to you.' Light dawned: the persistent, rude Canadian. Should she have guessed? 'When I said I was coming over I was told no one would be available for an interview if I did. An *interview*! Christ. I didn't want to say I was his son, not knowing how he was playing it, so I just set off for the airport,' he shot her an angry look, 'as if I didn't have a schooner to build and an overdraft busting its limit. Tried again from a call box at the airport and got the same goddam woman telling me no one was available. And then the phone went onto busy and it's been that way ever since.'

'Off the hook.'

'No kidding! So I travel all night and arrive at the gates to find the place crawling with press, and some fuckin' great chain and lock stopping me getting in. Tried going over the wall and got myself arrested. What the hell's going on?'

It was almost funny. 'I'm sorry—'

'No, don't do *sorry* again, Eva. Pull over.'

'What?'

'I said pull over. Those guys at the gate said something big's about to break. They've got some story – been shit-stirring from what I heard so you need to fill me in.'

A sign indicated a layby half a mile ahead and she pulled into it and stopped. Ross reached over and switched off the engine, then swivelled in his seat to face her. 'Right, go. From the start.'

She did her best, sketching for him the events of the past days, briefly describing Lady Maxwell and her sons. Ross listened intently, dismissed Keith and backtracked to Duncan. 'What's he been like?' She found it hard to give an impartial view but explained about the salmon farm and Tam's reservations about it, and concluded by saying much the same as she'd said to Tam. 'I think he's worried that Tam'll decide to stay.'

'And will he?'

'He says not.'

'But you think he might.'

'I didn't say that.'

He flashed her a speculative look. 'How's he doing? Is he OK?'

An impossible question. 'He's busy—'

'That's not what I asked. Is he drinking?'

'Not to excess.'

'Smoking?'

'A pack a day, I'd say.'

He stared ahead. 'Which'll kill him first?' he muttered. A large transporter hurtled past the layby, rocking the little Fiat.

'Was it bad? The drinking?' she ventured.

'Oh, it was bad all right.' He turned back to her. 'So what's kickin' off here? What's the story?'

He had to be told, or at least some of it; he'd find out soon enough. 'Someone's been doing some digging.'

He swore. 'Who?' She shrugged – ought she to tell him about Mallory? 'Don't you know or aren't you telling? Or have *you* been spillin'?'

She gaped at him. 'Are you serious?'

He returned her a grim look. 'Tam said he trusted you, though God knows why. I went along with you coming back with him because of that, then soon as he arrives here shit starts to fly. You were supposed to call me if it did, and you didn't. So, yep, I'm serious. Why didn't you call?'

She swallowed, keeping her temper in check, balancing it against the guilt. 'Things took off so suddenly. And I . . . I couldn't see what you could do.'

'Not your decision. I'd have come.'

'You're here now.'

He snorted. 'So none of this came from you, eh? You've told no one about any of it?' She looked away and it was her turn to stare out of the window. She was caught, and she knew that every second of silence condemned her. He reached over again, took her chin in his hand and turned her to face him, studying her expression, reading the answer there. '*Christ*, Eva!' His hand dropped back and his voice hardened. 'Better start talking, girl, cos we're staying here till you're done.'

And so she told him.

He listened without a word as she described Janine's phone call, what Mallory had written, her panicked reaction, then about Larry and the counterbalancing article they had drafted between them. It was a relief to put it into words, to confess, and she no longer cared what he, or Tam, thought. 'You can say what you like but I did it with the best of intentions and if it backfires then things are no worse than before.' She was shaking, angry now, daring him to judge her.

But Ross said nothing and was quiet for a long time. 'So he doesn't know what's coming down the tracks?'

'No.'

'Why didn't you tell him?'

'He'd have stopped me doing it.'

He digested that. 'And you trust this Larry guy?'

'He's one of the few editors I know with integrity.'

Another silence. 'D'ya find out why he left? Have they got hold of that too?'

She thought rapidly. Had Tam indicated that anyone besides Jillian Maxwell knew, except maybe Duncan, whose self-interest would ensure his silence. 'No. They can't possibly know.'

'But you do?' She bit her lip. 'Some woman, I guess? Usually is.' She said nothing and he snorted again. 'Bit late for keepin' secrets, don't ya think?'

'This one's not mine to tell. But from what I've heard it's not what the story's about.'

'OK. I'll find out for myself. Drive on.'

'Interrogation over?'

'Just drive, Eva.'

They drove in silence. Beside her Ross stared fixedly out of the window, giving nothing away. For a moment back there he'd looked dangerous, but now he seemed deep in thought, his brow furrowed and his eyes still stormy. Only Ross really knew how bad it had been fifteen years ago and what dragging the business up again might do to Tam. But at least now he was here to deal with the fallout. Perhaps she *should* have called him . . .

'So do I tell him about the article?' she asked.

'I'm workin' on it,' came the reply.

They continued on their way.

'You say no one here knows about the crap that happened back in Heart's Repose?' he asked.

'No.' Not yet, at any rate.

He grunted and went back to brooding. They arrived at the pig farm to find two vans parked up, off the road near the entrance. When it became clear that the Fiat was turning into the yard, two photographers leaped out and ran alongside the car, snapping cameras at the window. She accelerated away through a puddle, spattering them with mud, and Ross nodded his approval. 'Good one,' he said. 'But I still say you should've called me.'

'I wish I had.'

He said nothing more and as they approached Rosslie House she sensed him taking in its size and appearance. He made no comment, though, and she pulled into the courtyard and parked.

'So do I tell him?' she repeated.

'I'll sleep on it.' He twisted round and picked up his duffel bag from the back seat. 'We've twenty-four hours to decide.' We. He'd said *we*, which meant she didn't have to handle this all on her own any longer; the sense of relief was enormous. Ross might hate her for what she'd done, as his father undoubtedly would once her article appeared, but at least Tam now had someone else on his side. He raised an eyebrow at her. 'So we goin' in, or do we sit here all day?'

They entered the library and Tam leaped to his feet. 'Ross!' His face lit up and he gripped his son's shoulders as he examined him. 'Not sure I'd recognise you without a bruise or two, son. Arrested in less than twenty-four hours! Impressive, even for you.

Jilly, meet Ross McLeod. Shake hands nicely, Ross, then take a seat and explain why you're here.'

There were only four of them at dinner that night. Keith must have decided it was safer to eat in his cottage and Duncan had not reappeared. Ross had been given a bedroom on the other side of Eva and had come down, showered and changed but still in jeans. He seemed interested but by no means overawed by his surroundings, whistling as Tam introduced him to portraits of his ancestors on the staircase. 'I reckon I'd have taken off too,' he said, 'with them eyeballin' me every day.' Tam laughed and even Jillian smiled. He paused in front of the one of his grandfather and studied it.

'The image of Archie, don't you think?' Jilly said. 'It was painted just after we got married. They'd have been of an age.'

Ross nodded, looking back at her, but made no response. His own resemblance to the Maxwells was all the more marked as he sat opposite his father at the dining table and Tam appeared reinvigorated by his presence. The story of the phone calls, the fight and the arrest were all retold and he laughed with genuine delight. Ross grinned but then fixed him with a straight look. 'So what's the deal with those fellas at the gate?'

'I look on them as a welcoming committee.'

'They're a wretched nuisance.' Ross switched his gaze to Jilly and Eva watched him weighing her up. He flicked a questioning look in her direction, which Tam seemed to catch.

'Some better story will soon come along to draw them away,' he remarked. 'Can it be *that* interesting when a missing man turns up?' He leaned forward to refill Eva's glass, giving her a slanting look. 'But forgive me, I'd forgotten. Have you heard from your friend today, my dear? How's she bearing up?'

Eva left the three of them as soon as she could after dinner, aware of both Ross and Tam's eyes following her as she withdrew. She went up to her room but was unable to settle there, knowing that if Tam went searching for her, it'd be the first place he'd look. His question had come out of nowhere and she'd felt her face flush as she gave an unconvincing reply.

It could only be a matter of time before he cornered her.

So she headed outdoors, slipping unnoticed through the back door, and briefly contemplated taking refuge with Keith in his cottage but decided she needed to be alone to think things through. *Would* it be better to warn Tam now rather than wait for the axe to fall? Ross hadn't given an opinion in the end and she was finding the tension unbearable. She'd steeled herself to the task once before and could surely do so again – especially now that Ross was here to deal with the fallout. He might be hostile but at least he'd listened to her.

She went down to the river where, just two days ago, she had walked with Tam and he had entrusted her with all the pain of his past. Above her the rooks were returning to their roosts and she remembered his delight that first day, seeing the rookeries swaying in the tree tops. A fish jumped midstream and she watched the ripples spread, flattening as they reached the river banks; if only the consequences of past actions were as transient. She could do nothing more to change what would happen next, but tomorrow, whatever Ross might say, she'd warn Tam and give him a chance to prepare; she owed him that much.

She turned back and, as she approached the house, she saw a figure standing on the terrace. For a moment she thought it was Tam, come at last to demand answers from her, but as he stepped out of the shadow she saw it was Ross. He came swiftly down the steps and across the grass towards her.

'I've been looking for you.'

'Where's Tam?'

'Someone called by. Said he'd fixed to see him.'

Jim Kincaird? Tam must have asked him to come. 'Has Duncan turned up?'

Ross shook his head. 'Never mind Duncan. Tell me about the widow.' He gestured to a seat set back against the wall where they would be hidden from the house. 'I was expecting some old dame not a woman like . . . like *that*. What's the story?'

She prevaricated. 'How do you mean?'

'Don't play dumb. She must have been years, *decades*, younger than the old man.'

'Almost thirty years—'

'So more like Tam's age.'

'Yes.'

'So she's part of the picture, yeah?'

'She lives here; it's still her home.'

'That's not what I mean, and you know it.' He was starting to put the pieces in place and the slanting look he gave her was the mirror of his father's. 'Thirty marries sixty? She some kinda gold-digger?'

'You'll have to ask Tam.'

He grunted. 'There was the title, of course. Guess that meant something back then.'

'I've no idea.'

'Maybe still does.' He continued to consider her. 'The whole deal must have quite a pull.'

She looked back at him, and then guessed what he was thinking. 'Oh, absolutely,' she agreed. 'There's the house itself, a gem, isn't it, if a bit run down, as well as all the land right down to the sea. Quite a package, don't you think? I wonder if Jilly expected the old man to live quite so long, though? Must have good genes, you Maxwells. Tam, on the other hand, smokes a lot, and drinks a fair bit, though, so got to take that into the reckoning.' His eyes narrowed. 'There was probably more money around in Jilly's time too. I've not got a handle on that aspect yet, but I'm well placed to have the full picture by and by.'

His expression barely changed but she saw his lips twitch. 'You'd want to be sure about that.' She made to get up but he pulled her back. 'OK, but I never did get it, the two of—'

'Apparently you still don't. No one does.' She looked away then, thinking with anguish that whatever special thing there was between her and Tam, it was about to shatter.

'Can't blame 'em.' Ross sat back and stretched out his legs, abandoning his theory without apology. 'So who feels more threatened by you, d'ya reckon, the widow or the brother? Either way you could spike their guns.' She said nothing but he pressed on. 'There's the widow acting like she's got him hooked and landed, but it's Duncan you could really screw up—'

'He'll more likely feel threatened by you,' she replied. 'Especially now you've come all this way to check the place over.'

Ross acknowledged the hit but shook his head. 'I was straight with him when I took him off to the boatshed, told him I wasn't interested.'

'But now you've seen what's at stake . . . ?'

Her glare was met by a glint. 'OK, scores settled, Eva Bayne.' He might have said more but at that moment Tam himself appeared from around the side of the house, talking to a man who looked about Duncan's age. He caught sight of them, came over and introduced Jim Kincaird.

'We've been trying to find Duncan. Have either of you seen him?'

Neither of them had and, after a few exchanges, Jim took his leave and strolled off down the drive. 'Now that's a man with sound ideas,' Tam remarked, watching his retreating back. 'But where has Duncan hidden himself? I'd hoped we might reach a meeting of minds over a Scotch or two.'

Just as Eva was considering whether this might be the moment to tell Tam, with Ross here as a buffer, Jilly appeared on the terrace above them, looking down. '*There* you all are! Is Duncan with you?'

'He's not.'

'I tried phoning the Brodies but got no answer.'

'So he took off in a sulk!' Ross muttered beside her. 'What's the big deal?'

'It's complicated,' came Tam's soft reply, then: 'Stay there, Jilly, we're coming up. He'll turn up when he's ready, I suppose. Let's all have a nightcap, shall we, and wait until morning.'

He put out an arm to sweep Eva along but once inside the hall she made her excuses and slipped away. Tomorrow morning, then. For sure.

CHAPTER 34

But tomorrow proved to be too late.

She walked into breakfast next morning and straight into the eye of the storm. Tam was standing at the sideboard, a newspaper spread open before him and he swung round as she entered. His face was rigid with fury and she felt her knees buckling. 'Eva! My congratulations. An exclusive after all.' Her instinct was to turn and run but he strode forward and propelled her firmly over to the sideboard. 'Read,' he ordered, his hands heavy on her shoulders. The newspaper headline jumped before her eyes. *Unsung Hero Returns to his Own*. And below it her name, her own byline at last. 'And then be good enough to explain.'

Eva stared at the paper in disbelief. A day early, and not even the headline they'd agreed. She wished the room would swallow her up. 'It . . . it was supposed to be in tomorrow.' Jillian Maxwell had another copy of it spread on the table and was looking across at her.

'Today, tomorrow, what difference?'

Oh, *why* had she not told him! 'Because tomorrow, Tam, in the supplement, Mallory has a spread about you and everything that happened in Newfoundland. I wrote this to come out on the same day . . .' she faltered under his glare '. . . to defuse it.'

He stared at her. 'How do you know? About Mallory?'

'Janine . . .'

He expelled his breath and his jaw tightened. 'So *that* was it! And rather than do the obvious and tell me, you seized the opportunity to make your own splash. Very enterprising, my dear.'

She felt a hotness behind the eyes. 'If you think that—'

'Behold.' He gestured to the paper.

'But this is the *truth*, Tam, every word. Not a pack of lies about drink and abduction, making you out to be some depraved—' She was barely aware that Ross had appeared in the doorway and halted there. 'I *had* to do it! Left to yourself you'd *never* have contradicted what Mallory said, you'd have let everyone think it was true. You'd have taken the blows like you did before. Janine told me what Mallory had written – he'd dug deep and uncovered everything and he'd twisted it, crucifying you and swiping back at me.'

Jilly Maxwell was staring at her with a strange expression, but Tam continued to glare.

'I'd like to wring your neck,' he said.

'*Beastly Baronet returns: Maxwell's past revealed*, that's to be the headline—'

His face darkened. 'And you didn't think to warn me?'

'And what if I had? I couldn't stop it, and this was the only thing I could do.'

'You didn't think I could handle it, was that it?'

Her anger rose to match his. 'I didn't see why you *should*. And it's my story too, Tam! I'd a right to tell it, and believe me, it wasn't easy.'

For a moment she thought she'd reached him but he turned away. 'Go and pack your things, Eva. I'll pay you until the end of the month.'

'Whoa!' Ross came into the room. 'Listen to her, Tam.' His father swung back. 'Eva, stay there. She's right; this cost her! She told me what she'd written and . . .'

'*You* knew—' Tam was aghast.

'. . . and explained why she did it.'

'—and didn't see fit to tell me either!'

Ross stopped beside her. 'I was considerin' it,' he replied, unabashed. 'Timing came adrift.' Briefly he squeezed her arm as he went and poured himself a coffee, pulling the newspaper over and began to read. 'You said yourself she's smart, Tam, and I'm thinkin' this was a smart move.' He raised his cup, continuing to read while Tam stood by, speechless and unrelenting. 'She's done all right,' he remarked, reading on. 'Made a splash, sure enough, and not for the first time, eh?' He shot a look at his father. 'Bigger splash this time, but same reasoning, same thinking. Crazy on both occasions, maybe.' Briefly Eva met his eyes, astonished at his words. 'She's put herself on the line here, Tam.'

It had been Ross who'd pulled her out of trouble that day too, she thought, watching him read, but he had scowled at her then, and he wasn't scowling now. Tam looked blankly from one to the other as if they were strangers, then went to stand at the window with his back to them. The only sound in the room was of a newspaper rustling as Lady Maxwell closed the copy she was reading. 'He's right, you know, Archie, and it was brave of Eva. But gracious me, what a story! It might help. Getting your defence in first is always a sound move; it weakens the assault. And if Mallory tells lies tomorrow, we'll sue.' She pushed the paper aside, the matter closed. 'She's absolutely right about one thing, though, you'd have just taken it, absorbed the blows, hidden the scars and gone to ground again. From what she's written here you did nothing wrong. Quite the opposite in fact. You were badly used and this way she's absolved you even before the accusation's made.'

Tam went on standing there. 'Absolved me, Jilly?' he said, not turning round.

She replied in a low, almost confidential, tone. 'Of this, yes. So don't punish Eva for loving you.' He stiffened but still he didn't turn.

Eva could bear it no longer and turned blindly towards the door, Ross put out a hand to stop her but she evaded him, headed down the corridor and pushed open the door into the courtyard. She stood there gulping the cool air and fighting back tears.

Ross caught up with her. 'It's OK. You did fine.'

'He thinks I wanted a *scoop*!' she said, dashing an arm across her face.

'He's not thinkin' straight right now.'

'Can't he *see*—'

'He will.' Ross drew her over to the old water trough and sat on the edge, pulling her down beside him.

'That he could *think* it for a moment!'

'He had a shock, that's all.'

'He sees it as a betrayal.'

'Like I said—'

She glared at him. '*You* thought I was a gold-digger.'

'Can you believe it!'

That diffused her anger a little and she bit her lip. 'I *should* have warned him, I know I should. And I was going to.'

'Makes no difference now.'

'And Larry! *He* should have told me, he should have said.' Ross shrugged. '*And* he changed the headline we'd agreed on.'

'Yeah. Unsung hero, my ass! He's a fuckin' liability.' His arm came round her shoulders and gave a squeeze, and she found herself half laughing with him, half crying as the tension in her eased. Then the arm withdrew. 'But *do* you love him? Have I got it all wrong again?'

He'd stopped laughing. She looked at him and saw the question was a serious one. 'Yes, I think I do, but not how I think Jilly means, I'm not *in* love with him. I couldn't just stand by and see Mallory destroy him.'

Ross's expression, she was beginning to realise, could be every bit as opaque as his father's. 'It's Lady J who's in love with him, or was. Right?'

She looked away. 'Perhaps.'

'Knew there'd be a woman at the bottom of it,' he said, then his eyes narrowed again, 'but something's telling me there's more.'

CHAPTER 35

Rosslie, 1940

Archie

Archie slept poorly the night after the fateful picnic. But he couldn't hold the frights accountable; the turmoil was his own doing. A churning mess of guilt and confusion writhed together in his head as he tossed and turned, but as the night wore on less worthy emotions rose to the surface. Surely what had happened down beside the estuary could never be simply *forgotten*; it was a beginning not an end.

Of what he wasn't quite sure.

It was perfectly obvious to him that Jilly had made a terrible mistake by marrying Pa, and she must have recognised this. Had it been otherwise, what had happened would have been unthinkable. But how far was she prepared to accept that central fact, and what could he do to persuade her? Her attitude on the beach afterwards had been ambiguous and confusing, but it was clear that her vitality and her beauty were wasted on Pa. It could only be a matter of time before life with him became unendurable.

And so, after the war . . . It was at this point that his thinking stalled. After the war, what? He rehearsed and dismissed any number of conversations they might have, plans they might form, promises they could make once peace was restored. He racked his brain for a solution, a better outcome than simply remembering to forget. There had to be a future for them . . . But would he be able to persuade her of that? Could he convince her that, after the war, they should go off together, risk all, start again somewhere else, in another country, perhaps? Pa was what, almost sixty, he could live for another twenty, thirty years. And that thought brought a flood of guilt that he could even be having these thoughts . . .

All through the night he struggled, dipping in and out of sleep, restless and fevered, obsessed, remembering the soft touch of her, the urgency of her passion. The frights, sensing him suffering in self-imposed torment, stood themselves down and left him to it.

Had they not, he wondered as he dressed next morning, and had he called out as they assaulted him, would she have come? He almost wished it had been put to the test . . . Arriving downstairs for breakfast he was disappointed, but hardly surprised, to find that she'd already eaten and was gone. Sparing them both, he thought, and so he took his time over his eggs and toast, rehearsing again what he would say to her. They must talk, that much was clear – he needed to know how she was feeling, to reassure her if that was required, hint perhaps at where his thoughts had taken him in the night – but this morning he'd do the decent thing and give her some space. He'd spend his time fishing and then maybe, in the afternoon, there would be more deliveries to make and they could talk things through; it would now appear normal for him to accompany her . . . He raised his head as Roberts entered with a pot of coffee. 'I'll have another stint at the river this morning, I think, Roberts. I might even be able to stand long enough to cast.'

Roberts beamed at him. 'You're coming on very well, sir. Lady Jillian said she thought you might do that and left instructions for a chair to be taken down.'

'She's gone out?' he asked, reaching for the coffee pot.

'Well, yes, sir.' Roberts looked surprised. 'She said she'd told you.'

'Remind me. Where was she heading?'

'Why, to London, sir! She caught the early . . . Oh! Oh dear, never mind, sir. I'll get a cloth. Some fresh toast too, I think.'

London?

Archie set the cup back upright, his hand still shaking, as Roberts left the room.

London!

'Stupid of me,' he managed to say when the man returned with a cloth. 'I'd quite forgotten.' Roberts began mopping up the spilt coffee and, shielded by the fuss, Archie ascertained that Jilly had caught the nine o'clock train and no, she'd not said exactly when she planned to return, and no, she'd not left any specific message except to hope that the day stayed fine for the fishing.

He rose, telling Roberts not to bother about more coffee and went out onto the front terrace, his mind roaring. *London.* To Pa! But why, for God's sake? Not to confess, surely! The thought sent a cold shiver through him. A fit of sudden remorse? Unlikely given her reckless, almost brazen, behaviour yesterday. So why . . . ? A tide of fury swept over him. To leave and not warn him, not explain. She'd surely *know* how he'd feel.

Damn the woman!

He stumped down to the river, seething with anger and bewilderment, and arrived to find that John McAdam was already there. He watched resentfully as the man executed a perfect cast into midstream. So the conchie could spend the day fishing, could he, while better men fought and died for their country. 'Shan't be needing you today, McAdam,' he called out in his best officer tone as he approached and, with a mean-spirited satisfaction, watched the man reel in and set the rod aside.

'Very well,' he said. 'Although Lady Maxwell said . . .'

'Never mind what Lady Maxwell said.' He paused. 'You saw her this morning?'

'I drove her to the station.'

'In the Bentley?'

'In the dog cart.'

Archie grunted. 'Did she say when she needed collecting?' God, that he had to ask this man!

'She said she'd telephone.'

So would that be in two days' time, two weeks or what? 'Right, well, you'd better get back to work shit-shovelling or whatever else you do here. Do you report to Kenny?'

'I do. But are you sure you don't . . . ?'

'Quite sure.'

'I'd a nibble just now, close to the bank and . . .'

'Thank you. I know the river well enough.'

The man looked back at him a moment, nodded and then left, and Archie watched him go.

It was almost a week before Jilly made the promised telephone call. She rang early, while he was still dressing, so it was Roberts who took the message. Archie had spent the week in a sullen fury, his only outlet being to exercise, strengthening his leg muscles, fishing or making a pretence of reading. At night the frights renewed their attentions with gleeful savagery and he'd had to face them alone. In consequence he felt exhausted. Despite his anger he ached for the comfort of her presence in the night and the distraction of her company in the day, and missed her dreadfully. And in her absence the reality of Andy's death hit him hard and that, combined with the knowledge that his own behaviour had been indefensible, he was reduced to a state of misery. Roberts must have noticed this and passed on the telephone message in the tone of one offering much-needed solace.

'The train gets in at five o'clock, sir, and I'll send someone to collect them.'

'Them?'

Roberts beamed back at him. 'Your father is returning with her ladyship and will stay for a few days.'

Archie was in the library the following evening in front of a smouldering fire when he heard the commotion that heralded his father's arrival. His stomach had been churning like a schoolboy's all morning and he wiped sweaty palms against his thighs. What on earth had she told him? How had she explained her sudden appearance in London and what the *hell* would happen now, for this was no childish misdemeanour . . . He heard Jilly's oh-so-familiar laughter and then his father's voice asking where he was. He rose, composed himself, swallowing hard, and was halfway to the door when it opened.

Jilly entered first and gave him a bright social smile. 'Archie! Here you are.' She went across to the fire and bent to warm her hands. His father followed her in and Roberts brought up the rear.

'Sherry, sir?' he asked.

'Lady J'll have sherry, I imagine, but, Archie, you'll join me in a Scotch? How are you, son? You're looking a damned sight better than when I saw you last. Jilly been taking care of you?'

His father's face revealed nothing other than genuine pleasure at seeing him and his words skewered him. 'I'm doing fine, Pa. How are things with you?'

The question provided an opening for a long description of their journey, his father's role in London and the progress of the war while Archie nodded attentively, and took in not a word. So she'd said nothing . . . She seemed to have deliberately positioned herself just outside his direct line of vision, but with every fibre of his being he was aware of her. His father's monologue finally drew to a close and he rose to replenish their glasses. 'Been fishing, Jilly tells me. Jolly good, and all right for starters, but rather sedentary, you know. It's the leg muscles that need strengthening. Are you riding yet?' Archie had, in fact, got Kenny to saddle the mare a couple of times and he'd ridden a few, rather painful, miles, but at least he could report that he'd done so. Listening to his father braying his opinions was all too horribly familiar, recalling the time when he'd been required to give an account of his day, which was examined and compared, invariably badly, to that of his brother at the same age. It had been a bruising ritual and he felt no less depressed by it now.

'You look better than I expected, bit pale perhaps, but Jillian tells me you're chafing to be back with the action.' Archie fired her a look but she was examining the bracelet on her wrist, apparently fascinated by the catch mechanism. 'No point in going until you're fit, you know. Just a burden otherwise. We'll talk about it tomorrow. You'll have heard about the plans for the Division's rebirth, eh, well advanced now. The 9th Highlanders will be at the core, absorbing other brigades for reconnaissance and so forth.'

'Yes, I read about that.'

'Cunningham's all for it, so they're pushing ahead. The 51st is too important to be allowed to vanish. Might be some desk job there, you know, until you're fully fit. They'll be glad to have you back. Big initiatives are being planned. I'll make enquiries.'

Jilly rose then and said she would go and unpack, trailing an affectionate finger across her husband's shoulders as she went. 'Righto, m'dear.' The general acknowledged the gesture with a pat of her hand.

Archie felt rather sick.

Alone now with his father, the reality of what he had done overwhelmed him and he burned with remorse. The general was looking drawn, his face was thin, the skin stretched tight across his bones, and his eyes seemed to have faded. He looked older than his years, older than when he had visited him in hospital. Andy's death must have devastated him. His brother had been the apple of his father's eye, a fact Archie had never resented, being only too pleased to have ducked expectations he could never hope to fulfil. But now, when his father's need of him was greatest, he'd made of him a cuckold.

He could die of shame.

'Jilly's anxious about you, you know,' his father said, in ironic counterpoint to the thought. 'That's why I came up.'

'I can't imagine why she would be.'

'Said you're restless. Understandable, of course. But you'll have ample opportunity to settle scores, you know, and put St Valéry behind you.'

'Yes, sir.'

His father leaned forward earnestly. 'We must come about again, son, as a family and a country. It's all we can do – tighten sail and ensure that our boy's sacrifice was not in vain.'

'*Dulce et decorum est*,' Archie muttered below his breath. The big lie.

'We've held them off for the moment,' Pa continued, making no sign that he'd heard, 'and they'll not try an invasion now, not this year anyway, and so we've bought ourselves a little time. We must regroup and make best use of . . .' And he was away, describing possible strategies and scenarios as no doubt he did nightly in his club with other veterans who'd been put out to grass, speculating on move and counter-move as if a gigantic game of chess was being played on the world stage, seizing the distraction from his private grief. Archie watched his face and wondered what, when the war was over, he would ever find to talk about.

In ten years Pa would be seventy and Jilly just over forty.

Good luck to her.

It was not until the end of the following day that he managed to corner her alone and their encounter was brief, and brutal. From his bedroom window he'd seen his father outside, talking to Kenny, and he went onto the landing just in time to see Jilly entering the library. He hastened downstairs, followed her in and shut the door. 'What are you playing at?' She swung around to face him. Her face was pinched and peaky, and she looked as if she'd not slept either.

She didn't answer but picked up the cardigan she'd been wearing the night before and slipped it on, clasping her arms around herself. 'Work it out, Archie. You aren't stupid.'

'Bringing Pa back with you. Why do that?'

She gave a twisted little smile. 'Let's call it self-defence.'

He was utterly speechless. 'And so what happens now?'

'Why, absolutely nothing.'

He stared back at her. 'That's it, you mean?'

'What did you imagine would happen? It was a moment seized.'

She might as well have kicked him in the gut. 'And . . . and do you stay here now, or go back to London with Pa?'

She bit her lip. 'I want to go back with him, but he won't let me.'

'You *want* to go?'

She lifted her chin. 'Yes, very much.'

And he knew then that whatever fleeting thing there had been between them had passed. He'd been a fool to think otherwise, and he hated her for it. 'In that case, I'll make arrangements to leave at once. Get this bloody desk job Pa speaks of.'

She nodded, still hugging the cardigan to her, an odd look in her eyes. 'That would be for the best, Archie.'

His father's opinion of him took a sharply favourable turn when Archie announced these intentions at lunchtime. 'I'd feel the same in your position, son. I'll put in a word.'

'And since the estate can run itself perfectly well without me overseeing it,' Jilly interjected, 'there's no reason why I can't return to London with you. There must be *something* useful I can do – other women are doing all sorts of things.'

But the general had begun shaking his head even before she finished speaking. 'Air raids are becoming more frequent, my dear. I can't be doing my job and worrying about you getting caught in one. London's a good place to be out of at the moment.'

'Is that supposed to make me feel better? Knowing that you're in danger and I'm up here?'

'It really isn't up for discussion, Jilly,' her husband replied, apparently unaware that morsels of soup hung in his whiskers. And so this was how it would be, Archie thought, looking from one to the other. Jilly expressing a wish and Pa refusing to consider it. 'And besides,' his father was continuing, 'you were keen enough to come up here in the first place.' This was news. Archie had imagined she'd been sent.

'I love it here, but . . .'

'There you are then, my dear'. He reached across the table and patted her hand again. 'No more to be said.'

CHAPTER 36

An hour later Archie stood in the courtyard, feeling eviscerated, and waited for Kenny to saddle the mare. His leg was paining him but he was desperate to get away from the house, away from the two of them, away from her. So what had it been about, that reckless moment on the beach? For him it had been the culmination of something rather wonderful that had been growing up between them over the weeks of his convalescence, something more than friendship, crowned by a glorious moment. He'd convinced himself that that moment was inevitable and presaged some sort of future for them.

But he'd read it wrong. Hopelessly wrong.

He shook his head, incapable of grasping what was going on in Jilly's mind. Complicated and forbidden, yes, but had it just been sex for her? Sex with someone who would never broadcast the affair. A safe bet.

What sort of a woman was she?

And what sort of marriage would hers be? He couldn't imagine his father ever waiting for her, a towel over his shoulder, consumed by lust, while she swam naked in the surf. The thought of it still stirred him.

He led the mare to the old mounting block that had stood for decades in a corner of the courtyard and, with Kenny holding the bridle, he carefully swung his leg over the horse's back. The air was chill as he rode out and it sobered him a little, and the wind in his face served to gradually clear his mind. He was being unreasonable. Childishly so. She'd been right to kill the business, of course she had – he could even feel a reluctant admiration for the effective way she'd achieved it. But could they not have been more civilised about it? Her volte-face had been so abrupt, so apparently out of character. Or was it? He owed his sanity to Jilly during these last weeks, and perhaps he owed her his life, but in all essentials he barely knew her.

But she too had been seeking solace these last weeks, that much he knew.

So could they not have parted on better terms?

The wind was tearing the first leaves off the trees as he trotted along, the horse's movement beneath him jarring his leg but less painfully now than last time. Perhaps, after all, he had been convalescent long enough. Few newspapers found their way to the house and he had to rely on the crackling wireless set, which reported the daily pounding that London and the south coast were getting. There'd been sporadic incendiary raids on Scotland's east coast towns too, but here in Argyll such things were unimaginable and at Rosslie it was all too easy to forget the carnage and convulsions beyond its boundaries. Listening to Pa had made him realise just how out of touch he had become.

Time to return to the fray.

He rode on and through his misery discovered he could still appreciate the soft beauty of late summer, seeing how the bracken was already turning golden on the lower slopes. There was a melancholy to every autumn, a sense of time passing, an innate sadness, and today he felt it most profoundly. Andy would never see another one, and he too would soon be leaving.

Unless, by his actions, he'd forfeited his right to return. An unbearable thought.

Without conscious decision he found that he'd ridden towards the coast and he shortened rein to look down the estuary to where the sea stretched before him, calm and constant, and the sight of it soothed him. By the time he reached the ruins at Aber Rosslie, however, his leg was beginning to nag. He wanted to dismount to stretch it but wasn't sure he'd be able to remount on his own. Then the sound of hammering reached him and beyond the last building he saw John McAdam there, bending over one of the sheep fanks, repairing an internal stall.

He rode over. 'Lady Maxwell hiding you, eh?'

McAdam looked up and nodded. 'She thought it best. Saves awkward questions.'

'Like why you aren't doing your bit?' The words were out before he considered them but today he didn't care. 'I don't expect Pa'll stay long. He'll be back in London soon, doing *his* bit and dodging fire bombs.'

No response.

The pain in his leg was worsening. Damn the bloody thing – he'd have to dismount and walk about a bit, ease the muscles. He glanced across at a stretch of low wall and decided that if he could position himself close beside it, he might just about manage. McAdam sensed his intentions and put a hand to the bridle, urging the mare into position. It was an awkward, clumsy dismount and, if McAdam hadn't been there, he would probably have fallen. Having to lean on the man's shoulder and be assisted to where he could sit did nothing to improve his temper. 'You've made very good progress, by and large,' the man remarked. 'You couldn't have done that a couple of weeks ago.'

'It's bloody infuriating.'

And it was almost as infuriating to find himself once again liking the man, with his calm dignity and his infernal conscience. There was an intelligence about him, a directness that was attractive, and Archie's annoyance dissipated a little. But he stopped short of apologising. 'What brought the timberwork down?' he asked instead, nodding at the stall under repair.

'Storms, I suppose, and neglect. Might as well get it repaired while the weather holds good. Needs must before next year's lambing.'

Next year's lambing. Would the war be won or lost by then, or continuing on its relentless cycle of violence? The thought of lambs on the slopes bringing the promise of renewal raised his spirits a little, and he gestured to McAdam to sit beside him and they sat there in silence, looking towards the roofless houses, their stone walls stoutly built in expectation of permanence. If Hitler succeeded in his aims would Rosslie House stand empty like these places, open to the elements, burned out by a ravaging foe or, worse still, occupied by the victors? He'd passed houses in France, far larger than Rosslie, set aflame or abandoned, their shutters banging against empty walls, shredded curtains billowing through broken glass. In this world of the unimaginable, the unspeakable was happening.

But not every ravaging hand was of a foreign foe. He offered McAdam a cigarette, then lit both from a single match. 'Which house was your father's?' he asked, nodding towards the ruins.

'That one, nearest the water. They could pull the boats up the slipway and into the naust there.'

'Good position.'

'Aye, close to the stream for fresh water and the fishing was good. Sheltered too. He brought me out here once and showed me. Told me all about it.'

'And how the sun always shone, I imagine.'

'I don't suppose it did. But it was a good life they had here, he told me. Hard at times, but good. Folk pulled together.' Archie started counting the houses; at least seven, maybe eight. McAdam saw what he was doing. 'Forty were living here, at the time of the eviction.'

'Where did they go?'

He shrugged. 'They scattered. Some, like my father's family, went to Glasgow looking for work in the factories, some went to relatives, the rest moved down to England, or emigrated. Canada, Australia, New Zealand . . . It was hardest on the old folk, but I suppose it always is. Once their community had gone, they'd nothing, the bond was broken. No reason to live.' From where they sat Archie could see over a tumbled wall to an empty fireplace, besides which lay the coils of old bed springs. Rooms that had once housed lives were now knee-deep in sheep droppings with hearths long grown cold. On one wall a cupboard door still hung from its hinges, revealing empty shelves where a bird had built a nest. 'And it didn't have to be that way,' John McAdam went on, 'with a bit of intelligence and good intentions, if folk'd been given a little land of their own, and what with the fishing, they could have made a go of it, they'd have supported each other like they always had. But they'd no choice in the matter, they *had* to leave. The factories killed them, my dad said, killed their spirit and starved their souls. Made slaves of them.'

The man's eyes had kindled as he spoke. 'So you've a passion for something then,' Archie said.

'I've as much passion as the next man, Captain Maxwell,' he replied, and then he turned his head with an odd deliberation and Archie followed his gaze, stiffening as he realised that from here there was a clear view down the estuary to the small white-sand beach nestled beneath overhanging turf. His mind went on the alert but McAdam was continuing in the same casual tone. 'I like to come out here. I was here a few days back and saw the sheep fank needed repair, which was why I suggested mending it today. No one else comes here now, although occasionally Kenny walks over for a smoke.'

Damn.

Archie's mind raced as he absorbed what he was being told. Were the words a warning or a threat, and would an attempt at blackmail follow? Had McAdam told Jilly, and was that why she'd fled? He glanced sideways at him but McAdam simply went on smoking with unruffled calm. 'Resets the balances, I find, coming here. Away from it all. We need places like this. To escape. And I'm reminded here that there *are* things worth fighting for, things that matter more than politics, beyond the conflict – if ever we *do* get beyond it. We can't undo the past, of course, all we can do is survive the present – and then do better.'

Archie glanced at him. It might have been Andy talking. 'Getting beyond the conflict is the hard bit.' They smoked in silence for a while and, as no threat materialised, Archie added, 'You'll have the place to yourself from now on. I'm going back to work.'

McAdam turned his head to look at him. He seemed surprised. 'Are you fit?'

'Time I did, eh?'

Their eyes met and Archie held his breath, awaiting a response, but McAdam simply said, 'Perhaps.' And they carried on sitting there, looking out to the deep ultramarine expanse dotted with flecks of white. Then McAdam turned back to him. 'I don't take the stand I do lightly, Captain Maxwell, and coming here actually strengthens my resolve, but I'm finding it gets harder all the time. I tell myself the war was not of the people's making but of politicians' and yet it's the people who pay the price. And I keep returning to the central dilemma, that once reason and humanity have failed, how do conflicts get resolved without resorting to further conflict. It seems such a nonsense! An endless pattern of aggression met by counter-aggression that must be more aggressive than the original offence in order to succeed. And all it does is wreck lives.' He gestured to the idyllic scene spread out before them. 'I look at that view and find it intolerable to think of men out there on merchant ships being stalked by other men in U-boats, hunted down and blown apart just a few miles off our coast. Senseless! There must surely be a better way.' He turned back to Archie and gave him that clear direct look of his. 'Yes, I have a passion, but it's a passion for peace, and fairness, Captain Maxwell. And I don't judge others . . .' He paused. 'I know from what I saw in Spain what you'll be going back to, and, by God, man, I wish you well.'

Archie rode home slowly, going over their conversation in his head. He'd been struck by what McAdam had said and it was hard to argue with him. They'd continued to talk as the shadows lengthened and the encounter had taken him out of himself and helped him restore his sense of what was important. As he crossed the hall, his father emerged from the library. 'Ah, there you are, son. I've been doing some telephoning and the matter is fixed. You can report for duty at Rothes just as soon as arrangements can be made.'

* * *

It wasn't until the end of February that Archie returned to Rosslie. He'd hoped to go over Christmas, but in a brief telephone call Roberts informed him that Lady Maxwell had gone down to London, so he'd buried himself in work and allowed family men to go off duty instead. He'd written several times to his father, still nurturing a strong sense of remorse at what had happened, determined that after the war he would make an effort to grapple with his new responsibilities and forge a better relationship with him. His father had never been a good correspondent and his responses were brief.

After Christmas, they dried up completely. The war was keeping him busy.

Archie too had been fully occupied. His leg still gave him trouble, but he ignored it and could now get around quite well. Training men on the grey north-east coast had been a wearying business, not least the devising of ways of keeping up morale when his own was so low. The arrival of Wimberley as the new commanding officer, however, had been a shot in the arm and his demands had kept them all fully occupied and focused as the Division got itself back up to strength.

But he was feeling ready for a break from it all as he stepped down from the train at Rosslie station. He looked along the platform for Roberts but, as steam from the engine cleared, it was McAdam who came forward and took his bag. 'Welcome home, Major Maxwell.' Promotion had come with the job.

'Still here, then?'

'As you see.' And he gave Archie the familiar, open look that he remembered.

Milly and the dog cart awaited them outside the station and, as they approached Rosslie, Archie looked about him, recognising that the countryside was at that seasonal pivot point, poised to shake off the winter but not yet quite ready to burst into spring. Buds were forming at the tips of the twigs, biding their time until the warmer days before unfurling. Soon the rooks would be repairing their nests in the stand of old oak.

'How's the leg doing?'

Archie was so used to being addressed as sir that McAdam's withholding of it felt like insolence. 'It does fine. Better than my clerk who lost his at Dunkirk, or my requisitions officer who manages the paperwork with one arm. One of the orderlies lost an eye when half his face got burned away, so it would be a pretty poor do if I complained, don't you think?' The man made no reply. 'And yourself? Keeping the aphids at bay?'

'No one goes hungry on the estate, or the surrounding area – we've seen to that. The other glasshouse is repaired now and ready for spring. We've had to plough up the lower pasture, I'm afraid, the one facing south across the river, but it means we can increase the yield.' The lower pasture! Archie felt a pang and an absurd anger that he'd not been consulted, but, then again, if he had been, he'd have felt obliged to agree. It was a lovely spot, a riot of colour in the spring when vetches and clovers vied with cowslips and bluebells, giving way to silken grasses as summer progressed. Even they had become a casualty of war. 'It was a hard thing to do,' McAdam continued as if reading Archie's thoughts, 'but it can be restored in time.'

It could, of course.

All could be restored. Given time.

As they turned up the drive, though, and approached the house, Archie began to feel nervous. He'd written to Jilly, a formal letter asking if he might come, but it had been Roberts who'd replied, giving him a range of possible trains he might catch. He had set himself this as a test, a chance to show that he could behave well, put the past behind him and turn the page, but now the thought of seeing Jilly again set his pulse racing. He'd done his best to put her out of his mind, his future relationship with Rosslie and his father depended on it, but she, along with the frights, still haunted his nights.

He straightened his shoulders as he entered the hall, dropped his valise and spun his hat onto the hall table, before going through into the library. Jilly was standing in front of the fireplace with her back to him and she turned as he entered.

'Good journey?' she asked.

He stood, frozen in shock, and stared at her. Words failed him. Then, 'Jilly, I'd no idea. Pa never said—'

'Did he not?' she replied, coolly.

'How long? Or rather when?'

'April. Early or middle. Thereabouts anyway.'

'April? Good G— I mean *good*! Pa must be delighted.'

She gave an odd look. 'He's adjusting to the idea.'

'And you?' he asked, gulping, the words tumbling out. 'Are you pleased? I mean, I'm sure you are. You must be. Of *course* you are! Are you keeping well? I mean, you look well.'

'Yes, I'm well.' She stepped forward, a fecund Madonna, the bump neat and rounded beneath her soft woollen dress, and made to go past him. 'You're walking a great deal better, I see. You're in the same room, of course – it's been aired and the fire's been lit. I'll let them know in the kitchen that you've arrived. Dinner in half an hour?' And with that she disappeared.

He was glad, he told himself as he went upstairs, still in shock. It was good. Renewal! That was always good and the child would be something for Jilly to focus upon and Pa, in his dotage, would be kept on his toes. He tried smiling at the thought.

Yes, he was glad.

He dumped his valise and went to stand at the window, looking out, his insides churning as he resisted all thoughts of what had happened back in the summer, struggling to readjust his thinking. Remembering to forget . . . That would be key. Jilly had been right all along. But it would be an odd household after the war, nonetheless, and he played with the vision of Jilly filling the place with children, dispersing ghosts and bringing gladness.

How splendid.

The gong sounded and he pulled himself together and went downstairs to be greeted by Roberts, who expressed himself delighted to see him, referred to the forthcoming happy event and the plans to expand production on the estate.

'God, it's good to be back,' Archie said when he had gone, forking another potato onto his plate and forcing a smile. 'A touch of sanity in a mad world.'

She smiled a little in return.

'We should drink a toast. A glass of wine'll do you good.' He rose, filled another glass and brought it to her. 'To a healthy child, and a better world.'

She raised her glass and took a sip. 'To a better world.'

But something was wrong. She was playing with her glass, running her fingers up and down the stem, contemplating him with an odd, strained expression, biting her lip as if trying to bring herself to say something. Eventually she did. 'You know, every woman I know would have immediately started calculating back, given the circumstances. Men don't do that, do they?'

He frowned, uncertain.

'Try it, Archie.' He stared at her. 'Due April. Go nine months back.' Her tone had sharpened. 'Use your fingers if you have to.'

He counted: April, March, February . . . September, August.

July.

He felt his stomach turn over and his face flood with colour. 'Jilly . . . But Pa was here at the end of July. And . . . and you went down to London.'

'Damn good thing I did, don't you think?'

He continued to gape at her, desperate for what she was telling him not to be true. 'You've surely no way of knowing.'

'It's not his.'

He felt himself panicking. 'You can't be certain—'

'I can. Try as I did, I can assure you it's not his. He . . . he couldn't. Age, or weariness, or the shock of Andy's death, I don't know.'

Appalled, he said, 'Does he . . . does he know?'

'I went down and explained the matter at Christmas. Your father is a perfect gentleman and didn't ask questions. I fully expected to be shown the door but he has been most kind.'

He quailed, remembering suddenly. 'My last three letters had no reply.'

'There you are then.'

His guts turned to jelly. He rose unsteadily to fetch the bottle from the sideboard, and his hand shook as he filled the glass, slopping wine onto the tablecloth.

'That's why I went to London so suddenly, and insisted that your father came back with me.' Her face was flushed too and she was gulping at the wine. 'I thought it'd be fine if he would only make love to me, but it didn't work and then he refused to let me return to London with him. I . . . I tried to make it right.'

And he, he realised now, had never even given it a thought. 'What did he say when you told him?' he asked, still standing, his knuckles pressing onto the table for support. 'When he realised—'

'Nothing at first. And then *I see*, very quietly and he went on to ask if I was keeping well, and when the baby would be born and if there was anything I would need.'

'Oh God.' He sat shakily and stared at the dark stain on the tablecloth, watching it expand over the white linen.

'I tried so hard to redeem the situation! But he made some remark about the journey north being explained, and then I realised I should have been smarter still and claimed it was a fling with an old flame from London, but by then it was too late. I'd tried to be too clever. It was the only time he looked angry, when he said he appreciated the effort. *At least the thing will look all right then*, he said, and made me promise to say nothing to you until he had considered the matter.'

'The *thing*?'

'Appearances, not the child.'

Archie's head was reeling. He had written to his father again just before going on leave; a light chatty letter in which he promised to see that all was in good order on the estate, saying he was looking forward to renewing acquaintance with Jilly and other such pleasantries. In this context every single remark would appear the vilest insolence—

The phone rang in the hall.

Roberts appeared at the door. 'Your father is on the telephone, sir, asking if you've arrived.'

Archie pushed back his chair, exchanged a quick glance with Jilly, and went into the hall. His palm was sweating as he took the receiver from the stand.

'Pa,' he said.

'So, you've arrived. I just received your letter, regarding your leave.' There was a pause and then an arid tone. 'Something of a surprise for you upon arrival, I daresay, or perhaps not. Perhaps you already knew.'

'I didn't.' Prevarication was pointless.

'So she kept that promise at least,' his father said, and there was a longer pause. It seemed to last forever until he heard his father clear his throat. 'I've now had time to consider the matter . . . and how best to deal with it, and I've reached a decision. Here it is. Two things will happen, Archie. Jillian will have her confinement at Rosslie, I shall arrange for a nurse, and she will remain there. The child will be mine, legally, and in every way. Understood?'

How could it be otherwise? 'Yes, sir.'

'Secondly, in the morning, first thing, you leave. Make whatever excuse you like. Get back on the train and spend your leave elsewhere. Understand?'

'Yes, but—'

'And stay away from Rosslie. Not welcome now or in the future. And keep away from Jillian. After today no contact whatsoever. No letters, no telephone calls, no meetings. Got that?'

'Pa, I'll come down to London and—'

'I shan't see you if you do. I'm not sure when I *shall* want to see you, but that can wait until after the war. We'll see what transpires, and, in due course, I'll consider. No need to write again, you know. All you have to do is grasp those essential points. Leave Rosslie, stay away, and have no contact with Jilly. If you've got that there's . . .'

'Pa—'

'. . . nothing more to be said.'

CHAPTER 37

Rosslie, 1980

Archie left the dining room after Eva fled with Ross hard on her heels, and walked out onto the terrace. He stood gazing over the old parkland as the whole wretched mess he'd made of his life played like a film reel in his head, just as the frights used to do.

And now the whole world had been informed. Of some of it, at least.

That gut-punching shock of a headline and the thought that Eva – Eva of all people – had betrayed him . . . It had set his senses reeling and seeing the words, set out in print, had brought it all back – the whole ghastly sequence of disasters. St Valéry and Fergus. El Alamein and the bogus medal, a portrayal of heroics disguising the tragedies.

Andy, Pa, Duncan. The wasted years.

And now the chaos that followed had been laid bare for all to see. By Eva, who had been trying, yet again, to save him.

The irony was poetic.

But Jilly's words had stopped him in his tracks. *Why punish Eva for loving you.* He stood there and gazed grimly out over the tranquil scene. Was she right? Could he have missed something of such overwhelming importance as Eva being in *love* with him? He'd thought they understood each other, he and Eva . . . But he'd once thought the same of Jilly. Naïve, deranged, self-obsessed, he'd been twenty-two then, crippled and an emotional mess, and allowed an impossible situation to develop. But this time he had no excuse. *I've seen the way she looks at you*, Jilly had said once before, and he'd dismissed the idea as absurd.

But then Jilly wasn't always right. She was wrong about absolution. That would never be his.

He rested his forearms on the terrace balcony and watched a male pheasant strut across the grass, croaking its conceit. But Eva, what of Eva? Had Nemesis turned Athena when she picked up the cudgel to defend him? A child of light and shade who'd fallen at his feet and twice seemed to offer him redemption. He'd never once stopped to question the nature of their attachment but simply delighted in it until, years ago, he'd been accused of harming her! *Had* he done so? He was sure of nothing any more except that he'd as soon pull the wings of a damselfly than hurt her and the thought that he had was utterly unbearable. What was it he'd said to the poor girl? He'd known something was troubling her but he'd never have guessed what she was struggling with, or that she'd do something as mad as that without telling him! But it had been Ross she'd confided in and Ross who'd risen to her defence . . . He mused on that for a moment before turning back to the house.

He must find her, at once, and put things right.

But as he reached the door to the terrace it opened abruptly. 'Archie, you must come.' Jilly reached out and pulled him in. 'One of the tenants is on the phone. Something's going on down at the estuary. Someone's there . . . he thinks it's Duncan. Behaving oddly—'

Archie took the call in the office. 'Maxwell here,' he said and listened with a sinking heart. 'Right. I'm on my way. Thank you.' He grimaced as he replaced the receiver. Drunk by the sounds of it.

Jilly stood rigid in the doorway. 'What is it?'

'I'll go down and see.' He forced a smile but a strange sense of dread had crept over him as he'd listened to the man. 'Stay here, Jilly, no need to come. Tell Keith, perhaps.' He went quickly past her into the hall, swept up the Land Rover keys and headed out into the courtyard where Eva and Ross were sat on the horse trough, deep in conversation.

They looked up and he halted at the sight of them, immediately torn. 'Eva. God forgive me! We must talk, my dear, but later . . . Right now I . . . I must go to Duncan.' He turned away, making blindly for the vehicle but in his haste he tripped and stumbled, dropping the keys.

Ross was beside him in flash. 'What's the rush?'

'He's . . . he's behaving oddly, I'm told. Down at the salmon farm. Someone called through . . .'

He bent to pick up the keys but Ross moved fast and scooped them up. 'I'll drive you,' he said and headed for the Land Rover. Archie began to protest but Ross was already in the driving seat, checking over the dashboard. He started the engine and so, with a quick nod to Eva, Archie climbed in beside him. 'We'll talk. We must . . .' Eva nodded rapidly and raised a hand.

As they swung out of the courtyard Archie got a grip on himself, fighting back a rising sense of panic. 'You driven one of these before?' he asked, wincing at the grinding of the gears.

'Couple of times.'

'That third pedal's called a clutch. Use it.'

'Sure. So what's happening?'

'One of the tenants saw someone he thinks is Duncan, out on the pontoons, yelling and falling about, being mobbed by gulls. Drunk by the sound of it.'

Ross glanced at him but Archie's gaze was fixed out of the window, cursing now that he'd not made more of an effort to find the lad after their wretched row. He'd assumed that he'd sought a consoling bosom as he'd done before, but Jilly seemed to think not. The workings of his elder son's mind were a mystery to him and it pained him to acknowledge how little he knew him.

Ross, by contrast, was transparent and was now driving like a maniac as he always did, bouncing over potholes at a terrifying pace. But you knew where you were with Ross. 'Left here,' he said.

'There's a sharp— *Christ*, Ross, all right then, forget it. Right at the next fork and then the road narrows.'

'*Narrows!* Jeez.'

They continued in a tense silence. Then Ross glanced across at him again. 'She isn't, by the way, if that's what's eating you.'

They went up on the verge, brushing the hedge. 'Who isn't what?'

'Eva. In love with you.' Water from a puddle hit the windscreen. 'Cares about you, for some reason, but it stops there. Damned good thing too.' It took Ross a while to discover the wipers' stock, which gave Archie a moment to feel a profound sense of relief.

'That must have been quite some discussion you were having,' he said.

By now they'd reached the coast road and there was no time for more. The Land Rover leaped over the little bridge from where they could see one of the rowing boats tied up beside the pontoons and a figure out there who seemed to be carrying out some sort of frenzied attack on the cages.

It was Duncan, without a doubt.

A swarm of gulls had gathered above him, dipping and swooping down to feast on an unexpected bounty, and every now and then he'd wave his arms frantically to drive them off. Even from the shore they could hear him shouting. 'Rat-assed,' Ross remarked, his eyes fixed on Duncan as he yanked on the handbrake.

Archie flung open the door. 'Let's get that boat on the water.'

Together they dragged it down the slipway and Ross rowed swiftly out to the cages. It was only as they tied up beside the other boat that Duncan seemed to notice them. He yelled something that was ripped away by the wind, then flung his arms about again, batting at the gulls, then staggered and grabbed onto the collar to steady himself. 'Wrecked,' Ross murmured. 'He'll be in any moment now.'

'Stay here. I'll talk to him.'

'Watch yourself. He's lookin' ugly.'

Archie started along the walkway.

The wind was strengthening and the air was alive with screeching gulls, while in the clear water below he could see the lithe shape of seals arriving to share the feast. Duncan's cutters had created great holes in the mesh of the cages and salmon were escaping in their hundreds, scenting freedom beyond the gauntlet of the gulls. 'Steady, Duncan,' Archie called out.

In answer Duncan picked up an oar, jabbing it at Archie, keeping him at bay. 'Stay away,' he shouted. 'And fuck off back to Canada.' Wherever it was that Duncan had been last night, it had not been with Sarah Brodie. He was a mess – there was stubble on his chin and his eyes were bloodshot and furious. His clothes looked slept in.

'I'll do just that, Duncan, soon as we sort things out. Come ashore and let's make a start.'

But Duncan shook his head. 'Don't give me orders, damn you. Not some squaddie . . .'

'I've not ordered squaddies around for—'

'You come back, after all this time, buggering things up . . . and thinking I don't know!'

Archie paused. Know what? 'Duncan—'

'Got thinking, after what he said. Worked it out . . .'

'After who said what?'

'Pa.'

Oh God. He'd been right. And this, then, was serious.

'Seems my mother's a whore . . .' Duncan staggered as a gull swooped down and he batted it away. 'Thought at first maybe you . . .' he swung the oar as the bird returned, breathing heavily, his words blown away '. . . just a chancer . . . but now I've proof . . .' *Proof of what?* 'Rosslie's mine. Not in your gift, damn you. By *right*!' Archie stared at him, saw him stagger again, struggling to keep his balance. They had to get him ashore and he glanced over his shoulder at Ross. Duncan chose that moment to swing the oar again, the blade missing Archie by inches. It hit a gull, which fell, injured, onto the water where it swam round and round, crying out in stunned bewilderment, dragging a broken wing. 'Went looking, see. Women keep letters, I thought, and I was right. Found them. So I *know*.'

He was making no sense. 'OK, but let's get ashore and talk it all through. Rosslie's yours, whatever—'

But that served only to inflame him. ''Swat I'm saying, curse you. I *know!*' He was staggering wildly now as he tried to wield the oar. Archie took a step forward, quickly reversing as Duncan swung again, panting hard. 'All done here, though. Finished. Investors pulled out, you know! And Sarah . . . Bloody salmon can go. Tell Keith. He'll be happy 'bout that.' Archie sensed rather than saw that Ross had climbed onto the pontoon and was crouched down, removing his shoes. Desperately he signalled for him to stay put but Duncan saw the gesture, then recognised Ross and roared his fury. '*Christ!* The bastard's arrived! Come to check things over, eh? But then we're *all* bastards, don't you know! Maybe Keith's a bastard too. Fucking whore . . .' There was a splash as a seal leaped at an escaping salmon, ripping out its throat, sending a spray of blood onto Archie and Duncan gave a wild laugh. 'Mallory's out for *your* blood, you know, and that smart little bitch's too.' Archie kept his eye on the blade of the oar as he tried to unravel meaning in the stream of vitriol. 'Bloody war hero, but wait 'til they—' He jerked aside as another seal leaped, steadying himself with difficulty. So had Duncan been aware of Mallory's article? 'Didn't know the half of it, though.' He appeared to be sobering. 'And now you'll drag us all down, damn you!'

Archie's patience ran out. 'Right then, let's start putting things right by—' But he got no further as the oar, swung in a sudden vicious arc, caught him on the shoulder. He stumbled, lost his balance then fell head first into the nearest salmon cage. Numbed by the blow he started to sink, too stunned to kick, aware only of silvery forms, a hundred deep, receding into a dark infinity . . . Then the water exploded beside him and hands clutched at his clothing and he was being dragged, gagging, to the surface. 'Grab the mesh,' Ross shouted in his ear. 'Get a hold.'

Gasping and retching, Archie managed to hook his fingers onto the cage wire just as Duncan took another wide swing. But Ross saw it coming, ducked below the surface then shot back up and grabbed the passing blade. Unbalanced, Duncan staggered, his arms flailing wildly as he fell backwards into the water, on the seaward side of the cage.

Archie saw him fall and yelled out, but Ross shoved him from behind. 'Move!'

'*Duncan!* Get Duncan . . .'

'You first. Go!' They worked their way around the collar, hand over hand, as quickly as they could, Archie hawking and spitting with Ross right behind him.

'Duncan . . .' he gasped as Ross pulled him up onto the pontoon. 'For God's sake, get him!'

Ross looked back to where Duncan had fallen. 'What the fuck . . .?'

He had grabbed the floating oar and managed to stay afloat but even as they watched he released it, quite deliberately, and began swimming away from the cages, making slow, laboured progress towards the mouth of the estuary.

Just as his mother once had done.

'*Duncan, no!* The boat, Ross! *Go* . . .'

Archie kept his eyes fixed on Duncan. With every stroke he swam more slowly, his head now barely visible above the waves. '*Duncan!*' he yelled again in desperation. '*Turn back!*' Ross pelted along the walkway and leaped into the nearest boat and was pulling strongly around the cages but even before he reached the spot where Duncan's head had last been seen, Archie knew it was over, and shut his eyes in despair.

Three figures stood on the slipway, watching in silence as the scene played out. Eva clung to Keith and Jim Kincaird stood tense and silent beside them. He'd been on his way home, seen the commotion and come down to investigate, arriving at the same time as Eva and Keith, who'd been sent by Jilly. His battered ATV was now parked beside Eva's Fiat. Eva had screamed when Duncan knocked Tam into the sea cage, grabbing Keith's arm, and they'd watched, powerless to intervene, as events unfolded. Ross had rowed backwards and forwards for what seemed like an eternity, standing occasionally in the rocking hull to scan the empty seas.

Keith turned to Kincaird. 'We need the police here.'

'Aye,' the man replied, but his eyes were on Tam who sat on the walkway, his head in his hands, and he made no move to go. They saw Ross turn back at last and return to his father. They spoke for a moment, then Ross helped him into the boat, leaving the gulls and seals to their bounty. Keith and Kincaird went down the slipway to meet them and Eva waited, watching as Kincaird stripped off his jacket and draped it around Tam's shoulders. The four of them stood for a moment, conferring on the cobbles.

As they came back up the slipway she went towards them. Tam's hair was plastered onto his head and his face was ashen pale; she saw such pain there! She put out a hand to him, having no words, and he clasped it briefly. 'Go with Jim, my dear. He's nearest. Telephone the police.' His voice was hoarse and strained. 'Tell them I sent you, and ask them to come down here. You'd better come on to Rosslie afterwards, Jim – bring Eva back, they'll want statements from us all. There's been an accident, tell them. Duncan had been drinking and fell in. We went in after him. Couldn't find him. An accident.' He released her hand and waved her away. 'That's all. I'll do the rest.'

CHAPTER 38

The police went down to Aber Rosslie and later returned with the three men, and were then at Rosslie for hours, and Eva could see the toll it was taking on Tam. His face was still rigid with pain and she saw he was struggling to hold things together. They'd discovered an empty whisky bottle and some pills, Keith informed her, scattered on a heap of flattened cardboard in the re-roofed building, indicating where Duncan must have spent his final night. Jilly had gone into shock so the family doctor had been summoned. He supplied a sedative and ordered her to bed. Kincaird was eventually allowed to return to his farm and the officers departed to interview the man who had phoned originally, raising the alarm.

The news of Duncan's death spread quickly and once again the phone had to be taken off the hook, but not before Keith fielded a call from Sarah Brodie and listened, grim-faced, as she sobbed down the phone. 'Seems they'd quarrelled,' he said, hanging up, 'which I think is code for she'd broken it off and doesn't want to be blamed. He'd gone round yesterday, she said, in a foul mood, made some phone calls and then just blew his top. She said he'd frightened her. Full of remorse now, of course.'

'A perfect storm,' Tam remarked, without turning round. They were in the library and he was standing by the window, staring out to where clouds were gathering, masking the sun. He looked aged and worn, tense and distant, and had barely spoken since the police had left. But he seemed strangely preoccupied in a way that puzzled Eva.

He turned and caught her watching him. 'We must put out a notice. Eva, help me here, will you.'

'It can surely wait.'

'No, no, let's get it done.' He went to the bureau and assembled pen and paper, which he passed to her. 'What wording do we use these days? Notice is hereby given of the death . . . And the date, I suppose. Born nineteen forty-one . . . when was his birthday, Keith?' Eva and Keith exchanged puzzled glances but Keith told him and she wrote it down. 'Accidentally drowned sixteenth of August, nineteen eighty.'

Perhaps it helped him in some way to do this so she took his dictation and handed him the paper. He took it and studied it for a long time.

'Were the police satisfied with it being an accident?' Ross enquired from where he was sitting beside the fire in borrowed clothes, his hair still tousled. Was he too feeling culpable? Eva wondered. It had been him, after all, who'd grabbed the oar's blade. He caught her eye, making a questioning gesture towards the figure of his father as if he too was perplexed by his odd detachment.

'Uh huh,' Tam replied, not looking up. 'There'll be an inquest, of course. It was fortunate, perhaps, that someone other than family spotted him first, and that Jim came by.' He lifted his head as the portent of Ross's question struck him. 'It *was* an accident, Ross. Without question and no blame attached.'

'He was trying to kill you.'

Tam showed no sign of having heard. 'So drunk he could barely stand, and there's no need to distress his mother with anything else. Understood? We agreed . . .' He looked sternly at the three of them. 'I told the police that he and I had argued yesterday, and that he'd downed the best part of a bottle of Scotch, and whatever else he'd swallowed. All that is true.'

'And like you said,' Ross remarked. 'No blame attached.'

Tam gave him a bleak look and abruptly left the room.

Keith left a moment later saying he'd check on his mother, leaving Ross and Eva alone. 'He's taking it hard,' Eva said, looking across at Tam's son.

Ross grunted. 'Bound to, and he's taking it on himself, like always. Telling everyone that they'd argued and Duncan got wrecked, *not* that they argued, Duncan got wrecked, tried to *kill* him, then fell in and drowned.'

'He's sparing Jillian.'

'And blaming himself.'

'Duncan was out of his mind – he can't have known what he was doing.'

'You'd like to think so.'

They sat in silence, reliving those dreadful moments. How suddenly had this new disaster struck! But something else was troubling Tam, she was sure of it. She looked across at Ross. 'What was Duncan yelling out there?'

'Couldn't catch it all. Cursing Tam, mainly.'

'But Tam was genuinely trying to find a solution; surely Duncan could see that?'

'All I saw was murder in the guy's eyes – I know the look. *Crazzee* drunk . . . He was cursing his mother too, calling her a whore, so let's just level, shall we, Eva? He was my brother, not his, yeah? That's what this is all about.' She nodded, seeing no point in further prevarication and he whistled softly. 'Messed up badly there, Dad.' Then, after a moment, added, 'Sounded to me like Duncan had it worked out.'

She stared at him. 'What did he say?'

'He'd got proof, he claimed. Kept on about his rights.'

'Oh God. No wonder Tam looks so haggard.'

'And me showing up there made the guy flip.' He rose to refill his glass from the sideboard.

'You're not blaming yourself, are you?'

He shook his head. 'No way. He'd totally lost it by then. Greeted me as "the bastard", come to check things out. Said he was a bastard and maybe Keith too; God knows what was happenin' in his head.' He stood there, staring into his glass. 'My *brother* . . . God, the secrets that man keeps! They just keep on comin'.' He sat down again. 'But something else is eating him.'

'I know.'

'Any ideas?'

'None.'

He shrugged and they sat in silence again until Ross said, 'But I guess this changes things for him.'

'How do you mean?'

'This place, taking it on. And if the lady's wanting him to stay on and play house, like you said—'

'I don't think it's that. And I don't think he will.'

Ross grunted. 'Better not be, cos I want him where I can see him. Keep him outta trouble.' Would that ever be possible? she wondered. 'I hate to leave him in this mess but I need to be headin' back. I've a schooner to finish and a consortium baying for my blood.'

They were interrupted by a noise in the hall and a moment later Keith entered with a petite girl with springy red hair and an open, friendly face. 'This is Susie,' he announced, and introduced them.

'I drove straight back, soon as I heard,' the girl said, after giving both Eva and Ross a hug. 'What an awful time to meet you.' She turned back to Keith. 'Who's with Jilly?'

'She's had a sedative . . .'

'I'll go up to her in case she stirs. Bring in my bag, would you please, Keith. I'll unpack the rest later. And, Archie, where's he?'

No one was quite sure.

'I'd better go and see.' Eva rose and followed Keith and Susie out of the room.

'Come tell me when you've found him,' Ross called after her. 'And if you don't, I'll take a look outside.' But Tam, she discovered, had been seen by the cook heading off on foot towards the hills behind the house.

Eva reported back to Ross. 'Should we go after him?'

He shook his head. 'It's what he does, he walks, sometimes for miles, working things through. Leave him. I can go looking later if he doesn't show up. But right now I could do with some air myself. Come with me?'

They set off and, without intention, ended up on the field lane, which led down towards the estuary. Eva paused as they rounded a hedge and she saw the shimmering water ahead of them. 'I'm not sure I want to go back down there.'

'It won't make it any less real, you know, what happened. C'mon. I need to see the sea, can't get my head straight without it.'

They walked on, neither speaking, but after a while Eva turned to him. 'I'll not leave Tam, you know, if you have to go back.'

He nodded. 'And when he follows, assuming that he will, what then? What'll you do?'

She'd not begun to think about that. 'Look for a job, I guess. Mallory can't have poisoned all the wells.' She was far from sure she wanted that sort of job any more, although ironically her unintentional scoop might end up serving her well.

'And if Tam asks you to go back with him?'

'He'll hardly need a private secretary in Severn.'

'Wouldn't bet on it.' He lifted his eyes to follow the flight of a gull, making it hard to read his expression, but after a moment he went on. 'He'll not let you go easily, you know. He needs you and he's got this way of hookin' folk in. He's a self-contained old bastard in many ways, doesn't take help easily but you still end up stickin' with him.' She smiled a little, Ross was right and she hated the thought of losing him again. 'Did he ever explain to you what happened, between him and Jillian Maxwell?'

'Just the bare facts.'

'Maybe one day he'll tell me.' He shook his head. 'All those years, he's been carrying it, clammed up inside him, must have weighed him down . . . Actions have consequences, he used to say, drumming it into me when I was a kid and getting myself into trouble. You can wreck your life with a single act, he'd say. Catch yourself on! And I'd zone out thinking he was no great role model for all his preachin', and let's face it, he wasn't. I just wish he'd told me . . . I only learned he'd had a brother – a real one – after you turned up in Severn. And now I find I had one too. Maybe even two . . .' He opened a field gate and held it for her. 'As a kid I remember hearing him shouting out in the night, screaming sometimes, and my mother trying to calm him. She told me it was because of what he went through in Europe, in the war, but it used to freak me out – I can hear him now . . .' They passed a clump of gorse, its spring glory withered now and faded. 'You remember what a tuckamore is?' She nodded, seeing again the stunted, wind-blasted spruce trees, distorted by the Atlantic's salt-laden gales, their branches bleached and entangled, barely alive. 'That was Tam back then. Shaped by the storms, and hell-bent on self-destruction. Drove me crazy, he did, I'd take off and go fishin' with the men from the outport, anything to get away. Or I'd run off for longer.'

'But you always went back.'

'Like I said he hooks you in.' He paused and glanced at her. 'And then he changed and I never knew what the pivot point was until that night you showed up and he explained it to me . . . What he told me then was the only reason I trusted you to come here with him. Somehow, back then, you'd reached him, found a way through.' She saw Tam again reflected in his eyes, that same intense yet private, almost vulnerable, look. 'Saw you as a sort of talisman.'

She smiled a little. 'Despite always bringing him bad luck.'

Ross shook his head. 'There was a time, as a kid, I was jealous of you. I knew he talked to you – I used to see you sometimes and he'd be chattin' away to you in a way he never did with me. I wasn't easy, growing up, I know that, I drove him mad, skippin' school, getting into trouble. There was always some sort of stand-off between us back then, but he was different with you.' She must have looked stricken and he smiled. 'We talk plenty these days, Eva. All caught up. And maybe he'll tell me the rest one day.' The smile was Tam's smile.

'So he's hooked us both in . . .'

'Uh huh.' The expression in his eyes made her feel suddenly shy and she walked on.

He followed.

'I went back there, you know,' she said, 'to Heart's Repose.' They'd reached a point where they could look down on the expanse of blue water opening in front of them. 'I rather wished I hadn't, though, it was such a forlorn sight. And it felt strange, I could almost see myself, like a ghost child running about in the bones of the place, as if a part of me had died too, or never even existed . . . It felt like looking directly into the past, into another world, an abandoned one.'

He nodded. 'I guess it was more gradual for me. I saw it happening, up and down the coast, and it's still going on. Places being abandoned, folk leavin', trying to get started someplace else. Got used to it over the years, I guess, but it's not been an easy time for anyone.'

'What did you do, you and Tam?' She felt she could ask him this now that the hostility was gone.

'Felt rootless for a while, but we had each other. It brought us closer. Tam persuaded me an education was something worth havin' after all and I started workin' with this old timer, building boats down on the Avalon. He was an inspiration, was old Goron, and left me the yard when he died, and so between him and Tam, I settled down. Mostly . . .' He grinned briefly. 'And Tam did too. Which is why I need you to get him back where he belongs and let him get writing again.'

'He writes still!' She told him about the poem she had found.

'I used to find stuff too,' he said. 'Crazy stuff on scraps of paper, half-written, mostly when he'd been drinkin'. But he had something, even then. But yeah, he's good. Critics like him. He campaigns about the fisheries too. Writes their stuff for them, lobbying officials with big words they don't understand.' She sensed his pride in him. 'So he needs to get home and get writin' again, then he'll be OK.'

By this time they had reached Aber Rosslie and Eva stopped and looked out towards the damaged cages. Ross stopped beside her and they stood there, each reliving those terrible moments, and she was aware of him, very close. 'He thought if he came back here he'd find some sort of resolution, said he *needed* things sorted.'

'He didn't want this, though.'

'No.' After a few moments of silence he turned to her. 'But sometimes you've just gotta go back. And face it. Whatever the cost, or you get stuck.'

'I felt that at Heart's Repose. I was glad in the end that I went.'

'It doesn't change anything, but it helps you accept.'

Her eyes remained fixed on the cages. 'It'll haunt him, what happened out there. It'll weigh on him forever.'

'But he can't let it destroy him.'

She turned to him, suddenly needing to say what had been going through her mind. 'But the awful thing is that he'll be right, Ross. Duncan's death *is* because of what happened between him and Jilly.'

He looked back at her, his eyes very dark, and nodded. 'Secrets can be dangerous.' He turned away then and surveyed the ruins of the Aber Rosslie houses where police tape was still blowing in the breeze, caught on the door of the place where Duncan had spent his last desperate night, and changed the subject. 'So what happened here? In this place. You wrote about it, right? Folk got thrown out. Carrot and stick, you said. Made a connection to the outports.'

She nodded. 'These people got the stick – they were forced to go, didn't get a choice, though I'm not sure the outport folk had much of one. Tam wanted Duncan to consider renovating the place.'

He seemed diverted and looked more closely at the ruins. 'Those walls were built to last.' He left her and went to explore them, and she watched him turning over oil drums to inspect an old fireplace, examining a wooden shutter that still hung from a window. He disappeared round the back of one dwelling and Eva went to sit on the slipway, still thinking of all the intertwining threads that had brought them to this place.

It wasn't only Tam who'd be forever haunted.

After a while she went looking for Ross and found him crouched down inspecting the hull of a wooden boat which had been dragged ashore behind the houses. 'There's life in this little darlin' if someone gets to her soon. She was a beaut once.'

'Tam was telling Keith about your boatyard. Said he should consider doing something similar.' Ross rose and dusted off his hands, and looked speculatively at the slipway and at the ruins, and nodded again.

'I doubt I'll be coming back here anytime soon but Keith should come on over and see our set-up.'

As the light began to fade they headed back towards the house, saying little, and Eva felt her spirits lightening, glad that the last bit of constraint between them was gone. So she was surprised when he turned to her at the foot of the steps. 'Not sure about leaving Tam in your care, though.'

'Why's that?'

'You were told to call me.'

'Are we back on that? I thought we'd moved on.'

'You made me a promise.'

She caught a glint in his eye and saw that he was baiting her. 'I'll make you another, and I'll keep it this time. Though it's hard to see what else can go wrong.'

CHAPTER 39

Archie was relieved to find Ross alone in the dining room when he came down next morning; he wasn't sure he could face the others yet. Even the hours he'd spent walking among the hills yesterday hadn't helped him to come to terms with what had happened.

And Duncan's words kept ringing in his head. They could mean only one thing . . .

He'd returned home as the colour was fading in the western sky and seen Eva and Ross approaching the house from the other direction, walking companionably, side by side, deep in conversation backlit by the setting sun. He'd stopped and watched them from the shadows and, just for a moment, the darkness in his mind had lifted.

Ross looked up as he entered the dining room and pushed the newspaper across the table. 'Read.'

He groaned. 'Mallory! I'd forgotten, though frankly—'

Ross tapped the paper. 'I said read.'

He put on his glasses. '*Is our climate changing? Opinion is divided in the wake of Hurricane Allen, an immensely powerful category-five hurricane, currently tracking its way from the Windward Islands, through the Caribbean . . .*' He stared at it, then looked up at Ross.

'You owe her,' Ross folded the newspaper and put it aside.

'I do! God forgive me.' He put his glasses away, pulled out a chair and stared at the paper. 'So they withdrew it . . . although Mallory could announce to the world that I was the devil incarnate and I'd not give a damn right now.' He poured himself some coffee. 'And he'd not be far wide of the mark.' He looked across at Ross. 'I should never have come back.'

'Duncan came looking for you, you told him to walk away, and he didn't.' Archie said nothing; it wasn't that simple. 'And he *wasn't* your brother—'

'Ah. Eva told you?'

Ross shook his head. 'I guessed. And maybe one day you'll feel like tellin' me the rest of it. But no way does Duncan's death go on your account.'

'Then on whose, Ross? God knows, I wished him no harm! And if I'd known—' He broke off. Later, he'd explain later, but first he must speak to Jilly. He had lain awake last night, tormented by his suspicions – and an almost unbearable pain had built inside him. 'I handled things all wrong. Whatever else, he was my flesh and blood, Ross, and yet he saw me as a massive obstruction, an interloper. I should have got us past that and sorted things out with him. We should have been honest, the three of us. If only . . .' He broke off and raised his cup to his lips. 'Bloody refrain of my life!' His hand began to shake, spilling the coffee. He clattered the cup down, struggling for control. 'You heard what he was yelling yesterday, at the cages?'

'He was drunk.'

'He said things that—'

Eva appeared in the doorway and he broke off. She stood staring in horror at the folded paper but Ross opened it and spun it round so she could see the headline: *Is our climate changing? Opinion is . . .* She stared at it and then looked blankly from one to the other. 'I don't understand.'

'Pulled it,' Ross said, with a smile.

Archie rose and enveloped her in a hug. 'Ah, Eva. My guardian angel. How could I ever have doubted you?' He dropped a kiss on the top of her head and released her. 'Come and have some breakfast. Has anything been taken to Jilly?'

'She's up and out. Her bedroom door was open as I passed.'

Archie paused, set the coffee pot down, and straightened. 'In that case you must forgive me. We'll talk later, my dear.' And he left the room before either of them could stop him.

It didn't take him long to find her; he knew where she would be. She was wearing a red jumper, just as she had done all those years ago. How like her, he thought, as he limped towards the glasshouse . . . She looked up as he pushed open the door, registering no surprise at seeing him. She looked fragile, though, her face was drawn and so much older than yesterday.

'I hadn't really expected to see you this morning, Jilly.'

She was pulling off the last of the unripe tomatoes from potted plants and forty years dissolved between them. 'Did staying in bed ever help anything?' she replied in a distant voice and reached, like an automaton, for another pot, laying the green fruit in a box of straw beside her. It occurred to him then that her enduring enthusiasm for the walled garden was the four walls that defined it, enclosing it, her fortress against the world where the rhythm of the seasons could be depended upon. It was, after all, only when boundaries are overstepped that matters become unpredictable.

Perhaps she felt safe here. 'No words can express my regret, Jilly. Nothing comes close.' She nodded, not looking up. 'But we must talk, you and I.'

At that she lifted her eyes to his. 'Must we, Archie?' she said, and he glimpsed the depths of her pain.

'We must.'

'He was drunk, I'm told,' she said, 'and so you mustn't think I blame you, if that's what's troubling you. I don't hold you accountable.'

He pulled up a chair with a broken back and sat. 'We're both accountable, Jilly, there's no escaping that fact. And Duncan's death *was* avoidable.'

'But was it?' She pushed aside her hair, oblivious to the dirt on her hands and avoiding his eyes. 'I've been asking myself that. Perhaps his course *was* set at conception, but he was never a happy boy, you know, and he was a difficult youth. Then he grew up to become a dissatisfied and resentful man. Perhaps what happened was always his destiny.' She turned to reach for another plant, tipping out the soil and discarding the withered stalk. How often he had thought of her here, as he saw her now, composed and self-reliant. But not so hardened. When he hadn't been hating her all these years he'd remember how she used to come to him in the night, endlessly patient and comforting. Tender almost . . .

'If his course was set, who set it for him?' he asked, but she ignored him.

'You'll stay on, won't you, Archie? Rosslie is your responsibility now and Keith is no more capable of running it than I am, and I . . . I'm not sure how I'll cope—'

She broke off and bent again to her task, her hair fell forward, covering her face.

'I'll stay as long as necessary to get you through all this,' he replied quietly, 'but I plan to leave as soon as I can.'

She looked up again, stricken. 'But, Archie . . . we *need* you! How will Rosslie function otherwise? Duncan was essentially running things even before your father died.'

'And since then, believing it to be his right.'

She misunderstood him, or perhaps chose to. 'What would you expect him to do? He had it *all* to deal with, Keith was no help, and Duncan did his best. I suppose I never really recognised how he must have felt, running things with your shadow hanging over him, aware always that you might return . . . Rosslie was his, but *not* his. The pressure must have been building in him for weeks, but I'd no idea the strain he was under.'

Her words skewered him. 'Was that how he saw it? My shadow hanging over him . . .'

'He never said as much, but I suppose it *must* have felt that way. While Andrew was alive, Duncan had some autonomy since your father had been leaving things to him more and more as he aged, more or less rubber-stamping whatever Duncan proposed. But after he died, the reality – the wretched *impossibleness* of the situation – must have hit home.'

'And yet you say his death's not on my account!' Was it intentional, he wondered, this twisting of the knife.

'That's not what I meant. It was an accident, Archie, a stupid, tragic—'

He paused, seeing that her eyes had filled, but he'd not spare her. 'You told me he didn't know.'

'About us? He didn't.' She brushed an arm across her eyes.

Archie shook his head. 'Yesterday he made it very clear that he did know. Pa seems to have said something before he died.'

'*No . . .*' She looked back at him, horrified. 'He promised me he never would.'

'Dying men break promises.'

'Duncan would have come to me; he would have asked—'

'And what would you have told him, Jilly?' He had to keep the pressure on until he knew.

'It would have depended on the question.'

He grimaced. 'Things never were quite straightforward with you, were they?'

She returned his look, unabashed. 'I've had to chart my own course, Archie, sailing solo for so long. And I had my sons to consider.'

'Survival being everything?'

'Exactly.'

'Andy's maxim.'

'Was it?' She reached for another plant.

He hesitated for just a moment and then went in deep. 'Duncan said he had proof.'

She shook her head. 'There was no proof.'

'Called me a chancer. Said Rosslie was not in my gift.'

She raised a shoulder and tipped out another pot. 'He was drunk.'

'Said he thought at first it was me . . . then went looking for evidence. Women keep letters, he'd decided.'

He was watching carefully and thought he saw her stiffen. 'You never wrote me any letters.'

'You once told me, Jilly, that men never think of counting back, only women do that. Count nine months back from mid-April, you said, and you reach July.' He saw that her hands had grown still. 'But count back from *March* and you arrive in June. In late June nineteen forty I was on my way up to Rosslie, drugged up to the eyes and unable to walk. You went away for a spell around then, as I remember, visiting a friend.' He paused again. 'Keith informed me yesterday that Duncan's birthday was March twenty-second.'

'He came early.' She focused more than was necessary on pulling off the green tomatoes. 'I expect it was the stress.'

'Still manoeuvring, Jilly?' She stayed silent but dropped her hands and clasped them tightly together on her lap. 'You're on the rocks this time, my dear . . . But you're right, I only ever wrote one letter to you, asking if I could come home on leave, which I did and found you pregnant. I don't suppose you kept that one.' She was holding herself together well but with every second he grew more certain. 'And it was unwise of you to have kept *his* . . .'

He went on watching her, letting the silence lengthen, determined that it would be she who broke it. And as he watched he thought again how, on the night they'd learned of Andy's death, she'd sat staring into the fire, lost in a world of her own, while he sobbed in Andy's armchair with Roberts' hand resting on his shoulder. And later as he passed her room, the anguished keening he'd heard had not, after all, been for the lover who had disappeared in the snows of Norway but for another, lost over the Channel, flying like a maniac, reckless to the end.

But he needed to hear her say it.

She was staring dead ahead. 'I'm not sure I can make you understand.'

He felt the blood drain from his face as the glasshouse began to spin. Duncan had been a Maxwell, it was written on his every feature, and that alone could mean only one thing. Pain exploded in his head and he wanted to grab her by the throat and shake the truth out of her . . . ! It was several moments before he trusted himself to speak. 'Did you know, Jilly, right from the start?' She made no reply and a white-hot anger began to flow, molten through his veins. 'You *did*, damn you! You *knew*! And yet you let me believe – you let *Pa* believe – that Duncan was *mine*.'

She returned his look, pushing aside her hair again, leaving a dirty mark on her cheek. 'What else could I do? I couldn't destroy Andy's child, he was all I had left, and I couldn't destroy your father by telling him the truth.'

'So you destroyed me instead.'

'You destroyed yourself, Archie.' The scorn in her voice seared him and suddenly the restraint in her was gone. 'You always said you wanted your freedom, you never expected to inherit Rosslie, you wanted to be out from under your father's thumb, out as fast and as far away as you could get. *Give him sons*, you said. *Then he can disown me and leave me in peace*. And I did, didn't I? Isn't that exactly what happened?' She put her hands, palms down on the potting table, as if to steady herself and her eyes blazed at him. 'You wanted to be a writer, you told me, and so I solved both our problems and set you free.' He looked back at her, shaking his head in disbelief. 'A feted war hero, you could have done anything with your life! But instead, you sank into—'

'Jesus *Christ*. Jilly!'

She raised her chin, fighting back. 'Better that you left when you did, you know. I believe you were a little in love with me.'

'I was, damn you. I wanted you to run off with me after the war, even *before* I knew about Duncan, I was that stupidly besotted! I loved you and I hated you for years, depending on how much I'd drunk. But for the rest . . . yes, I went down a road of self-destruction, because I was longing for you, for Rosslie, my home, and for my *son* – I'd have done anything to wind the clock back. And I felt such *shame*.'

She reached for another pot, her hand trembling. 'I could never be ashamed of loving Andy. And we did what we did, Archie. We were no more innocent, you and I, than Andy and I were guilty. Duncan *could* have been yours.'

'But you *knew* that he wasn't. You threw me to the wolves!'

'I had to survive. Your brother's maxim, as you just said.'

He was breathing hard now. Being certain was so much harder than suspecting, and yet there was one more thing to be confronted. 'But Andy didn't, did he! He *failed* to survive. Don't you ever ask yourself *why*, Jilly? He was flying like a madman, we were told, the day he died.' The thought had occurred to him in the night, that perhaps they had considered the same route to oblivion, he and Andy. 'Did you never stop to think that he found the wretched coil *un*survivable?'

Jilly paled a little, biting her lip. 'Andy never knew I was pregnant. I didn't know for sure until just before that day at the beach, *after* we knew he'd been killed. I was in despair that day, I'd lost everything and I was pregnant with his child. It came to me that I could swim out into the estuary and just keep on swimming.' As Duncan, her son, had done . . . Dear God, the echoes kept reverberating. 'It would have been a clean way out, an end to it all. But I was carrying *his child*! And then I realised it didn't have to be that way. As long as Andrew and I were intimate as soon as possible, I could claw something back, find some joy in the future. I would have that part of Andy with me always, my secret to cherish, and it would hurt no one.' Archie let out a strangled sound. '*You* were a mess, crippled in more ways than one, but I'd looked after you for *his* sake, and because you were so young and hurting, so messed up and vulnerable, and since I was already caught I thought there could be no harm in giving you what you so clearly wanted.'

She was quite extraordinary. 'You mean I was there, on hand, a convenient stooge—'

'No, Archie.'

'And did you pretend that day that it was Andy between your legs, Andy inside you?' He couldn't help himself. That pivotal moment distilled at last into concentrated bitters, a sour bile at the bottom of the glass. 'And was it there that you learned how sand feels on naked flesh? Same bloody beach?' It had been a random shot but he saw that it had found its mark. Dear God! The same beach, the same sand and he a surrogate Andy. He turned away no longer able to look at her, but stared, sickened and shaking, out across the walled garden with its neat raised beds, ordered and tidy – hurting every bit as deeply as his younger self had hurt.

She seemed to sag at last.

'No, Archie,' she repeated, but in a softened tone. 'It was you. And I didn't only care for *his* sake. I'm sorry I said that . . . I cared for you for yourself. I saw in you a different Andy, a more sensitive, sweeter man. You were so terribly young and had such courage, you'd been damaged by the horrors but not broken. I wanted to help you, to nurture you – I *so* wanted you to come through! Your frights granted me a sort of release, a sense of purpose, which I could set in the balance against the sinning. I could actually *do* something, I saved you from yourself and I liked to think I helped you heal.' *You'll thank me one day*, she had said and he had, times many, despite it all. 'That moment on the beach was a reckless sort of madness, you wanted me, I knew you did, and I . . . I was grasping at something with no thought for the future, because the future held nothing.'

They sat in silence and the molten anger in him began to cool, leaving him heavy with sorrow. 'Giving and taking, you once called it,' he said at last.

'And was that so *very* dreadful?'

He made no reply and after a while she spoke again. 'We met just after the wedding, Andy and I, and I knew straight away that I'd made a ghastly mistake marrying your father. It had been a craven act, and I paid the price of cowardice; I *could* have survived alone but I was in despair; I weakened and was lost. Later, though, Andy said it was the same for him, meeting me. A thunderbolt. Inescapable. Hopeless . . . We were in complete turmoil, no idea what to do. Your father was very busy in those early days and so, when Andy was on leave, he would escort me to functions in his place. We were constantly being thrown together.' They had become lovers, she told him, swept along by their passion and then mortified by it, but quite unable to stop. Andy was transferred to Oban to assist in training flying-boat pilots for Coastal Command. 'I persuaded your father I should go and live at Rosslie for a while, keep an eye on the estate and it became easier to meet. We told ourselves we'd work out what to do – as if there *was* a solution! We fooled ourselves. There wasn't, of course, there was no way out . . . He came here just once. Not to the house as your father would have come to hear of it but we met by Aber Rosslie and walked, and talked endlessly. He couldn't stay away, he said . . . Then the last time I saw him was the time you mentioned, when he came down to John McAdam's tribunal. He was on his way back south to crank up training there, and to bolster the Channel sorties, just after you arrived. We met after the tribunal and I agreed to have John at Rosslie, putting right an older wrong, as Andy put it.' She paused, staring down at the potted tomato plants, reliving the memory. 'He was different then. He looked dreadful, gaunt almost and very tense. And I knew what was coming: he broke things off, said he'd come to his senses and it had to stop. After the war he'd leave Rosslie—'

'But Rosslie was his *life*, his everything!'

'I knew that. And I knew what he proposed would destroy him. I told him he mustn't, for your father's sake and for yours, though he saw through me and said I was protesting for my own ends and that the situation was impossible, and so we argued. It was dreadful . . .' Her voice cracked a little. 'He kept insisting that he could never be at Rosslie while I was there and I told him it would destroy his father if he left and he said he . . . he could count on Archie to step up to the mark.' Archie squeezed his eyes shut. 'I thought, though, that after the war I could win him round and persuade him to stay.'

Neither of them spoke for a while after that. 'But he made another plan,' he said at last, 'and so he flew that last mad sortie.' His brother was a risk-taker but a cool one until, perhaps, the poison of remorse corroded his reason. Archie knew all about that. Jilly said nothing, but he knew he was right.

A flock of starlings landed on the roof of the glasshouse and began squabbling.

'Why did you stay with Pa?' Archie asked.

She met his eye unflinchingly. 'Because I had no choice. Andy was dead and you might well be killed too. What else could I do? Besides I owed it to him; he'd given me shelter and a home, and I repaid him poorly. You weren't the only one who cried out in the night, you know, your father relived the hell of the trenches on many a night and Andy's loss devastated him. He clung to the notion of his son's valour and heroic death – it sustained him and I had to let him keep that, anything else would have destroyed him; I'd done damage enough. So I couldn't leave him – not after all that. I *had* to bear the consequences, and I had a child to consider. Duncan was the only thing that mattered.' Her voice became increasingly strained as she spoke. 'I spoiled him, I know I did, yet somehow I neglected the important things. I brought up both boys more or less on my own; your father spent a great deal of time in London, at his club. He *tried* to love Duncan, I think, who, God knows, bore none of the guilt, but he didn't seem able to, and . . . and Duncan was a difficult, moody child.'

Archie listened despairingly. What chance had the poor lad to thrive?

But Jilly was continuing. 'I was a terrible mother but I promised myself that Rosslie would be his one day. We owed him that much, I thought, and I owed it to Andy.'

'I'd *never* have challenged Duncan's right to inherit!' he said, the anger flaring up again. 'And had I known Andy had a son— God, Jilly, I'd have confronted Pa head on, despite my own guilt, and between us we could surely have found a way through. God knows, I'd have done anything for Andy's boy, and you denied me that chance!'

She looked back at him, her lips a thin line. 'How easy it is to sit there and pass judgement. I couldn't take the risk, Archie. Who knows how your father would have reacted.'

Having been cuckolded by both his sons.

Archie turned away and was silent.

'I thought you might get in touch after the war. I'd hoped we might patch things up.'

'And I was hoping to hear from Pa.'

'Perhaps if you had—'

It was too late, like so much else. 'He'd forbidden me, I felt I had to respect that. And the thought of seeing a boy I believed to be my son, and not to be able to claim him, was just too painful.'

But had he known him to be Andy's . . .

The unspoken words hung there and the silence stretched out.

'And then there's Keith?' he said at last, but she made no reply. 'Who bears a striking resemblance to John McAdam.'

She made no attempt to deny it and gave him a brittle look. 'Do you imagine you were the only one who felt remorse, Archie, the only one to consider self-destruction? After Duncan was born, weeks after, Andrew came up, for form's sake, then returned to London burying himself in war work. He'd forbidden me to join him, said it wasn't safe, but it was more than that, of course – he didn't want me there. I grew desperately lonely and found motherhood a terrible strain. Duncan was so demanding . . . John discovered me one day in the potting shed where I'd already cut one wrist, rather ineptly, and was attempting the other but my hand was slippery and I couldn't grip the knife.' She took off the broad bracelet she always wore and revealed a white puckered scar. 'He'd seen us, you and I, down on the beach that day so there was little I needed to explain. He blamed the war for all of it and gave comfort in a wonderfully detached, neutral sort of way and it steadied me. But when news came of the death camps his resolve cracked and he joined up.' She played with the bracelet, snapping and unsnapping the clasp. 'He left before I knew I was pregnant so there I was again, on my way to London to tell my husband the same story as before. We had a showdown. I told him he must either divorce me or start living with me again, otherwise I'd take comfort where I could and he must be prepared for a string of bastards. I showed him the scar on my wrist and he knew I was serious. Eventually we reached an accommodation.' Another . . . 'We'd salvage what we could of our marriage, bring up the two boys as best we might, and I swore that I'd never leave him. There would be no more children, that was the deal, and we never again shared intimacies.' She paused, then reached for another plant, and Archie began to recognise the high price that she'd paid for loving his brother. 'When John came back from the war I told him about Keith and I thought he might ask me to go away with him but he didn't. He was married and living in Switzerland last I heard. And anyway I'd made a promise.'

'So you remained faithful to Pa?'

'I remained careful,' she replied. 'And developed an interest in art.'

And there he had it, Archie thought, and he looked across at her, her chin up and defiant, a woman who had just lost a son but who could still look him in the eye, daring him to judge her. He felt his anger dissipate. Her life had been as much a wasteland as his, both of them casualties of war.

John McAdam had been right.

But then she spoke again. 'We tried to find you, you know, when he started to fail.'

'At whose instigation?'

'Your father said that we should.'

His interest quickened. 'Just that? That you *should*?'

'He foresaw difficulties, he said, once he died.' Bloody right! 'Perhaps it was around then that he said something to Duncan, though he'd promised me he never would.'

Archie digested that. 'Did he ever mention me?' The question had been tormenting him since his arrival.

'Only if others did. He'd say you'd gone to live abroad and would leave it at that. We'd agreed between us it was better if we didn't discuss you. Duncan grew up looking like a Maxwell because he was a Maxwell so no one had reason to ask questions.' That wasn't what he'd asked. Would Pa have loved Duncan better, he wondered, if he *had* met his end in North Africa? Perhaps then he could have forgotten that the lad was his dead son's son, not his own. And what if he *had* known Duncan was Andy's . . . ? But Jilly was continuing. 'Duncan had your father's personality, you know, which made them too similar for harmony.' She reached out a hand to him. 'I know what you want me to say, Archie, and I don't have an answer. But that photograph in Mallory's original article, the one of you with the medal . . . we found it after he died, in a box together with photographs of you and Andy as boys, and some of your mother. He'd kept it safe and written "Archie" on the back. It was well thumbed.'

It was little enough but perhaps counted for something, and was all there would be now. He stared out into the walled garden seeing shades of his father there, with his mother, inspecting the blossom on the apple trees, a sweet but distant memory, and he saw Andy and himself searching in the nettles for a lost cricket ball, laughing as Kenny chased them out. And John McAdam, shovelling shit, wrestling with his conscience.

As he would forever wrestle with his own.

'So, Jilly.' He felt he'd aged a decade in the closeness of the glasshouse. 'Here we are, back where it all began, still struggling with it all, and bearing the consequences. We've survived, I suppose, you and I, in a ramshackle sort of a way. Perhaps Andy would have approved . . .' She smiled a little. 'I can't help thinking, though, that we did it very badly and there should have been a better ending. For Duncan, anyway.'

'But perhaps there's still time, for us, if not for him.' She reached out to him again. 'Stay, Archie. Make your peace with Rosslie. Live out your years here, somewhere you love. Rosslie needs you and it has such a deep place in your heart.'

Briefly he covered her hand with his. 'It has, and it will remain there. I'll not leave it in a mess and I won't desert you entirely, I promise. But leave it, I will, as soon as I have things in order.'

She drew back her hand and was silent for a moment. 'And will you take Eva Bayne with you when you go?'

He met her look, and nodded, remembering the sight of Eva and Ross in the golden evening light, coming across the grass towards him, and felt again that surge of hope. 'I shall ask her to return with me, and very much hope that she'll come.'

CHAPTER 40

Ross left the day after the inquest, not waiting for the funeral. Duncan's body had been recovered by fishermen and brought home to lie in the estate's ancient little chapel. Archie had thought his heart would break as he stared down at the plain oak coffin of his brother's son and Jilly had crumbled at last. She'd clung to him as she had done once before and he held her close, letting her sob. Ross had offered to stay on but Archie had shaken his head. 'You'll be a distraction, son, there'll be another feeding frenzy by the press as they speculate on what happens next. It's Duncan's funeral and nothing must detract from it. I'll follow, just as soon as I can leave things in good order.'

They stood together in the courtyard on the morning of his departure, waiting for Eva to get the Fiat out of the stables. 'I've told her she's under orders to bring you back,' Ross said.

Archie raised an eyebrow. 'Have you indeed? She'll doubtless please herself. But I'll return as soon as I decently can, with or without Eva.' The Fiat drew up in front of them. 'Godspeed, son, and no more heroics, eh? I'll stay out of trouble.'

'It'll be a first if you do.' Ross eased himself inside, looking up as he pulled the door shut. 'But make it soon, eh, and with, yeah, not without.'

Archie laughed and waved them on their way.

'With or without what?' Eva asked as they left the courtyard. There were still press vans at the front gate so they were taking the pig-farm route.

He gave her a slanting look. 'Never mind. But he gets it, I think.' He was booked on an early flight, giving him time to make the connection in London, and a soft autumnal mist was rising off the fields as they bumped along the track. 'He's gonna find it hard to leave all this.'

'I think a bit of his heart will always be here,' she replied, 'even if it is overshadowed by the past. But we must get him back to Severn soon.' The *we* had been accidental but Ross glanced at her again. 'He's told you he plans to come back every year?' He nodded. 'That'll work well for him. He's pleased to have taken Jim Kincaird on board as estate manager, for a number of reasons. Keith's pretty self-contained, he reckons, and he and Susie can look after Jilly. So, don't you worry, he's planning his escape.' She swerved to avoid a pheasant which flew off with a startled rattle.

'Has he asked you what you'll do?'

'Not in so many words.' Tam had in fact, begun to drop hints which had set her thinking, indulging herself in the various possibilities.

'Meaning what?' he persisted.

'Meaning he said we'll discuss things properly in due course. Too much going on right now.' Possibilities which might or not transpire; she was making no assumptions.

He digested that, staring dead ahead. 'And would you come back with him if he asked you?'

'If he does, I'll decide then.'

He glanced across at her with a frown. 'That's no sort of answer.'

'There's been no sort of question yet. And besides, he's perfectly able to look after his own correspondence, so what would my role be?'

'That might depend,' he said, looking ahead again. 'You got ties here?'

She thought fleetingly of her mother. Their paths had sharply diverged in recent years and so if she decided to return with Tam, she too could travel back and forth as her mother grew older. 'Not binding ones.'

He grunted and the subject was dropped; there was time enough, after all, and some things could not be rushed. He said little more and an hour later she pulled up outside Departures. 'No point in you hanging about,' he said. 'Just dump me here, and then head on back.'

'Back on Tam watch?' She smiled and he nodded.

'Full-time job. You promised, remember?' He opened the car door and paused. 'And just so you know I told him he *should* bring you back with him.'

She looked at him, registering the glint in his eye. 'And what did he say?'

'That you'd please yourself. But since you've not got bindin' ties, you should come.'

You know where you are with Ross, Tam had said. But did she? From an icy north, Ross's compass point seemed to be swinging in a southerly direction.

It was that change which had been dominating her thinking. 'And do what?' she quizzed him.

'I'll find you a job on the schooner if Tam runs out of ideas.' He gave her that smile – Tam's smile.

She let it warm her. 'But I heard the boss's a bit of a bastard.'

'Money's crap too.' His eyes had not left hers.

'Threw me out when I went there, told me never to come back.'

'Maybe he's changed his mind.'

Their looks held for a moment. 'I'd like to think so.'

He smiled then. 'Guess we all make mistakes, Eva Bayne.' He lifted her chin with his thumb, contemplating her. 'Worth another shot, eh?' he asked, and in answer she slipped her hand behind his head and pulled him down to kiss her.

EPILOGUE

Severn, Newfoundland, 1981

Alerted by the scrunch of car wheels, Archie looked through the kitchen window and saw a taxi was pulling up beside the boatyard. It disgorged an elderly lady with a stick, who eschewed the taxi driver's hand and walked stiffly towards the house.

It took a moment for Archie to recognise her. He raised a quizzical eyebrow and went to the door. A moment later the old lady was standing in the kitchen fixing him with a severe look. 'You've become something of a celebrity, Tam Nairn. In all the days I wondered what became of you I'd never have imagined *that*.'

'But you suspected I'd hidden depths, eh?' He gestured to a chair. 'Why don't you sit, Ada, and tell me why you're here?'

'I've not come to see *you*, I've come to see Eva Bayne. Where is she?'

'Somewhere around.' He looked across at the old woman he had last seen the day he'd left Heart's Repose. Must be well into her eighties now. She'd housed him and Ross for three weeks in her tiny back bedroom after their cabin had been burned out, feeding them and trying to reform Ross, who had lit out in protest after a couple of days. Ada Sinclair was a pain but she'd been one of the last to stand against signing in favour of the resettlement programme and for a short while they had been unlikely allies. 'Shall I go and find her?'

He was amused to see that she was still eyeing him with a missionary zeal. 'In a moment, yes. But first I have things to say to you. I've read several articles these last weeks and pieced together your very chequered career . . .'

He sighed. It was inevitable, he supposed. The press on both sides of the Atlantic had had a field day after Duncan's death, especially when word had got out about Ross's existence. He'd escaped Rosslie as soon as he decently could, bringing Eva back with him – causing a frenzy of rumours among the press. Some determined journalists had followed them to Severn from where Ross had definitively despatched them. Interest had died down since then, the wedding had been kept very private and at last they'd been allowed some peace. Ross had threatened to drown the next journalist who appeared, although the boatyard had benefited from all the interest.

And now here was Ada Sinclair with *things to say*. He put up a hand. 'Look, if this is going to be one of your sermons, Ada, I suggest you sit down so you can give it full rein. Being a gentleman, I can't sit until you do.'

Ada Sinclair, with an air of dignity, sat. 'As I was saying . . . a chequered career and you're apparently still avoiding your responsibilities.'

Archie pulled out a packet of cigarettes, offered them and shrugged at the cold look he received. He lit one for himself. 'How's that?'

'I remember Rosslie as a girl before I left Scotland. My aunt lived not far from there and we used to visit. I had, of course, no reason to connect you with it. I remember it as a very beautiful place and now that you're not only a baronet but a landowner, it is your duty to return there, assume the reins, look after your father's widow and train your son.'

He batted away the smoke. 'Train my son? *Train* Ross! You once told me he was the rudest, most ignorant and ill-disciplined boy you'd ever had the misfortune to try to teach. Anyway, why would I?'

'You neglected his education shamefully. I never said that he was unintelligent, just unruly and very badly brought up.'

Archie gave her a grim smile. 'You know, Ada, I think you're the only woman on earth I'd take this from.'

Her expression didn't change; if anything it became more severe. 'I had to come because I read with considerable dismay that you have brought Eva Bayne back with you to be your private secretary. A cynical euphonism, I expect, for what is an extremely unsuitable—'

His eyes began to dance. 'Now you go too far . . . Eva is extremely suitable and a first-rate secretary dealing with correspondence between myself and a very able estate manager I've left in charge at Rosslie. I intend to return regularly but otherwise leave the running of the place to the son of a man who saved my life, and leave my rather vague, if well-meaning, half-brother-of-sorts to look after his mother while I remain here.'

'With Eva?'

'With Eva.'

'Who is considerably less than half your age.'

He nodded. 'I'm sixty-three, she's twenty-six so that counts as considerable, I reckon.'

She pursed her lips. 'I *had* hoped the newspaper articles were wrong.'

'The story had gone a little flat, you see,' he said, apologetically. 'They needed something to spice it up and they've rather latched onto that aspect of things – and ran off with it. She's pregnant, by the way. Gotta look after her, don't want her getting upset. Wish me joy?'

'I shall do no such thing. It's disgraceful.' Ada's lips formed a thin formidable line and she reached into her handbag and pulled out a folded document, which she put on the table, keeping her palm pressed down on it. 'After reading what was printed I became intrigued enough to do some research . . .'

He rolled the cigarette to the side of his mouth. 'Been snooping, eh?'

' . . . and I'm surprised that no one else made the connection. Major General Douglas Wimberley of the 51st Highland

Regiment was known as Tartan Tam, and you served under him.'

The humour in Archie's eyes faded. 'I did, and I'd have followed the man to the ends of the earth.'

'And Nairn was the objective set for your men to achieve.' He nodded briefly and she looked smug to have her speculation confirmed. 'I've read accounts of the battle in which you were awarded this.' She opened her palm. 'And from what I deduce, your actions that day were nothing short of heroic and saved a great many lives.'

But he wasn't listening. He'd gone cold, his eyes fixed on the medal. 'Where the hell did you find that?'

'In Eva's trouser pocket the night I came to your cabin with her mother and found her in your bed. I couldn't imagine where it had come from and concluded that either you'd given it to her or she'd stolen it, and either explanation would only confuse an already spiralling situation.' Or, Archie thought, if the wretched woman had left it where it was, it might have spared him a very great deal of— 'Just the day before she'd asked me the meaning of the word "valour" and so I made the connection and realised she must have already seen it. I could not imagine under what circumstances and it never once occurred to me that you, of all people, might have been awarded it.' He narrowed his eyes but then again gratuitous insults were a speciality of the elderly so he let it go. 'The article Eva wrote last year made all clear but at the time it was impossible to discover easily who had been awarded them. It seemed so improbable that it was yours – and you'd a habit of taking things that weren't.' Dear God! Was she still harping on about that damned book? 'It was only after reading about you that I remembered I still had it. I suppose if I'd *not* taken it, you might have been identified many years ago, and since then it's rather preyed on my mind.' It was almost an apology but Ada was the sort who never quite managed one.

And what then might the trajectory of his life have been, he wondered bitterly. His father would still have been alive . . . He reached out, took up the medal and examined it. As one grew old, he was discovering that the number of 'what ifs' had an unfortunate way of multiplying in the mind. Hours could be wasted trying to follow the routes life might have taken. And there lay madness . . . 'Like many things in my past, this medal is a travesty. I'd rather hoped to get myself killed that day in North Africa and decided I might as well do something useful before I did. To be awarded a medal for what was, in effect, a failure seemed to be all of a piece. Keep the damn thing; it's got me into enough trouble already.'

She took it back from him and put it in the centre of the table, apparently uninterested in what he'd said. 'It's time to acknowledge your responsibilities, Archibald Maxwell, and behave as you should. Go back to Rosslie, take Eva with you if you must—'

His eyes gleamed again. 'Take Eva? I doubt Ross'd like that. It's not my bed she's in these days, you absurd woman.'

If chagrin was what he expected, he was disappointed. Ada Sinclair's face lit up and she took up the document, unfolded it and laid it flat on the table. 'In that case, all the more reason to stop this ridiculous pretence.'

Archie pulled it towards him and saw what it was. His face hardened. 'You *have* been snooping, haven't you?'

'Are Ross and Eva married?'

'Is that your business?'

'I can only hope so. If not, don't let Ross cut things too fine.'

Archie looked back at her. 'You really are an unconscionable old busybody.' He tapped the table. 'What put you onto this?'

'Those articles got me to thinking. I remembered when your . . . your *wife* was expecting, I spoke to her and told her that since she was about to become a mother, she should demand that you make an honest woman of her—'

'*Christ!* By what right did you—'

'—and she was every bit as rude as you and said that folk like me knew nothing, always quick to judge, or some such words, and I thought no more about it. When Ross was registered at school as Ross McLeod, I assumed that she'd ignored my advice. But reading all the various articles I remembered what she'd said and so I applied to see marriage records for that year, and there it was. September nineteen fifty. Surprisingly easy, if you have the date and know where to look.' Archie snorted. 'Why ever did you let everyone think Ross was illegitimate?'

'I can see no reason whatsoever to tell you.' He was no longer prepared to be amused. 'And I'd rather like you to leave.'

'You can*not* allow Ross to remain in ignorance of this, Tam Nairn.'

He went and opened the door and held it for her. 'If I replace your damned poetry book, will you go away and leave us alone?'

She walked through the door, head erect. 'I replaced it myself, years ago. And I'll not go until I've spoken to Eva.'

Eva shifted position again, put down her brush and moved her neck, easing the tension in her muscles. It was hard to find a way to kneel and varnish the schooner's deck planks without getting indigestion and a protesting kick from within. 'You all right?' Ross asked, sensing her movement, but not looking up from where he was working.

'Just having a stretch.'

'I don't pay you to stretch.'

'You don't pay me at all.'

She saw him smile, that slow Maxwell smile which, from Ross, could still turn her bones to water, but he didn't look up. The schooner was months late and the consortium buying it was running out of patience. The men had been working on her all hours but today Ross had sent them home while he stayed on and addressed some of the last outstanding snags. Which would come first, she wondered, the baby or the ship? It would be a close-run thing. 'Take a break,' he said. 'I could do with a coffee myself.'

He helped her down the ladder, giving the bump a passing caress as she landed, and went to put the kettle on. The schooner was out on the slipway now and it was possible at last to appreciate her perfect lines, the long sharply angled bow, the undercut stern, and the sight of it made her fiercely proud. Ross's schooner. His first love, she'd teased him. 'You come a close second,' he'd assured her, 'and I'm not sure I'd make a profit selling you on like I will with this beauty.'

'Will I be your first love when you do?'

He considered. 'Guess so. Until I start the next one.'

'By then there'll be other competition.' She patted the bump.

He bent and kissed her. 'Have to start another of them too.'

Ross had come to the airport to meet them when she and Tam had finally managed to leave the constraints of Rosslie behind them and had made his intentions clear from the start. She'd seen Tam watching with amusement as his son wooed her over the next weeks as, he told her later, Ross had never wooed a woman before. And Eva had basked in the delight of being wooed . . . While they'd remained in Rosslie, Tam himself had been hardly less subtle. 'He needs civilising, does Ross, but he's a good man at heart. Badly brought up, I'm afraid.'

'You'll tell me next he just needs a good woman.'

'Should I advertise?'

'If you think that necessary.'

A week after her arrival she accused them of a conspiracy.

'Absolutely,' Tam agreed.

'Whatever works, eh?' Ross grinned and led her off across the boatyard towards the cliffs where it had become their custom to walk once he'd finished work for the day. They'd found a sheltered place among the rocks where they could look out across the ocean, away from curious eyes. Cloudberries were growing there and he picked some for her. She remembered what her mother had said and shook her head, teasing him. 'I was told the berries here are poison.'

'Some are.' He'd bid her open her mouth and watched her as she'd savoured the bitter-sweet taste. 'Not all of 'em though.' And he had pulled her to him.

The kettle had just started to boil when she heard voices and looked up to see Tam approaching with an old woman, and it took her a moment to believe the evidence of her eyes. 'Gosh . . . I . . . Heavens. Miss Sinclair!'

Ross appeared from around the stern, wiping his hands on a rag. Ada Sinclair stood there, taking in the two of them, the bump, and then the ship. The latter seized her attention and she stepped forward to run her hand along the smooth varnish. 'Why, Ross, this is very fine.'

He gave a slight nod in acknowledgement, raising a quizzical eyebrow at his father. 'Ada came to bring you this, Eva,' Tam said, 'which has been weighing on her conscience since she nicked it from you fifteen years ago.' He ignored the old woman's indignant protest and handed Eva the medal. 'I think you'd better keep it for me, after the effort you took to recover it.' She stared at it in disbelief and then up at Tam, but he had turned to Ross. 'And being an unprincipled busybody, she brought something else, which can loosely be described as being for you, son. I left it on the kitchen table, you'd better go and have a look. It has . . . implications.'

Ross gave him a searching look, threw down the rag and went across to the house. Tam waited until he had gone then turned to Ada Sinclair. 'Say whatever it is you came to say to Eva but if you insult her, or upset her in any way, I'll throw you into the bay.'

'*Tam!*'

Miss Sinclair, however, was still examining the schooner with a softness in her eyes, unmoved by Tam's threat. 'I remember seeing the fishing fleet setting off, like a flock of wild geese spreading their wings, those great sails cracking as they caught the wind, the hulls cutting through the water like blades, men running about on the decks, water creaming past their bows. What a sight they used to be!' Then she turned and looked at Eva, taking hold of both her hands. 'You look radiant, my dear, your father would be very proud of you. He was a fine man, and I wish you and Ross good fortune.' She turned to Tam. 'There, was that all right? And now my taxi, I think.'

Tam escorted her to where the taxi was waiting then waved her off and returned, gesturing a bewildered Eva to a bench beside the slipway. He sat down beside her and slung an arm across the back of it. 'What was that all about?' she asked him, sensing a tension in him as he glanced back at the house from which Ross had yet to emerge.

'Meddlesome old trout.'

'How odd. She looked just the same, so disapproving and . . . and so sure of herself.' He laughed. 'When she took my hands I thought she'd tell me to go and scrub my nails!'

Tam grunted. 'She was checking for that.' He pointed to the ring of her left hand, but as he spoke the back door slammed and Eva turned to see Ross striding towards them.

'Jesus *Christ*, Tam!' he said, reaching the bench to stand glaring down at his father. 'Full of surprises, aren't you?' His eyes were stormy and he was breathing hard. 'Anything else you want to tell me? Any other little detail you've overlooked?' He had a piece of paper in his hand, which he thrust at Eva. '*Implications*, the man said!'

Eva took it and read it, then read it again, and looked up at Tam in astonishment.

But he was calmly returning Ross's glare. 'Can't think of a single thing, son.'

'Jeez.' Ross sucked in his breath and looked away.

'Not a concern for you yet, of course. I've a few years in me, might even last another twenty—'

Ross snorted. 'You'll be lucky. I need a drink.' He flicked a glance at Eva. 'We'll talk . . . ' he said, and strode off. A moment later the truck shot out of the yard, sending up a spray of gravel.

After he'd gone Tam and Eva sat in silence while Eva, equally stunned, digested the enormity of this latest twist. 'This counts as a bombshell, Tam.'

'Do you mind?'

'That's hardly the point. Why didn't you tell him?'

'You know perfectly well.'

'Well you should have. Were you going to?'

'Not while Duncan was alive. Ross being a bastard cleared the way for Duncan. Rosslie was his, whichever way you came at it.'

'But even so . . .'

'And him being known as McLeod, not Maxwell, helped me stay hidden – until you came looking.'

'So had I not found you . . .'

Tam gave her that crooked half-smile. 'Ross'd never have known and so not given a damn. But that's all changed now . . .' She caught that fleeting look of sadness she sometimes saw. 'I *was* planning to tell him, Eva, but finding it hard. Guess I should be grateful to Ada.'

Had he really expected to get away with it? she wondered. 'Surely when you *did* marry, you left a trail.'

He shrugged. 'Not a clear one. And who'd go looking except for the wretched Ada! Once we left Heart's Repose I thought we'd successfully vanished. I'd dropped Nairn for McLeod too by then, after all the furore . . .' And but for Billy Norton and Ross's boatyard, and her own pursuit, he would have remained undiscovered. Beside her, he gave a sigh. 'I'd found no repose in Heart's Repose but I cherished high hopes of Avalon. It amused me to think of King Arthur being taken to a mythical Avalon by a bevy of enchantresses for his wounds to be healed, and I rather took to the analogy. It was lost on my son, of course . . . The myth never says whether Arthur's wounds were healed or not but if he could vanish so could I.' He paused. 'Though I'd reckoned without one persistent wound-healing young enchantress who hunted me down and gave the game away.'

She absorbed that with a smile, knowing herself forgiven.

'Tell me about her. Ross's mother. I should like to know.'

He was silent for a while, then removed his arm from the back of the bench and sat forward, staring ahead. 'Her name was Molly McLeod. Daughter of a native woman up on the Labrador and a Dundee whaler who called in there a few times a year, got drunk, beat her mother up, got her pregnant and then abandoned her. Molly had it tough from the start. I was at a low ebb when I met her, drinking and fighting, out with the sealers or the whalers, living a bad, hard life.' Punishing himself, Eva thought. 'She'd patch me up when I came ashore, feed me, care for me, drink with me, and eventually we moved south, ending up at Heart's Repose. When she got pregnant I thought I could do rather better than the Dundee whaler so I took her to St John's and married her. Told her I was on the run and let her think what she liked, but she never asked. When Ross was born we registered him as Ross Maxwell McLeod, which I thought was close enough to be legal and not give him, or me, trouble in the future.' He let out a long breath. 'We'd not a lot in common, Molly and I, but she was good to me in her way and so we stuck by each other and had a life of a sort, until she got sick. Then it got bad.' He stared out over the ocean, his eyes looking back into a past that Eva could not imagine.

'And now this . . .'

He straightened, and put his arm around her shoulder and chuckled. 'Poor old Ross. Not a bastard after all, despite his best efforts. But Sir Ross McLeod Maxwell sounds rather well, the ungrateful whelp. And is it such a poisoned chalice? Rosslie's a gem, you saw that for yourself, and I hope you'll both cherish it.'

'We will, of course, but not—'

Tam laughed, cutting her off. 'And you can encourage him to cherish me, keep me going a while longer, putting off the evil day. I might even go home to die, in poetic counterpoint to Arthur. How would that be?'

She rested her head against his shoulder and thought how comfortable it was, and he dropped a kiss on the top of her head as he was wont to do. Avalon *had* healed him, she decided, healed them both perhaps, and made them whole. She'd told him once about her rockweed – seaweed dilemma and how Ross had made the question irrelevant, and he had laughed at her. He'd countered by saying he liked to think of himself as a wild salmon, that king of fish, returning home each year. 'Not to breed, of course, but to maintain the cycle of life.' He'd paused and looked serious for once. 'You know we never leave the places we love, my dear, we carry them in us. They go into the making of us, the very fibre of our being, so the dilemma was illusionary. Besides, the weed remains unchanged whether it's on the rocks or in the sea, only the circumstances shift around it. All we can do is enjoy and endure as required, while the tides ebb and flow.'

She sat beside him now, cradling the bump with one hand, the copy of his marriage certificate in the other. Would Ross mind so very much once he'd absorbed the shock of this news? She doubted it. He often referred to Rosslie, and there were plans for Keith to come over and look at Ross's set-up at the boatyard. Finding the old skiff Tam remembered as a boy behind the ruins at Aber Rosslie, had inspired Keith to consider Tam's idea of setting himself up in boat-building, down beside the estuary. The sea cages had gone from there now.

First though, he was planning a trip to Switzerland.

Rosslie was moving on in other ways. Eva knew it would take many years to clear the various debts but there were reasons for optimism. Jim Kincaird had employed ghillies to guide sportsmen onto the moors and along the beats of the river and Susie had proved to be surprisingly practical and was busily refurbishing two of Rosslie's unused bedrooms. Tam told her that Jilly had sold the McTaggart for a good price at a London gallery and Keith reported that she was putting her energies into smartening up the dining room. Eva had seen letters arrive and guessed that she and Tam corresponded too, though these she never saw.

Duncan's death would, for Tam, forever cast its shadow over Rosslie and before they left for Newfoundland she had gone with him and waited while he stood before the newly erected headstone. It stood in the Rosslie graveyard beside a memorial to Andy and the grave of his grandfather, and recorded only Duncan's name and dates. Tam had stood, in silence, for a long time, and then simply walked away leaving Eva to return to the house alone.

Since then he'd seemed to find peace here along this rocky coast, and perhaps, at last, he would find his elusive redemption. He had begun writing again. He'd not shown her what he had written, perhaps the act of writing had, of itself, fulfilled a purpose. Feeling the same need for completion, she'd set herself the task of recording stories of the resettlement, the personal experiences, and had returned as promised to talk to Shelagh Doyle. Perhaps that way the voices from the outports would be preserved.

As she had grown bigger, she often came and sat with Tam as they sat now, looking out over the waters of the bay. They needed to say little to one another but could let their individual thoughts wander as they watched the boats lift and fall on the swells, listening to the sawing and hammering from the boatshed where a thing of beauty was taking shape. Ross had come out one day and stood contemplating them.

'Sometimes, Eva, I wonder which one of us you married.'

Eva had smiled up at him, recognising that glint in his eye, and Tam had laughed. 'Well, son, the fates threw her at my feet, not yours. But since they've brought us to this point, I reckon they knew what they were about.'

AUTHOR'S NOTE

During the late 1970s/early 1980s, my father worked as a doctor up on the Labrador and in Newfoundland; my mother helped out in the orphanages and with the disabled members of the community. This book is dedicated to them. Visits to settlements along the coast were, by then, no longer by boat but by sea plane and my father returned with stories of the places and individuals he encountered. I was lucky enough to come down the Labrador coast myself a few years ago, calling into one or two abandoned settlements which once teemed with summer fishing activity. Most poignant in these places were the little graveyards with their white marble headstones and faded black lettering, eloquent of the people who once lived there. Newfoundland is a very beautiful province and now attracts many summer visitors who go there for the hiking trails, the majestic scenery and Newfoundland's rich culture and history. Indigenous groups harvested the sea resources for centuries, Scandinavian Vikings came looking for land and timber, and then European explorers discovered the fishing grounds and Newfoundland became known throughout the western world.

The Forgotten Shore is a work of fiction, none of the characters existed and the events in the book, other than historical events, are all imagined. Heart's Repose, Doyle's Point and Severn were creations based on the many small harbours and outports that once existed along Newfoundland's rocky coast. Rosslie and Aber Rosslie are also fictional and were inspired by similar places along the west coast of Scotland. I drew on many sources in writing this book, and here are just a few of them. Mark Kurlansky's fascinating book (1999) *Cod: A Biography of the Fish that Changed the World* shows the vital role that the Newfoundland fishing industry played in European history. The Newfoundland government's twentieth century Resettlement Program is discussed in many sources, including the excellent Newfoundland and Labrador Heritage Website www.heritage.nf.ca which gives access to documents, old images and videos and provided a valuable source of reference material. Scott Walden's photographs in his book (2003) *Places Lost: In Search of Newfoundland's Resettled Communities* are beautiful and poignant, and his text is both informative and sensitive. The story of the 51st Highland Division is told by, among others, Eric Linklater in (1942) *The Highland Division*, Patrick Delaforce in (1997) *Monty's Highlanders 51st Highland Division in the Second World War* and Richard Doherty in (2006) *None Bolder: The History of the 51st Highland Division in the Second World War*). Stephen Drummond Sedgwick's (1988) *Salmon Farming Handbook* gave invaluable insights into salmon farming in the 1980s. These and many other sources were consulted in order to provide a backdrop to the novel but nothing can replace actually going and seeing the places for oneself. I am grateful to two dear Canadian friends, Jenny and Toby, who came and explored coastal Newfoundland with me last summer, putting up with my insistence to stop and photograph yet another old salting room and jetty as we investigated abandoned root cellars and collapsing houses as well as hiking the trails that once linked vanished outports, seeing icebergs drift by off-shore and finding traces of a way of life that was disappearing before our eyes. The people we encountered were ever welcoming and always friendly and I am grateful to the man who took us inside his grandfather's salting room which, in the 1960s, had been floated across from an offshore island when the community there was re-settled. It still contained the old salting barrels, boat and fishing gear – and the twine loft still stored nets. Sadly he was there to oversee its dismantling as the roof was collapsing and the old place was no longer considered safe.

I am indebted to these scholars, researchers, locals and friends who helped me formulate *The Forgotten Shore*. I am grateful, as ever, to my agent Jenny Brown and to Lisa Highton, of Jenny

Brown Associates, for their invaluable comments, feedback and guidance. The brilliant team at Hodder and Stoughton, especially my editor, Olivia Barber, copy-editor Suzanne Clarke and cover designer Becky Glibbery, deserve a special thank you for their continuing support and patience.